THE CROWN OF FIRE & FURY

BOOK TWO
OF
THE RUNEWAR SAGA

J.D.L. ROSELL

Illustration © 2021 by René Aigner
Book design by J.D.L. Rosell
Map by J.D.L. Rosell
Map elements by StarRaven (on DeviantArt)

Published by Rune & Requiem Press
runeandrequiempress.com

CONTENTS

Part II
FURY

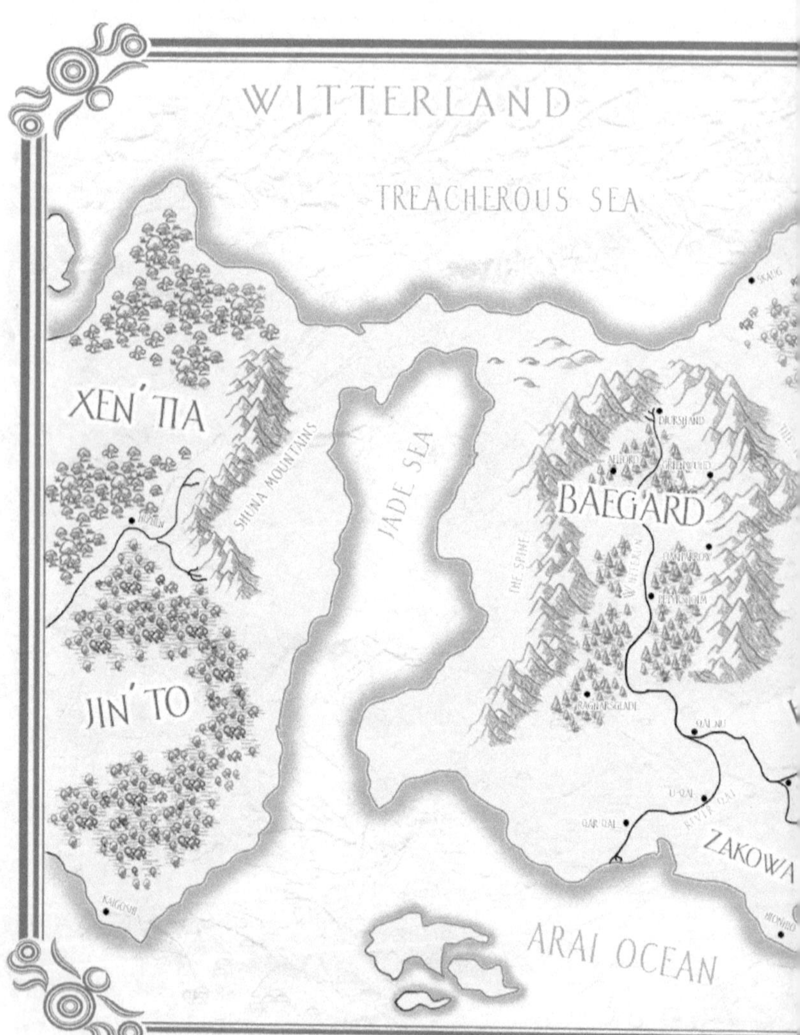

WITTERLAND
TREACHEROUS SEA
XEN'TIA
JIN'TO
SHUNA MOUNTAINS
JADE SEA
THE SPINE
BAEGARD
DJURSLAND
ALFORD
GREENWOOD
CANTHRISBY
PEPPERHOLM
RAGNAR'S GLADE
KAIGOSHI
QAI NU
U-QAI
KWIT QAI
QAR QAI
ZAKOWA
MEONHID
SKAUG
ARAI OCEAN

ENEA
THE MIDDLE LAND
N
W E
S
THE ELDWEALD
THE HUMMOCKS
TAIGARTEN
KARSEL
MAX IRU
THRAX IRU
NORTH VINAXI
SOUTH VINAXI
THE ANTALPS
PICCO
BAIA
SUN OCEAN
SUMERLAND

To my incredible wife, whose high standards never let me slack off in my writing. This book is what it is because of you.

PART I
FIRE

"A sword age, a wind age, a wolf age. No longer is there mercy among men."
— Snorri Sturluson, *The Prose Edda*

PROLOGUE

Ragnar Torbenson leaned against the stone railing and watched the sun claw its way atop the Teeth. Wolves ran on the morning winds, biting at his exposed skin. Though spring was late in coming, and Ragnar wore only the long tunic he had slept in, he did not flinch before the cold jaws, but welcomed them. His father, long buried — *thank the gods* — had told him one night after he had cried over his hunger-racked belly: *Quit your weeping! Be a weakling and I'll treat you as one!* Then he had shown Ragnar just how weak he was, beating him bloody until he ran out of mead and ventured out to fetch more.

Ragnar's lips curled, remembering the night the old man had cowered before him. *A good night. A red night.*

He had hated his father; every son did, his own included. But like the frigid wind, his father's cruelty had forged him into the man he was today. Adversity was a gift.

So long as you survive it.

He had done more than survive. He was Ragnar Torbenson, Lord of Ragnarsglade, the first man to found a jarlheim in three hundred winters. He had built his city from the ground up, gathered men and their families to him through vision and strength, and braved the nearness of their southern enemies to forge the strongest and most prosperous province of all — or it would be, someday.

He wrung the stone railing as if it were a chicken's neck and looked balefully over his surroundings. Petyrsholm, where he presently stayed, likely could claim those honors he envied. It was a grand and ancient metropolis. Though its stone was dun and worn, it possessed a stateliness his own city of wood and straw had many years yet to achieve.

His father, rapacious louse that he was, had a saying for that as well. *If you can't grow it, take it.*

Slowly, Ragnar pried his clenched hands from the balustrade and straightened his spine. His father had been a forceful brute, a warrior renowned, but he had been unprincipled and malicious. Though born to a highborn family, he had allowed anger and bitterness to poison his prospects, and thus lived and died a pauper. Ragnar had learned from his failures. He had bent his head to lessons while their village still had a gothi who would risk coming to the manor to teach him. He had trained in the yard until he overcame the older boys, then even the battle-tested men. He had learned the art of spinning coins through lending and trading. He had prospered. And through it all, he remembered what it came back to.

Hunger — and the will to leash it.

Ragnar Torbenson, Jarl of Ragnarsglade, smiled over a city that was not his own as he thought of the coming day when it would be.

1. THE JACKAL KING

We are endless and We are ceaseless
We are many and We are One
For Our children, We splinter
We fall, Stars to the Ocean

To you, We give a piece of Our Heart
A Sliver of the Sun
To you, We give the Karah
A god born of your own

- Words in the Sand, refrain 12;57-58

Sehdra smelled the giantess even before she entered the throne room.

She hesitated at the arched opening as the stench filled her nostrils. The trace of sulfur made her stomach turn, and not only from the stink itself. Sehdra had always tried to make of herself a shadow, one that might disappear into an alcove or corner as soon as she entered a chamber. Most of the servants, slaves, and ministers in the palace aided her in it, wanting to see her as little as she wanted to be seen.

But her brother had always delighted in pulling her back into the light.

"Royal Sister?" a voice spoke by her side. "Sehdra, are you well?"

She produced a smile as she turned to Teti. In her people's eyes, the man was her slave, one of the servants castrated to serve the women of the royal family. But it had been a long time since she had seen him that way. In the twenty-one floods since he was assigned to her, when she was a girl only just receiving her womanly cycle, Teti had become the brother she had never had.

Or, she mused, *at least the brother Physt could never be.*

Sehdra smiled at Teti, not wishing to worry him. Yet she wondered how ugly she must look as the deformed side of her face crinkled. Teti never seemed to mind. He returned the smile, saying with his eyes what it would be dangerous to utter with his mouth.

He will not lay hands on you. He will not spill royal blood. He will not tarnish the image of the karah.

Neither were fooled. She knew as well as he that her brother had many ways to harm beyond words.

She had been summoned by the karah, and could not delay entering. Drawing in a breath, Sehdra summoned her courage and, with Teti a step behind, walked inside.

No matter how many times she visited it, the karah's throne chamber awed her. Golden morning light streamed in through triangular windows lining the walls. Columns framed the wine-hued carpet that bisected the room. Braziers blazed between the columns, making shadows dance and the murals, expertly brushed onto the walls and columns, come alive.

Sehdra knew every story depicted in those paintings.

The hunt of Yeshept and Pawura. The creation of the world by Wise Qa'a. The struggles between Red Bek, White Aya, and Black Gazabe. All the ordeals of the Divine were drawn along these stones, each a reminder of the insignificance of mortal striving.

The room had been designed to draw the eyes toward a single point at the far end. The Ascendant Throne possessed the same angularity as the rest of the room, the seat as bluff and strong as the power it conferred. Gold and silver lined the stone, and emeralds splayed across the top in a crown. Yet it did not detract from the man who sat upon it, cushioned from its hard surface by pillows, but added to his mystique.

Sehdra's eyes did not rest on the karah. Inevitably, her gaze rose to the dark alcove behind the throne. There loomed a greater shadow, hidden but for the occasional glint of jewels and precious metals, silent but for a heavy, thrumming respiration that filled the air with its bitter scent.

Do not look, Sehdra cautioned herself. *Do not draw attention.*

It took an impossible effort, like looking away from a stalking lion, but Sehdra managed it. She continued forward, tottering and wincing each time she put weight on her withered leg.

No sooner had she entered sunlight than did her brother call to her. "Sehdra Ohkweht!" crooned Hephystus, his voice pitched high in mockery. "Come here, sister. I wish to look upon beauty this day!"

As he laughed, the others in attendance followed suit. *You are cold,* Sehdra told herself as her face burned. *You are ice.* She felt every lancing gaze from the guards, servants, and ministers who swayed to their karah's every cruel whim. Shadowed behind the columns, they seemed like the interred bodies of the dead risen at their descendant's behest, come to join in the debasement of his own blood.

But she knew the only bystanders of any importance were the two men to either side of the throne. On her brother's right was his vizier, Zosar of White Aya, the enactor of the karah's will and his principal councilor. Zosar carried himself like a cat through an adoring crowd, every part of him oozing self-satisfaction. His clothes were rich and sun-bright, as if in defiance of the dust that covered the city below. The largest opal Sehdra had ever seen sparkled in the center of his headwrap. He kept a short scepter tucked into his wide belt, shaped like the cobra god he professed to serve.

To the left of the chair stood a man opposite of the vizier in every way. Known only as the Ibis, he was a Suncoaster, and his strange ornamentation showed it. Though the throne room bore a morning chill, he wore no shirt, putting on display the bones woven into his ebon skin, which formed a pattern like a pair of elephant's tusks. A short skirt tucked around his waist, ostrich feathers its only decoration. He held his chin low, like a boar preparing to charge. His onyx eyes betrayed nothing of the intentions beneath.

Sehdra kept her gaze locked on her brother. She knew how mottled the cursed flesh became when she flushed. Scaled and puckered, color only worsened the look of the birth defect. She had hidden it for most of her life under an assortment of extravagant masks, hoping it added an air of mystery rather than appearing as ornate bandages, as it often felt. But since her brother's crowning, he had forbidden her from wearing masks in his presence. And the karah's word, as all knew in the Ascendant Empire, was absolute.

Yet she was protected even without them. Long ago, she

had learned to make a mask of her flesh. Her face showed no emotion. Only her cursed skin might betray her.

Sehdra limped forward and conjured a respectful smile. Nothing in the way she carried herself could be worthy of reprimand. Yet still, her brother found ill with her.

"You must walk as befits the ohkweht." Familiar ridges appeared above his nose, a foretelling of the morning's tidings. "You make it seem as if I keep a court of aberrations and invalids."

It was another of the legacies of her unfortunate birth, that twisted foot and leg. It pained Sehdra to walk on it, ground her joints together, and made her look ridiculous.

"My deepest apologies, Divine One." Sehdra spoke without irony. Her brother had keen ears for ridicule, being seasoned in it himself, and mocking a god had dire consequences.

The karah watched her in disapproving silence as she stopped at the appropriate distance before the throne, then bowed, descending to her knees and prostrating herself before him. She breathed in the musk of the red carpet, already showing enough wear to soon be replaced, and waited for his dismissal. Her withered limb screamed in protest.

It felt an eternity before he spoke. "Look at me, dear sister."

Sehdra rose, repressed a wince as her leg throbbed, and met her brother's stare. Karah Hephystus the Third had grown into his role as the ruler of Ha-Sypt over the past five years. When he had first ascended at sixteen floods, he had too much resembled a boy playing a man's role.

Now, the royal trappings fit him. The leopard skin draped over his narrow shoulders did not swallow him, but signified the power and authority he possessed, even over those deadly and majestic creatures. The lion's tail that hung from his belt showed no beast could compare to Physt's prowess.

The Ascendant Crown, too, accentuated his appearance. It was a work of beauty, constructed of fiber at the beginning of his reign and stiffened into its symbolic shapes. The conical base was painted black in honor of Gazabe the Jealous, the god Physt had taken as his Inspiration. The wings flanking it represented the ears of Red Bek. Last rose White Aya, curling out in a deadly leer from Hephystus's forehead.

The karah was held as a god among men. Though Sehdra had always struggled to accept that, her brother at least looked the part. Yet, no matter what the gods conveyed through the sands, she had to look no further than his eyes to see the mortal she knew so well. They burned with the same casual cruelty he had always fostered.

As Hephystus beheld Sehdra, his expression spasmed. "Your face repulses me, Royal Sister. Had I not something you must witness this day, I would command you stay to the shadows. At least you must turn that beetle-flesh away from me."

Sehdra obeyed at once. His insults slid off her like water over oiled leather. "Of course, Divine One."

"*Of course,*" he mocked. Then, abruptly wearying of the torment, her brother leaned back and dismissed her with a casual wave of his hand. Already, his cold eyes had flickered up to the chamber's entrance. Sehdra bowed again and scurried out of the way before looking around. Once sheltered behind the columns, relief flooded through her. She tried not to appear as if she hid, but maintained the regal posture worthy of the Royal Sister. Her stomach twisted, wondering what spectacle her brother had planned this morn. That Teti slipped up next to her brought only marginal comfort.

The vizier roused, clapping his hands once. "Bring him in!"

Sehdra understood her brother's game as soon as she recognized the man who was dragged forth and thrown to the ground. Raneb, high chanter to Wise Qa'a, had never more resembled his deity than on his hands and knees. His black robes and headdress, stiffened into the mandibles of the beetle god, made him seem as if he were a scarab searching for scat.

Not likely to find any on Physt's floor, Sehdra thought, *though there is plenty in his words.*

"Raneb Nautjer!" sneered Vizier Zosar. "You are accused of a most grievous crime. You have been found stealing from the Holy Karah himself."

Raneb remained on his knees, but rose to clasp his hands before him. "Please, Divine One," the high chanter begged, ignoring the vizier. "Please, spare me. Show the Wise Scarab's mercy. I have done Qa'a's will all my life. I only needed coin for a short time, then I would—"

"*Silence!*" roared Zosar. He approached the prostrating priest and, withdrawing the scepter from his belt, whipped it across the man's face. Flecks of blood caught in the sunbeams as the bronze cracked across Raneb's jaw. Sehdra barely flinched. She had come expecting violence.

"Enough, Zosar."

At the karah's command, the vizier backed away. Sehdra's brother smiled. His eyes were bright with more than the wine he so often drank now.

"Zosar says you have been skimming the top of the temple coffers. Is this true, Raneb? Answer yes or no only, or I will take your tongue."

Raneb remained on his knees, though he drew upright. Still, he visibly trembled as he whispered, "Yes."

"And from these coins, you are to cede your seasonal

tithe to me, your karah. Yet, if some are missing, you will not pay the full amount — is that not so?"

"Yes."

Hephystus leaned forward in his throne. His smile reminded Sehdra of a jackal slavering over a fresh carcass. "I am your god, Raneb. I am the first of your gods, ahead of your beetle, ahead of any others. *I am the first!*" His voice rose to a shout, then lowered as he continued. "I am the god who is here before you, priest. And so I am the last god you should steal from."

Sehdra's every muscle was taut as she watched the drama play out. *Like a scene from a slave play.* Yet this was no act. Her brother embodied this reality and ruled it.

She knew the scene's inevitable conclusion.

Physt leaned back. The smile had faded and malaise returned as he waved a hand. "Take his head."

Raneb all but squealed then. "Please, Empyrean Soul! You are first among the Divine, of course you are first! I repent — I will pay back every coin, every last one, even if it paupers me. But only spare me, I beg of you—"

Guards stepped up to either side and seized the high chanter's arms, wrenching them back and drawing short his pleas. A third guard drew his khopesh, the curve in the blade settling lightly on the back of Raneb's neck. Sehdra's pulse raced. She found her hand reaching behind her to grip Teti's, sharing their horror.

I should speak. I should stop them. She was only the ohkweht, sister to divinity. She had not the authority to defy the karah's will.

Yet neither could she let a man die because of her.

As the guard's arm drew back to swing, Sehdra lurched free of the shadows. "Divine One, wait!"

The guard, seeing who had spoken, hesitated and looked at the throne. Physt looked annoyed, while the vizier smiled. The Ibis's expression did not shift, nor did his stance.

"Speak quickly, sister," her brother grated. "The apostate's head must roll!"

"You know Qa'a is the god to which I am devoted." She hesitated, swallowing the next words she had been about to say. While their mother had often said it was Qa'a who blessed Sehdra at birth, and not cursed her with deformities, her brother had never shared the opinion. But, conscious of the blade waiting for the high chanter's neck, she rushed on. "Seeing as such, I request that you allow me to inquire into his reasons for taking from you."

Physt's eyes narrowed. "I cannot refuse a humble request from such a *beauty*. Very well, Sehdra. Ask."

She bowed, pretending he had graced her rather than delivered the same stale insult, then looked back to Raneb. "I put my question to you, Raneb Nautjer. Why did you do as you say?"

The high chanter's head raised just enough to look at her. "The widows, Royal Sister, and the orphans. With the recent riots, there are more than usual requesting food and fewer offerings made. I thought to borrow what they needed from the temple."

Sehdra's heart cried out for the man. That he possessed a kind spirit had seemed clear to her every time she had visited his temple before. She was certain it was the truth. All knew of the unrest among the population under her brother's harsh rule.

Physt barked a laugh. "Do you believe your god and king soft-headed, priest? Surely, you can lie better! Men who rise as high as you do not risk death for *widows* and *orphans*. I have heard enough."

Her brother waved a hand again, and Sehdra's hopes

plunged. Yet she remained where she was, even though she would be splashed by the beheading.

If all I can do is wear a good man's blood, then I must.

But a sudden rumble, like the groan of the shifting earth, stiffened everyone in place.

"Wait!" cried the Ibis in his shrill voice. He skittered forward on legs that bowed outward, making him seem more like the bird for which he was named. "Great Oyaoan speaks!"

On the spot, the Suncoaster spun around and bent down on one knee. Sehdra followed the Ibis's prostrations to the source of the rumble. She did not want to look; she could not help but look. As the shadows roiled behind the throne, a monstrous shape took form.

She rose four times the height of the tallest man Sehdra had ever seen. Her tusks came into the light first, yellow as picked-over bones, and glittering with the jewels that hung from them. The macabre necklace came next, swinging with each heavy step, the skulls making a chilling, rattling sound. Then came the dozens of clinging bracelets, made of gold, bronze, silver, and copper, catching the light as one arm, then the other, came into view. Her skin was gray and rough and seemed to defy illumination. Her eyes, dark as an oasis pool on a moonless night, seemed to absorb the scene before her. A trunk, writhing like a viper, hung down the front of her face, and wide ears, heavy with rings, framed it.

Sehdra's withered leg felt as if it would lose what little strength it possessed and send her sprawling to the ground. No matter how many times she stood before Oyaoan, she never grew used to it. Her brother was supposed to be a god, but as he sat with the huamek's shadow cast over him, she could only see him as a man with a god's crown.

Oyaoan rumbled again. Though Sehdra knew it to be

speech, none but her translator, the Ibis, understood what she said.

"Great Oyaoan speaks!" the Suncoaster shouted from the floor. "The beetle priest is to pay his debts, then return to his duties. There is need for him soon, and Great Oyaoan does not throw away lives. Great Oyaoan has spoken!"

The giantess stood not a dozen paces from Sehdra. She longed to bolt, though she made for a poor runner. By an effort she had thought beyond her, she remained where she was as Oyaoan stretched one gargantuan hand toward the high chanter. Sehdra's nose detected a whiff of urine as the thick, gray fingers grasped Raneb's shoulder and wondered if it came from the priest. Despite what the Ibis had declared, the high chanter shuddered violently under the huamek's touch. Tears streamed down his face.

As easily as Sehdra might lift a knife, Oyaoan hoisted Raneb and set him on his wobbling legs. Then she rumbled in her foreign tongue again.

"Great Oyaoan speaks!" the Ibis said, still bowed. "She is merciful and wise. She will not waste good hearts. She bids the high chanter, Raneb, to remember her graciousness in the seasons to come. Great Oyaoan has spoken!"

With that, the giantess turned and lumbered back into the darkness behind the throne.

Only once the huamek returned to the shadows did Sehdra suck in a ragged breath. Her gaze traveled first to Raneb, who swayed as if he would faint, then to her brother. Hephystus leaned forward on his throne, hands clenched into fists. Rage was written in every crease of his face.

"*Get out!*" he screamed. "*Leave*, you blighted worms, or I'll tear off your heads myself!"

As her brother reached for his goblet and drained it, Sehdra felt a hand on her elbow. "We should go, Royal Sister," Teti murmured in her ear as he led her to the door.

She did not resist, but let her friend sweep her along. The occupants of the throne chamber thronged the door, frantic to obey their karah, but none impeded her passage. No one wished their head to be the next to roll, and offense given to the ohkweht might be all the provocation Physt needed just then.

But as pain stabbed up her twisted leg, Sehdra knew it would not be long before the sword fell on someone's neck.

2. STRANGE COMPANY

*The babe conceived out of wedlock must be acknowl-
edged, for it is the father's responsibility to care for his
seed. Such a child shall be brought under roof and heel,
and made into an oath-sworn daughter or son.*

*- The Inscribed Beliefs; Verse the Second, Line the
Twenty-first*

Bastor wiped the sweat from his brow and shifted
the satchels digging into his shoulder. Over the
many days he'd been walking, the bags had pulled
his muscles every which way, like bread kneaded by a baker.
Truth be told, he felt he had about as much strength as
dough now.

But long ago, his father had instilled the lesson in him to
never show weakness. Around his father, after all, that had
been liable to end in a beating.

He glanced over his unoccupied shoulder and
accounted for his companions. *We're a ragged bunch,* he

thought as he surveyed the small party. *Even by my low standards.*

Walking ten paces behind him came the old Jarl of Oakharrow, Lord Bor Kjellson, and his attendant, Uljana. Every step that the sprite-touched man walked on his own was a miracle to Bastor's mind. The past several days had seen many fits and starts in their journey westward, most of them dictated by the jarl's shifting moods. Once a renowned warrior and leader, he often devolved into fits and tantrums. Bastor felt shamed merely witnessing them.

And the gods know I feel little shame these days.

How Uljana tolerated it, much less this sojourn, Bastor could not say. Other Baegardians would see in her only a mule's stubbornness, for they saw thralls as less than human, if not quite beasts. But Bastor knew better.

Put any highborn in her hole-ridden shoes, he thought, *and they'd be as broken as the jarl by midnight.*

He had flashed the Sypten woman smiles when he could spare them, and he tried to speak with her when they stopped at night during the initial days of travel. But she had learned to be suspicious during her years of enthrallment. In him, she saw another highborn man trying to take advantage of a slave woman, no matter how old and worn she had become. Though he understood, Bastor could not shake his regret, like a pebble hidden in his boot. Still, he had abandoned his attempts to engage her after the third night.

Behind the jarl and thrall came the last two members of their party. *The courting doves,* Bastor thought wryly as his eyes flickered over their distant forms, nearly lost among the trees. Though they never acknowledged it, something lay between Lady Aelthena and her guardian, Frey. He had seen them sneak off that night some days ago, and they had not come back the same.

But beyond his usual teasing, Bastor kept quiet about the occasion, nor did he inquire into what had happened among the dark pines. The jarl's heir — if she could still be called that — was prickly at the best of times, and even more when it came to her affections. Even after roughing it in the wilderness between Oakharrow and Petyrsholm, with her silver-threaded dress fraying at the hem and her fur cloak spattered with mud, she remained unbowed. Her jaw was set, her verdant eyes bright, her steps unfaltering.

She's either mad or hardier than she looks. Despite himself, his admiration for her had sprouted and grown.

Frey noticed Bastor's gaze and gave him a hard look. Bastor answered with a droll grin before facing forward. The guardian was a different story. Though Bastor had sometimes walked beside him, Frey had not spoken a willing word. The man saw him as a smuggler and ne'er-do-well, and would not budge in that opinion.

To be fair, he's not far wrong.

Yet, for all the young warrior's resistance, Bastor saw a kindred spirit in him. Frey, he felt, would do whatever was necessary to make things right. From what Bastor had heard, he had already abandoned his aging parents to the Jotun back in Oakharrow out of duty to Aelthena.

Duty, and his other interests in the jarl's daughter.

Bastor focused his attention ahead. His companions remained alive and well. The travel had not been easy, especially as they had often walked next to the road rather than on it. But through an unforeseen blessing of the Inscribed, it had remained uneventful.

All good fortune ended, however, and theirs was no exception. For through the canopy, Bastor caught his first glimpse of Petyrsholm.

He had only visited the city once. Bastor had been seven, and his father had hauled him out to make the rounds among his fellow jarls, courting them for future favors and ambitions. The city had struck him as older and grander than his home jarlheim of Ragnarsglade, and he had stared around in wide-eyed wonder — at least until his father put an end to it. *You're not a straw-headed plowman,* Lord Ragnar had said. *You're my son. Act like it.*

Bastor's lips twisted in a smile. *How I look forward to our reunion, dear father.*

A discordant sound scattered his bitter musings. Bastor halted, listening. Beyond the rustle of the wind through the pine needles, he heard a distant rumble.

Hooves, pounding up the road.

He squinted beyond the trees to the wide dirt path. He could see no one yet. But they would arrive soon.

Bastor turned back to his companions and motioned, gesturing toward the road. Uljana seemed to understand at once, but she ignored Bastor to smile at Lord Bor and gently direct him behind a large oak. The jarl shrugged off her touch, muttering protests and wandering off — toward the road. Bastor watched with a resigned smile as the old man went to alert the very people from whom they sought to hide. With a sigh, he took his axe in hand and wondered if the feeling in his gut was dread or anticipation.

Both, probably.

Frey seemed to have heard the horses as well, for he laid a hand on Aelthena's shoulder. Predictably, the heir did not listen. Shaking him off just as her father had his thrall, she shifted the bag hanging from her shoulder and strode off to intercept the jarl. Bastor closed in on their other side. He knew better than to try to stop Lord Bor from doing anything; he had seen his violent side more than once during the trek. But if there was to be blood, he meant to be there.

You could flee, whispered a part of him. *Leave them. What good can it do to stay? Save yourself.*

But for all his flaws, Bastor was not gutless. And Aelthena, by benefit of her position, mind, and resolve, could accomplish a great deal. Even when she had threatened to expose him and his father, he could not turn away from her potential. His father may have coerced him into undermining Baegard, but at his core, Bastor never wanted to betray his homeland.

He would stand by it now.

The noble warrior, he taunted himself. *Who would have believed it of me?*

The jarl neared the road, undeterred by his daughter's attempts to dissuade him. Bastor came swiftly behind. He lowered his burdens to rest behind a tree and tightened his hands on the axe's shaft. He could see the riders now. The jarl would show himself before they could pass. His breath came quick. The blood pounded in his head, in his muscles, hard and ready for sharp use again. An eager grin pulled back his lips to bare his teeth.

Lord Bor emerged and roared, "*HALT!* Who goes there?"

The horsemen pulled up — a dozen of them, by Bastor's quick count. He considered himself a hard man, as such things were reckoned, but he was not so mad as to believe he could sway such odds in his favor. Still, he did not put away his weapon. If they were foes, he would be ready.

The voice that called forth was high-pitched with surprise. "Lord Bor?"

Aelthena, who had been watching from behind a tree, suddenly burst forth. "Asborn?"

Asborn. As the situation became clear, a sigh escaped Bastor, and a feeling almost like disappointment swept through him as he hooked his axe onto his belt. He watched as first Frey, then Uljana, revealed themselves to Thane Asborn and the men with whom he traveled. The guardian spared one last look back at Bastor, his thoughts hidden behind a wariness, then moved out of sight.

Bastor turned away from the party and went off by himself, the satchels left behind. *She'll be cared for now,* he told himself. *And you have your own path to walk.*

To accomplish what must be done to unite Baegard would require many things that Aelthena, and even Frey, would not dare to do. That was the path Bastor must walk. No matter how little he wanted to.

He made for the nearing walls of Petyrsholm, already anticipating the horn of mead awaiting him.

3. A WOMAN'S WILES

The Jarlmoot is an older tradition even than the jarlheims themselves. I have seen scraps of writing referring to "moots" dating back to before our ancestors sailed across the Treacherous Sea. In origin, they are meetings of leaders, be they clans, tribes, or simply heads of families, and were reserved for matters important to the applicable communities.

The Jarlmoot specifically refers to the gathering of Baegard's jarls to address nation-wide issues. On occasion, this has related to betrothals broken, indiscretion in the bedchamber, or other pettier affairs. Most frequently, however, it is for waging war, and the election of an Arkjarl to lead their warriors into battle.

- Commentary on the Jarlmoot, by Alfjin the Scribe

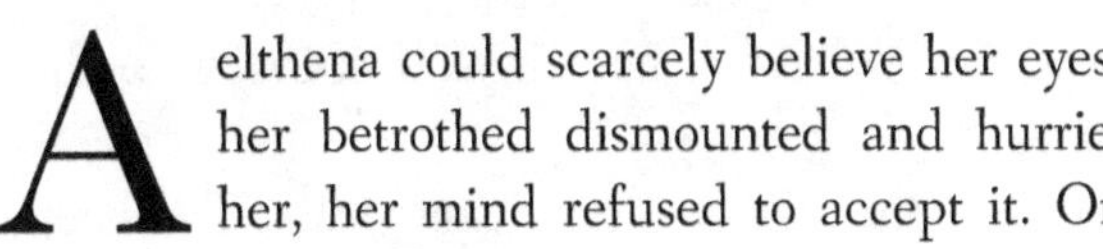

Aelthena could scarcely believe her eyes. Even as her betrothed dismounted and hurried toward her, her mind refused to accept it. Only as his arms closed about her and his chainmail pressed hard against her ribs did she believe it.

Asborn. He's here. We've arrived.

She lifted her arms to embrace him back as relief flooded through her. She had not known how much she craved even a small piece of home, of the familiar. Asborn gave that to her. He smelled mostly of the road, of dust and sweat, yet beneath it, his earthy scent was just detectable.

But something spoiled the moment. Something held her back. She tried to push it from her thoughts.

Not now. Time enough for it later.

But the memory of that night had lodged once more in her mind.

Just as she could no longer endure the embrace, Asborn pulled away, only to hold her at arm's length. His eyes sparkled with tears. "I heard the news. I was coming. But now you're... Aelthena, I can't believe you're here."

"I know."

Tell him you missed him, a part of her urged. *That you cannot believe he's here as well.*

But somewhere in the leagues across the wide Baegardian valley, she had shed, along with the softness of her flesh, some of the hard resolve that had defined her. Or perhaps that change had come before, when she witnessed the Jotun destroying the Teeth Gate with dragonfire and splattering Skarl the Savage across the cobblestones.

I'm different now. She wondered if the man who held her truly knew her anymore. If he ever had.

As Asborn's brow creased, Aelthena searched for a better response. "It's been a long journey," she said, eking out an apologetic smile. "I'll be more myself once I've bathed and had a meal."

"Of course. Forgive me — how thoughtless I've been." His natural goodwill touched upon, Asborn brightened.

Releasing Aelthena, his eyes traveled past her, and she turned to see he looked at Frey.

"Thank you, Guardian Frey," Asborn said gravely. "For keeping her safe when I could not." In a rare show of respect from a highborn to a lowborn, he held his fist to his heart.

Frey mimicked the thane's gesture and grinned. "The pleasure of duty is its own reward, my Thane."

Aelthena seethed silently. She hoped only she heard his hidden meaning. Asborn, at least, seemed unaware.

"I brought an additional horse for you, and one for Lord Bor as well." Asborn glanced at Frey, then Uljana, his brow creasing. "It appears we'll have to double up on our way back to Petyrsholm."

"Frey can take my horse. I'll ride with you." The words came before thought. Her instincts for politics and society, rusted away in the wilderness, were quickly being polished and primed. She wondered if she lost something as she regained them.

"We had a fifth companion." Frey frowned into the woods. "But it appears we've lost him."

Bastor's absence suddenly became obvious. She wondered where he had gone off to, and why. *To return to his dastardly ways, no doubt.* They had been companions of convenience, nothing more. She wondered why that stung. She had barely known the man, even if he had saved their lives.

But she knew he would not go far. Petyrsholm was the rogue heir's most likely destination. And she did not doubt that, whatever his declarations of reformation, he'd entangle himself as thickly as ever in the darker side of Baegard's politics.

"Check if he left anything behind, then we'll be off," she said to Frey, glad for an excuse to order him about. He took a bit of the satisfaction out of it as he grinned, his bright eyes dancing.

You won't forget that night, they seemed to say. *And neither will I.*

She set her jaw and turned away, going to her father to set about the onerous task of mounting him atop his horse.

She had not thought to find Petyrsholm and its holdings to her liking. In Oakharrow, they spoke of the plains city with sneering disregard. It was a jarlheim of soft people, Harrow-folk said; they did not have to suffer the harshness of living in the mountains, closer to the elements and at the mercy of the sprites of ice and air. She had seen the city once before, and as a child, she had believed her people's declarations.

Yet if Holmsfolk were soft, there were benefits to softness. Spring had already stretched forth into the vale. Hollyhocks, dandelions, and bluebells bloomed in colorful displays, like girls dancing at the Blossombirth in their new skirts and smocks. Broad-leaved trees were not bare skeletons, but spawned fresh growth, a merry chartreuse in the stirring breeze. Oaks and alders proliferated, as did aspens and maples, though pines were not left behind.

Even as the forest gave way to fields and farms, Aelthena looked forward to every rise in the road and the sweeping views they afforded. The pastures were green and rippled in the wind. She had never seen a sea, but she could easily imagine it as she held to Asborn and watched the grass sweep this way and that, like the ocean's waves.

Cutting through the land was the Whiterun, sparkling as brightly as its name. It wound like the great serpent Lavaethun through the Baegardian valley, curving to the west of Petyrsholm to run from Djurshand in the north all the way past Ragnarsglade to the south. She had seen it from Oakharrow, and from afar, it had seemed as thin as a thread. In truth, it stretched half a league wide at its broadest, and even at its narrowest, it still exceeded Oakharrow's Honeybrook many times over. Boats and rafts, dark against the sun-dazzled waters, drifted up and down the river. She felt a stirring in her as she recognized one of them as a drakkar, a longship fitted with a dragon figurehead, which her ancestors had long ago employed on raids to earn a fearsome reputation. These days, they sailed not the sea, but the Whiterun, patrolling the waters for incursions from Ha-Sypt, Zakowa, or one of the western nations, and occasionally harassing the Sypten cities downstream.

They rode closer, and the city itself drew her eye. The plains city could not match the austere majesty of Oakharrow, yet even Aelthena had to concede Petyrsholm possessed a beauty born of abundance. The walls that surrounded the city were of a chalky limestone. Homesteads crowded around the walls like youngsters at the feet of a favorite elder. From atop one rise, they could peer over the walls and see the inner city was even more densely populated, buildings stacking one on top of another. Above all rose the bastion that had precipitated the town: the Elkhorn, home to the jarlheim's leader, Lord Petyr Petyrson, and where the Jarlmoot was taking place.

As they arrived at the open city gate, Aelthena observed the peasantry milling about them. Some wore pinched expressions, but as many smiled and laughed and called greetings over the bustle. Their party gathered curious stares, and only a few of the lowborn thought to bow or show signs of respect. Aelthena scarcely noticed. She might be highborn, but the title that validated her blood was far from certain.

A street ran through Petyrsholm toward the castle.

Paved with the same gray stone as the walls, it twisted like a river around the buildings. Like in Oakharrow, the main road was a gathering place for stalls and shops, and a market like the Dusty Wares sprawled in an overwhelming mixture of sounds, scents, and sights. Aelthena was surprised as a glimmer of nostalgia stole over her. She had never been fond of the Dusty Wares, preferring quieter browsing. But with her home stolen from her, even those poor memories were gilded.

They ascended the hill to the castle grounds. The Elkhorn was of lackluster lime and boasted more wooden roofs and supports than either the Harrowhall or Vigil Keep. Sprawling along the crest like an enormous stretching cat, it lacked the artistry of the Harrowhall's spires and facades and Vigil Keep's bluff walls. But arrow slits lined every fortification, and guard towers erupted from amid the chambers. It was a castle built to endure war.

Just the castle we'll soon need.

The guards seemed to know Asborn, for at his hail, they cranked open the portcullis and admitted their party. Aelthena wondered if Bastor could enter so easily. Would he return to his father? Or find a drinking hole somewhere in the city to drown in?

He's not your concern, she reminded herself. *You have enough to worry about as it is.*

Riding into the main courtyard, which was surrounded by plain walls on three sides, Asborn dismounted, then assisted Aelthena. She had never enjoyed accepting aid of any kind, but grudgingly consented to the offer, the concession better than risking a twisted ankle. Besides, as she stood on her own legs again, she realized just how much the journey had worn on her. They had walked from dawn to dusk and eaten worse fare than she was accustomed to. She tried not to let her weakness show, but straightened her carriage as her mother had long ago taught her a highborn woman should.

Would you could be here now, she thought to her departed mother as Asborn and his keepers passed off their horses to the castle grooms. It was a wish she had scarcely imagined she would make before. But now that Bestla Of'Bor was gone, she craved the advice she had before refused. She walked through a foreign castle in uncertain times with only the haziest idea of what she must do. She was tired and hungry and afraid. Her brothers were likely all dead, and her father corrupted by spirits. She wanted nothing more than to fold into her old bed in the Harrowhall, draw the covers over her head, and sleep.

Stop it, she chastised herself as grooms led the horses away and Asborn turned back to her, familiar creases in his brow. *Be strong. You know the next step. Take it and do not hesitate.*

To hesitate now would mean to stumble and fall. And she was not sure she could rise again.

Aelthena prepared as if going to battle — for, though it would be conducted with words, she suspected a fight awaited.

She left no detail untouched. She bathed, ate, dressed in a clean, if plain, dress. Under it, she strapped a small knife, used for trimming the candle. The hard edge of the blade pressed against her wool undergarments, and the strap pulled tight, but she felt better for it.

When she exited the small chamber given to her, Aelthena found Frey already waiting. "M'lady," he greeted her with a smile.

"Guardian." She did not return it, but looked him over

while pretending not to. He had replaced his travel-stained clothes with fresh ones, though from their threadbare appearance, he had pilfered them from a servant's chest. The sword belted around his waist was the only sign that he was her protector. Telling from his damp hair and the scent of juniper wafting from him, he had bathed as well. Part of her wanted nothing more than to breathe him in and step into the circle of his arms. She kept her thoughts hidden.

Yet Frey stepped closer. "Don't tell me you mean to pretend we are merely lady and guard now. Not after all we've been through."

Aelthena squashed the soft part that wanted to fold into his arms. She lowered her voice. "That *is* what we are. What we have to be. I'm promised to Asborn, remember?"

Her resolve was quickly fracturing. Frey seemed to see it, and his mockery disappeared.

"I'm here, Aelthena," he murmured. "By your side. Guarding your back. I said I would always be loyal. I don't mean to contradict that now."

Aelthena tried clearing her throat, feeling as if some of her earlier meal had lodged there.

"Good," she said, tone harsher than she intended. Frey raised an eyebrow, yet she refused to apologize. "We must go. The jarls will be waiting."

The guardian bowed his head — sardonically, to her eye. But as he again spoke, no hint of impropriety escaped. "Will Lord Bor be joining us?"

"No. The others will know from Asborn that I am Lord Bor's heir. I doubt his presence will make any difference in their acceptance."

Doubts seemed to stir behind Frey's eyes, but he only shrugged. "As you will, Lady Heir."

Aelthena stepped past him. She could not entertain his

doubts, not now. Not when her own mind was overflowing with them.

Asborn had earlier given her directions to find the Jarl-moot. Yet despite being certain she remembered the way, she and Frey soon became lost. Aelthena looked around with mounting frustration as she entered not the base of a tower, but the bustling castle kitchens. Perplexed servants stared at her like a flock of sheep until Frey stepped up and halted one thin-faced girl.

"Hundred pardons," he said with a pleasant smile, "but my mistress is seeking the tower where the jarls meet. Might you show us the way?"

The girl, nervous as a doe, glanced back into the kitchens. A short woman there, who stood like a stone amid a swirling stream, had been watching them, and approached at that moment. Aelthena guessed her to be the head cook.

"What is it? M'lady," the cook added after an appraising look over Aelthena, then Frey, intuiting who stood before her.

Aelthena ignored the woman's patronizing tone. "I require directions to the Jarlmoot. Can you lead us there?"

"Not I, m'lady — the kitchens are my kingdom, and require a firm hand." The cook let loose a small, proud smile at that. "But I'll send Ipu here to lead you. Ipu, take them up at once."

"Thank you." Aelthena turned after the nervous kitchen girl, who muttered for them to follow her.

Ipu proved a competent guide, and within a matter of minutes, they had reached the base of the tower. "It's right up there, m'lady," the kitchen girl mumbled, her eyes downcast.

"Thank you, Ipu. I never would have found it without you." Aelthena was about to head up the stairs when she paused. "Many try to sever the tallest stalks, but we should not bend for fear of the scythe. Do you understand me?"

Ipu's eyes flickered up to meet Aelthena's. With a mite more confidence, the kitchen girl murmured, "Yes, m'lady."

Aelthena gave her a tight smile. Her reaction, and Frey's grin, somehow settled her own jitters. "Good. I shall see you again."

With that, she rallied her strength and mounted the first step.

The Jarlmoot, Asborn had informed her, took place at the top of Antler Tower, the tallest in the Elkhorn. She recalled from her first visit to Petyrsholm that it was the place from which rebellion had once been orchestrated against the King of Ice by Calder Coppereye before the insurgency was squashed. She hoped the war council held now would have the goal of unity rather than division.

And that I will have a place among them.

Up and up, the tower ascended. A golden evening shone through the narrow tower openings, and gusts, chill with the height they had gained, stirred through her damp braids. She welcomed the cool relief after the laborious hike.

At the top, a landing appeared where two castle guards stared hard at them. She could hear raised voices from the final staircase. Aelthena tried to rein in her galloping heart as she approached the guards. Their eyes grew harder as she neared. She tried not to quail.

Do as you told the girl. Stand tall.

"I am Lady Heir Aelthena." She peered beneath the helms of the guards to meet their eyes. "Heir to Lord Bor Kjellson, the Jarl of Oakharrow. I seek admittance to the Jarlmoot."

The guards exchanged a look. "We were told to expect

you, Lady Heir Aelthena," one of them spoke, a man sporting a dark, wiry braid off his chin.

She should have felt relieved at his statement. But something in it gave her pause. "Good," Aelthena said as she took a step forward.

The men moved between her and the stairs.

"Lord Petyr has forbidden you entrance, Lady Heir Aelthena," the same guard said. She detected a hint of satisfaction in his words.

Her blood rose. "On what grounds?" she demanded.

"You're a woman," the second guard grunted.

"You don't say," Frey retorted from behind her.

Though she appreciated the support, Aelthena ignored him and continued to stare with all the heat she could muster at the two men. "I am a jarl's heir, and my father is unwell. You cannot deny me entrance on account of my sex."

"All the jarls agreed," said the dark-braided man. "'These are men's affairs,' they said."

"That, they did." The second guard bobbed his head.

Her anger was bubbling over. Words were blunt instruments against thick skulls. She would get nowhere through speech.

She made a dash for the stairs.

They shouted after her, but Aelthena ignored them, racing toward the door above to wrench it open. She would not be barred, no matter how improper her entrance. She would not be excluded from "men's affairs" any longer.

She flung the door wide, then came to a halt. A dozen eyes stared at her. She tried not to wilt before them.

Asborn was the first to stand and speak. "Aelthena?"

She nodded toward him, then studied the other men in the room. She recognized them, most from the carvings given to each ruling family for just such meetings. Some of their likenesses had been overly flattering, but not so much that they were not familiar.

Petyr. Hother. Harald. Alrik. Siward. She fixed each of their names in her mind as her gaze slid over their faces.

She stopped at the last man. His hair, golden and radiant in the evening sun, was combed and slicked back down his scalp. A neatly trimmed beard with a hint of red framed his broad jawline. His clothes were as fitting for a warrior as a jarl, but for the lack of armor. Yet it was his eyes that were most arresting, the stormy blue of them familiar from his son.

Ragnar.

Lord Ragnar stood after Asborn, but with more decorum. While he did not reach Bastor's height and breadth, he remained a powerful and intimidating man.

"Lady Heir Aelthena," he said, his rich baritone containing both honey and iron. "Your presence is... unexpected."

She clawed through her swirling thoughts to find a reply. "It should not be. Thane Asborn has done admirably in holding my place, but as my father's heir, it is I who belong here."

She noticed the table then. Unfurled across it was a yellowed and cracked vellum scroll as long as she was tall. She recognized what it depicted immediately. *Enea.* Placed upon its surface were a spattering of stones in gray, white, and black. *And her armies.*

War reached its greedy hands over the lands.

Lord Petyr cleared his throat. "I believe I had made the situation clear to my guards."

Aelthena tried not to glare as she met his eyes. The lord of the Elkhorn rather less resembled the bull elk of his insignia and more a fox. His features were narrow — lips, eyes, nose, and chin all. The hair on his head was thin and dark, and the beard on his chin fell in three thin plaits. Where Lord Ragnar dressed like a warrior, Lord Petyr made no such intimations. He seemed a wealthy merchant in his silver-lined cloak and rich clothes.

"I am far from clear on it," she shot back. "I fail to see how my sex weighs against my authority."

She looked to the men who were supposed to be Oakharrow's allies. Lord Alrik of Aelford, a man who resembled a bear even more than her father, had never seemed one to balk at speaking his mind. Yet now, he frowned down at the stones on the map as if searching for an answer. Lord Harald, who sat next to him, was said to be a meeker sort. And though he met her gaze with his large, moist eyes, he stayed true to his reputation and remained silent.

"Lord Petyr is, in this respect, correct," another of the jarls spoke. "As is written in the Beliefs, 'A woman's place is at the hearth.' And politics, I trust, do not happen around the cooking pot."

Aelthena turned her gaze upon Lord Hother, a man who as much resembled an egg as she had ever seen. Round and bald, he interrupted the impression with a red fox skin draped over his shoulders. Gold buttons lined his cloak, and a silver circlet sat atop his head as if he were a king and not a jarl. She took it to be a reminder that when Baegard was first founded, his jarlheim of Djurshand had been the seat of royalty, though many centuries had passed since that had been the case.

"I met a cook downstairs," Aelthena said quietly. "She rules her domain like a queen, and I daresay she's accomplished far more than you have, from the looks of it." She gave a meaningful look down at the map, though she had hardly had time to become acquainted with it.

The last man in attendance grunted at her words,

though in affirmation or dismissal, Aelthena could not tell. Lord Siward was a difficult man to read. Known as the Black Ram for both his insignia and his role in holding a shield wall during the Sack of Qal-Nu, he was as scarred and bare-headed as any veteran. Metal clanked as he moved, telling of the precious metal bands layering his arms in the old way of preserving and showing one's wealth. A man as entrenched in ancient custom as he was unlikely to be an ally of hers.

She realized then there would be only one argument she might win, one by which she might gain a seat at the table. And from the blackening expressions of even Oakharrow's allies, she had to make it at once.

"But I did not come here to squabble over the Inscribed Beliefs," Aelthena said. "I came because war is upon us, and Baegard must unite behind one shield."

"I was under the impression that you came because you were driven from your city." Lord Petyr's tone was deceptively mild for his biting words.

She tried not to show he had found his mark. "Yes, I was. And I can see how that might seem like cowardice or weakness. But I have seen our enemy, and they are like none we have encountered before. Not since the days of our ancestors have we fought against them."

"You mean the Jotun!" Lord Alrik finally spoke, his voice booming through the chamber. "This 'King of Chieftains,' as Lady Kathsla's messenger named him."

Aelthena had forgotten that Asborn's mother had snuck out a messenger. She hoped it would corroborate her story.

"Yes. I first thought 'the Jotun' was a mere title, as you do. But I tell you now, my lords, it is not. I have seen the Jotun with my own eyes. He is not a man, but a giant, a *true* giant — humanity's ancient enemy come down from the Witterland."

Her gaze wandered to Asborn. She wondered if even he believed her. Though his brow was ridged as a washboard, he nodded at her glance.

But it was Lord Ragnar who spoke first. "It is a hard thing to believe. But I have had word of these creatures for some time among the Syptens. The surtunar, too, have risen from the old tales."

Aelthena eyed the Jarl of Ragnarsglade. Traitor that she knew him to be, his was the last support she had expected. Only as she parsed through the web of politics did she understand. *He has had contact with the giants; he must have.* Did that truly mean the surtunar were real? Her breath came quicker at the thought. But the colder part of her speculated on what Ragnar's game was in admitting knowledge of the giants now and backing her claim. Perhaps he sought to placate her.

She would not be so easily satisfied. Not when he had given her city and its people over to their enemies.

Calm, calm. She could not accuse Ragnar, not now. She had too little influence to succeed. And, as incredible as it seemed, she had larger goals to achieve.

Baegard had to unite.

The jarls muttered among themselves in the intervening pause. Sensing this might be her only chance, Aelthena drove her point home.

"The giants would be enough to contend with on their own, but they also bring dragonfire. Through his machinations, the Jotun destroyed the Harrowhall and broke through our city gates. You cannot know the power of this sorcery." She clamped her jaw. The last word had come out trembling with her fear and revulsion.

"Thank you, Lady Heir Aelthena, for bringing your concerns to us." Lord Ragnar afforded her a small smile, though his eyes remained flat. "But Thane Asborn has already presented Oakharrow's situation to this council and is suitably representing the plight of your people. Now, if you are finished, we must proceed with deciding what we must do about the threats facing Baegard — and, as you say, how we may unite behind one shield."

Aelthena began to respond before she caught herself. Staring into their eyes, she saw herself as they did now. *A woman's hysterics, not an heir's injustices.* Even Asborn seemed embarrassed for her, his eyes downcast.

She tightened her jaw. After the fall of Oakharrow, she knew a lost battle when she saw one.

"Very well," she said, her voice tight. "I expect to hear of your progress soon."

With that, Aelthena turned on her heel, strode out of the chamber, and left the door hanging open behind her.

She would not convince the jarls with a man's earnestness. Yet though Aelthena had suffered nothing but defeat after defeat of late, she found herself more full of resolve than ever before. Opposition did not grind her down; it only made her will stronger.

But she was a stranger to Petyrsholm, an heir without a jarlheim or allies. She could not bull ahead as she was inclined to do. No — she had to employ different means, one that Asborn's own mother had advocated: a woman's wiles.

Aelthena smiled and strode past the guards, who eyed her nervously at the bottom of the stairs. No doubt they wondered what she had to smile about.

"Come, Frey," she beckoned to the guardian, and smiled all the wider as, like a dog, he trotted obediently at her heels.

4. A PRIEST'S HOME

All words are fallible. Even holy words such as these, inspired by Djur and his progeny, are subject to error.

Thus it is the responsibility of the Silvers to reinterpret the Inscribed Beliefs for each generation, to ensure any mistakes, such as they are, may be corrected.

Life is ever-adapting; so must we be.

- Counsel on the Inscribed Beliefs, by Silver Vigilance

Bjorn was the first to mount the ridge and see the lights in the valley, but it was Loridi, coming shortly behind him, who called it out.

"Look'ee here, my fellows — and dear lady, of course," the jester spoke between panting breaths. "The fires of Eildursprall burn just below!"

A grin broke free on Bjorn's face, crinkling the unfamiliar, frost-tinged hair on his chin and cheeks. It had been eight days since he and his companions had parted ways with the remaining Hunters in the White and Skyardi.

Eight days since they had left behind the smoking ruins of Chasm Valley and the sorcerous dust that had proliferated there. They had trekked through the Teeth along treacherous paths, the warming days triggering avalanches near and far and turning the ground to slush beneath snowshoes and hooves. But they had not been attacked by beast nor barbar, and Bjorn was glad to suffer any amount of peril to avoid further violence.

He leaned forward to stroke Clap's muzzle. "We made it, boy," he murmured as he pulled off ice from the horse's mane. "You'll have a nice, warm stall soon."

"We can only hope."

Bjorn turned to see Hoarfrost appearing beside him. The Skyardi leader wore as cold an expression as the blustering wind atop the ridge. But through their experiences leading up to Chasm Valley and the days afterward, he realized that behind the icy eyes lay a warm heart, even if it was far from gentle.

A fourth figure joined them, loping through the snow with indefatigable strides. "They will welcome us," Yonik said, his unnaturally keen senses having allowed him to overhear the conversation. "After all, they are my family."

"They are Yewlings," Hoarfrost countered.

Bjorn, undecided in his opinion, studied the town below. In the gray light, he could pick out little more than the shapes of the buildings and the light escaping from their boarded windows, but it seemed an ample town, stretching the length of the snow-covered vale beneath them.

"Even so," Yonik murmured, "it is a town of two halves. The eastern half is mostly Yewling townsfolk, true. But the far end is our destination: Heim Numen, the compound where the Silvers reside and all gothi are trained. They would never fold to demands from the Jotun, no matter the penalty."

Bjorn nodded, hoping the priest was right. His eyes traveled up the opposite side of the valley to where a mountain loomed. Even as he craned back his neck, he could not see the top of it, swallowed as it was in low-hanging clouds. He had sometimes wondered how it would feel to stare up at Yewung, the tallest peak in the Bones of Nuvvog, as he glimpsed it from afar. Now he knew.

Awed. Small. Powerless.

Would he feel the same standing before the Jotun? He shook the dark thought from his head. *I didn't abandon them. I didn't forsake Oakharrow.* He was doing all he could, the *only* thing he could. He would find the truth behind the coming of the giants. He would uncover all there was to know regarding this ancient enemy. And then, when he knew how to defeat the Jotun, he would return.

Like a hero from the tales.

Then he thought of Keld, the boy's bloodied face and still eyes, as he'd appeared after the greatbear mauled him. The smile faded as quickly as it had come.

A gust stirred up, clawing at the raw skin of his face and curling within his hood. Though he tried not to listen to its whisper, he could not stop the words.

Fire, the wind wheezed. *Fire in the valley.*

Bjorn squeezed his eyes shut. He had hoped he might be free of the omens that had plagued him all his life, that they had only been because of inadvertent exposures to *khnuum.* Now, he had evidence to the contrary.

He would never be free.

Puffing sounded behind Bjorn. Desperate to escape the wind's whispers, he turned to see that Seskef, the last of their small party, had finally reached the ridge. As the big man stopped next to Loridi, he bent over, barely glancing down at their destination, much less keeping hold of his mount's reins.

"Now that you're here," Loridi said cheerfully as he clapped his friend on the shoulder, "it's time to keep going!"

The big man only groaned and waved a hand, pleading for mercy.

"With warmth and shelter right before us?" The tall man shook his head mournfully. "I'm afraid there's no pausing now, my friend. But perhaps we should roll you down?"

Hoarfrost made a disgusted sound as she stalked past the pair of jesters and led her horse down the curving path to the town.

Loridi looked at Bjorn and grinned. "Some folks have no sense of humor, eh, Lord Heir?"

Bjorn grimaced. With his jarlheim under threat by the Jotun, perhaps even fallen to him, and self-exiled to boot, he had no right to the title. "Best if you don't call me that."

"Ah! Trying for anonymity, are we? Very well, Lor — erm, *Bjorn.*"

With a look that was not quite repentant, Loridi ushered Seskef down after Hoarfrost.

Bjorn prepared to follow, but glanced at Yonik first. The priest still stared down at Eildursprall with a queer expression. The town's light seemed to gather in his eyes, reflecting like full moons in a lake. He often wondered at the oddities in the gothi's appearance and abilities. With half a greatbear's head as a hood, his reputation as a renowned hunter was plain on display. But since learning of *seidar* and the true face of sorcery, he wondered if the man had been born with his deviances, or if an experience had brought them about.

If he trained with the gothi, would the same thing happen to him?

Already, he felt changes within him. After Egil had shot

a fiery arrow into the Chasm and ignited the incendiary dust within it, a persistent cough had claimed Bjorn's chest. It had lasted for days afterward, sometimes rising so severely its passage left him weak and shaking. Yonik had brewed him a tea with leaves he had hauled all the way from Oakharrow for coughs, and though the gothi was not prone to worrying, his brow had creased often as he watched him.

But on the fourth day, Bjorn had risen with his lungs clear and feeling as nimble and spry as he ever had. Since then, he had marched at the front of the company and outlasted even Hoarfrost. His increased stamina was not the only difference. The cold touched him less, though Loridi assured him his nipples felt as frigid as ever. The hair on Bjorn's chin, soft and sparse before, had thickened, to Seskef and Loridi's amusement. He received no end of teasing about it as they marveled at what a specimen he had so quickly become, and they often asked if they needed to teach him how to shave. Thus far, he had rebuffed their attempts, though the situation was swiftly becoming untenable.

Yonik noticed Bjorn's stare and smiled. "Best not let Hoarfrost arrive first," said the priest. "Baltur knows that for all her other qualities, she's not the finest speaker."

Bjorn let the moment slip away. They all had worries enough of their own without burdening each other. Instead, he grinned. "Lead the way, old wolf."

For a moment, the gloom of the wind's omen had dissipated, yet as the silence of the march down surrounded him, the ominous words returned. He tried to shut them out. What good had prophecy ever done him? It only foretold what would happen; it did not tell him when or how to avert it. If fire would come to Eildursprall, as he suspected the warning meant, he could do nothing to stop it.

Yet for all his rationalizations, the guilt remained.

The snow firmed with the departure of the sun, but scarce light meant the going was slow. The lights of Eildursprall disappeared from sight as they moved around a cliff, then reemerged as they came out on the other side. Bjorn raised his head, gladdened to see their destination near, when he noticed Yonik had halted. Clap whinnied and pulled back on his reins as if spooked. Heart racing, Bjorn looked around for what caused the alarm.

Four silhouettes stepped before the fires of Eildursprall. Long objects in their hands spoke of bows and spears. Bjorn itched to reach for his shield, hanging from Clap's saddle, but did not dare, lest an arrow was aimed at his heart.

One spoke, a man by his voice, but in words Bjorn could not understand. One of his eyes was covered by a patch, while the other darted toward Yonik. It had sounded like Yewling speech, yet he feared it was Woldagi waylaying them, or one of the other tribes under the Jotun's command.

After a brief pause, Yonik replied. Where the barbar had been rough and accusing, the gothi was soothing. *We are not enemies*, his tone said, even if his words remained unintelligible to Bjorn's ears. *We come as friends.*

The barbar replied as gruffly as before, this time in stilted Djurian. "You think we believe Harrowmen are out in the winter mountains?"

"Our task is urgent," Yonik said, as calm as if weapon points did not bristle toward them like a threatened porcupine's quills. "The Silvers may possess knowledge Enea has dire need of now. We could not delay."

Silence greeted the priest's plea. Bjorn felt his companions' fear as if it were Chasm-fog, sticky and foul. His own terror throbbed like a second pulse. But something else, something molten and fierce, coursed through his veins beneath it. He itched not only for his shield, but his sword as well.

Fear and fury. It was a concoction with which he was becoming all too familiar.

Finally, the Yewling answered. "The *Seyfuli* will decide. Come. Give over your weapons."

"Do as he says," Yonik advised, removing the pair of long knives from his belt. "The Silvers will not have us harmed. They are just being cautious."

For a moment, Bjorn would have preferred to fight all of them alone rather than yield his sword and seax. But as the Yewlings approached with weapons at the ready, reason flooded back in. He sighed and, looping Clap's reins through an arm, set to unbuckling his belt, then slipping off the loops of his blades. His knife and shield followed quickly after. A barbar edged near, one hand outstretched, and Bjorn gave over his weapons and watched the man edge back. Only then did he realize the Yewlings were as afraid of his company as he had been of them. The realization squashed any fight remaining in him.

"Come," the Yewling said after his fellows were burdened with their weapons. The man's face briefly came into the firelight, showing a glimpse of a dark, thick beard and scarred features. Then he turned away, and two of the barbars positioned themselves behind Bjorn and his party to herd them into town.

Trying to ignore the spearpoints at his back, Bjorn observed what little he could of the town. The buildings were similar to those occupied by Oakharrow's lowborn, but the thatched roofs sloped nearly to the ground. These seemed to be the homes of the ordinary townsfolk, for after a while, they reached a low wooden fence that encircled a wide set of grander abodes.

"Heim Numen," Yonik breathed in his ear. "Home to the gothi order."

Opening the gate, their Yewling escort led them inside the compound and among the houses. Here, torches were mounted every dozen strides, and by their light, Bjorn tried to identify the buildings' functions as they passed. Two on either side promised to be the longhouse and the brewhouse, often the largest edifices in Baegardian towns. Others he could only guess at their functions. One square domicile was made almost entirely of stone. Whatever was kept in there, he expected to be quite valuable to be worth the effort.

The Yewlings took them to a round hut that looked barely sufficient to contain their company. As they were ushered inside, the sentries led away their horses. "See you soon," Bjorn murmured to Clap as the gelding whinnied in protest. The barbar who grasped the reins eyed him strangely, but it could have been the way the torchlight caught on his scar-lined face. Bjorn stepped inside with the others, and the door closed, sealing them into darkness. He heard something scraping outside before a heavy weight settled against the hut's single door.

They were trapped.

For several long moments, the company remained silent in the darkness. But Loridi was never quiet for long.

"Well," he said with false cheer, "that wasn't the warm welcome I'd been looking forward to. But at least we're out of the wind!"

"Unfortunately," Seskef noted, "we're stuck in here smelling you all night."

"Sprallfolk have always been protective of the priesthood." Yonik sounded defensive, something Bjorn had never observed before in the priest. "When the Silvers hear my name, they will release us."

"I'm sure 'Yonik' is the magic word they've been waiting for," Loridi said drily. But not even Seskef chortled at that.

Bjorn felt around him blindly until he found the walls. The hut was sealed well, no cracks between the boards to let in the scant light from outside. With a sigh, he sank down to the floor and rested back his head.

It promised to be a long wait.

He jolted awake as whatever had blocked the hut's door was dragged away.

Heart thumping, Bjorn listened into the darkness. *Will they slaughter us? Free us?* His companions remained silent, awaiting their fates with the same trepidation.

Unhindered, the door swung outward. The world outside was still couched in darkness. A barbar face looked in on them, illuminated by the torch in his hand. Bjorn recognized him as the man who had spoken before.

"Come," he grunted in Djurian. "The *Seyfuli* wait."

Bjorn glanced at Yonik, and sure enough, the priest exited first. Not wanting to be more a coward than he had already shown himself to be, Bjorn went out next. He flinched upon seeing barbars surrounding him. Their mounts and possessions were nowhere to be seen. It seemed Yonik's name had not earned them that much trust, then.

After all his companions had filed out, the lead Yewling grunted and gestured. "This way."

"I remember," Yonik murmured, his protest soft. If the barbar heard it, he did not show it.

They headed back down the same path they had come in upon, only now they stopped at one of the long buildings. The Yewling did not knock at the door, but pushed through and gestured sharply for them to follow. As Bjorn pressed inside, a shiver stole over him at the sudden change in temperature. As he had earlier guessed, they stood in the longhouse, and it seemed a merry environment on a chill night. Hearths on either side of the hall poured out flames and heat into the grand room and warmed the pots hanging next to them. Long tables and benches occupied most of the space, and sitting at them were a dozen people, both men and women. Bjorn stared at the women until he came to his senses and looked away, blushing. Aside from Hoarfrost, he had scarcely seen womenfolk since leaving Oakharrow, and the Skyardi was hardly a woman he dared look long at. The Sprallwomen did not have the same compunction about gaping at him and his companions, and their mutters grew at their passage. He hunched his shoulders and hoped he came off favorably.

The sentry led them down the middle of the hall to the far end. There, the floor raised to a platform, where a shorter table sat perpendicular to the others. Mounting the stairs, they were forced to navigate around this table, then back down the stairs on the other side. A door sat in the middle of the wall, two braziers framing it. To this door, the Yewling stepped forward and knocked before pulling the door outward.

"In," he growled, his dark eye staring first at Yonik, then Bjorn. The gothi did not seem to share Bjorn's hesitation, but entered as if he had every right to be there. Bjorn wordlessly followed.

The chamber beyond was not as tall as the rest of the longhouse, but had a roof that sloped to the ground. A smaller fireplace nestled into the alcove and put off heat. An oval table took up the majority of the space. Around it were seated three people. All sported white or gray hair, and despite the stifling warmth from the fire, they were bundled in furs. As aged gazes looked up from their abruptly ceased conversation, Bjorn had the sense of a lifetime of knowledge simmering behind each pair of eyes. He knew them to be the Silvers even before Yonik bowed low.

"Honored Mothers, Honored Father," the gothi said, as respectful as Bjorn had ever heard him. "Thank you for admitting me and my companions on so late and cold a night."

"Brother Yonik," one of the two women greeted him with a thin smile. "It has been long since you last visited." She had the same coppery hue as many of the Yewlings Bjorn had met, but her hair was a striking contrast, curled tight against her skull and striped with fading orange, blonde, and gray. Though she had clearly seen many winters, her green eyes were bright and acute. She spoke Djurian as one born to it, despite appearing to be a barbar.

Yonik returned the smile. "My apologies, Mother Iron. My duties have occupied me."

Mother Iron gave no sign of whether she accepted the gothi's excuse as her gaze turned on Bjorn and the others. "And who are your companions?"

Yonik spoke their names in a swift sequence, inserting Bjorn's among the others with no surname nor adornment. Bjorn did not object. He was relieved that here, at least, he need not be the jarl's heir.

When he had finished, the sole man among the Silvers spoke. "You return in the middle of the night in the heart of winter." His voice was rough with smoke, and he cradled a pipe in his hands. Between his pale skin and his accent, Bjorn guessed him to have Baegardian blood. His hair and beard were the flat gray of morning fog, and both hung long, only just kept tame with thin braids embroidered with beads that made a tinkling sound as he turned his head. "A poor time to travel, I think. Especially when we have reports of hostile men on the prowl, serving some 'King of Chieftains'."

"You are right, Father Temperance," Yonik replied, a slight wince in his voice. "Our journey has been long and difficult. Yet my duties called me to come as soon as I could."

"Do not peck at him like cocks at a hen!" the last woman all but barked. She was most striking of all, with skin dark as flint and hair white as bone. Her eyes were clouded, as if she saw through a perpetual mist. The cane leaning against the table confirmed her blindness. Illustrated upon her skin were various likenesses of beasts and objects, the most apparent of which was a wide, blue eye upon her forehead. He wondered what tribe she was from. Her appearance and accent were like none of the barbars he knew.

"We must listen," the strange Silver continued. "Brother Yonik brings dire tidings for us all. Heed him, or spell our own doom." Ominous as her words were, she immediately undermined them with a cackle.

The other two Silvers frowned, but neither replied. They turned toward the gothi and waited expectantly.

Yonik cleared his throat. For a wonder, Bjorn thought he seemed nervous. But as he spoke, Yonik seemed to master whatever hesitation had stolen over him.

"Mother Iron, Father Temperance — Mother Sign is correct. I will explain more in the coming days, but I will start by saying this. An enemy to all of humanity has returned. We have seen their sorcery in an attack on Oakharrow. We have seen where the army they have assembled left to assault the city. And Hoarfrost here" — Yonik gestured to the Skyardi — "has seen his face."

"What enemy is this?" Father Temperance leaned forward, clutching at his pipe.

"The same as I have long warned of," snapped the blind

Silver — Mother Sign, if Bjorn had understood correctly. "The jotunar come. That is why there have been so many attacks this season. That is why the animals change and grow fearsome and large. The giants have come to Enea, and they have brought with them the *seidar* we have always quailed at using."

Bjorn tried to repress his shiver. The reputed size of giants was worrisome enough. That they possessed unknown magic, perhaps even beyond the dragonfire they had already witnessed, struck a dread through him such as he had not felt since the battle against the jotunmen and greatbear.

"We have heard only of the Jotun thus far," Brother Yonik said. "But I fear more of his kind will soon follow. And already, he has united tribes that have feuded for generations. Even one giant is a great threat."

"You have come here seeking the legends," Mother Iron said, calm despite all the startling news that had been shared. "You come to learn more of the giants."

"If, indeed, this is a jotun we face," Father Temperance said, his bushy brows lowered.

"It *is* a jotun," Mother Sign declared. "And we will help you, Brother Yonik. I will make sure of it."

The other two Silvers looked over at her, Mother Iron with mild annoyance, Father Temperance with more overt disdain. "This is a council, not a monarchy," the man muttered. But neither contradicted her declaration.

Bjorn's knees felt weak with relief. Despite an uncertain welcome, it seemed they would have the resources of Eildursprall at their fingertips, after all. *And hopefully, we can learn what we must.*

The vision he had glimpsed within the Chasm-fog came back to him then, filling his eyes until the chamber disappeared. Figures, tall as mountains, loomed out of the mist.

Their voices were thunder, their footsteps the rumblings of a volcano. They leaned down, and where their hands swept, men and women died.

"Bjorn."

He blinked, and like a slate with a cloth wiped over it, his eyelids wiped the mirage away. He found Yonik staring at him, mouth pinched with concern.

"I'm fine," he muttered.

Mother Sign pointed at Bjorn, her finger finding him when her eyes could not. "And him, I will have. Bring him to me tomorrow, Brother Yonik."

Still disoriented, Bjorn felt he had missed something. "Why?" he blurted before he could think better of it.

Mother Sign only smiled, her face wrinkling with dozens of laughter lines. "Because you have the Sight, bear cub. Or it has you."

Before he could think of a reply, Yonik's squeeze on his shoulder silenced him. "I will bring him, Mother Sign," the priest spoke. "Thank you, Mother Iron, Father Temperance. May Djur bless you for your kindness."

"It is the Wild God's will," Mother Iron replied.

Father Temperance sighed, then leaned back in his chair and brought his unlit pipe to his lips. "May he shelter and protect us."

Mother Iron looked at the barbar sentry. "Flint, show Brother Yonik and our guests to lodging. You may help yourself to any food within the longhouse. I trust you remember where everything else is?"

"I do," Yonik answered. The smile that pulled at his lips seemed bittersweet.

"Very well. We will hear a more complete report from you tomorrow."

With that, the Silvers dismissed them. The lead barbar, Flint, grunted and led them out of the chamber. Bjorn followed him and Yonik through the longhouse and between the staring priests, priestesses, and acolytes.

He hoped Eildursprall would prove welcoming, though the gods knew they had yet to encounter any such hospitality in the Teeth.

5. THE SCARAB

A child of Qa'a may bear
His blessing in their flesh
The eye will see it in err
Yet beauty hides in unsightliness

- Words in the Sand, refrain 53;231

Sehdra leaned on the balcony and squinted into the cool wind. Nights in the Bounty grew cold, but she had always treasured the relief from the day's heat, when Hua, Creator of All, stared down with disapproval upon humanity. All her childhood, the chanters of Hua had warned of the Desolation, when the Bright Maker would tire of his children's sins and wipe the world clean by sending his servants, the huame, to burn it and begin anew.

The priests did not preach their prophecies any longer. The Desolation was already coming to pass.

The moment of serenity faded as Sehdra's eyes settled on the dark, seething mass that interrupted the pale Bounty. Pawura's Pasture was typically reserved for the grazing of livestock, grasslands being a treasured resource in the Bounty. But the karah had sent out the call, and armies needed somewhere to gather. Those shepherds who depended on use of the meadows would either find another grazing place or starve.

Casualties before the war has even begun.

Dawn burned orange on the horizon, yet she was not surprised when she heard the door open and close as quietly as a river breeze. Despite her somber thoughts, a smile curled Sehdra's lips as she turned to greet her visitor. Teti was already immaculately dressed and his eyes bright, if still puffy with sleep. He returned the smile and stepped up to the balcony next to her, shivering.

"You will catch Aya's chill standing out here, Royal Sister. Let me bring you something to wrap in."

"Best bring something for yourself as well." She spoke to his back, for he had already turned to rout through the chest at the foot of her bed. "You run colder than I do."

"Bek's fire blazes within you," Teti called as he straightened, a leopard pelt cradled in his arms. Closing the chest, he returned to the balcony and draped the soft pelt over her shoulders before settling a rangy hyena's hide over his own. Though the chill had not seeped through her skin yet, Sehdra tugged the skin close about her, grateful for its warmth.

"Thank you. And I have told you — don't be so formal when it is only us. I may begin to think you do not like me."

She glanced sidelong at him. As usual, Teti had positioned himself on her left side, the side of her face that did not suffer the birth-curse. *Considerate as always.*

Teti flashed her a wide smile. He trembled slightly under his hide, his spare frame having little meat by which to warm his bones. "Impossible. Gazabe himself could not stand between me and you."

Sehdra rolled her eyes. "You've a foolish mind. Perhaps if you did not serve me, you would have told tales to children, like a pauper by the baths."

"But I would not be so happy and carefree if I did not serve you."

She shifted her weight to lean into his side. "Serve me like a tentpole, then. You already have the look."

Teti lent his support and placed his long arm lightly across her leopard pelt. They were quiet for a long moment before his inevitable question came.

"Are you weary of standing, Sehdra? Would you like me to fetch a chair?"

She adjusted her stance, hiding a wince as her twisted leg twinged. "No. I am fine, Teti."

Silence fell between them again. Sehdra looked over the long city laid out below them. Annax-Nu had grown off the life-giving River Nu and stretched for leagues in either direction. It was not without its faults; life could be harsh for the commoners and slaves who lived too near the floodplains. But it was also a city with much beauty. The temples, built into grand pyramids, dominated the landscape. The karah's palace itself ascended only a little higher than most, and not as large as Gazabe's. The Black Jackal, as the Jealous Lord of Death, did not suffer impetuousness even from the karah. Though the Sypten ruler was a god among men, Gazabe was lord of all the Divine, and one offended him at their peril. Chanters had interred many sarcophagi within for the ushering of souls to the Jackal's Delight, the life beyond life. She wondered how long it would be before it was her turn to be locked within the temple's dark belly.

Not long with the huame among us and Physt at our head.

As if privy to her thoughts, Teti murmured, "All storms pass, Sehdra. Even this one."

"Not before many innocents drown." But even as she voiced the thought, she turned away from it. Such despair was fallow soil, and before her mother had died, she had often impressed upon Sehdra that she must always think toward the future. *Sand does not grow fruit, Sehdra,* she had told her more than once. *Plant your plans where they might blossom.*

"Three days ago," she spoke into the brief silence. "When Oyaoan spared Qa'a's high chanter. Do you remember?"

Teti's laugh was bitter. "How could anyone forget? I thought the huamek would kill you."

She had believed the same when the behemoth had emerged from behind the throne. "But she did not. She sided with me. Did you not see it? My brother would have killed Raneb, but Oyaoan decided I had the right of it."

"I suppose," he agreed reluctantly. "But Royal Sister — that is, Sehdra — I would not place your hopes on a huamek. She is a servant of the Bright Maker, and all the prophecies say they are here for one thing: to burn the world clean, then begin anew."

Sehdra looked over the long city. "Perhaps that is not entirely a bad thing."

His horror reeked like a perfume. "What can you mean?"

"What if the Divine are not wrong? Sin *is* rampant throughout the empire. Nomarchs and chanters feast while farmers starve. Soldiers take advantage over any woman they please — and, if the rumors are true, even children. This is an infernal land, Teti. Perhaps Ha-Sypt must be managed like how peasants maintain their fields. Half the world must burn for the other half to thrive."

Teti's silence was hard to bear, but Sehdra kept her chin high. She would wait for him to deliberate. Only by tempering her beliefs against his could she hope to make them strong enough for what would come.

"Do you agree we must slaughter the mountain savages then?" he asked quietly.

Sehdra blinked. "No. The Winter Holds pose problems, of course. The savages are ever thirsty for our people's blood, and we can never burn enough ships to stop their raids. But I speak of illness here in our own empire."

She wanted to say more, but the words retreated from her lips. Even here, upon her private balcony, she could not speak treachery. *I mean the karah. I mean my brother.* She held the thoughts as firmly as she could in her mind, hoping somehow that Teti might hear them.

When Teti spoke, his words were so soft she had to lean closer to hear them. "Men cannot stand against the will of the Divine, Sehdra. Not even a god of flesh and bone. Certainly, he cannot defy a servant of Hua herself."

She thought of all the spiders on the web in which she was entangled. *Physt. Oyaoan. The vizier. The high chanters.* They, and the generals who led their armies, were like the soldiers of a Duaat board, positioned in an eternal game for power. But she was no player sitting at the table; she was little more than an insect on the board. Unwanted, often unnoticed, and without the strength to do more than nudge.

But if nudging was all she could do, then nudge she must. She had seen what the future was in Physt's visions as well as the Oyaoan's fathomless eyes. Neither was a fate she could abide by, not for her people.

"You know what they call me," she said aloud. "*The Scarab.* Half of them mean it as an insult. The other half know better. It is said a scarab beetle can survive a hundred floods by burying under the sand." She turned to the man who meant so much to her — servant, friend, confidante, brother in all but blood — and smiled the twisted smirk that was all her cursed face could manage. "I will survive, Teti."

Without invitation, the tall man wrapped an arm around her shoulder and squeezed her against his side. His familiarity warmed her more than the leopard pelt ever could. Though servants to royal women were always castrated, it was not that fact that put her at ease with him, but the unfailing loyalty he'd shown her over the two decades. She closed her eyes and leaned her head against his shoulder, hoping her body might warm the stubborn servant so that he stopped shivering.

The door rattled, giving a moment's warning for Teti to withdraw his arm. Before he could stride across the room, the door burst open, and a shaven-headed boy stumbled in, a small scroll clutched in his hand.

"Boy!" Teti snapped as he stepped up next to him, covertly letting the hyena hide slide back onto the chest. "What do you mean by coming into the Ohkweht's rooms uninvited?"

"Leave him be, Teti." Sehdra limped over to the pair. Internally, she cringed; the lad would have to endure her face, for she had no mask at hand. But if she could suffer it within the throne room, she would survive one messenger boy's gaze. "What is your message?"

"A summons, Royal Sister," said the boy between panting breaths. He darted a look at Teti, then held out the scroll to Sehdra. "From the karah himself!"

The cold, which had left her untouched all that morning, finally crept in. Sehdra edged forward and accepted the scroll. She knew what it would say even before she unfurled it.

"It is time." She raised her gaze to meet Teti's. "The

armies march. And my brother means for me to go with them."

Her companion's brow furrowed. "We go to war with the Winter Holds?"

Sehdra nodded. "As ever."

She was to be dragged along, like a beetle in a boat's wake. Likely it was because her brother did not trust her to be left behind, to scheme in his absence. He was shrewd enough to see he had never entirely squashed her spirit. He would go as well; she knew that for a fact. He had hungered for blood too long to do otherwise.

And there was another reason. With Oyaoan and the huame in their midst, this would be the final war with the mountain savages.

A sigh escaped her, yet she held herself erect. "Best start packing, Teti. A long road lies ahead."

Her friend nodded and hurried to the task.

6. OLD HABITS

The duty of blood comes before all but that to god and king. A son's life is his father's to spend.

- The Inscribed Beliefs; Verse the Second, Line the Twelfth

Bastor stood before the door for several breaths, ignoring the stares of the guards to either side, before he raised his hand to knock. Within, he heard faint voices, and his stomach clenched in anticipation. He noticed he was slouching.

Stand straight. Don't give the bastard the satisfaction.

Bastor drew himself up to his full height and hardened his expression. Gods knew he had enough practice at it.

The door swung open. Instead of his father, whom he had expected, a youthful face appeared. The sneer curling his lips was all too familiar.

"Ah, but look who's returned, Father," the lad called over his shoulder as he stepped aside. "The lost mongrel, his tail between his legs!"

"As merry a greeting as ever." Bastor stepped inside and shut the door. "'Welcome home, brother' would have done fine."

His brother only waved over his shoulder before slumping down on the divan. A full goblet and a half-full pitcher of honey wine sat on the table before him. Next to it lay a lit pipe, smoke curling from the bowl. The lad picked up both the pipe and the cup, then indulged in one after the other. It was hardly a surprising display. Ragnar the Younger had always had a proclivity for vice.

The rest of the chamber spoke of similar luxury. Rugs littered the stone floor, cushioning every footstep, and arrases featuring the violet lynx of their family sigil draped over the walls. In addition to the divan, two cushioned chairs were set before a roaring fireplace. Bastor found the heat stifling after so many days out in the open air, yet he dared not let his discomfiture show. The ceiling rose a dozen feet high, giving the entertaining chamber a grander feel than most guest quarters.

War made its presence known as well. Two shields hung from a rack, along with two pairs of sheathed swords and seaxes. Ragnar's gilded armor adorned a mannequin, gleaming with oil, the repaired marks in it only elevating its allure rather than detracting.

Next to this display lay an archway, from which another figure stepped into the room. Lord Ragnar studied Bastor for a long moment, eyes cold and calculating.

"So," his father said at last. "You survived."

Bastor did not advance further into the room. He wished he had never come. "Yes."

"Why did you come here?"

He had, in the intervening months since he had last seen his family, believed he had hardened toward them.

Now, as the sting of the question drove under his skin, he saw how he'd deluded himself.

"I thought you might wish to celebrate," said Bastor, forcing a smile. "After all, I am your heir."

Young Ragnar snorted into his cup at that. Their father ignored him, as he ignored all of his second son's flaws.

"You are." Lord Ragnar's voice was frigid. "But do not expect me to be overjoyed when you have failed me."

"Failed you?" His pulse quickened. He wondered if some report had escaped of his activities in Oakharrow. Which of his father's contacts had he missed killing?

"Don't feign surprise." His father's words whipped out like a biting wind. "You knew my intentions. Yaethun Brashurson was to be the Jarl of Oakharrow, not this Jotun the girl speaks of."

Bastor did not have to force his next smile. "'This Jotun'... you don't even know what you face, do you, Father?"

Smiles were rare in the Jarl of Ragnarsglade outside of the public eye, and rarer still did they portend anything good. As his father smiled now, Bastor had to repress a shiver.

"Of course I do, Alabastor," he spoke softly. "I suspect I know far better than you."

He could not help a bubble of laughter. His younger brother stared up at him incredulously, but as their father had done, Bastor ignored him. "The name is no boast. It is a giant, Father. Plucked right from the Scribe's tales."

"And I said, I know."

Bastor eyed his father, his smile fading. He could not detect any signs of a lie in Lord Ragnar's face, and he had long grown adept at identifying them. *So he knew. How? When?* Until he uncovered those answers, his father kept the upper hand.

The jarl eyed him a moment longer, then nodded as if satisfied. He lowered his gaze as he began pacing the room.

"Though you have failed me once, you might redeem yourself still. My fellow jarls remain obstinate. Thane Asborn seems amenable to my ascension as the Arkjarl, but he carries little weight. Lord Petyr and Lord Hother both dream of the privilege themselves, but have even less support. Eventually, they will concede, once I find the right incentives. Lord Harald would never have the ambition for it, and Lord Alrik lacks the wits.

"Only Lord Siward poses a significant threat. *The Black Ram.*" His father spoke the title spitefully. "Reputation matters more than aptitude in this. He is seen as battle-hardened and shrewd, yet who knows his values and his own mind. He has the admiration of Alrik and Harald, and perhaps of the others as well. Only his lack of interest in the Iron Circle has kept it from his head."

Bastor watched the jarl pace, back and forth, back and forth, the boards creaking with his steps. As comprehension of what he was leading to settled in, icy dread wound tight around his gut.

"I suppose you want me to take care of it," he muttered.

His father paused and glanced at him, but it was his brother who spoke first. "You!" Young Ragnar spluttered, leaning forward from the divan. "As if he would entrust such a task to *you!*"

"Quiet." His father's rebuke was mild, especially compared to those he had leveled toward Bastor at his age. Yet his younger brother wilted before it, sullenly puffing away at the agas in his pipe, its piney musk prickling Bastor's nostrils.

As usual, Lord Ragnar ignored his youngest's behavior. "Yes," he said to Bastor. "But subtly, and in a way that none can connect the act to me. I hear Lord Siward has brought his daughters with him. Perhaps, if something were to happen to one of them, the promise of further reprimand will compel him to withdraw his claim."

With the words, foreboding turned to fury. Bastor could barely unclench his teeth long enough to speak. "I won't harm his daughters."

Lord Ragnar went still. Then he strode toward him and struck Bastor across the face.

He had seen the backhand coming. He had dodged others like it often in the past. But old habit made Bastor stand still and accept the blow.

Like a beaten dog, knowing I deserve it.

The right side of his face burned, and the coppery taste of blood was on his tongue. Yet as Bastor straightened and met his father's eyes, he did not quail before the iron in them, nor did he acknowledge Young Ragnar's cackle from the couch.

"You will obey," the jarl said calmly. "Or have you forgotten all I've taught you?"

Bastor's marred lips twisted into a wry smile. "'Our first loyalty is to our blood,' you mean?"

Lord Ragnar nodded, his gaze never leaving Bastor's. Though the older man had to look up into his heir's eyes, somehow he made it seem as if he looked down on his son.

"Do what must be done." The jarl turned away. "And I expect a full report on your previous failures at a later date. What consequences they warrant will be determined then."

Bastor stared at the space between his father's shoulders and wondered if it wouldn't be better for Baegard if he buried a blade there. *I could do it.* A numbness had washed through him, deadening the pain in his face. *I could kill him. I want to. I crave it.* As the jarl's heir, he could bear weapons, so his blades still hung from his belt. His father had never been half the fighter Bastor was. He could kill him long before any guards could intervene.

But he felt other eyes on him, and like a moth to the flame, Bastor looked over at the divan. Ragnar the Younger watched him, a lopsided smile plastered on his slack face. In those green eyes, which he had inherited from the serving woman who had birthed him, he saw understanding of what had been passing through his mind, and the taunting for him to do it. There was no brotherly understanding, no shared suffering; Ragnar, pale as snow, had always been the favored of their father's scions. With how Lord Ragnar used him, he knew neither father nor brother would shed tears if he were to never return.

Bastor dropped his gaze to his feet. Despite his resolution to stand tall, his broad shoulders rounded. He felt like meat pulled to shreds between starving wolves, leaving little recognizable behind.

Baegard needs him alive. It was the conclusion he had never wanted to face, but known deep down. No other man up or down the valley was as cunning or as cruel. Only his father could be the Arkjarl they needed for the Seven Jarlheims to prevail. Though he doubted that even Lord Ragnar, with all his secrets and schemes and authority, could prevail against the unconquerable creature he had seen.

But what choice do we have?

He thought of Aelthena, and all the qualities she shared with his father. The resolve, the sharpness of mind... with a good heart rather than a rotten one. But as soon as he thought it, he wanted to laugh. Men would never ride to battle in her name. No woman in Baegard would be respected as a jarl, much less the Arkjarl who was to be their commander.

Bastor thrust a fist to his chest and raised his head. "For our blood's glory then, eh, Father?"

Not waiting for a response, he turned and strode from the room.

7. BEHIND EVERY GOOD MAN

The role of the Arkjarl is a curious one. Temporary by design, the Arkjarl is intended to provide the missing component for such times as our nation has been without a monarch: a single leader who dictates the course of Baegard during a war.

But it does not work as smoothly in practice as in theory. Either the Arkjarl finds himself hamstrung by his fellow Jarls and unable to perform his function, or he seizes more authority than he has been granted and becomes a king in all but name.

Yet, when war is upon us, and no king leads the charge, we have returned to this practice repeatedly. I see no signs of its dissolution.

- Commentary on Djurian Culture, by Alfjin the Scribe

Aelthena closed the door behind the last entrant, then girded her smile before turning back to face them.

Six chairs, five of them filled, sat arranged around a

warming fireplace. The chamber they occupied was wide and austere, softened only by the morning light filtering in through the narrow windows and an elk-emblazoned arras hanging in rich green from the wall opposite the hearth. The fire reached from around the dun stones that sought to contain it, as if eager to lick up every word they uttered.

Better the fire hear than anyone else.

Though they met openly in Lord Harald's room at his wife's behest, each woman in attendance knew the peril in their congress. It was conspiracy they now engaged in, and not even women were safe from punishment for it.

Aelthena looked over the attendees as she walked toward her own chair, carefully composing her expression to be warm and welcoming. These were the jarls' wives — all except Aelthena. She had met privately with each of them, urging them to attend this meeting, and one by one, they had agreed. Kathsla's initial contact with them back in Oakharrow had primed them for Aelthena's outreach now.

Yet she had the sense that implementing her plans would be far from simple. These women made up their own minds, and they were not always set the same way as their husbands. She had traded one group of stubborn goats for another.

Only this herd might listen to me.

"Thank you for coming," she said as she settled into her chair. "I know it is difficult for some of you to get away." She arranged her dress neatly, as her mother had long ago taught her a highborn lady should. Aqua and adorned with silver threading, she had purchased it for just this occasion to represent her kin and jarlheim. Though she had winced at its cost to Asborn's flattening purse, it was a necessary investment to be presentable among highborn women, lest she be laughed out the door before she even spoke.

"Oh, you need not worry on my account," Iona Of'Siward said cheerfully as she bounced the babe on her knee. The boy, Olle, could not have been much more than a winter old. He giggled and stared up with delight at his mother, who smiled back at him. Like his mother, he had blonde hair and a bright disposition. Whether the mother had any significant thoughts behind her pretty face remained to be seen.

The other women looked at the child, most adoring in their expressions. Aelthena valiantly held onto her own smile. *A conspiracy of mothers.* She hurried on before her hopes flagged.

"Time is pressing, so I won't bandy words. I spoke to each of you regarding my intentions. Now, I mean to make those more clear."

"Do," Olga Of'Petyr said tartly. "You were quite vague before." Like her husband, she seemed as warm as a viper.

"My apologies, Lady Olga." Aelthena's smile tried to flee, but she held it in place. "What I wish to discuss may go against the wishes of your husbands. Politics, according to the Inscribed Beliefs, are the affairs of men. Yet the plight facing our nation forces we women to put forth our own hands."

"Oh, m'lady, you need not be apologetic about that." Nanna Of'Alrik reached out to pat Aelthena's knee. "We are all used to meddling." She also resembled her husband, sharing his warm personality and his big bones. Her thinning brown hair was tucked inside a scarf, exaggerating her eyes and smile to toady proportions.

"Men need guidance," Olga affirmed.

Inkeri Of'Hother, younger even than Aelthena, let loose a simpering chuckle. "Behind every good man is a good woman, isn't that right?"

Olga only stared at Inkeri. Aelthena had to hide a smile. The two were opposite in both manner and appearance.

Hother's wife was plump where the Lady of Petyrsholm was bird-thin, and the young woman was sweet to the point of cloying. Only the silver circlet atop her head, mirroring Lord Hother's own, made Aelthena wonder if husband and wife shared the ambition of reclaiming their ancestor's authority as monarchs.

"Not a good woman," the last of their assembly spoke. "A better one." Sigrid Of'Harald was as different from her husband as Olga and Nanna were alike. Dark in hair and eyes where he was bright, bold where he was timid, she seemed a woman to speak her mind and never apologize for it. Despite her somewhat aloof manner, Aelthena found herself drawn to her.

I am not content to hide behind a man. The words were on the tip of her tongue. But no matter how strongly she felt them, she could not speak them. Not unless she wanted to ostracize the only allies she seemed likely to win. Still, she had to seize the oars of the conversation and turn it back the way she needed.

"Be that as it may," Aelthena said, "as the women connected most closely to those in the Jarlmoot, we must do what they have failed to. I don't know what they've told you, but this is the truth: Baegard faces a threat such as we've never known."

She told them all then, all she had seen and experienced. Of Nuvvog's Rage and the destruction of her home. Of the Sypten sorcerer dressed as a barbar and the great fire he summoned. And finally, of the giant who stepped clear of the smoking wreckage of the Teeth Gate, who killed Skarl Thundson with a single sweep of his axe. Her tongue stumbled over the words, hardly able to believe them even as she spoke them. She could only imagine how the tale must sound to the others.

But as she lifted her gaze from the dancing flames and

looked at the surrounding women, she found far more sympathy than she had dared hope for. Her chest warmed at their nods, and her spirit soared.

They believe me. She had not realized how much she yearned for validation.

Only Olga seemed stubbornly defiant. "I hesitate to say it," she said, sounding anything but hesitant, "but your eyes must have played tricks on you, Lady Heir Aelthena. Jotunar are a fable."

The warmth in Aelthena's chest flared, and it took an effort to keep her voice even. "I assure you, Lady Olga, I know what I saw. I am not one to believe in rumors and sprite tales. I did not believe giants existed anymore than you do now. But you must believe me when I say this was a true jotun. He rose taller than Oakharrow's walls and had tusks like a woolith. His axe was as tall as a tree, and he was shaggy like a beast. But he's clever as well — he united the Teeth barbars into an army and took my home."

The Lady of Petyrsholm seemed far from convinced, but she only pressed her thin lips together.

"I believe you, Lady Heir," Iona spoke up. Her little boy had fallen asleep in her arms while Aelthena had said her piece. "My pa always believed the giants were up there in the Witterland, biding their time. Why else would we have so many stories about them?"

It was hardly a stout defense, but Aelthena smiled all the same, grateful for any support.

Sigrid made a small noise that turned heads toward her. "I have not believed in the jotunar, but my husband has received strange reports these past days. Merchants bound for Oakharrow were turned away or met by barbars at the gates. Some spoke of this Jotun as if he were in command. Those admitted saw the Harrowhall's destruction. It is as the Lady Heir has said, the rock melted by fire. Two stones are barely left standing together." She pressed her lips together for a moment before continuing. "Perhaps 'Jotun' is merely a title. Perhaps, in the battle, Lady Heir Aelthena did not see what she believed she did. But it does not change the fact that she speaks true of the threat against Baegard. With barbars in Oakharrow and Ha-Sypt somehow involved, we face a war on two fronts. And we cannot stand with each jarlheim on their own for any longer."

As she finished, Sigrid glanced at Aelthena and nodded, a gesture Aelthena returned. The woman had not taken her at her word, but could she blame her? Wouldn't she question it if she sat in her place?

She stands with you, Aelthena thought. *Right now, that's all that matters.* Soon, they would see the truth for themselves.

"Perhaps," Olga muttered, unwilling to yield the last word.

Ignoring the severe woman, Aelthena glanced at the two who had as yet remained silent. "Lady Inkeri, Lady Nanna? What are your thoughts?"

Inkeri glanced shyly at the older woman, while Nanna gave a heavy shrug.

"A mother never wishes to hear that her sons will go to fight. But I, too, have heard too much, both here and before, to ignore the truth. War is coming to Baegard. Wishing otherwise won't change that."

The matron's words instilled in her a seed of doubt. *You didn't bring this war, just word of it,* she told herself. Yet she could not help feeling somehow responsible for sending Nanna's sons off to fight and, gods forbidding, to die.

Only then did she wonder what that might mean for the other men in her life. *Asborn. Frey. Bastor. Bjorn, if he's survived this long*. They would fight as well. Perhaps they would be one of those who fell.

Can't think of that. Not now. Her resolution, which had become iron-hard since the rejection by the jarls, wavered and cracked. She clung to it, holding it together. She could not balk at the cost. She had thought through what was coming for them — for Baegard, for all of Enea. It was inevitable. The Jotun had gathered an army and pillaged her home. Ha-Sypt had never sued for peace in the previous Summer Wars, and from all she had heard of its present karah, they would not do so now. Blood was inevitable; it would spill in rivers on both sides.

We must make sure they suffer more.

"What can be done, Lady Ael — that is, Lady Heir Aelthena?" Inkeri finally spoke into the silence.

She raised her head and emerged from her bleak thoughts. "What can be done?" she repeated softly. The answer had seemed so clear before. Now, it was a pale hope, but it was the only solution she had.

"Baegard must unite behind one shield." Aelthena looked at each of the wives gathered before her. "The jarls must elect an Arkjarl to lead our armies as a unified force. And we, the women behind them" — the words, necessary as they were, tasted like ash — "we must choose the best man to hold that shield."

She said "man," even as she longed to put herself forward for it. But she knew that if she could not muster support to even be present at the Jarlmoot, she would never gather votes to become the Arkjarl. Once again, Aelthena tempered her ambitions. *For now,* she reassured herself. *Because I must.*

But it had seemed a game, even then, a contest to win. With all the lives that would be lost, her own accomplishments paled in importance.

"Who?" Sigrid asked sharply. "Your father might have once been the best man, but forgive me for saying, I do not believe he is any longer."

"And Thane Asborn lacks the pedigree," Olga observed, a hint of satisfaction seeping through her frost-bent disposition.

Aelthena answered with forced calm. "I'm not here for personal gain. We must all set aside ambition to do what we must. The jarl we put forward should be the best man for the position — the cleverest warrior, the most charismatic leader, the most cunning general. Even among such venerable men" — sarcasm edged into her voice, and she tried to dampen it — "there is one obvious choice to my mind."

The women looked at one another, each wondering who she might name. "Not Lord Ragnar?" Sigrid finally queried.

"No." Aelthena spoke with far more vehemence than she intended. "Not Lord Ragnar. I mean Lord Siward."

Iona brightened with a sudden smile. "My Siward! Do you mean it, Lady Heir?"

Aelthena gave the woman a smile that felt like a grimace. "I do. He is a veteran of the Sack. He is competent and respected. There should not be many objections to his election."

"And not Lord Petyr?" Olga interjected. "He is just as distinguished, if less scarred."

The Lady of Skjold, so often cheery, showed the first hint of another side. "Scars are badges of warrior's courage. My Siward is more handsome for them."

Olga pressed her lips together. Aelthena was glad she had the sense not to respond.

"The others, as I said, possess admirable qualities," Aelthena said, hurrying to placate the Lady of Petyrsholm. "But Siward is a tested warrior. He is called the Black Ram for his stand during the Sack, a stand that held against all odds. It is just such a defense that we need now, with my home taken and other enemies lurking on our borders."

Olga had no answer to that, though she looked far from convinced.

Aelthena glanced at the others, hoping to find agreement. Nanna shrugged. "Alrik is brave and tough, but he has never had much of a mind for strategy, and no aspirations beyond Aelford's borders."

Satisfied, Aelthena looked at the other two. Sigrid did not object, likely realizing that Lord Harald was far from what was needed in the Arkjarl, though she appeared annoyed by the knowledge. Inkeri's confidence in her husband also seemed to fail, for she wilted into her chair.

Just as Aelthena thought it decided, Sigrid finally spoke. "Why, again, do we not consider Lord Ragnar? His accomplishments are impressive. He has grown a town into a jarl-heim within his lifetime, and he guards the southern border against many a Sypten raid."

Because he's a Djur-burned traitor. Aelthena bit back the words and tried to find a more palatable line of defense. "Guarding against skirmishes is not the same as winning a battle and taking a city. And Lord Ragnar is new to his position. He doesn't have the same support or established lineage as Lord Siward."

"He is cunning," Sigrid pointed out. "None can deny that."

Cunning, indeed. It took an effort for Aelthena to unclench her hands from her seat.

To her surprise, Olga came to the rescue. "Look around, Lady Sigrid," the Lady of Petyrsholm said in patronizing tones. "Lord Ragnar has no wife. Ask yourself: would we prefer a man to wear the Iron Circle whose ear we have access to, or one beyond our reach?"

Sigrid, a woman who seemed at least as proud as Aelthena, bristled at the rebuke. But she still gave a tight nod. "Very well. Lord Siward it is."

Only as the Lady of Greenwuud said the words did Aelthena realize what they had just accomplished. *We've done what the men could not,* she thought in awe. *I've done it.* It was only the first step; the work was far from done. But if Kathsla's declaration of wives' influence over their husbands held true, they were well on their way to a united Baegard.

There will be an Arkjarl, and I will have picked him.

But as Aelthena's gaze drifted toward the fireplace and she watched the dancing flames, she saw again the Jotun looming from the smoke. All she could do was hope it would be enough.

8. WHISPERS OF THE STONES

"The stones whisper their secrets to me, and I confide in them my dreams."

- Torvald Geirson, the Last King of Baegard

Bjorn had barely lifted his spoon, laden with the most delectable stew he had smelled in weeks, before a slap to his back spilled it back into his bowl.

The longhouse was fairly full that morning. Acolytes, gothi, and guards broke their fasts together and filled the hall to the rafters with their chatter. They crowded around the fireplaces lining the walls, where pots of soup simmered. The place smelled of smoke, food, and humans recently hard at work. Bjorn had found an unoccupied spot at one of the long tables and sat alone. It suited him well enough; he had spent years on his own and was comfortable with his own silence.

Yet he had been so determined to ignore his surroundings that he had not noticed Loridi until it was too late.

"There you are, Lord Heir!" the jester whispered as he slipped onto the long bench next to him. "I wondered where you'd gone when your bunk was empty." Only then did Loridi seem to notice the spilled broth on the table, and he raised an eyebrow. "You realize that should go into your mouth, right?"

Bjorn only sighed. "It's just Bjorn, remember?"

"Oh, he remembers, but chooses to forget." Seskef sat on the bench with rather less grace. His gut, resilient despite the lean days they had lived through, bumped into the table and sent more broth slopping over the edges of Bjorn's bowl.

Bjorn slipped a spoonful into his mouth before Loridi gripped his shoulder and shook him fondly. "He will always be the Lord Heir in my heart, and that's what counts."

"In this case," Seskef retorted, "I believe a greatbear cloak and a piece of parchment matter a great deal more."

"You think so? Yet is not leadership made possible by the belief of people in it? What does ink on paper matter if—"

Having stolen three more spoonfuls, Bjorn found he could not remain silent any longer. "The pot's still warm and half-full. Best grab bowls while you can."

Loridi looked as if he would continue for a moment, then grinned and winked. "Ah, I see — someone's still grumpy." The thin jester shook Bjorn's shoulder again as he stood. "See, Lord Heir? We're beginning to know each other well."

"Huddle together with a man while his fruits freeze off," Seskef opined as he, too, stood, though far less nimbly, "and you're bound to know him a bit."

Loridi chortled and ran a hand over his friend's hair as the two of them headed for the stew pot.

Bjorn sighed into his bowl and took another sip. He closed his eyes and enjoyed the sensation of the warm steam against his face. He had slept poorly the night before and was paying for it now. Though he shared a room with his three male companions, Hoarfrost being housed elsewhere in a lodge for women, there was something about being surrounded by barbars, even friendly ones, that put him on edge.

Yet if the Silvers meant to stick by what they said the night before, he would soon be the pupil to one. And through her, he would learn more of the Sight.

Seidar. The Old Djurian word whispered with hidden meanings that flitted beyond his comprehension. He wondered what Mother Sign would teach him. If her name was any indication, she knew much of the old sorcery. She would help Bjorn become a *Volur*, like the seers of old.

Only... he wondered what it truly mattered. Even if he possessed the talent Yonik believed he did, and the visions he saw were not just the delusions of a sprite-touched mind, what could it do for their cause? Visions would not save Oakharrow from the Jotun and his army. Visions would not stop Nuvvog's Rage from burning all of Enea to ashes. They needed to understand their enemy as their ancestors had. And magic, as much as it drew at his curiosity, could not deliver that knowledge.

Can it?

Loridi and Seskef returned with full bowls, then gabbed over Bjorn's head as he bent to his stew. Minutes later, his spoon was scraping the bottom of his bowl, and Bjorn rose to claim a second helping. Before he could reach the cauldron, someone else entered the longhouse. Bjorn hesitated, hand on the ladle, as Yonik crossed the hall toward him, only pausing to give a cursory greeting to their fellow Harrowmen.

The gothi paused before Bjorn, regarding him for a long

moment. Bjorn, unnerved by this scrutiny, held up the ladle, stew dripping over the edges. "Hungry, old wolf?"

Yonik grinned, his teeth bright amid his pinecone beard. "I never did grow out of a boy's hunger. Just a small bowl, then we'd best be on our way."

Bjorn asked where they were headed as he picked up the cleanest of the bowls stacked by the hearth and poured a small helping each for him and Yonik. He remembered Mother Sign and her words from the night before all too well. *Because you have the Sight, bear cub. Or it has you.* He had wondered all the night through whether they were the words of one sprite-touched or a prophetess, and what either case might mean.

They returned to their companions, Bjorn reluctantly sitting between the pair of jesters, knowing it put him in their line of fire. Sure enough, Loridi scrutinized his bowl as soon as he had set it down with a disapproving stare. "Not becoming one of those mad, starved priests now, are you? How are you going to last till lunch?"

Before Bjorn could think of a rejoinder, Yonik interceded. "Duty calls. Had you been listening last night, you might remember Mother Sign bade that Bjorn visit her this morning."

"What, that old bat? I thought anyone with a stone of sense would know better than to listen to her prattling."

Bjorn winced and looked up and down the table, hoping none of the priests or acolytes had overheard. A few glanced their way, but none scowled. In fact, one of them, a young woman, pretty with fiery hair and seeming about his age, had been staring at him until he'd looked. He turned away just as quickly, wondering if it had truly been embarrassment he saw from her. A small smile appeared on its own.

"Lord Heir? Come now — you can't think yourself so high and mighty as to not even *respond*."

Bjorn startled to find his companions all regarding him. Loridi, who had just spoken, had his eyebrows raised. The flush that had crept up on him deepened.

"Told you not to call me that," he muttered.

A grin quickly replaced Loridi's mask of hurt. "And when have I ever listened before?"

Yonik stood, barely making the bench creak. "Come, Bjorn. Best escape this one's brambles before we're stuck in them."

"Alright, alright." Loridi held up his hands. "If you two are making progress, Seskef and I shall have to as well. Perhaps the clerics might have a library to peruse?"

Seskef snorted a laugh. "Oh, you'll be plenty useful in a library."

Loridi shrugged. "I'll fetch you books, and you can read them. It's a perfect system."

Bjorn, who had never realized Loridi was illiterate, smiled awkwardly as he stood. Most Harrowfolk could not write more than their mark, yet the jester had always been so deft with a phrase and bursting with stories that Bjorn had figured he was as avid a reader as himself. He wondered where else Loridi had accumulated his trove of tales.

"I'm sure you'll find a way to occupy your time." Yonik gestured for Bjorn to follow as he made for the longhouse entrance. "You've never lacked ways to waste it before."

"A fair point!" Loridi called at their backs as they stepped back into the cold.

Bjorn breathed in the crisp morning air, welcome after the stuffiness inside. Eildursprall, still covered in snow despite the coming spring, had a fresh scent only winter could bring. Now that he could see the town, it had a cheery look to it. Smoke puffed from chimneys, and firelight flickered from boarded windows and doorways. Men and women milled about on their business; Yewlings and Baegardians both, distinguishable from one another by the color of the faces peering out from under hoods. Since they stood within the borders of Heim Numen, Bjorn assumed most were acolytes and gothi. He had never wondered how many lived at Eildursprall during their years of training. Having already glimpsed dozens, he thought at least a hundred might lurk among the sprawl of buildings.

Yonik led the way, walking with his head turning from side to side, like a man taking in all the changes to his home after a long trip away. Bjorn watched him, wondering again at the priest and his life. Judging from his expression, Heim Numen was more home to him than Oakharrow was. He wondered what it must be like to live the majority of your life away from the place to which he felt most connected. Already, he had begun to miss Oakharrow like a dull ache in his chest, but even more, he missed the people from it. He thought of his mother and brothers, of Keld, of Aelthena and his father. He wondered if they were still alive.

Nothing remains the same, he thought, *whether you leave or stay.*

The priest led him to a hut that struck Bjorn as familiar. When he realized why, he had to laugh. "The same place they locked us up last night?"

The gothi gave an eloquent shrug. "Life is full of small ironies, isn't it? But best not keep Mother Sign waiting. 'Slight a Silver, lose your liver' — or so we acolytes used to say."

Bjorn tried to imagine Yonik scuttling around on menial tasks, but even his imagination was not up to the task. "Hard to picture you as an acolyte."

Yonik grinned, then jerked his head toward the hut. "I think you'll have your fair share of it soon enough."

With no small amount of trepidation, Bjorn stepped up

to the door and knocked. He waited for a long moment before the answer came.

"I invited you before, did I not?" called a wizened voice.

Bjorn pulled open the door, then paused in the doorway. He had seen little of the hut during his confinement the night before, but it turned out there was little to see. The walls were bare, devoid of the decorations he would have expected of a witch woman, like feathers, bones, and skulls. Chests lining the walls were the only furniture. A cane leaned next to the door. A lit firepit occupied the hut's center and illuminated the space. Over the fire hung a pot of steaming water.

And behind it, sitting cross-legged, was a bent and grizzled woman: Mother Sign, the uncanny Silver from the longhouse.

Bjorn's attention, however, had caught on the fire and the steaming cauldron. The memory of Yonik's hut arose, when he thought he had become sprite-touched like his father. Sweat beaded his brow. He held his breath, afraid to breathe in the steam lest the visions return.

Mother Sign raised her head at their entrance, though her clouded eyes stared above them. "I can hear you holding your breath, cub. Don't faint on my floor."

Bjorn, chagrined, sucked in as quiet a breath as he could. "Is that steam... *khnuum?*"

The Silver barked a laugh. "Soon, you'll wish it was. No, cub — you'll not be doing any Seeing for a while yet. This pot is for tea. Sit and help me with it."

Bjorn glanced at Yonik, who only shrugged, then did as he was instructed. After retrieving two cups from one of the chests, Mother Sign produced a pouch with brown, dried leaves and twigs inside. She tumbled a bit of the mixture into each cup, then had Bjorn pour in water. Glad to be holding something warm, he took the cup in his hands and breathed in the scent, pleasantly surprised by the spicy tang to it. Yonik, now leaning against the wall, did not ask for any, and Mother Sign did not instruct to prepare a third cup.

Bjorn held his tea and waited for the Silver to speak. But Mother Sign seemed content to bend over her tea and breathe in deeply. Finally, he could endure it no longer.

"You wanted to see me?"

Inhaling once more, Mother Sign's eyes found his, seeming to see him despite her blindness. They wandered away a moment later. "Yes. The Sight has you strong, Bjorn of Oakharrow — like a deer in a wolf's jaws. You are *Volur*, true as they come. And in here" — Mother Sign rapped her temple with her knuckles — "there's much I must pass on to you. I have seen my apprentice coming for a long time now, the greatest I will know. At last, you have arrived."

Bjorn shifted, suddenly uncomfortable. *She can't mean me.* He had never been the greatest in anything.

But haven't you wanted to be? another part of him whispered. *Aren't you curious to see?*

He found himself speaking, his decision already made. "Then I guess I'd better learn."

"So you will." Mother Sign gave him another gap-toothed grin, then reached into a satchel propped against her leg and pulled out a flat, gray stone about the size of her hand. She held it out, her thin arm slightly trembling.

"Here. Take this and look closely."

Hesitantly, Bjorn accepted the stone and did as she bade. The stone was not completely smooth, but had intricate lines and arcs etched into one face. He frowned at the carving. Almost, it looked familiar to him.

"Is it an Old Djurian rune?"

Mother Sign shook her head. "Feels like you should know its meaning, doesn't it? But it's not Old Djurian, but of the language before, written by your ancestors before they crossed the Treacherous Sea and carved homesteads from Enean hills. It was they who discovered the secrets of the runestones, the knowledge which we have preserved here at Heim Numen these long centuries."

Secrets of the runestones. Bjorn lifted the tea to his lips and let his eyes linger upon the stone in his hand as he considered it. "What does this one mean?"

"Mean?" Mother Sign chortled, a slight hiccup escaping her. "It *means* nothing, cub. It only *is.*"

It sounded very much the same to him, but Bjorn let the point slide. "Then what *is* it?"

The blind Silver sent a questing hand forward. Bjorn, guessing her intent, held the runestone out to her. But instead of taking it, she traced a fingertip along the spindly lines for several long moments.

"This one's name is *gramur* — 'Frenzy,' we would call it."

Frenzy. Now that he had its name, Bjorn believed he *did* feel it: a deep-burning sensation, like lava locked in a volcano's heart. But no — it came not from the stone, but from *within himself.* The rage was his; the stone only awoke it.

If he just reached for it, then—

Bjorn dropped the runestone and jerked away. His head felt hot and slightly feverish. He inhaled a ragged breath and was relieved as the feeling swiftly subsided.

Mother Sign was quiet for a long moment. From the corner of his eye, he thought she glanced toward Yonik in the corner.

"Well," she said at length, "you do have it strong. You sensed it even without *khnuum,* didn't you, cub?"

"Don't call me cub." The words slipped free before he could think better of them.

The aged woman only laughed. "Prod a bear and get the claw, eh?"

Bjorn wondered if the axiom had more intent to it than it seemed. How she could know who he was without even seeing his face was beyond him.

If Mother Sign knew, she gave no indication of it as she spoke again. "But I have not truly answered what a rune-stone is. For an impatient young one, I will be as brief as an old woman can be."

She sipped her tea, then continued. "Those ancient people used runestones for many things beyond what is permitted today. Their warriors peered at runes like this Frenzy stone before charging into battle. Priests and priest-esses healed with them, both of body and mind. Seers and seeresses gazed upon them to catch glimpses of possible futures, by which they steered the path of their society. And indeed, the Inscribed Beliefs themselves were transcribed in just such a way. A dozen gothi many, many generations ago engaged in a collaborative Seeing, and together perceived the gods' instructions that guide our laws and lives to this day."

Now that he no longer gazed upon the runestone, Bjorn felt his pulse settle into its normal rhythm. He wondered at the aged woman's words and if any of them could be true.

"If they are so powerful," he asked after a silent moment, "why don't we use them today?"

Mother Sign smiled, her face wrinkling like old vellum. "Fear. Runestones unlock our potential, cub — *all* our potential. We are capable of far more than we know. Yet there are barriers in the way, walls put up by ourselves and others, limitations that hem us in and chain us to mediocrity. When used properly, runestones break down these barriers, and from behind them emerges something both terrible and wondrous."

Yonik, silent thus far, added his own contribution. "Like a butterfly from a chrysalis."

Bjorn cast him a skeptical look, to which the gothi only grinned.

A smile touched on Mother Sign's thin lips as well. "Ah, how I have missed your florid observations, Brother Yonik. But the principle is correct: as a key turns a lock, a rune-stone opens a *Volur's* potential. Some believe the runes are gifts from the gods, the language by which they command us and help us grow. Perhaps, to borrow Yonik's turn of phrase, it is in the same way that a caterpillar emerges from a chrysalis transformed into a butterfly, or how a babe grows within a mother's belly. *How* is not ours to know — only that it *is*, and it is the will of the Inscribed that it remains a mystery."

"But not all believe it so," interjected the priest.

The Silver's eyes wandered toward him. "True. Others, like Alfjin the Scribe, have thought they are inventions of our own minds, that *Volur* long ago stumbled upon the Hall of Doors and learned the runes from it."

"The Hall of Doors?" queried Bjorn.

"Ah, have I not mentioned it? Yes — *Hael Ek'dyrr*, it was called in Old Djurian, but the meaning is the same. *Volur* have long envisioned the same place during Seeings. The Hall of Doors appears as a corridor lined with rune-inscribed doors. A seer finds a door by looking upon the corresponding runestone, then pries it open to access its ability — if they dare."

Bjorn could imagine it, but questions crowded his head. "But I did a Seeing with Yon— that is, Brother Yonik, and I didn't visit this hall."

"You are lucky you did not." The Silver's head tilted toward where the gothi leaned against the wall. "As I understand from the circumstances, the rune was imperfectly carved. Had you entered the Hall of Doors, you may have gone to the wrong portal — or, worse still, to the right one, and never been able to shut it."

"What happens then?"

"What our ancestors feared. The unlocking of potential may bring about ruin as well as wonders. The gods, speaking through the Inscribed Beliefs, feared the Sight would make men's wars too devastating, dooming them to repeat the wars they fled from in the Witterland. So they made a fateful choice that day and forbade the use of all runestones but those involved in visions, and these were permitted only that they might continue to stay true to the gods' intentions."

Bjorn breathed in his tea as he mulled over all the Silver had said. "If their use is forbidden, why do you still have runestones like that?" He gestured toward the gray stone lying facedown on the ground next to the fire, then remembered she could not see him. "That is, the Frenzy runestone."

Mother Sign nodded, as if she had been waiting for this question. "We gothi have always preserved knowledge, for there is inherent value in knowing. But we have also known that what is forbidden in one era may be permitted in another, should the need arise. The Witterland Runestone tells of a time when the giants return. Always, we hoped this vision would not come to pass, that the world would divert from its course. But, like many of the things we fear, it proved inevitable."

The Silver's clouded eyes wandered to Bjorn's face and strayed over his chin before resting somewhere above his head. "The time for change has come — and it changes with you, cub. If the Wild God has taught us nothing, it is this: all must adapt or perish. Even a god's guidance may be right for one age, but wrong in the next."

Chills fled over his skin like elk before a winter storm. Even with her being blind, Bjorn found it difficult to meet Mother Sign's eyes. *It changes with you,* she had said.

As if the world rested on his shoulders.

Too much — it's too much. Bjorn had never reckoned himself strong by anyone's measure. He had endured the trek through the Teeth and stood up to the jotunmen and their greatbear, but had only survived by the barest thread. Maybe he was a *Volur*; maybe the Sight was strong within him. But it did not mean he could defy the wisdom of the gods and forge a new path.

"I..." he began, but trailed off. *I think you have the wrong man,* he had been about to say. But those were a coward's words. Whatever else he was, he could not consent again to being a coward. "I'll try to learn," he said instead. "Though I'm not sure I'll succeed."

Mother Sign smiled widely. "Of course you are not sure! Neither am I certain. But all we can do is try, is it not?"

Bjorn shrugged. Even knowing she could not see the gesture, he could not find words to explain.

"Then let us begin." The blind Silver reached forward and found the runestone by touch, then held it up. "You will learn each of the major runes and trace them. You must know them as a vain woman knows her face — something I once knew well! Once you have showed mastery, we will proceed to the minor runes — here, carved around the edges — which supplement the major rune's effect, some tempering, others exaggerating. Then, and only then, might we test them upon you."

Sharing a wince with Yonik, Bjorn repressed the rest of his simmering questions. But emotions still churned in his stomach. *What will the runes unlock in me?* He could not decide if the thought filled him more with excitement or apprehension.

But it did not change that he had to learn. Bending over the runestones before him, Bjorn set to his task.

9. GODS WILLING

I

For each facet, a priest shall reign
To speak on Our behalf
A temple they must maintain
They are known by mask and staff

High chanter shall be their name
And high their station shall be
Below the Karah in acclaim
Above the rest of thee

- Words in the Sand, refrain 14;21-22

Sehdra felt as if she traveled in the Jackal's Blight as servants carried her through the karah's military camps.

Though she had never felt comfortable elevated on a palanquin borne on the shoulders of slaves, it was a relief now. Teti plodded next to her along the banks of the Nu, where the muck had mixed with all manners of soldiers' waste. The men had only just settled down for the evening, yet like an infestation of rats, they had already defiled the riverbank. Sehdra breathed through a veil scented with myrrh, draped over the scarab mask that covered the cursed side of her face, but it did little to ease the eye-swimming stench. She pitied her friend, yet the dictums of society forbade him from riding beside her.

Men and their instruments of death thronged the landscape, as populous as locusts in a plague. Each was filmed with sweat, the heat still fading as the sun fell, and most dragged with exhaustion from the day's march. Sehdra picked out the divisions among them, passingly familiar with military structure from lifelong exposure and the past few weeks of reading up on generals' accounts in the royal library.

The infantry made up the largest group, one hundred regiments of one hundred men each, composed of spearmen, lancers, and archers. Standards flapped in the hot wind among each camp, the stitched shapes of the Divine providing identification. Most had not chosen this life — Sehdra had glimpsed in her tours of Annax-Nu the deals given to prisoners both foreign and from the People of Dust: a life of hard labor in the quarries, or military service. Many preferred a soldier's life.

Many will not outlive that choice. Though, having visited a quarry once, Sehdra could not say they had made the wrong decision.

Second largest among the army were the mercenaries. In numbers almost equal to the infantrymen, they had flocked to her brother's call from across the continent and beyond. A score of nations were represented by their foreign banners. Men close at hand from Zakawa as well as North and South Vinaxi. Warriors from the western nations of Xen'tia and Jin'to. The most came from the dozens of lands she only knew by name from the sprawling Suncoast to the south. She thought of the Ibis standing before Oyaoan's shadow as she glimpsed the tattoos and piercings and clothes strange to her culture. When viewing others from his continent, he did not seem so out-of-place.

But these twenty thousand men were not alone, but supported by a spattering of much smaller, yet still powerful divisions. The chariotry congregated in their own camp, though the thousand men were officially assigned to various infantry regiments. They tended to be the sons of nomarchs and wealthy merchants and captains, and thus preferred the company of their own class to those one step above slaves. Their chariots were lined up in neat rows, as they were each night, and their horses hitched to posts. She wondered how well the division would fare in the Baegardian valley. From all she had heard, the land was rocky and forested, both poor grounds for chariots. But Karah Hephystus had commanded they come, and so they did.

Horses were not the only beasts in the host. Easily seen from her view atop the palanquin were the gray behemoths from the Suncoast that Sehdra's father had begun importing, breeding, and training throughout his reign. It had been one of his proudest achievements, and she knew the origin story well. In one of his many campaigns to the south, Karah Sharek had seen how effectively elephants trampled his men and broke their lines. He began gathering them at the first opportunity, but encountered many problems in transporting them across the sea and keeping them alive when they landed on the shore. But her father, like her brother, had never been a man to be told something could not be done. Eventually, after much coin spent and many lives lost during the sea voyages and breeding experiments, the elephant division began to thrive. Now they numbered a hundred strong, enough to be deadly to the shield walls the mountain savages were famous for using.

Forces on land were only one arm of the military. Along the Nu, a bristling forest of masts emerged above the sea of tents. Forty feluccas sailed upriver toward the Winter Holds. As several of their cities were built along the upper reaches of its shores, and the enemy would bring to bear their dragon-ships in the coming battles, a fleet provided a tactical advantage. These ships, though similar to the common vessel fishermen used, had been adapted based on the boats of the mountain savages, doubling the men housed aboard and adding more oars to aid in the passage against the current.

But mighty as these forces were, and as many wars as they had won, they paled before the last branch of the army. Sehdra's eyes were drawn toward the great tents she knew sheltered the huame. A dozen of them, more than she had ever seen in one place, had come at Oyaoan's call. Though the giantess was the largest among them, each of the others rose higher than the elephants and looked just as strong. Exposure to Oyaoan had shown her that Hua's Children possessed as much intelligence as humans, if not more. Combined with their awe-inspiring strength, their impregnable hides, and the dark armor they carried with them, she could not see how they would be stopped.

With their help, Physt will conquer all our enemies. Perhaps all the world. But she had seen the price of such aid, and knew it to be a demon's bargain.

Finally, having crossed much of the long camp, she arrived at her destination. The slaves grunted as they lowered the palanquin, and Sehdra rose and tried not to let show the feebleness of her leg. After their arduous trip, weakness was the last thing she wished to display, even before servants. Teti had moved around the palanquin to spread a mud-spattered rug at her feet. A sigh escaped her as she stepped onto it and crossed the churned earth to the tent's flap.

All we do for show, she mused. *Like peacocks before their mates.*

But she paused at the entrance to lift her veil and adjust her mask. Posturing was important in a game where the slightest mistake could be fatal.

Teti moved to open the tent, but hesitated, making it seem as if he barred her entrance. "I will be right outside, Sehdra Ohkweht," he murmured.

Despite his return to formality, she smiled. "If this endangers me, it will not be from within."

"I know you can look after yourself, Royal Sister. I merely worry."

"Perhaps overmuch." She gently touched his arm, then faced forward. Teti relented, opening the way, and Sehdra entered.

The tent was sized for its occupant's status, roomy but barring luxury. The soft glow of several rushlights illuminated the gloomy interior, and it was stuffy with heat, despite the cooling land outside. Sweat accumulated at the edges of her mask, threatening to drip into her eye. She wished she could wipe at it and find some measure of relief, but formality saw her striding forward instead.

The tent's owner rose from a desk in the middle of the tent, the sole furniture besides a chair and a cot behind it. He looked both pleased and nervous to see her.

"Sehdra Ohkweht," he said as he bowed low, his nose almost tapping the desk. "I am honored by your visit."

"I wished to speak with you, Raneb Nautjer." She was dismayed to see no chair other than the one he stood before. Her withered leg already throbbed.

The high chanter to Qa'a, however, had always been a perceptive man. No sooner had the wince crossed her features than he was bringing the chair around to her. "Please, Royal Sister, sit. You have preserved my life and are elevated far beyond my poor station. You must be as comfortable as I can provide."

Despite herself, she murmured her thanks and gratefully sank into the seat. It would have been most proper to tug her legs against the chair, but with how poorly her bad leg was behaving tonight, she had no choice but to keep it extended.

Raneb's eyes caught on her mask, and a smile lit up his face. Though his hair was graying, she thought he would have been comely in his youth, particularly when he smiled.

"A fine mask for your visit, Royal Sister," he observed. "The Wise Scarab would be pleased."

Sehdra returned his smile. "Qa'a be praised. How are you finding your duties in his name?"

The high chanter's cheerfulness flickered away. "I hope you will not mistake me for ungracious, Royal Sister, but serving the Divine here is... a challenge. There are many duties I leave back in Annax-Nu, duties I worry will not be entirely filled. And I am sure you are aware that it is not precisely an honor to be chosen as priest to the karah's armies, nor pleasant."

"I am." She imagined how it must be to bestow blessings upon the soldiers, grimy from their marching, and after traveling all day himself. It was a punishment to force Raneb onto the war trail, just as it had been for her.

"As it happens," she continued, "this relates to my aim in coming here. There are things we must discuss. Divine willing, we will survive Hua's Strife, as they're calling this campaign — but if we do not, we must at least set our plans."

Raneb grimaced. "It is my turn for a confession, Sehdra Ohkweht: your words fill me with foreboding." His eyes darted to the tent's entrance, and he took a step closer, his voice pitched softer. "What is it you speak of?"

She drew in a breath, then exhaled it as quietly as she could. It did little to alleviate the nerves jangling inside her. But through long hours spent in the karah's court, she had learned to steel herself against discomfort. This was the least of the risks she had taken lately.

"As part of your duties as a high chanter within Nome Qa'a, you are tasked with aiding the nomarch, are you not? Primarily through the administration of people where their well-being is concerned?"

Raneb looked as cautious as a hunted gazelle. As if to counteract it, the high chanter strained for another smile. "Yes. So I am blessed to do."

"So you are privy to many of the inner workings of the territory, are you not?"

Raneb bobbed his head. "I might be called so. But please, Royal Sister — what are your questions regarding?"

She had been stalling, unwilling to ask her question. Now it seemed that Raneb, in the hopes of permanently forestalling it, was pushing the conversation to a point.

He will regret that.

She spoke without preamble. "Why are there so many widows and orphans in Nome Qa'a? What is happening to its men?" She resolved to leave it there, the inquiry dangling, yet she could not help but add, "It is such a shame for so many to be lost and without reason."

Raneb grew still. His eyes, the brown of wet sand, flickered back and forth between hers. He seemed to be taking her measure, to see if she might lash out like a cobra should he respond improperly. Finally, he closed his eyes and breathed out deeply before reopening them.

"You saved my life and soul, Sehdra Ohkweht," he murmured. "Without you, I would have been ushered to the

Land of Blight, no matter my years of service to the gods. I owe you a debt that cannot be repaid. And though these words will further endanger me, for you, I will speak them."

Sehdra's heart fluttered. Her curiosity had been ignited by the mystery, it was true, and all the more so since Oyaoan had shown uncharacteristic mercy toward the high chanter. But it seemed her question drove at something far deeper than she had suspected.

Raneb took a step closer and leaned toward her, his voice pitched low. "Within Nome Qa'a, there is a pit far into the desert, far away from any oasis or shade. Many men are required to go to this pit, and most do not return. Those who do return drive wagons to Annax-Nu and head directly into the palace vaults. These caravans are accompanied by a huamek — perhaps to guard, perhaps to oversee, most likely both. Sometimes even after the loads are deposited, the men do not survive to go to home."

It took an effort to keep her voice level. "Are all those men killed? And what for? What lies in this pit?"

The high chanter shook his head. "I do not know, and I do not ask. Not even the nomarch knows, and I suspect he, too, does not wish to. All I know of it is this: other huame guard it, permitting none to see it and remain in this world." He paused and screwed up his eyes. "Ah, but there is one more thing: no fire is permitted there. The nomarch let that slip when he complained of the impossibility of the Great One's demands. He seemed quite nervous when he realized what he had admitted, but we have not spoken of it since."

Sehdra mulled over his words. She realized she was kneading her withered leg and stopped herself. *A pit where no fire is permitted... A pit that kills the men excavating its ore, or perhaps are killed for the knowledge of it...* She could not fathom what metal or stone would be so valuable as that. Even gold did not warrant such stringent measures, and despite how much of that precious metal Oyaoan wore, the giantess had never seemed to yearn for it. *Diamonds and other gems?* An unprecedented quantity, perhaps, might be worth killing hundreds for, particularly to the huame. And such a trove of wealth could fund the wars they now engaged in.

But why would she forbid fire?

None of Raneb's revelations made sense. But if she had learned anything since the Children of the Sun had come to Ha-Sypt, it was that currents moved of which she was only half aware. Whatever was in this pit was likely something she had never seen, a secret known only to the giants. All she could do was try to unravel it. Perhaps it would help her understand why Oyaoan wanted this war.

The giantess's motivations were key, after all. She knew why Physt wanted to invade the Winter Holds. Even before he heard the reports of the savages' weakness, he was bored and bloodthirsty, and longed to spread his glory throughout Enea. But Oyaoan's goals were opaque. Power, she certainly strove for, but not that she might be lauded for it. As far as Sehdra knew, the huamek cared nothing for humans except for how they served her needs. And if the giants wanted power alone, why had they not marched north from the Suncoast long ago? Less than a flood had passed since Oyaoan had led her dozen giants and their caravan of servants to the gates of Annax-Nu and, through the Ibis, demanded an audience with the karah. If what she had heard of their long lives was true, they could have ruled for centuries, if they wished.

Something changed. She knew it, knew it in her bones, and had long ago learned to trust her instincts. Yet what that change was still eluded her.

Sehdra's head jerked up as voices spoke from outside the tent. She recognized Teti's raised voice, so she had a moment's warning to stand before the tent flap swept open. The ivory robes of the vizier swished around him as he entered the tent. Zosar's cruel eyes scanned the spare surroundings, falling on Qa'a's high chanter, then Sehdra. His lips curled.

"Sehdra Ohkweht." The karah's advisor bowed half as low as Raneb had. "I was honored to hear you were within."

"Vizier, please," Raneb protested. "The Royal Sister requested a private—"

"Thank you, Raneb Nautjer," Sehdra interrupted before looking to Zosar. "As much pleasure as it gives me to see you" — *That is, none at all,* she thought to herself — "I am afraid you lack the authority to interrupt me in a private conference with the high chanter of my Inspiration. Am I not the karah's kin? And thus, sister to a god?"

The royal advisor's sneer dripped away like river fog before the morning sun. "My sincerest apologies, Royal Sister," he said with blatant insincerity. "But as I come at the karah's behest, I fear I must remain and speak all the same."

Sehdra smiled at him, though her cursed flesh, hidden behind her mask, remained cold and unyielding. No matter how puffed up Zosar became on his borrowed authority, her words had reminded him of the tenuousness of his position. But he had the ear of her brother, and before the karah's word, hers carried little weight.

"I am always grateful for my brother's messages," she said at length. "Please, if you would convey it."

Zosar seemed to recover some of his bluster as he straightened. "His Sanctity does not wish his high chanter distracted from his many duties. War is an unsettling matter, and the men need much counseling from the gods."

Sehdra nodded, understanding the reprimand for what it was. *He suspects. He knows I plot.* Even though her brother had summoned her to accompany the war host, she had not truly believed he paid her much attention. Now, she saw he watched her closely indeed if he sent his highest advisor to cut short her meetings.

He fears me. Never had she believed it possible of Physt. All her life, he had taunted her, most often for her decrepit appearance, and lorded his power over her. He had never shown signs of fearing her before. The answer to why that had changed loomed large, both in size and power.

Oyaoan.

A greater authority reigned in the Plentiful Land than the karah these days. Even her brother, obsessed with his own divinity, understood that. He worried Sehdra plotted with the huamek against him. No doubt the incident with Raneb had only heightened his suspicions.

Sehdra, who had always sought the shadows in any room she entered, now found herself thrust into the full strength of the sun. And no one could have been more shocked than her to find she basked in it.

Even as she stood on her quivering leg, even as she was forbidden an ally by her brother's orders, Sehdra glowed with victory. Yet she kept her composure meek as she spoke. "Of course, Vizier Zosar. Tell my brother I will no longer disturb Raneb Nautjer, but leave him to his tasks."

The royal advisor looked surprised, then suspicious, if the widening and narrowing of his eyes was any sign. "Very well."

He remained at the tent's entrance, as if unsure how much he could prolong his stay, even with their karah's authority. But Sehdra had pushed the confrontation far enough. Granting Raneb a respectful nod, she limped with as much dignity as she could muster back to the tent's entrance. She caught Zosar's pungent perfume as she passed, a mixture of wood, cinnamon, and musk, and just managed to not wrinkle her nose.

Outside, the cool air was a relief. Darkness had swept across the camp while she spoke with the priest. Teti still stood, waiting with anxious eyes. He quickened to her side and glanced over her shoulder, no doubt wary of the lingering vizier.

"Are you well, Royal Sister?" he asked.

Sehdra met his gaze and let a glimmer of her true feelings show. "Never better, my friend. We claimed a victory this day. A small one, yes, but a success nonetheless."

Smiling at Teti's astonished look, she limped up to the palanquin, but hesitated before pulling herself into it. She turned back to her friend and spoke in an even softer voice.

"Physt burns too brightly. If his light should go out..." Sehdra reined in her dreams with a shake of her head. "I should not speak of it. Still, I plan for the day when it comes. I will not be without allies when power falls into my hands. Now come — let us return to our tent so you may wash away the camp's grime."

"The camp's grime," Teti rejoined, "and the reek of a certain advisor."

Her smile widening, Sehdra mounted the palanquin. Easing out her aching leg, she found a rare enjoyment in being carried through the war camp.

10. FIRST LOYALTY

Bastor pretended to take another sip of his honey wine as he watched the guard down the hall.

The daylight peering through the narrow windows down the passage had long ago faded to darkness. Now, only intermittent torches lit the corridor. His inclination was to hunch down in the pools of shadows between them, but he resisted the urge and instead remained next to one of the mounted lights. Soon, the night patrol would come by to extinguish them. Then it would be his time.

From the look of the huskarl, he had judged his approach well. The man had touched a hand to his stomach often over the past hour. Now he hunched over, his face scrunched in pain. Bastor could sympathize. He knew how effective the syrup of ipecac was that he had administered to the man's stew.

"A job well done," he muttered to his companion as he took an actual swig of mead.

The wooden statue, probably depicting one of Lord Petyr's ancestors, did not have the decency to respond.

Bastor had been building his reputation for days now. Indulging in ale and mead in all manner of indecorous places, he was quickly becoming known as the no-good drunkard son of Lord Ragnar. His father, from all the scowls he had sent Bastor's way, did not approve of his methods, but he did not interfere. It made Bastor all the more determined to continue.

The soiled perception came with the requirement of enduring snickers and ostracization from finer society. He did not find it difficult to deal with until he found Aelthena passing by with a frown. He knew that look; she thought she had overestimated him. Somehow, it stung more than it should have.

But such a reputation also had its perks. Expectations had met the floor, then been buried beneath it. As his fellow highborn began to ignore him, he grew able to move throughout the Elkhorn unobserved. Thus he had consorted with servants and stood watch in corridors, and all anyone would do when he was caught was shake their heads.

Little as it seems possible, he mused, *but they've still underestimated what a scoundrel I am.*

"At least I have you, my stiff friend." Bastor knocked his drinking horn against the arm of the carving, then took another swig.

"Partaking alone again, eh, Lord Heir?"

He blinked and looked around, as if too befuddled to have noticed the footsteps and muted conversation of the patrolling guards. They both grinned at him, half in mockery, half in roguish comaraderie.

"Ah, Thorpe, Kustaa!" Bastor flashed a lopsided smile.

"I'm not drinking alone — if you care to join me?" He held out the horn with raised eyebrows.

The one who had spoken first, Thorpe, laughed and accepted it, though not before casting a furtive glance to either side. Taking a long draught, he finished with a sigh and handed it to his companion. "Harrowmead, isn't it? Volkur's tits, but that's fine stuff."

"'Tis the truth. Don't know how they do it." Bastor took the horn back after the second guard, Kustaa, had finished, then scowled down into it. "Crooks! I've nothing left to wet my throat with."

"Guess you'll have to move your lazy bones. Be good for you." Thorpe knocked him on the shoulder, as if they were both down in the guardhouse and Bastor did not soar ranks above him. "See you on the next round, Lord Heir."

"If I'm not collapsed in the cellar by then, I en't drinking right."

Bastor grinned after them as their laughter echoed down the hall. His mirth slackened away as they passed the guard standing at the door and ribbed him for looking green. The swirling anxiety had fully returned by the time the footsteps faded from hearing, and the door guard's groans could be heard even from his position.

Our first loyalty is to our blood. His lips twisted as he levered himself away from the wall and headed down the corridor.

Some minutes later, he returned with a different aspect. Gone was the highborn frillery, the mead, the drunken smiles. In their place were dark clothes and a gray hood. He covered his hands in rough leather gloves, and his only ornamentation was two knives strapped beneath his tunic. He moved like a skittish cat, halting at every intersection and peering around the corner before proceeding. Though the watch was not supposed to return to this section of the

Elkhorn for half a candle, as he had observed on previous nights of pretended debauchery, in a citadel this size, one never knew what kinds of criminals might be prowling about.

Myself as a prime example.

Carefully, Bastor peered around the edge of the stone. The door guard was leaning over, and something glistened on the stone and his boots in front of him. Bastor wrinkled his nose. He had hoped the stomach ills would drive the man off to a chamberpot, not make him sick at his station. The man was stubborn in his duty.

Damned shame he'll pay for it.

Knowing he was unlikely to sneak up on him, Bastor pulled the hood tighter about his face and turned the corner. He kept his pace casual and his eyes down so the torchlight did not catch on his features. The door guard, even in his misery, noticed him approaching. The stout man even tried standing upright, to only marginal success. Bastor felt as if he would be sick to his stomach as well. His guts twisted like a boatman were making knots with his intestines.

"Good evening," the man said hoarsely when Bastor was a dozen paces away.

He pitched his voice deeper and scratchier as he responded. "Doesn't look that way for you."

The door guard gave a sickly grin. A bit of spittle had caught in his beard. "Bad stew's my guess."

Bastor only shrugged and made as if to pass him by. His pulse quickened as he came within reach of the guard. And, despite all his nerves leading up to this moment, now that it had come, he found the heat that flooded through his limbs and filled his head to be far from displeasurable.

A smile won free of him — then he struck.

Bastor's fist thumped first into the man's gut. The door

guard, robbed of breath, wheezed in surprise and pain as he doubled over. Bastor used the opportunity to wrap one arm around his neck while the other sought to disarm him. But even sick as a dog, the man was a fighter. He bucked under Bastor's headlock, kicking against Bastor's shins and the wall. The huskarl's efforts loosened Bastor's grip enough that he sucked in a shaky breath, and one of his hands scrabbled at Bastor's face. Gritting his teeth, Bastor strengthened his hold by bracing it with his second arm. Like the jaws of a bear trap, he squeezed the man's neck closed. Strength blossomed as exhilaration, fury, and fear bubbled through his veins. The guard drew his nails across Bastor's face, thin lines of fire, while his other hand pulled feebly at Bastor's forearms. His efforts grew weaker, then went slack.

Bastor did not let up even as he grunted with the effort and slumped to the floor under the man's weight. Finally, the last spasm before unconsciousness truly set in. Only as the door guard went limp a second time did Bastor release his hold.

He caught his breath as he gazed down at the guard. There was always a possibility that he had killed him rather than knocked him out, but he'd known the risks. Rising, he patted the guard's waist until he located a ring of keys. Three of them hung from the metal, one for each of the daughters' rooms that he had guarded. Without checking for a pulse or breath, not wanting to know, Bastor stood and made for the door he had earlier identified as belonging to his mark. He tried two keys in the lock before the third finally turned.

Gentle as a merchant with his coins, he pushed open the door and peered inside. The chamber was softly illuminated by several candles mounted along the walls and a banked fireplace. Like his rooms, there was only a small entertaining room with no more furniture than a table and a few chairs. A green banner bearing Lord Petyr's elk insignia hung from one wall, while a mounted bull elk's head decorated the hearth. An archway lay past the fireplace, telling of the bedchamber just beyond.

No sooner had Bastor shut the door than a voice called out from the archway. "Mother, is that you?" It was a young woman's voice. "Did you check on Destin on your way in? Poor fellow sounds like he's had some bad—"

The woman emerged into the room and let out a startled yelp. But Bastor had positioned himself next to where she would emerge, and he clapped a gloved hand over her mouth. The woman bit at his glove and tried to knock him with foot and elbow, but as soon as he pressed cold steel against her throat, she went as still as a vole spotted by a wolf.

Bastor tasted a hint of sick in the back of his throat. It made his voice all the rougher as he spoke. "No sudden moves. We need to talk, you and I. About your father. I'm going to uncover your mouth, but don't make a sound, hear me?"

The young woman did not move, but Bastor removed his hand anyway, gripping her shoulder instead.

"Did you kill him?" she asked as soon as she could. "Destin?"

"The guard? Best concern yourself with your own safety." She smelled faintly of apple and winterlily. The innocent scent made his guilt churn all the more. Worse still was the fear-sweat permeating from her. But he could not quail now. He had come here with a purpose. To fail it would mean far worse for far more people.

"What do you want?" The young woman's voice trembled, but she spoke with conviction.

He braced himself and said the rehearsed words. "I know you, Helka Of'Siward. You're a dutiful daughter, loyal and proper, even if you've a will of your own. You respect your father and love him, and he loves you. Which is why you're going to convince him to relinquish his claim to the Iron Circle."

He waited for her response. For several long moments, she remained silent. When she spoke, the words came out slowly, almost thoughtfully.

"You work for another jarl, don't you? Someone who doesn't want my father to become Arkjarl over him."

Bastor's lips pulled back in a snarl. His father preferred he slit her throat. *A clean finish,* he would have called it. In some ways, he was right. Helka promised to be clever enough to guess Lord Ragnar was behind the attack. She could unravel the Jarl of Ragnarsglade's carefully laid plans and ruin his chances for power — and thus, doom the entirety of Baegard.

But even against those stakes, he would not take his father's path. He strayed too close to becoming him already. *And I'll go screaming to Ovvash's hells before I let that happen.*

Roughly, he shook her, though he tried his best not to cut her on the blade. "Don't *think,* Helka. Think too hard on this, and I'll be forced to kill you. Neither of us wants that. All you need to concern yourself with is convincing Lord Siward to remove himself from consideration. Do it by whatever means necessary. And know that, in doing so, you will help Baegard survive."

"I don't believe you." Against all reason and fear, the young woman stood strong. "My father is the best man to lead Baegard's forces. Who among the jarls is better suited? None have his experience and mind."

But in war, Bastor thought, *one must also be ruthless.*

"Last chance," he warned, pressing the blade tighter against her neck. "Agree, or I'll have no other choice."

For a moment, he braced himself for the worst. Then she broke.

"Fine!" Helka gasped, her throat quivering under the blade's cruel touch. "I'll do it!"

Bastor repressed a relieved sigh as he eased away the dagger. "Good. Now I'm going to leave, and you won't scream or alert anyone. Do that, and the next knife that comes for you won't stop at your skin. Understood?"

"Yes."

He guided her toward the door, careful not to trip over the rug in the center. When he reached the exit, he removed the knife from Helka's throat and shoved her away. "Not a word," he gave a final warning, then opened the door to step back outside.

The young woman spun around, no doubt hoping to identify her attacker. Their eyes met before Bastor bowed out of the room and shut the door with a louder noise than he intended.

Back in the corridor, Bastor looked down to where he had left the guard. He had only a moment to register the missing body before he heard a grunt on the opposite side.

He reacted on instinct. Dodging back, a sword whisked by Bastor's face, the steel sparking against the stone. The door guard had evidently recovered, for he quickly readied another blow. Bastor skirted out of striking distance. With only a knife against the man's sword, he was at a severe disadvantage. And all the huskarl had to do was shout and it would be over. The gods smiled on him that he had not already.

He had not wanted to kill this night. But if it was between this man's death and his, Bastor knew the choice he would always make.

Baring his teeth, he feinted a charge, counting on his poison to have slowed the man's wits. The huskarl took the bait, trying for the easy skewer. It overextended him, giving Bastor the opportunity to surge around him and lash out toward his exposed armpit. His blade bit deep into the man's flesh, finding the gap in his chainmail. The man grunted, and as his mouth fell open, a bit of spew dribbled out of it. Now Bastor knew why he had not shouted: he had been trying not to heave up his guts.

It almost awoke pity in him, but he smothered the spark. *His death or yours*, he reminded himself, then moved to finish the job.

Bastor grabbed the huskarl's sword arm with his free hand and wrenched the blade free. The man struggled against him, but his strength was swiftly fading. Bastor drove the guard against the wall and wrenched his blade free from his side. His hand was slick with blood; the hilt was becoming difficult to grip. He clenched his fist tighter around it, then drove it toward the man's neck.

As his knife came away, fresh blood gurgled out.

The door guard slumped down the wall, one hand grasping at the spurting liquid. He looked surprised, but in a distant way. Bastor tried not to think as he stepped around the dying man and secreted away his weapon. He tried to deny the screams sounding in his head.

He fled down the corridor.

Though he had all the caution of a charging bull, Bastor ran into no guards before he made it to his room. His head pounded, and a roaring filled his ears. He fumbled open the lock and pushed it open. Just before he shut it, he noticed the dark smear he left on the lock. He lifted the corner of his tunic and wiped at it until the metal shone dully again, then stepped inside.

Once there, he stood for a long moment. The blood that stained his clothes was wet, but beginning to crust on his skin. He raised his hands, and by the smoldering light from his fireplace, he saw the dark streaks upon them.

He dropped his hands. His legs trembled. Chills traveled down his limbs.

I killed him.

He had tried so hard not to, had carefully planned his approach for days. Yet it had not mattered in the end. At his core, Bastor was a killer. Just like his father.

Don't think. Not now. The danger was not over. Later, he could succumb to guilt and self-loathing. *Later.*

For now, he had to finish what he had started.

He stripped off his clothes. He undid his belt and set it aside with his knives. Gathering the soiled garments into a pile, he tossed them into the fireplace, then built up the coals so that the cloth caught flame. He moved to his washing basin and scrubbed at his hands. He was glad for the scant light; he would not see how the water turned pink. He splashed it over his face, appreciating the sting of the scratches from the huskarl. Pain felt like a penance, even if this was something he could never atone for. After his skin was as clean as he could manage, he retrieved the knife he had used and washed away the blood from it, then secured it in the chest at the foot of his bed.

His tasks complete, Bastor returned to his sitting room, naked but for his underclothes, and watched the clothes burn in the fireplace. He felt horribly thirsty. Returning to his chest, he fetched the cask of Harrowmead he kept there and uncorked it to fill the same horn he had used before, left behind when he had changed clothes. He filled it to the brim, then drained it, and filled up a second one.

Sliding down the wall opposite the hearth, cold stone scratching against his back, Bastor leaned back his head and closed his eyes. But he could not ward away the memories that rose to haunt him. Though his limbs dragged and his mind screamed, he leveraged himself up again and reached for a log from the woodpile, then crawled over to his chest. Opening it, he stared at the knife he had just placed there, unwilling to reach for it for several long moments.

Let it do some good, he thought. It finally compelled him to seize the hilt and draw it from its sheath.

Bastor set his horn in a holder positioned by the hearth, then took the knife in one hand and the wood in the other.

He began to carve.

It was a rushed and sloppy effort at first, but soon, his anxiety relented to the flow of the work. He had carved countless blocks before. He knew the pattern, and it always settled his nerves to conform to it.

For a time, he became lost in it, and almost forgot himself.

11. BEST LAID PLANS

Aelthena had only just smoothed out her borrowed dress when the lock in her door turned.

"A moment!" she called, frantically ensuring she had secured her clothes. Only a second afterward did she recognize the impropriety of the intrusion. "Who is it?"

The trespasser did not answer until he had entered and closed the door behind him. When he had locked it, Frey finally turned around. Her scowl deepened until she realized he did not wear the teasing smile she expected, but a grave frown instead.

Worry gnawed at her. "Is something wrong? You look as if you've seen a corpse risen."

"Not risen — one buried in a fresh grave." Frey scanned

the room as he spoke. "Have you left your chambers today yet?"

"Does it look like I have? Quit playing coy, Frey — out with it."

As usual, the guardian ignored her and continued his search farther into the room, though she had not granted him permission. There was little to look through. Of all the jarls and their relations, she swore she had been given the smallest accommodations. Her sitting room could be crossed in several strides and only seated four at most. Her balcony had barely enough space upon which to stand, though it at least boasted a view of the farmland to the south. Her bedchamber sufficed to fit her lumpy bed and no more. The garderobe affixed to the chambers was dark and never quite smelled clean. She did not even have her own bath, but had to use the ones shared by the other highborn in the castle. Having arrived at Petyrsholm with few possessions, what little furnishings there were flaunted the emerald elk of Lord Petyr.

Frey poked his head behind curtains and the green arras opposite the fireplace, then moved toward her bedroom. She stopped him with a firm hand on his arm.

"Before you rifle through my undergarments," she said crossly, "tell me what you're looking for."

A rueful smile edged onto his lips. "I doubt I'll need to search there. Assassins tend not to be that small."

"Assassins?" Aelthena looked back toward the door. "Why the blazes would you be worried about assassins?"

"A huskarl was killed last night, Aelthena. One of Lord Siward's. He'd been protecting his daughters' rooms."

Her pulse quickened, and her mind churned. *Lord Siward's huskarl, slain.* This was no coincidence. Not with what she and the jarls' wives had been up to.

"Were any of his daughters injured?"

"His eldest, Helka, but only slightly. I think she was more frightened than anything else. A man held her at knifepoint, but the blade only nicked her neck."

She felt sick imagining the scene. She remembered Helka; the girl was as golden and lovely as her mother, but had her father's hard countenance, even though she had only seen sixteen winters. Aelthena had liked the little she had seen of her during meals with the jarls and their families.

"What did he want, this assassin, if not to kill her?"

Frey had done a circuit of the bedroom and seemed satisfied no one lingered in the shadows. "Can't say. If he said anything to her, it has not spread with the other news. All I know is that he had a Sypten look to him. Perhaps he was an escaped thrall. More likely, I'd think him an agent of the karah. Either way, it doesn't change that my first duty is to ensure your safety. With your leave, I'll be sleeping at your door."

Despite the dire news, Aelthena found a very different feeling warming her now. "If you think it necessary," she said with forced calm.

Frey glanced at her, then smiled in that infuriating way of his. She looked aside, refusing to engage, even as her cheeks pinked.

Desperate for a fresh line of thought, Aelthena grasped at the first subject to come to mind. "Much as I enjoy your intrusions, I must request that you leave. I have to do my hair, then attend a meeting. It's more important than ever that Lord Siward becomes the Arkjarl, and as swiftly as possible."

Over the intervening days since the jarls' wives had agreed to pull for Siward to wear the Iron Circle, progress had been slow, too slow. Every couple of days, Aelthena gathered the women together again, yet the reports remained the same: each was gaining traction, but their husbands were slow to convince. In some ways, Aelthena could sympathize with the jarls' plight. Relenting power to any of them took theirs away, perhaps permanently.

But haven't I sacrificed to serve Baegard? she thought irritably. *Is it so much to ask the same of them?* Yet she could do nothing but wait and hope she was doing enough.

Frey looked around at her. "I can't leave, Aelthena. What if the assassin comes for you next? I need to be by your side from here on out."

"You really think he'll come by daylight?" But she had to admit, a tendril of fear threaded through her at his words. *Assassins in the Elkhorn.* She knew that, with all her machinations, she was as fine a candidate as any of the jarls to be the next target.

A knock at the door startled her back to the present. Trying to dismiss images of a Sypten man pushing into the room and diving at her with a knife, she held her breath as Frey drew his sword and cautiously approached.

"Aelthena!" a familiar voice called through the door. "Please open up!"

She let out a sigh of relief. "Put it away, Frey. It's just Asborn."

The guardian did not look pleased, nor did he sheathe his blade as quickly as he should have at her betrothed's arrival. All the same, Frey opened the door, and Asborn pushed inside. He spared the guardian a narrow-eyed look before striding forth and grasping Aelthena's hands. She tried to ignore Frey's watchful gaze as she pressed Asborn's hands back.

"I'm glad to find you well," he murmured. "When I heard the news last night, I feared — well, after all you've been through, I couldn't bear another thing to happen."

"I'm fine, Asborn." She felt both embarrassed and

annoyed, though she knew she should feel neither. "The killing happened on the other side of the castle. You don't need to worry about me."

His brow wrinkled. She noticed that his hair hung untidily about his face, and how it seemed aflame in the sunlight that snuck between the curtains.

"Of course I do," he said. "We're sworn to each other, you and I. And I care for you. If I found you harmed—"

"But I'm not." Though she knew Asborn had the best of intentions, she wished he had not come.

He seemed to sense her annoyance, but when he frowned, he turned it on Frey. "Guardian, I would like a private word with my betrothed."

Frey glanced at her, waiting for her small nod before putting a fist to his heart. "Of course, Thane Asborn." The guardian ambled toward the door and let himself out, securing and locking it behind him.

When Frey had left, Asborn turned his gaze back to her. "You should stay in my chambers. I cannot protect you down here."

Her mind raced to invent excuses. "But my possessions are all here."

She knew it was a feeble argument even before he smiled. "Then we'll have them brought up. It will be tight, but I don't think you have many clothes at the moment, do you?"

"But Asborn," she rushed to say, "we're not in Oakharrow any longer. We cannot sneak into each others' beds, not with the jarls and their wives watching, not to mention the other highborn trailing their heels."

He only gathered her closer. "Then we'll marry! I've missed you, Aelthena. I've missed how close we were back home. Since reuniting here... Well, I've felt something has come between us."

Not something. But she was not so cruel as to say the truth aloud.

Is that what stops you, kindness? part of her mocked. *Or practicality? You cannot afford to lose Asborn as an ally, after all, not when he is Oakharrow's voice in the Jarlmoot.*

She spoke aloud a different thought. "Of course something has come between us, Asborn. Our home was taken. Our people suffer gods only know what at the hands of that Jotun. Our nation is under threat, and still, *still* we cannot unite. How can I think of intimacy when all of that is crowding my head?"

How abashed he looked almost made her take back the words. Almost.

"You're right," he relented as he took a step back. "Of course you are. It's just that sometimes..." He looked aside, seeming to reconsider his words. "It feels that things may be coming to an end. That nothing will be as it was before. And I cannot help but think that I don't want to have any regrets."

Aelthena released his hands to grip his face. "Don't say that. Nothing's ending; neither of us are going to die. We just have to fight for now, alright? Fight like Djur himself. We'll come through this."

He looked at each of her eyes, then dropped his gaze. "Of course we will. Of course."

A knock came at the door. Aelthena dropped her hands from Asborn's face and called out, "Yes?"

Frey poked his head in a moment later. As she debated if his intrusion should irk her, he spoke. "A messenger awaits you, Thane Asborn. The day's Jarlmoot has been called early. Your presence is requested in Antler Tower at once."

Asborn nodded. "Thank you, guardian." He glanced

back at her. "No doubt it is concerning the night's grim affair. I must go."

Envy reared in her. Up in that tower, decisions were being made, and by her sex alone was she forbidden from taking part in them. But it was not Asborn's fault that things were as they were, so Aelthena kept her voice steady.

"Come back here as soon as you're finished," she said. "At once, hear me?"

He smiled faintly. "You are the Lady Heir — how could I refuse you?"

She returned the smile, though it was strained, and watched him leave the room. Frey shut the door behind Asborn, but stepped inside himself. Aelthena raised an eyebrow.

"Still worried about assassins?" she mocked.

"It's my job to worry."

"Then worry while I meet with the wives. And you will be the one needing protection if you think you can make me stay here," she added at his expression.

Frey sighed and leaned against the wall, arms crossed. "That, m'lady, is exactly what I suspected. Very well. Braid your hair, and we'll be on our way."

Aelthena turned away, not wanting him to see her smile. *Insolent man,* she thought fondly as she wove her golden hair.

Aelthena wondered if she would wear a line into her floor with her pacing by the time Asborn returned.

Frey, who had remained by her side while she met with the jarls' wives, excused himself without being asked, though he spared her a sardonic look. Aelthena ignored him. She did not have time for her guardian's jealousy.

"Well?" she demanded when the door sealed shut. "Was anything decided?"

Asborn's expression was grave. "Yes. Lord Siward has asked to be excused from consideration for the Iron Circle."

Aelthena stared at him for a long moment, uncomprehending. Then the implications sank in.

"Why? Why would he do that?"

He sat in one of the chairs before the hearth. "He never gave a satisfactory answer. All he said is that, with his family's safety at risk, he cannot dedicate himself to the duties that the Arkjarl must undertake."

Aelthena sat next to him and stared into the banked fire. Amid her shock, the tiny dancing flames were almost mesmerizing.

"If Lord Siward is no longer being considered," she said slowly, "only one choice remains."

Asborn sighed. "Yes. A vote is coming, Aelthena, perhaps as soon as tomorrow. And when it does, I feel I must put Oakharrow's support behind Lord Ragnar."

The bald declaration inflamed her. Her hands clenched into fists, and she raised her gaze to meet Asborn's. "You can't."

He winced. "What else can we do? He's the only one with the necessary skills and influence. And perhaps the man's son was wrong; perhaps he's not a traitor. This Alabastor hardly seems trustworthy himself. Have you seen him prowling about? He reeks like a mead hall, and not an upstanding one."

At the name, Aelthena went still. An epiphany stole over her.

"A Sypten," she murmured, more to herself than Asborn. "And who benefits?"

Asborn's brow wrinkled. He leaned toward her. "What's that?"

She shook her head and stood. "Something I need to look into."

He stood as well, his brow furrowing. "And you cannot tell me of it?"

"I'll explain later. Just promise me something, Asborn. Don't vote for Lord Ragnar until I say to. Delay the vote, do whatever you must — just don't commit to him."

"Very well." He looked far from pleased at the prospect. "Though I wish you would tell me what you're up to."

"Nothing that Frey cannot protect me from."

Asborn all but scowled at that. But pliable as he was, he allowed her to usher him toward the door.

"Be careful," he warned. Then, standing in the open door, he leaned down to kiss her forehead before sweeping away.

Frey's eyes followed Asborn until he turned out of sight, then he stepped within. "Yes?" he asked without even a veneer of formality.

She ignored his sulking. "Find Bastor. I need to speak with him now."

The guardian frowned. "That may be difficult. I heard he left the castle this morning. I suppose highborn living didn't suit him as well as his roguish ways."

She gripped his arm. "Even if it's difficult, we have to do it. Otherwise, I don't think I'll be able to stop Ragnar from claiming the Iron Circle."

Frey held her gaze for a long moment, then nodded. "Fine. I'll go fetch him. But stay here and lock the door while I'm gone."

Aelthena raised an eyebrow. "Who was the jarl's heir again?"

"Where your safety is concerned," Frey said as he opened the door, "my obedience has limits."

She smiled to herself as she closed the door behind him.

12. BY THE SCRIBE'S HAND

If, as I have proposed, the giants are taken as metaphor, what shall we make of the "Warriors of the Stone" and "the One with the Farthest Sight?" Here, I believe the rune-stone is referencing tales known to our ancestors that have been lost to time. Perhaps these "Warriors" were well-known folk heroes, or an order of fighters like the berserkers found in our own age. And "the Farthest Sight" implies that this man or woman has access to magic, and perhaps was part of a savior tale.

But once more, we stray into speculation. I suspect the truth is lost — yet I ever strive to understand.

- Commentary on the Witterland Runestone, by Alfjin the Scribe

I t felt like a homecoming as Bjorn stepped inside Heim Numen's library.

Stamping his feet free of snow, he raised his gaze and breathed in deeply. Almost, if he closed his eyes, he could imagine himself again in the Harrowhall archives by the familiar bouquet that greeted him. The bite of the chill in his nostrils, locked within the stone walls where fire was forbidden. The faint scent of mildew, a librarian's greatest fear, yet unavoidable in the snowy clime. And pervading it all, the earthy musk of vellum and parchment.

Works of writing packed every corner of the squat stone building, organized onto shelves, chests, and scroll cases. His mind ran free as he wondered at all he could learn had he the time. That a person could inscribe all the learnings of their life, all the reachings of their imagination — it seemed just as magical as *seidar*.

Yet in the past two weeks, more of his focus had been on that truer sorcery. Mother Sign had bade that he come to her hut in the mornings, and there, she taught him all he needed to know of the Sight and runelore. It was harder work than expected. Not only were the runes finicky in their shapes, but they played tricks on his mind as he studied them. The Mend runestone was the most soothing of the score of stones; whenever he gazed upon it, a warm sensation, like being enveloped in an embrace from head to toes, slowly filled him. The Endure runestone also uplifted him, firming his will as he painstakingly traced it again and again. The Farhearing and Farsight runestones were less pleasant, for his senses betrayed him upon their study. The Frenzy runestone affected him worst of all. He had to clench his hands into fists against the inexplicable anger that bubbled up inside him, and more than once, he had snapped the charcoal stylus with which he had been writing.

As he traced each rune on his stone slab, Mother Sign informed him of its function. The Frenzy runestone had been one long out of use — centuries had passed since a *Volur* had gazed upon it with the Sight open. According to her, though, Frenzy was what berserkers, renowned warriors of old, had used to invoke their battle rage. It did not impart fury alone, but allowed the warriors under its influence to feel no pain and freed their minds of the doubts and fears that would hold them back in battle. All barriers to violence were removed, and all the training throughout their lives became accessible. Bjorn tried to imagine himself as such a warrior. Though he had received training as befitted a son of a jarl, his natural timidity had always held him back. With those effaced, what might he become?

He could not decide if it terrified or thrilled him.

Step by step, he progressed in his studies. He learned first the twenty major runes and now proceeded to a more careful study of the minor ones that ringed each stone. He had begun to understand how to use *seidar* as well. It was a similar ritual to the one Yonik had led him through in the wilderness, if more refined.

"First," Mother Sign instructed, "you must breathe in the steam." She demonstrated the act herself, leaning forward over the stone heated in the firepit and inhaling deeply.

Bjorn had followed her lead hesitantly, remembering how it had affected him the first time in Yonik's hut behind the Tangled Temple. But he had lived too long in fear. Breathing in, he tried to detect if he felt any different.

The aged woman smirked at him. Even blind, she seemed to sense what he was doing. "This is not drascale ore, Bjorn; there is no *khnuum* trapped within."

"Oh." He was glad she couldn't see his flushed cheeks, though Yonik, who stood by the wall, might still glimpse them. "If it were *khnuum* steam, I would then focus on the runestone?"

"Yes. When we perform a true Seeing — which we will soon, never fear — focus is vital. Allow your attention to wander, and doors will unlock that you cannot close."

"And what happens then?"

Mother Sign only smiled, her cloudy eyes staring at the ceiling. It was Yonik who answered. "Let's not find out, shall we?" he suggested lightly.

Bjorn only shrugged and hoped he wouldn't have to.

"Brother Yonik is correct — such things are best left untouched. But what we do here is not without risk. There is always danger in magic, cub. If you learn one thing, let it be that."

As if I need the reminder. Aloud, he contritely agreed.

Outside of studying runelore and *seidar*, Bjorn was dragged over to the training yard by Loridi and Seskef. Contrary to Loridi's earlier declaration, the pair had not invaded the library, but spent most of their time in the small square brushed clear of snow, trading jokes and blows with the Eildursprall watch. Flint, the one-eyed guard who had greeted them so coldly upon their arrival, turned out to be less frigid than he had seemed, though he was far from warm. Bjorn avoided sparring against the barbar veteran or any of the watch, opting for his Harrow companions as often as he could. With Loridi and Seskef, his natural hesitancies subsided, and he rediscovered the skills his old blademaster had drilled into him. More often than not, he won against the two men.

Of all those in the yard, Hoarfrost remained dominant. Not even hard Flint had the prowess to overcome her. With a staff in hand to emulate a spear, she took down pairs of men at a time, often barely receiving a blow in return. Bjorn would lean on the fencing surrounding the yard and shake his head, while Loridi muttered, "Now *there's* a woman for you!"

More often, however, the Skyardi leader could be found with Yonik in the Silvers' room in the longhouse. His highborn status hidden, Bjorn was not privy to all they discussed, though the gothi sometimes caught him up during mealtimes. The topics ranged from politics and prophecies to fables and figureheads. Though their small village was tucked away into the wintry Teeth, the Silvers were far from isolated. Gothi regularly made the trip up to Eildursprall even in the dead of winter, and folks hailing from all across Baegard made the pilgrimage, bringing news from their jarlheims with them. They also had other sources of information, such as Mother Sign's regular Seeings, by which she could see the probable events of even faraway places like Ha-Sypt. From these snippets of information, the Silvers had formed a picture of Baegard's capacity to face the threats rising against them. Though Yonik tried to present them in a positive light, the facts fell with dread weight on Bjorn's ears.

"Between the Seven Jarlheims," Yonik said one evening, "ten thousand soldiers might be mustered; more, if the call is extended to young women. It will not match what Ha-Sypt has to offer, not with their deeper pockets and the Sumerland supplying an endless line of sellswords. But if they come, we have the walls, and that will count for much."

"What about Nuvvog's Rage?" Bjorn pressed. "And the jotunar?" Privately, he worried about surtunar as well. If the giants of the north existed, why not the southern giants as well?

At his words, Yonik's shoulders sagged. "I don't know," he admitted. "The Silvers only have one hope, but it is pale. Runelore has long been restricted in their traditions. Even now, Mother Iron and Father Temperance do not believe we should explore it."

"They don't?" As they were sitting in the longhouse, Bjorn glanced toward the room where the Silvers congregated. "Then how am I being taught?"

The priest flashed a rueful smile. "Mother Sign was never one to abide by the rules."

Bjorn found the revelation further spurred his interest. He threw himself into his studies and endured the unpleasantries that accompanied them with gritted determination.

Yet he could not spend all his time at *seidar*, nor could he learn everything Baegard needed from runelore. Thus, in his spare time, Bjorn had often visited Eildursprall's library.

It entailed far more exploration than he had expected. Even when narrowing his search to ancient texts and those relating to the jotunar, it was a tedious process. For one, locating appropriate writings was nearly impossible in a library where age was about the only distinguishable organizational element. Making matters more difficult was that artifacts other than scrolls and books were also frequent, as parchment had not been as widely available in their ancestors' time. Instead, bone and stone were often used, which were more difficult to store and organize efficiently.

But though the search was slow, Bjorn did not mind. The hunt for information was not his only reason for visiting the library.

As he entered, a young woman rose from her seat and came toward him. Her beeswax candle illuminated her smile.

"Good day, Bjorn."

Bjorn returned it. "Hello, Tyra."

She had captivated him from his first visit. The acolyte assigned the care of the library, Tyra shared his love for knowledge and books. They had first caught each other staring in the longhouse, and she carried a shyness about her to which he instantly related. Her hair was the auburn of ferns in autumn, and her gray-green eyes seemed deep forest pools. Though he felt guilty for looking, Bjorn could not help but notice her slim figure beneath her furs and robes.

The gothi-in-training let out a nervous laugh. *"Acolyte*

Tyra. Just because we're alone doesn't mean you can leave off my title."

"If you insist." His daring surprised him. Something about Tyra seemed to bring it out.

A smile played on her lips. "I assume you're here for the same? Legends of giants?"

He nodded. With the Jotun looming large in everyone's minds, he and the others had not felt it necessary to keep their mission secret. Seskef had made the point that the more people who knew, the more likely crucial information would filter their way. Still, Bjorn worried. Yewlings had aided the Jotun's men in Jünsden. They likely had agents in Eildursprall, if not Heim Numen itself. But some risks had to be taken.

Tyra held out an unlit candle, and Bjorn took it, lighting the wick off hers. Her eyes flickered up to rest on his for a moment, and his stomach lurched. He felt the urge to say something, *do* something, though he hardly knew what.

She broke the spell by turning away. "I have something for you today. Something you'll appreciate."

A lump appeared in his throat. Bjorn pushed down his roguish imaginings and followed the acolyte through the library and to the basement. The lower level was where he had been doing most of his research. Since it was underground, the temperatures remained regulated, and so the older pieces were stored below. The darkness was almost complete. If not for the feeling of earth surrounding them and the muted sound of their footsteps on the stone, Bjorn could have imagined they stood in an endless cavern, fascinations waiting to be uncovered all around after lying in dust for centuries.

Tyra led him to the farthest corner of the cellar, between the dust-battered shelves of scrolls, through the urns and gravestones, to the place where the gothi kept the most ancient artifacts. Bjorn had come to this corner often during his visits, but he found items had shifted since his last exploration. Tapestries, weavings, and rugs folded into a neat stack had been cleared away, revealing a large stone shaped like a rounded door that came half as high as Bjorn. Down its center ran a large crack that interrupted the faded runes carved into its face.

He stared at it for a long moment, wondering if it was another grave marker, before something stirred in his head. A slight pressure built behind his eyes, and he touched a hand to his forehead. *Musk must be getting to me.* Thinking through the pain, he wondered for whom such a large stone had been raised when he looked up to find Tyra wearing a coy smile.

"Well?" she prompted.

Bjorn shrugged. "You want me to guess what it is, or will you tell me?"

"I thought you would know." Excitement bubbled in her voice. "It's the Witterland Runestone! The one that Alfjin the Scribe translated?"

He struggled with the revelation, his imagination flailing at the task. *The Witterland Runestone.* The object was mythologized in texts he had read in the Harrowhall archives. He had scarcely believed it existed.

"I didn't realize it was real." His words were slow as his thoughts flew. "I thought it had been lost. It must be, what, a thousand winters old?"

"Or older." The acolyte put her hands on her hips and looked down at her find with a smile. "Something written by our ancestors' own hands. Someone who lived in the Witterland and crossed the Treacherous Sea. One of Baegard's very founders. Can you believe it?"

"Hardly." Bjorn grinned as well, heady with Tyra's discovery. His chest felt lighter than it had been in years.

Kneeling, he brought his candle closer and studied the runes for a moment, then frowned as his head again ached. "I can almost recognize these from" — just in time, he remembered not to disclose Mother Sign's instruction in runelore — "from my, uh, studies in Oakharrow, but they're different. Can you read them?"

"No. But since you know Old Djurian, you might be able to read this."

Bjorn looked up to see Tyra holding a sheet of cracked vellum supported by a slate tablet. His stomach lurched.

"Alfjin's transcription?"

"See for yourself."

The acolyte held it out to him. Carefully, almost reverently, Bjorn stood and accepted it. His hands were shaking, yet he grinned as he stared at the glyphs. These had been written by *the Scribe himself.* He had imagined just such a moment a hundred times locked away with the dusty tomes of his childhood, but he had never truly thought it might come true.

His scholar's courage flared to life, so strong he felt as if he witnessed the transcription himself.

A tall, fair-headed man in dark robes hunched over a desk. A single candle cast a pool of light over the paper before him. His quill darted over its surface, moving to the inkwell near at hand at regular intervals with barely a spilled droplet or blotted letter. The Scribe's face was in shadow, but his feverish haste was apparent in every movement, the tension held in his back like a cat about to pounce.

Bjorn blinked, and the vision disappeared. Had it all been his imagination? *What else could it be? The Sight?*

But it was not the most important thing just then. He focused his eyes again on the vellum and the faded ink upon it. With all the time he had spent in Heim Numen's library, his Old Djurian had quickly lost its rust, and he spoke the words with the conviction of a gothi telling a high tale:

> *"The earth in protest did shake its hide*
> > *Tossing off its plains and hills*
> > *And fire reigned across the sky*
> > *Peaks left charred, black on the fells*
>
> *And from her pits arose the drakes*
> > *Chained to serve the masters tall*
> > *The horde that gnaws on silver roots*
> > *Till anchors of the sky break loose*
>
> *Jailers of dragons, spare the light*
> > *Blind her not; uncover her spirit bright*
> > *Jotunar and Surtunar, keep your fire and frost*
> > *Men cannot survive the Eternal Night..."*

Bjorn looked up from the page to meet Tyra's unblinking gaze and could not keep away a wide smile.

"The words aren't quite as I've heard them before," he said. "And there are additional passages that I didn't know existed."

Tyra waved an impatient hand. "Well, go on!"

Clearing his throat, Bjorn squinted at the runes again, then continued:

> *"Though light be lost, and darkness palls*
> > *The moons still shine and cross the sky*
> > *Warriors of the Stone harken to the call*

They charge into battle to fall and die

The dragons' flames are the greatest thefts
For the lines lie not between man and master
But those who choose Life and those who choose
Death
A world blessed by smoke and ash and alabaster

And still comes One with the Farthest Sight
Whose eye can penetrate the Eternal Night
A vision of the Bright Age etched in his soul
He will lead us through war, through fire, through
cold."

As he finished speaking, Bjorn's thoughts wandered back to the broken stone from which Alfjin had pulled the prophetic words. His thoughts blossomed as he tried to divine what the passages meant. They could not be mere poetry; after all, had this not foretold the times they now lived in? The giants had returned — or one had, at least — just as the unknown carver had told. And the Jotun had brought fire as surely as if he did rule dragons. What, then, did this buried prophecy offer?

Hope.

Despite the grim predictions, these new passages practically rang with hope. Still, death clutched at the spaces between the runes. "Warriors of the Stone," whoever they might be, would rise in defense, but still they would die. Dragonfire would steal lives and homes, and many would "choose Death" if the world came to ruin as the augury implied.

And yet, Bjorn felt a glimmer of optimism. *One with the*

Farthest Sight. There would be a hero, a hero who could guide the world through the war and into better days beyond. *One with the Farthest Sight.* Surely, they must already exist somewhere, as the Eternal Night had already stretched its shadow over Enea. Bjorn wondered who they could be. The choice of words, clear even through two interpretations, put him in mind of the Sight, of *seidar*, and the *Volur* who wielded it. For a moment, he wondered if Mother Sign could be this proclaimed hero of legend. As far as he knew, she had the strongest grasp on the ancient magic. But a smirk stole the thought away. He had trouble imagining anyone following the aged woman's advice on forging a new world.

He finally noticed Tyra watching him with wide eyes. "What's amusing?" she asked.

Bjorn's grin broadened. "Just imagining Mother Sign as the hero of the stone."

The acolyte burst into a laugh. "That would be a surprise!"

Bjorn's thoughts turned back to the somber message. "But even despite the hero, it doesn't sound good."

Tyra sobered quickly. "No. But the second half is better than the first, isn't it?"

"So long as we can figure out what it means."

They stood there in silence. Bjorn's gaze wandered back to the old, timeworn vellum, eyes tracing the fading runes. "I should make a copy of this," he said in sudden realization. "What happens when the ink fades?"

"I could do it."

He looked at Tyra in surprise. "You'd do that?"

"What else am I supposed to do, stuck in this tomb all day?" Her pupils seemed to soak up all the light, wide and dark.

He wanted to reach and hold her hand, touch her shoulder; something, *anything*. Would he be a coward if he didn't? Or respectful of her oaths to become a priestess of the Inscribed?

The door upstairs squealed open.

They both startled and looked at each other, then away. In that moment, he saw his guilt reflected in her eyes, like they were children caught stealing sweets from the kitchens. He tried to shake the feeling as he moved toward the stairs.

"Who is it?" Tyra called up the stairs, following behind him.

"Only me, Brother Yonik."

The gothi was already heading down the stairs. Bjorn was only slightly surprised to find Yonik did not carry a candle, but navigated the darkness with nothing more than his prenatural eyesight. The priest leaned down to look at them, but he did not grin as Bjorn had supposed he might.

"Is something wrong?" Anxiety flared in him as he realized anything could be happening outside and he'd never know.

Yonik shook his head, shaggy hair falling about his face. "No danger. I only wish to satisfy my curiosity."

"Brother Yonik has often visited the library," Tyra rushed to explain.

The priest's eyes flickered to Tyra, then back to Bjorn. A shadow of a smile touched his lips. Yet if he bore any suspicions, he did not voice them.

"Indeed, I have," Yonik said. "The archives of Heim Numen are deep and dusty, and there is danger in their depths, yet I must delve into them all the same. As for you, Bjorn, I believe Hoarfrost was asking after you. Something about whooping you in the yard?"

Bjorn winced and was glad for the gloom to hide his blush. "Sounds like her."

He turned back to Tyra, reluctant to leave. He wished he had reached out to her before; with Yonik watching, even innocent intimacy was impossible.

"Thank you," he said instead, flashing an awkward smile. "For showing me... all that."

Tyra smiled, and he wondered what made her eyes pull downward as they did. "I was happy to. Return as soon as you can. I'll write up that copy for you."

Bjorn nodded, then avoided Yonik's amused gaze as he fled up the stairs and out into the cold.

13. A SERVANT'S PLACE

Born to Hua are Children tall
Huame, they shall be known
Long their limb and large their maul
Strong as bone and stone

The Children come to do Our will
When Desolation falls
To burn and burn the world until
We send to them Our call

- Words in the Sand, refrain 5;63-64

Sehdra was tired to death of war camps.

Each day proceeded like the one before it. In the mornings, she sat in her wagon, watching while servants packed away her tent, as useful as the whorls she traced in the wood. When at last her possessions were secured, she and her retinue joined the general procession. Their pace was as sluggish as the River Nu in drought. Time dragged, and Sehdra often nodded off as she bumped along. Yet though the hours stretched long, the leagues proved longer, and they covered little distance for their efforts. There were too many wheels broken, animals injured, and fights breaking out to move faster.

Only at night could she escape it all.

Sehdra had ordered a bath drawn up and warmed. It was an extravagance while on the road; but then again, she *was* the sister to a god. *And Qa'a knows I have worries enough to shed.* When she was not dozing, Sehdra's mind spun around the mysteries and problems abounding before her. Physt. Oyaoan. The war. The reasons behind it.

She had only just closed her eyes and begun to relax into the warm water when the tent flap ripped open.

Sehdra startled as her attendants squawked their surprise. Assassins had come for her; Physt had tired of her, or the mountain savages struck an early blow. But as the figure straightened and his face was illuminated by the twin braziers mounted inside, she sighed and sank back into the tub.

It was only Teti, entering with dramatic style.

By reflex, her arms crossed over her breasts. Though her friend had seen her naked often enough, she found herself strangely reticent to reveal herself any more than the bath forced her to.

Teti scarcely seemed to notice. His narrow features were scrunched even tighter as he stopped next to her tub, and sweat shone from his brow.

"You look as if you could use a wash as well," she said lightly.

"I'm afraid this is no time for levity, Royal Sister. Your pardon." Teti mopped at his face with a silk square that looked to have seen frequent use. "If I may be so bold, you must come at once to the karah's audience pavilion."

"Now?" Sehdra shared his frown. "What's happening,

Teti? Retrieve my bathcloth and leave us," she said, aiming these last words at her attendants.

The women set the long length of fabric next to the bath, then bowed and left. Sehdra hesitated a moment, then let her arms fall away so she could exit the water. To her relief, Teti turned aside while she stepped free of the bath and wrapped the bathcloth around herself. He moved to her chest to retrieve clothes for her.

"Explain," she said as she followed him.

His eyes darted up to meet hers for a moment. "It is poor news, Sehdra. Quite poor."

Her chest tightened. "What happened?"

"Oyaoan ordered Nekau Baka to march on an outpost town of the mountain savages, Godanglan — Fairglen, in translation. Only, it appears the huamek did not consult the Divine One in these orders. He is not well pleased, as you might imagine."

"Easily." Sehdra used the bathcloth to dry the rest of her body and hair before accepting the robe from Teti. He helped her dress, slipping the fabric over her shoulders, then tying it in place. With expert hands, he bound back her hair, opting for expediency rather than style by implicit agreement. Only when it was secured did she turn back to him. Her hair dripped onto her robe, but she was moderately presentable. Except for one thing.

"The scarab mask, please."

Teti eyed her for a moment, then nodded and moved to another chest. He returned with the inky black, stiffened cloth in hand and proffered it to her. Sehdra accepted the mask and stared at it. *Qa'a*, she prayed as her gaze ran over the prominent horn, the beady eyes, the broad carapace. *Please, share your wisdom tonight. I feel this camp may be short of it.*

She placed it to her face, and Teti moved behind her to

secure it. With the ties knotted, she turned back to him. "We must hurry."

He nodded. "Your palanquin awaits."

In her haste, she almost slipped on the carpet crossing the muddy ground and was clumsy in mounting the platform. Yet she made it, and soon, the slaves were lifting her and the palanquin onto their shoulders and marching through the camp. She felt a glimmer of pity for the men, called from their beds and whatever levity they engaged in to carry her. At least the karah's tents were near her own.

She heard her brother long before the audience pavilion came into view. Even before the palanquin had settled and the carpet laid out, Sehdra stood and dismounted, her crippled leg nearly crumpling as she went off balance. But Teti was by her side, steadying her and keeping a hand to her elbow until they entered between the stony-faced guards and into the din.

During their weeks of marching, Sehdra had only had the misfortune to enter the karah's audience pavilion a handful of times. Each time, it amazed her that such a display could be arranged day after day. The lofted ceiling rose several times a man's height, and the entrance was large enough to admit even one of the huamek. Carpets layered the floor, letting no mud or sand show through. A throne, not nearly as grand as the one in the palace, still dwarfed all other objects in the room. Tables overflowed with food and drink, while others were littered with maps and figurines denoting the movements and numbers of troops. Smoke hovered in the air, cast off from a brazier laced with her brother's favorite influencers. To her disappointment, though not surprise, she saw no chair other than the throne. Sehdra pushed the dread of oncoming agony from her mind. It was the least of her present concerns.

As in his throne room, Physt had gifted her at least a

few barbed comments at her every appearance, though he had been tame in his abuse. Now tame was the last word that could describe him. He stood in the middle of the pavilion, glaring up at the figure of Oyaoan, who dwarfed him in both size and presence. The karah's fists were balled up like a child throwing a tantrum. And what a tantrum it was — Sehdra winced at his screamed words, wishing she could cover her ears, wondering why she had bothered to come.

Hephystus did not notice her arrival, but only kept up his tirade. He pointed at a man standing in the corner, who looked as if he wished to disappear into the shadows, his shining armor making it impossible. Sehdra had seen him before, yet would have known him even had she not by his crest and the peacock feathers set in his helm: Nekau Baka, the chief general of the karah's armies.

"*My* men!" her brother was shrieking. "Whom *I* command! I tell the generals their course, and *I do not want* them to march on a goat-pricking village in the middle of nowhere. We must conquer a great city to glorify my name! We march to Petyrsholm!"

Sehdra looked to the huamek's face. With all the lit braziers lining the grand tent, she was better illuminated than most times Sehdra had seen her. Her jewelry seemed set aflame, and her broad features even more foreign. Her gray skin looked as tough as stone, and the thick limbs beneath as unbreakable as trees. But it was the eyes, dark and small within her immense skull, that made Sehdra run cold with fear.

Oyaoan boomed her reply, her unknowable words vibrating in Sehdra's limbs and chest. As she finished, her translator sidled up next to her leg; the Ibis was never far from his mistress's side.

"Great Oyaoan speaks!" the Suncoaster declared. "The supply lines must be secured as our eminent host presses into the heart of enemy territory. Petyrsholm is our ultimate destination, as the karah has most justly stated — but one minor town must first be assailed."

Physt took a step toward the Ibis. For a moment, Sehdra thought he would hit him, and she wondered how the huamek would react. But he stopped short, instead thrusting out his chin to stare up at Oyaoan. Though he still quivered with rage, a dangerous calm had settled back over him. Long experience warned Sehdra that her brother had reached his most malign mood, a balance between fury and cunning.

He thrust a finger back at Nekau once again. "You leave me no choice, Oyaoan." Physt's head followed his hand. "Nekau Baka, consider yourself disgracefully dismissed. I suggest you flee this encampment before I decide to make the penalty more severe."

Sehdra carefully hid her wince as her eyes slid back to the general. The aged man remained erect despite the weight of his oiled bronze armor, like a stubborn palm standing long after the oasis pool had dried up. His face was leathery and tanned from his decades of service, yet he had not grown stone enough to stop it twitching, betraying the simmering feelings beneath.

"Your Sanctity, if I may ask that you reconsider," Nekau began in his bass voice, almost as deep as Oyaoan's.

"Reconsider?" Physt fully faced the general, a hyena's smile spreading over his lips. "Are you sure you would like that?"

The general's throat quivered. He seemed to be chewing through all the words that might punctuate his death.

Sehdra knew then why she had come. She had to intervene, for the sake of Ha-Sypt — and for her brother. Taking a step farther into the pavilion, her movement drew the eyes of all those present. She did not quail, but stood taller.

"Your Sanctity, I must also suggest a different course," she said, calm and firm. "Nekau Baka has served you admirably for many floods, and led your troops to victory in Enea and the Suncoast. To make no mention that he was only following orders."

Her brother's smile widened as he crossed the pavilion to stand before her. She longed to back away. She knew that expression, knew it portended ill for her. But she stood as strong as her twisted leg would allow.

In a sudden movement, Physt snapped his arm out and ripped the mask free of her face. Sehdra bit her lip to keep from gasping as the rough fabric tore against her tender cursed flesh.

Do not flinch before a lion, her mother had told her when she was little, after she had cowered before one of her brother's moods. *You must stand with as much pride as he.*

She tried not to think of how her mother had bowed before her son after he stole the throne from her husband. How she had allowed his torments to continue and expand, while she had withered away and finally expired of a failing heart. She had learned long ago that people spoke more wisdom than they followed.

Sehdra held herself tall and awaited her brother's condemnation.

"I told you not to wear a mask in my presence." His voice began softly, then abruptly rose in volume. "And never, *never* speak against what I have decreed!"

Despite her mother's advice, Sehdra cringed. She thought he would hit her, no matter how ill it would look to treat his sister so.

But before he could lift a hand, Oyaoan moved behind him. For a brief, terror-stricken moment, she thought the huamek reached for her to do the karah's will. But the giantess had another target. Toward the side of the tent where a retinue of servants lined the walls, Oyaoan reached, and the slaves' training was insufficient in repressing their natural fear as they fled before it.

One older man, taken from the Winter Holds judging by his complexion, was not quick enough. Her hand enveloped his chest, then Oyaoan lifted the slave and raised herself to her full height again. All eyes in the pavilion were on her now, the karah's included. Sehdra had not breathed since the huamek moved, waiting for what would come next. Tiny, pathetic noises escaped the captured slave's lips.

Fast as the falcon soars, Oyaoan flung the screaming servant into one of the pavilion's posts.

As the savage crashed into the wood, there was a crack, and his body bent unnaturally around it like he were filled with sand. His shrieks abruptly cut off as he slumped limp to the floor. Sehdra's mouth hung open, watching blood seep from his body to stain the carpets. Her heart clambered to escape her chest. Even her brother appeared speechless for a long moment.

Oyaoan spoke into the silence. Her foreign words were soft at first, then rose to a point at the end. Sehdra suspected the message even before the Ibis delivered it.

"Great Oyaoan says that all servants are expendable, and will be treated so, if their usefulness expires." The Suncoaster bent his bandy legs in the mockery of a bow.

Her brother looked from the translator up to the giantess. Defiance had not disappeared from him, but now it burned like a banked fire, cautious and low. Without a word, the karah turned and exited the tent. His servants, cautious and fearful as they glanced up at the huamek, edged around the pavilion walls to follow their master out.

Sehdra glanced at Teti, then took one last look at

Oyaoan, only to startle as she saw the huamek's gaze leveled at her. She froze, not daring to move, wishing for nothing but to flee.

Oyaoan rumbled a short sentence, and the Ibis smiled before revealing it. "Great Oyaoan wishes you, Sehdra Ohkweht, to watch and to learn."

Sehdra bobbed her head like a servant. "Of course, Great Oyaoan."

She turned and exited as quickly as her tattered pride would allow.

14. ALE'S COMFORT

"A cup of ale gives as much comfort as an ample bosom."

- Common expression among Djurian men

His hand seized his knife before Bastor recognized what had woken him.

Pounding on the door. Or was it the pounding in his head? Both were so furious he had trouble distinguishing one from the other.

He rolled off the lousy cot all the same, landing in a crouch, then falling to his rump as his balance pitched and his stomach kicked. He bit back a groan. *Damn Petyrsholm and their Djur-burned ale.* Bastor righted himself and approached the grimy door to his room. *And damn me for drinking so much of it.*

The door shook again under heavy blows, threatening to come off its dubious hinges. "Bastor the Bastard!" a familiar voice called through. "I know you're in there. Now get off your sodden arse and open up!"

A grin pulled at his lips. Bastor shook his head and lowered the knife. Of all the visitors he might expect — and he had hoped for none — Frey Igorson was the last among them. Tottering over the last distance to the door, he unlatched it and swung it inward. He could not quite repress a groan as dim daylight filtered in from the hall.

Aelthena's bodyguard stood with his arms crossed. His eyes darted down to Bastor's knife, and he visibly tensed.

Bastor barked a harsh laugh. "I'm not going to stab you." To illustrate his point, he tossed the dagger behind him, where it carved a new notch into the planks before skittering back to the cot.

Frey relaxed, though his arms remained crossed. "I've been looking for you."

"Never thought you'd miss me." Bastor flashed him as wide a grin as his headache allowed.

The guardian shook his head as he attempted to hide a rueful smile of his own. Though they had never been anywhere close to friendly, Bastor liked to think a mutual understanding had grown between them during their escape from Oakharrow and the trek to Petyrsholm. Rogue and traitor Bastor might be, but he had done them several good turns, and even Frey had come around to that.

Of course, that was before Bastor split from them before reaching the city. And considering all his father had done — and what he'd done himself, from the shadows — he could hardly expect any warmth to remain between them.

A lonely man can hope, he thought with acid irony.

"Here on business, actually," the guardian said. "Need you to come with me."

Bastor glanced down at himself. He was still dressed in the clothes from the night before — clothes, he realized in the light of day, that were not entirely unsoiled. Beer had dribbled down his chest at one point, and spots decorated his shins from when his stomach had rejected the poison he had been filling it with for the past two days. *A wonder,* he thought, *but you do still have a glimmer of shame.*

He looked up and gave the guardian a once-over. Frey's clothes were plain, but they were at least clean and well-darned. Gods, but he had fallen far to compare so unfavorably with a common guard.

"Give me a chance to change." He waved at his bedraggled person. "And to splash my face."

Frey raised an eyebrow. "It'll take more than that to remove your grime — but fine. I'm sure the Lady Heir's nose will appreciate the effort, and it may lessen the scandal of your return."

Bastor snorted as he beckoned the guardian inside. Frey moved as cautiously as a fox entering a bear's den, despite Bastor's earlier reassurances. Bastor himself had no such compunctions, but put his back to the man as he staggered over to strike up a candle and provide some dim illumination.

"Since when have you worried about scandals?" Bastor asked as he ruffled around the clothes strewn about the floor, trying to locate the cleanest shirt and trousers among them, with little success.

"Not my choice; it's just that Petyrsholm is rife with them. Seven jarls and their retinues, to make no mention of legends and wars, will do that to a city, I suppose."

Bastor finally found a pair that, if not acceptable, would suffice. He pulled off his shirt as he spoke. "That's not what I meant." Pulling his head through, he met the guardian's eyes. "I mean considering what happened between you and Aelthena in that forest."

The guardian stiffened. Bastor grinned, then yanked

down his trousers, grinning all the wider as Frey looked aside, his face twisted into a scowl.

"Come now," he taunted as he pulled on the fresher pair. "Don't hold out on the details. I may be a rogue, but I'm not such a bastard that I followed you."

"You're drunk." Frey's voice was low. He still didn't meet his eyes. "And miserable. So I'll let those comments slide this once. But don't mention it again, Bastor. I will not have you dishonor the Lady Heir."

Bastor shrugged. Though he had been digging for a reaction, now that he had gotten it, he found it did not live up to expectations. *No wonder you're alone,* he thought, *when you drive knives into anyone in arm's reach.*

"I'm not quite drunk anymore." Bastor fished about for an overtunic, stockings, and boots. "But I'm close enough to it to be sorry for what I said. I don't intend dishonor toward Aelthena. Believe it or not, but she's gained my admiration. And though that may be worth dirt to most, it's all I have to offer."

Frey turned back to meet his eyes. Slowly, he nodded. "Fine. I'll let you get dressed, then we'll be off."

Bastor paused until the guardian left and closed the door behind him. Then he let out a long, heavy sigh and pulled on the rest of his clothes.

The walk through Petyrsholm was frosty, and not only from the chill weather. Frey remained silent as he walked a step ahead of Bastor and led the way to the Elkhorn rising above them. Bastor screwed up his eyes against the daylight. Though the sky was overcast and clouded with the smoke from a thousand lit hearths, the light still felt like knives carving into his skull. He vowed never to have another drink even as he scanned the buildings lining the streets, searching for signs denoting alehouses and mead halls.

Pathetic as he was, still more miserable cretins crowded the streets. Beggars, some missing limbs, others missing teeth, and still more with a lack of both, held out their hands and bowls, most not even bothering to mutter their pleas any longer. Bastor hunched his shoulders and turned his eyes away. *Give an alm and you'll be thronged,* his miserly father was fond of saying. Though Bastor scarcely believed the axiom, for the moment, it would serve as his excuse.

But it was the other feelings in their hollowed eyes that raised his walls higher. Most people thought they masked their expressions as they stared at Bastor, or perhaps that he did not notice. But he saw all of them. He rose half a head taller than most men and had shoulders to rival an aurochs. Where he walked, men and women flinched away, like deer before a wolf.

They're not wrong to fear me.

But the color of his skin was seen as the worst of his sins. He was a Sypten bastard, plain enough, and no amount of powder would hide that fact had he bothered. That he was a brute of a man to boot only further inflamed their hatred.

Yet even as his heritage brought him censure, it also fostered a secret society of sorts. He was not the only half-breed to walk the city streets. Most of those with Baegardian fathers remained in thralldom, and these avoided his gaze, as if afraid of it. But those few fortunate enough to walk free gave him subtle greetings: a small nod, a quirk of the lips, a fidgeting hand, a blink of the eyes. Bastor returned the signs in like. They were strangers, yet somehow, the brief interactions reminded him he was not entirely alone.

Others of Petyrsholm's underbelly watched him with different intent. Cutpurses and cutthroats waited in shadowed alleys, watching with hungry eyes as people passed them by. They shrank away, though, as the guard patrol wandered near their space with hard looks of their own. *No jarlheim is without its criminals.* Bastor pursed his lips. He wondered how he might use that fact to his advantage should the need arise. It seemed he could put his drinking to better use than simple oblivion.

The thought brought a sudden insight, and he looked sidelong at Frey. "You know what our problem is?"

The guardian met his gaze with obvious reluctance. "What?"

"We never really drank together." Bastor grinned. "Share a flagon and you can be friends with anyone."

Frey looked ahead again without answering. Just as Bastor thought he would ignore him, he finally replied. "If you didn't frequent such disreputable alehouses, perhaps we might."

He could not have been more astonished had the warrior begun dancing in the street. Bastor took care to hide it, though. "I might be swayed to a fine establishment as suits a high-living fellow like yourself. But I would not wait long in naming a place — I have a hunch that the time for casual drinking is almost past."

"If it even remains." Frey's eyes gathered a distant look. Bastor wondered if he thought of those he had left behind in Oakharrow.

It made him think of their other companions on the road. "How is the good jarl faring here in Petyrsholm? And Uljana — is she coping with his care?"

The guardian glanced at him oddly. It only occurred to Bastor a moment later how strange it must seem to the average Baegardian to inquire after a thrall's health. A bitter smile sprang to his lips.

How quickly we dismiss those we deem our lessers.

"Lord Bor has been complacent of late," Frey said. "And his thrall takes care of him well, from all I can tell."

"Oh, very good." He could not wholly keep the sarcasm from his voice. Telling by Frey's frown, the man noticed.

"Did I offend you?" the guardian asked stiffly.

"I might wonder the same thing. You think it odd that I ask after Uljana, don't you?"

To his credit, Frey seemed to think it over. "Yes," he admitted. "Few ask after thralls. But perhaps you're right — she is a loyal servant and has done much to keep the jarl comfortable. Perhaps she deserves more concern than she's given."

Bastor shrugged and looked forward. Frey's surprising turn gave him much to think about himself. *Perhaps he's not so pig-brained as I first thought.* The man's loyalty to Aelthena and his bravery in a scrap had already inclined Bastor toward him. He found himself almost liking the man.

He wondered if that would make it harder when it came time to betray him.

At last — though too soon, to Bastor's mind — the Elkhorn gate rose above them. The guards posted there recognized Frey from his passage out, but it took them a moment to identify Bastor. His coloring and hair seemed to trigger the memory in the end, telling by their darting eyes. "Lord Heir Alabastor," one said with a fist to his chest. "Welcome back."

He gave them a toothy smile. "Pleased to be back."

As they entered the sprawl of gray buildings, Bastor found his thirst had grown to a height he could no longer ignore. "This way," he said to Frey, turning off into a corridor that led to the kitchens.

The guardian, who had already taken several steps in the other direction, hurried to catch up. "The Lady Heir's rooms lie that way."

"And ale lies this way."

No matter what they had shared before, Bastor saw he was ruining it now. Frey's face twisted through a variety of familiar emotions. *Disgust, pity, anger — ah, old friends, how I've missed you.* He turned away, hiding the small smile he knew would only be misinterpreted.

One of the kitchen maids, shy and kindly Ipu, was obliging, and soon they were back on their way to the building where the jarls and their relations were housed. Bastor was surprised to find security had increased in their quarters. Despite himself, a nervous tingling started in his spine. He hid his face in his horn of mead whenever he could, but soon found it drained to the last drop.

Hide it, he told himself. *Hide it as you always have. As Father taught you to.* His resolve had turned sodden by his indulgences in the past couple of days, but through a last effort, he smoothed away his emotions.

"Lord Heir! I've been wondering which corner you slunk off to!"

Suddenly sick to his stomach, Bastor plastered on a smile. "Thorpe, is that you, you ugly bastard?"

"I'm not the only bastard in this castle, I hear." The guard, who strolled up with an unfamiliar fellow, grinned at his jape.

Bastor's amusement abruptly dried. Gods knew he behaved poorly for a highborn, but insulting his ancestry was a step too far. Still, for appearances, he clung to the smile.

"Despite how it looks" — Bastor shook his empty horn with a cocked eyebrow — "I'm in a bit of a hurry. But I'm sure I'll see you around."

"At the mead halls at least." Thorpe gave a mocking salute, mimicked more sincerely by his companion, before they carried on with their circuit.

Something unloosened in Bastor's chest. It was all he could do not to sigh out loud.

"You're on close terms with the castle guards," Frey noted, his tone flat. "And the kitchen staff."

Bastor shrugged. "I'm a man of the common folk."

The guardian's silence was response enough.

They turned down a hall, and suddenly Bastor found himself struck with a dizzying rush of memory. *Knife in the throat. Blood on the stone.* He stopped, staring, his heart racing, his vision spinning.

This was the hall where he had threatened Helka. Where he had murdered the huskarl. Unbidden and unwanted, his name sprang to mind. *Destin.*

"Bastor?"

Frey had stopped to stare at him. Bastor could not find a smile for once. He wondered what a mask of horror his face must look.

"Let's go," he croaked, motioning for Frey to continue.

The guardian obliged, but not without another studying look. Bastor followed on his heels. He kept his eyes carefully forward as they passed the doors of Lord Siward's daughters, or at least where they had been. By the two guards standing before them, it promised to be where they remained, unless it was a decoy. He hoped it would be the last he saw of them. *Please, gray gods, if you have any scrap of mercy, let that be the last of it.*

As they left the corridor, the panic that had gripped him eased its hand. By the time they reached Aelthena's door two corridors away, his breathing had leveled, though his heart still beat as if it would never have another chance.

Frey held his hand up to the door. "I hope the liquor put you in a good mood. I think you'll need it."

Bastor managed a ghastly grin. "Don't worry about me. Gotten this far, haven't I?"

And what a wonder that's been.

The guardian shrugged, then rapped on the door three times in quick succession. At the call from within, Frey unlocked the door, and Bastor set his jaw and strode inside.

15. TRUST

"The best sort of man is the one you keep sober."

- Common expression among Djurian women

Aelthena turned from her window as the knock came at the door. She swallowed and steadied her thoughts before answering.

"Enter!"

A moment later, Frey came in with a familiar man in tow. Her jaw tightened at the sight of Bastor. The days since their last meeting had not been kind to the eldest son of Lord Ragnar. His acute eyes were bloodshot and ringed with shadow. His tanned skin had a yellow cast to it. His broad shoulders bowed like the sagging roof of a poorly made hut.

The sight of him sparked her anger into flame. She hated seeing him like this. Bastor was talented and clever. True that he was brutal and too quick to violence, yet in their time together, she had glimpsed beneath his rough edges and knew a red heart beat in his chest.

You're better than this.

He could not hear her thoughts, and she would not speak them aloud. To assume the best of Bastor would be to underestimate him, and as she suspected his reason for being so downtrodden, that might spell a lethal mistake.

"Lord Heir Alabastor," she greeted him. She made no intimation to cross the room.

"Ah, but surely we haven't devolved that far, have we, Aelthena?" Bastor sauntered ahead of Frey to stop six paces short of Aelthena. The guardian's eyes were hard on the reprobate man's back, a hand gripping his seax's hilt.

She tried to dismiss her own misgivings and raised her chin higher. "You look well."

Bastor barked a laugh. "Now I know you're pulling my tail. Dispense with the games for once, m'lady. What do you want with me?"

"I'm sorry — do you have something more pressing to return to?" She looked pointedly at the empty horn in his hand.

"Several somethings, in fact." Bastor tossed the horn to her table and crossed his arms. He even pulled himself somewhat upright, as if to remind her just how much he towered over her.

Aelthena steeled herself and spoke, slow and calm despite the storm tossing inside her. "Fine. I'll get straight to the point. Lord Siward rescinded his claim to the Iron Circle."

"Is that right?" Other than a slight sway to his stance, a lingering unsteadiness from his intoxication, Bastor did not react to the news.

"He changed his mind after an assassin killed his daughters' guard and held a knife to his eldest's throat. I don't know what that looks like to you, but it seems far from a coincidence to me."

"Astutely observed." Bastor's shoulders had slumped again, and his gaze flickered toward the fireplace, where several chairs were positioned around the hearth. He looked on the verge of collapse, but his pride, soiled as it was, was too stubborn to allow him.

A sliver of cruel amusement curled through her. *After everything he's done, a little discomfort is the least he deserves.*

"Frey brought you here, Bastor, because I thought you might know more. You have always been... advantageously connected."

"That's one way to say it. But rogues don't get a brisk trade from morals." The large man shrugged. "I'll need something from you in return."

She spoke through clenched teeth. "Which is?"

"Assurances." Bastor wore a ghastly smile. "You must swear to me you will never reveal the ills I did in Oakharrow, nor try me on any account. I want a fresh snowfall. I want exoneration."

Aelthena frowned. At the end, his voice had cracked, betraying the depth of that desire. She found her own hardened anger crumbling, no matter how she fought against it.

"Fine. Despite what you did, you also saved mine and Frey's lives. It does not even the scale, but it goes far enough. You have my word."

A tension ran out of the big man. His shoulders slumped further still, and his gaze fell to her feet.

"Before I say what I know," he murmured, "I need you to understand one thing. Lord Siward cannot be the Arkjarl. If he is, Baegard will lose the war, and we will be its last generation. Only my father can prevail against what lies ahead."

Just like that, all her softening sympathy dissipated. "Then it *was* you," she breathed.

Bastor's eyes alighted on hers for a moment, then

wandered to the ceiling. "No one was meant to die. But yes. It was me."

"How could you, Bastor?" It felt personal, this revelation, though she knew it could not be. Anger still stirred in her chest. "You told me you had turned away from your father. He's a Djur-burned *traitor* — you said it yourself!"

Bastor's head snapped up as he roared, "I *have no choice!*"

Frey's seax sprang from its sheathe, but the heir did not seem to notice. A moment later, he swayed again and had to brace himself on a chair. "No choice," he repeated, the words coming out hoarse.

Aelthena tried to remain firm. "You always have a choice. It's not too late. With your help, we can still turn this around. We can still elect Siward as the Arkjarl."

But Bastor was shaking his head before she had finished. "I told you. It must be my father."

"But why?" She wanted to shout as well and only just refrained. "Why must it be him?"

The large man's eyes were filled with depths she could not plumb, as hard as she tried. "I know what he is — never think I don't. I had to grow up under his hand. His *bastard.*" His teeth bared in a snarl. "Replaced as soon as my brother, with his skin milky white, was born. Didn't matter that he was a bastard, too; he got his name."

Aelthena dug her fingernails hard into her palms, clinging to her anger. Yet a swell of softer emotions washed away its buttresses.

Bastor shook himself, as if awakening from a dream. "He may be another kind of bastard, my father — but he's the devil we need. And I think, after a fashion, we can trust him."

Whatever sympathy had been growing in Aelthena dissipated with the words. "I very much doubt that."

He shrugged. "Trust in his nature, then. You can always count on my father for one thing: doing what's in his best interest. Before, it was to ignite war, for in strife comes opportunity. Now, it's to win the war. He'll have gained nothing if Baegard becomes a vassal state of Ha-Sypt."

Trust. She could not apply the word to Lord Ragnar. *And if his son takes his side, then the same goes for him.*

She took a step closer and held Bastor's gaze. His sour breath wafted to her nose, further inflaming her fury.

"I will never yield Baegard to Ragnar." She kept every word as sharp as a hunter's knives. "I will never support that traitor."

Slovenly and sottish as Bastor was, he remained a stone wall to her fire. "And yet you once trusted me." He turned away and only just seemed to notice Frey's alertness. An acid smile touched his lips. "Though I would never expect the same of you."

"No," Frey said with a smile of his own. "Not even you are that much of a fool."

The heir's eyes remained devoid of mirth as they traveled back to her. "With trust or without, believe me when I say this is the way it must be. My father... he would burn down the world to achieve his aims. Oppose him, and he will ruin all of us."

"So he holds the jarlheims hostage," Aelthena said tightly.

Bastor barked a laugh. "Of course he does! Would you expect anything else of him? But my father is not bluffing, not in this. He has... resources. A secret that I believe will secure our salvation."

Aelthena wished she could slap the man into reason. As it was, she kept her hands clenched at her sides. "You ask us to be allies, yet withhold information. If you want us to trust you, then you must first trust us."

The tall man grimaced and shook his head, his filthy locks flapping against his face. "Look at me. So used to keeping his confidence, I do it long past when I should." Despite his self-flagellation, his eyes still held cunning as they found hers. "But it could give you a weapon against him. You could undermine his position and doom us all."

Not such a sodden fool, after all. "I could," she conceded. "But we should be allies, Bastor. I want to work with you and not against you. Back in Oakharrow... you betrayed my city, yes, but you also saved me and those I care for. Let us put the past behind us. Tell us of this secret so we can move forward together."

Despite her words, she hoped those barbs of guilt of his prior actions would provoke him into speaking. Judging by his wince, they had found their mark.

Bastor glanced at Frey, then looked back at her. "Fine. But only if you swear to me you will not use this against my father."

Her pulse quickened. But she only hesitated a moment. "I swear it."

The Heir of Ragnarsglade studied her with bloodshot eyes, then nodded. "We discovered a pit not ten leagues from the hold. Others must have seen it before, for its stench could be detected from a great distance, but no one seemed to make anything of it. Not until my father caught wind of it. He saw its oddities as opportunity and began exploring its qualities and potential uses. When I left home for Oakharrow, he had not yet mastered its use. But that was two seasons ago. By now..." He shrugged. "He must have found something."

Aelthena pursed her lips. "What does it mean? What qualities could this pit have?"

Bastor smiled, and the firelight dyed his teeth red. "It is

the substance within it, Aelthena. We call it firesand, for when flames are brought near, it ignites."

She stared at him. Behind her eyes, she saw her home once more aflame, the Harrowhall burning to the ground. She saw the Teeth Gate erupting into a cloud of dust and smoke, and the Jotun sauntering through it. *A metal orb*, Yaethun's son, Egil, had said was the form the sorcery took. She had wondered what such an orb could contain.

Now she knew.

"Nuvvog's Rage," she breathed. "Ragnar has dragonfire."

She met Frey's eyes and found her horror reflected there. *Ragnar has dragonfire.* The man responsible for her home falling to the Jotun possessed the one weapon that could turn the tide of the war. Every time she felt herself drawing near to exacting the change that Baegard needed, her campaign was dealt another blow.

But a sword has two edges.

A realization turned her despair on its head. Bastor had given them a more potent weapon against his father than she had hoped for. Hiding a deception of this magnitude, the other jarls could never hope to trust him as their Arkjarl.

Then we can raise Siward in his place.

All the while, Bastor carefully watched her, only slightly swaying from his uncertain state. Had he read her intentions? She tried to show only the despair still swirling through her. There was always enough of it she did not have to stretch far.

"Thank you for trusting me, Bastor," she said softly. "I will keep my silence. But even knowing this, I cannot support Ragnar. I doubt I ever will be able to."

The heir donned a rueful grin. "Can't say I'm surprised. I'd hoped to be allies, Aelthena. But it seems like in this, we stand on different ends of the field." He turned to the door, then paused. "Remember your oath. Deny it, and you might kill us all."

With that, Bastor stepped past the guardian. Aelthena kept her lips pressed together as he yanked the door shut behind him. The sound reverberated throughout the room.

Aelthena released her act and strode over to the hearth to stare into the dying flames. Her ambitions had been dampened, but not yet vanished. Bastor had given her fresh fuel to work with.

If it took oaths broken and friendships betrayed to save her people, she would consider the price a bargain.

She raised her head to find Frey standing by her side. "You don't actually mean to keep your promise, do you?" the guardian asked quietly.

"Of course not."

"I should have expected nothing less." His gaze traveled to the door. "You know, you can hardly blame him for this."

That raised her eyebrows. "Can you not?"

"How could you?" A knavish light appeared in his eyes. "He was born a bastard."

She sighed, though with a small smile of her own. "And here I thought we were past your buffoonery."

Their mirth quieted as their gazes returned to the flames.

"I could stoke the fire," Frey offered.

She shook her head. "Don't bother — I won't be staying. Too many things to do." She met his eyes again. "I think we can convince Lord Siward to reconsider now. Barring that, we'll expose Ragnar for the scoundrel he is. If we cannot do either, whether or not I will it, Bastor will win."

The guardian again wore a frown. "I'd rather he not."

"Nor I." She nodded toward the door. "I suppose we had best be plotting, then."

"Lead, m'lady, and I shall follow."

Aelthena knew it well, and she felt better to have Frey watching her back as they spilled back out into the Elkhorn.

16. FORBIDDEN DOORS

"I yearn to open forbidden portals. I flirt with temptation till dawn. They murmur and whisper, just beyond the threshold... soon, I must let them in."

- Torvald Geirson, the Last King of Baegard

Bjorn sensed there was something different to his lesson that morning as soon as he entered the small, round hut.

He paused at the entrance after pulling the door shut behind him and studied the room. As familiar as he had become with it over the past weeks, the changes were immediately obvious.

First, Yonik did not lean against the wall, watching as he had on all but one occasion.

And second, a small, silver-veined ore sat next to a steaming pot of water and the blazing firepit.

Mother Sign, who sat cross-legged before these implements, snorted a laugh. "I cannot see, but I can practically *smell* your hesitation. Sit, cub, sit — this will not hurt... much."

Bjorn took a step closer, but not to fold onto the rug that marked his usual spot. He was reluctant to speak, but he had been open with his teacher thus far.

"Has Yonik told you what happened at my first Seeing?"

"No."

Her ensuing silence was an invitation to continue.

Bjorn muddled his way through the blurry memories. "I saw visions. Visions of a terrible dragon as tall as the sky, and a wall of fire that consumed the Baegardian valley, and all those I knew and cared for falling dead from the sky."

"Horrid dreams, to be sure." Mother Sign raised her eyebrows. "But you will not suffer them this time. Not under my watch."

He drew in a breath. "I attacked and almost killed someone." To his surprise, his voice was nearly steady. "The man was innocent, but caught in the visions, I couldn't see that."

Mother Sign stared toward the wall for a long moment. Bjorn wondered what thoughts swirled behind those cloudy eyes; if she feared him now, or feared for him.

Finally, she sighed and gestured to the mat again. "Sit, Bjorn. We will talk of it. And only when you're ready will we make any attempt at Seeing."

It was too reasonable a request to deny. Bjorn folded onto the rug, drawing his legs in close, and hunched over the fire. The snow had begun to melt outside as spring stretched its influence over the Teeth, but winter was far from gone. As things stood, he soaked up every scrap of warmth he could.

The Silver was silent for several long moments. "Was it rage that made you attack the man?"

Bjorn shrugged. "I suppose."

"Then you need to fear it now. That door within you is sealed shut; were it not, I would have seen it. We will be careful, very careful, when we use the Wrath runestone. Yes, we must eventually," she said, seeming to sense Bjorn's recoil. "We must explore its potential, and you are the *Volur* who will do so."

His fists had clenched without his realizing it. With an effort, Bjorn pried them apart. "If you think that best," he muttered.

"I do." Mother Sign smiled, her eyes straying past his shoulder. "Now, we practice to prepare for that time. Here — take this."

She leaned around the fire to hold out another of the flat, round stones he had been so carefully studying with her. Bjorn accepted it and read aloud the primary rune carved into it. "*Brenamun.* Heartfire."

"So you have learned something." The aged woman gave him a thin smile. "And what is its effect?"

He could already feel it tickling his innards, tantalizing, inviting. "Warmth. It makes the seer warm."

"Good. *Brenamun* is one of the simplest to use, and the least dangerous — though nothing of *seidar* is without its risks. Should you open the door too wide, you may boil your insides. So take care, and maintain your focus and vigilance at all times. All times!" she repeated, loud enough that Bjorn startled, to her cackling delight.

Mad old bat, he thought fondly as he considered the other implements resting by the fire. "So I suppose you must heat the drascale ore, then pour water over it to produce *khnuum* steam."

"I am warmed that you so closely heed my words. Yes — but we will only heat the ore a little, for it is a little Seeing we do now. You need not carve me any shorter than I already am." Mother Sign grinned off toward the door. "But so an old woman doesn't burn herself, if you would..."

Bjorn doubted the Silver would do anything of the like — she had started the fire by herself, hadn't she? — yet he still obliged. Picking up a pair of short iron pokers resting next to the ore, he lifted and placed the rock at the edge of the fire. He thought he should probably scoot it deeper into the heat, but fear stayed his hand, even as he glanced guiltily at his teacher.

Mother Sign, with her usual preternatural sense for hesitation, did not seem fooled. "Nestle it in the middle of the coals. You must heat it evenly and thoroughly to produce any effect."

Grudgingly, Bjorn nudged the stone into the center of the pit, then cast down the pokers as if they were to blame for the change of affairs. For a long minute, he watched the ore slowly heat while he and the Silver sat in silence.

"As you begin to train in Seeing," said Mother Sign, "there is something you must remember, Bjorn. Yes, I used your name," she noted with a smile, "because I am quite serious about this. So listen well, as you have listened before."

Hearing a note of formality, Bjorn kept his own words sober. "I am listening, Mother Sign."

The Silver nodded gravely. "Heed your teacher's warning, *Volur*, as I once heeded mine: Do not make frequent use of the runestones and *khnuum*. You know that the Sight may unlock doors that have long been shut within your mind, that it may tap your hidden potential. But some doors, once opened, can never fully close."

A slow, familiar anxiety rose in him. "Should we not avoid Seeing entirely then, if it is so dangerous?"

"No!" Mother Sign all but shouted the word as she leaned forward. "No," she repeated softer. "We *must* use the runestones. It is the path, the *only* path, to our future."

Whose path did she mean — *Volur*? Baegardians?

Humanity as a whole? The words he had read on the Scribe's vellum, that contained the prophecy of the Witterland Runestone, came back to mind. *Warriors of the Stone harken to the call; they charge into battle to fall and die...* He wondered if runestones were what "the Stone" meant. And later, *still comes One with the Farthest Sight...* That had to mean a seer. And what good was a *Volur* without using runestones?

It is the path, the only path. He echoed her words in his mind and tried to believe them.

"Yes, Mother Sign," he said aloud, quiet but firm.

The Silver sighed suddenly. "I am adamant, cub, because I sit before you as proof of what might happen if you are not careful."

That caught his attention. "You... you opened a door you couldn't close?"

She nodded grimly. "More than one. And long have I paid the price."

Curiosity had its hooks in him now. Though he knew perhaps he should not ask, still, he had to. "Is that how you lost your vision?"

Mother Sign's eyes almost found his, and she wore a rueful smile, heavy with memory and regret. "It's the least I've lost. But when you live fully, you always lose some things along the way. The trick is to discover more and fill in the gaps."

She went silent then. Bjorn wanted to pry the full truth from her, but thought it best not to push. Yet the question did not cease to rattle around his head. *What doors did she open? And what else has she lost?* He had begun to feel he knew his aged mentor. Now he wondered if he understood her at all.

Mother Sign suddenly shook like a dog after a bath and

grinned. "But enough of an old woman's regrets. Time to make your own!"

"That's not exactly reassuring," Bjorn muttered as he lifted the pokers and rolled the drascale ore free of the flames. He let the smoking stone rest at the edge of the ashes. "Should I pour on the water?"

"You *have* become the compliant pupil, haven't you? A dose of terror is healthy for you, it is." As if she had not just been deadly serious moments before, Mother Sign waved her hand airily. "Yes, yes — you remember the steps, I'm sure."

He gritted his teeth, but moved to comply. Picking up the pot with a cloth rag sitting nearby, he carried it over to the other side, where the hot ore waited. Nerves pranced about his stomach like Clap in a meadow. "I pour it on and breathe it in?" he could not help but ask. "Then focus on the runestone and the meaning of the primary and secondary runes?"

"Are you nervous, cub?" Mother Sign jeered, leaning forward slightly. "Yes; those are the steps, and you know it. Only remember: once in the Hall of Doors, and you feel the rune's door open, have a care to keep it only cracked, no more — unless cooked liver is to your liking! Now, scoot around the fire within my reach."

Wondering what the aged barbar had in store for him now, Bjorn did as she instructed, leaving his rug to sit on the cold boards next to her. She reached out and, with unnerving accuracy, set a hand to his forearm. Bjorn tried not to flinch from her touch as her fingers worked under his sleeve. The Silver had removed her glove, and her skin was cold and dry.

"Through direct contact, one *Volur* may sense the *seidar* in another — to a limited degree," she explained. "But I cannot control it; that task remains to you. Understood?"

"Yes." He wondered nervously what she had in mind that would necessitate it.

"Good. Proceed."

With her hand still on his arm, Bjorn tilted the pot to pour a small stream of water over the hot stone. As soon as the water touched the stone, steam erupted over the surface. Bjorn hesitated, then leaned forward to breathe it in. A sensation like a breeze on hanging laundry passed through his mind. Almost, he could see a corridor lined with rooms that faded into shadows, each door inching open a crack as if curious children hid behind them.

As the initial burst of steam faded, he looked up to Mother Sign through swimming vision. "Again?"

"Once is enough," she said, her unseeing gaze settled on the round walls of the hut. "Quickly, now — the rune!"

Bjorn nodded, more to himself than her, and swiftly replaced the pot. Then, settling into a seat again, he drew in a deep breath and lifted the rune before his eyes.

As had occurred in the wilds on the way to Chasm Valley, his gaze seemed yoked to the rune as soon as he looked. It took an effort to remember all of Mother Sign's lessons and carefully examine each part of the rune and build the entire meaning. It was a circular shape, formed of soft arcs and waves, that mimicked the dancing of flames.

Brenamun, he repeated to himself. *Brenamun. Heartfire. Heartfire.*

Again, the shadowy corridor leaped into his mind. In each direction, shut doors extended, seemingly without end. One door, however, appeared to be easing open. As soon as he focused on it, his perspective shifted so he stood before it.

The Heartfire rune was carved into the door. This was the one he intended.

Open, he willed it.

The wood swung free of the frame. At once, changes swept through his body, the sensations filling it. *Warmth.* He sighed as heat, blessed heat, flooded through him. From the skin of his scalp to the ends of his fingers to his feet and toes — everywhere was warm. He could not remember the last time he felt so warm outside of the hot spring baths. *Warmth.*

Without conscious thought, Bjorn reached invisible hands forward and eased the door open a little wider. He grinned as a fresh wave of heat curled through him. *Heartfire* — yes, he could understand the name now, for his chest felt warmest of all.

Mother Sign said something, and with a colossal effort, Bjorn tried to heed his teacher.

"Careful... only cracked..."

He understood her repeated warning through those few words, and even caught in the ecstasy of the Heartfire, he knew their wisdom. With a heavy sigh, he reached forward again to the door and pressed it almost closed. As most of the heat left his bones, he felt an ache set into his body. Bjorn gritted his teeth and refrained from opening the door wider again. A sliver of his fear had reasserted itself, rooting him in the world and the very real consequences if his attention slipped even a fraction.

With the easing of *seidar's* grip on him, Mother Sign's words came clearer. "...hear me, cub?"

"I hear you," he mumbled. His mouth felt detached from him, like a separate limb he could only move through conscious effort.

"Good. The door is open, but only slightly?"

He nodded. Caught in the magic's thrall, it was a long moment before he remembered she could not see the gesture. "Yes."

"Very convincing," the Silver noted drily. "That's enough for now, then. Shut it entirely."

Bjorn did not want to release that last bit of heat. Yet he returned to the shadowy corridor and, like he set a shoulder to the door, he shoved it closed.

At once, he felt the difference. Bjorn wrapped his arms around his middle and hunched over, his teeth chattering. He felt even colder than before now that the *seidar* heat had left him. That the Hall of Doors remained in his mind, inviting him to return and open the door again, only made it harder to bear.

He knew Mother Sign listened to his suffering by her silence. "It is not a pleasant experience, shutting a door," she murmured. "But it is necessary. I think you have done many unpleasant and necessary things in your life, haven't you, Bjorn?"

He clawed to regain a semblance of himself. "I've come here every morning, haven't I?" he quipped through quivering lips.

His teacher chortled. "And I have many more irksome lessons planned yet, my ornery pupil. But we are not yet done with today's niceties. I want you to return to the *Brenamun* door. When you do, open it slightly more."

Bjorn was surprised at how eagerly he leaped to obey. Returning to the shadowy corridor, he found the Hall of Doors had grown hazier since the minutes before. The effect of the khnuum steam seemed to be fading. Eager not to inhale anymore than he had to, Bjorn tried to find the Heartfire door. But the hall, falling into darkness either way he turned, had returned to the endless line of doors, each the same as the next.

"Look again upon the runestone if you cannot find the door," his teacher advised.

Careful not to break her contact, Bjorn reached back

around the fire and took the runestone in hand, then gazed upon it. The gripping effect, too, was weaker than before, yet it swept him through the corridor to stand before the Heartfire door once more.

"Open the door." Mother Sign spoke in a whisper.

In his mind's eye, he reached forward and pulled slightly on the handle. As the door opened a crack, heat seeped into him, and all his hesitancies eased with it. A sigh escaped his lips, and his shivers disappeared.

"Focus." Her words had become murky again, but clearer than when the *khnuum* had more strongly affected him. "Open it wider."

He forced his numb lips to make a response. "Wider?"

"Yes. But not too wide! Always keep control. Only open as far as you can manage."

Bjorn went to do her bidding. But in his haste, he moved faster than was wise, wrenching on the door so it sat a quarter ajar. The heat that inundated him burned away all other thoughts for a moment. A grin appeared on his lips. *This* was what he had been waiting for! His entire life, he had never known warmth or elation like this. *Seidar* — how could he ever have feared it?

He wanted more.

He set a hand to the door handle, ignoring the buzzing voice in his ears, and opened it wider still. His very skin seemed to burn with glorious power. He felt as if he walked through a blazing wildfire, but instead of finding pain, only ecstasy awaited. He eased it open a fraction more, so it stood perpendicular to the adjacent wall. White light poured out from the portal, searing away the shadows in the corridor and illuminating it for hundreds of paces in either direction. But Bjorn had eyes only for the open passage before him. *What lies beyond it? What if I stepped through?* He took a step forward, and another, his toes on the threshold—

Pain. The sensation came suddenly, violently. It felt as if something had bitten his arm. At once, Bjorn's senses reasserted themselves, and he looked down at his arm to see blood trickled onto his knee, staining his trousers. Bjorn shut the door in his mind as self-preservation sprang into action. He stumbled to his feet and put a gloved hand to his forearm, where the gouge had formed.

Mother Sign felt around the fire until she located the rag Bjorn had used to move the pot, then wiped off the blood from her hand and knife. "Are you returned, cub?" she asked matter-of-factly.

He stared down at her, baffled. The shivers left in the wake of the Seeing claimed him again, and the wound on his wrist prickled.

"You made me bleed."

"I did." From her tone, his teacher had no regrets about it. "Pain, past seers have found, is the only reliable way to bring back a *Volur* who has strayed too close to becoming lost. I felt what you were doing, Bjorn. You opened the door wider than you could control. Did you think to step through it?"

He swallowed hard. His body felt all wrong. His joints were too loose, and his head spun. He whispered his answer.

"Yes."

Mother Sign shook her head. Disappointment radiated from her like light from a campfire. "Never open a door so wide that you can enter. Even more, never step through. Do you hear me, Bjorn? Many great seers have been lost to the allure of the light beyond them. Once the threshold is passed, you cannot return."

"Why?" The word came out in a croak. "What happens?"

"No one knows. Perhaps they join the gods. Perhaps

sprites purge their minds." The aged woman looked up at him, and it seemed as if the eye tattooed upon her forehead peered into his spirit. "I pray to Baltur you have the wisdom and strength not to find out."

Bjorn turned his head aside. His pulse felt erratic in its rhythm, its gait like a horse gone lame. "I won't do that again," he said quietly, forming the resolution as he spoke it aloud. "I swear it to you on my mother's stone."

Mother Sign went quiet for a moment. "A powerful oath. Good. Then you understand what is at stake here."

"Yes." He understood all too well. If he stepped beyond the door, if he accepted all the promises it whispered, he could not help Oakharrow, or Aelthena, or their father. He would abandon them as surely as it seemed he already had. And he would be spitting on the memory of his brothers and mother. Of all the shames he had endured, that was one he could not live with.

"That's enough for today." Mother Sign waved a hand at him. "Go. Take a rest; you'll need it. And if you again appear in the Hall of Doors before *khnuum's* influence dissipates, do not open any of them. I will not be there to pull you back."

"I won't."

Without asking if she needed assistance cleaning up, as he usually did, Bjorn pulled open the hut's door and stumbled outside.

A wind had found its way into Eildursprall's vale, making the day chillier despite the sun shining through the thin clouds. Bjorn pulled his cloak tighter under his neck and tried not to shiver as he made his halting way through Heim Numen. A few passing gothi cast him strange looks, but he kept his head lowered, and none of them stopped him. Conversation was the last thing he wanted just then.

The baths. It was the only way he could think of to

warm his bones. Hot water never ran out there, fed as they were by underground springs. And seeing as it was in the middle of the day, they were likely to be deserted, which suited his present mood.

He reached the twin shelters a short while later. Positioned at the cliffs at the foot of Yewung, they boasted roofs and walls, but were open to the elements facing the cliffs. The shelters shared a wall, but were built so that the sexes could bathe separately, a necessary requirement for priests committed to chastity. Bjorn appreciated the privacy. He had always been shy bathing around women, and he had avoided any such situation where he would have to since he was a child.

Entering the men's shelter on the left, a haze of steam greeted Bjorn. This steam smelled nothing like *khnuum*, so he breathed it in gladly. Already, he felt the chill easing away, the walls trapping in some of the heat and blocking out the wind. As he had hoped, no one else sat in the pool. The water, clear and glacier blue, beckoned him with spirals of steam curling off its still surface.

As quickly as he could, he stripped off his clothes and settled them into a pile on the bench by the door. As he turned to dash for the warm water, a splash sounded through the wall. Bjorn glanced over and found a gap in the boards there, just large enough to see through. Though he shivered in the chill air, the sight beyond the wall froze him in place.

A young woman stepped free of the pool, wearing nothing but the steam that wreathed her body. Her skin was pale where light scarcely touched it, her figure lean but shapely. His eyes could not help but linger on the movement of her hips as she padded across the stone to retrieve her clothes. As she leaned over, her breasts swayed into view. Bjorn felt a hot stirring in him and was yet more grateful for the wall that hid him from view.

Then she turned just enough that he could recognize her. *Tyra.* His heart beat faster still. Somehow, knowing her identity brought him abruptly back to how wrong his accidental peeping was. Moving slowly so that the movement would not attract her attention, he moved away from the wall, then slunk quietly into the pool, wincing at every slight sound it made. He hoped the howl of the wind outside proved loud enough to cover them.

As he stood in the hot springs, the warmth of the water sinking through him, his thoughts circled back to Tyra. One day, she would be a priestess. Nothing could ever occur between them; he had always known that.

But now, having glimpsed her devoid of her cloak and robes, he could no longer deny the attraction that had been there all along. An ache built inside him.

Long after he had reclaimed warmth again and *khnuum* had eased its hold on his mind, Bjorn remained in the pool and thought of Tyra, yearning for all that could never be.

17. THE FIRST TO FALL

Seven are We when We Splinter:

Pawura, the Dreaming Antelope,
Goddess of Art and Love
Yeshept, the Prowling Lioness,
Goddess of the Hunt and Wealth

Qa'a, the Wise Scarab,
God of Justice and Foresight
Aya, the White Cobra,
God of Cunning and Deceit

Bek, the Red Behemoth,
Goddess of Might and War
Gazabe, the Black Jackal,
God of Death and Decay

And Hua, the Bright Creator,
Father of the People of Dust
Mother of the mighty Huame

Seven Splinters are We...

- Words in the Sand, refrain 2;5-8

From atop the hill in her brother's war tent, Sehdra witnessed all the might of the People of Dust as their armies converged on the hapless outpost.

The mountain savages' town, Fairglen, had never stood a chance. Its walls were of timber, roughly hewn and hammered into the ground with sharp, uneven tops a dozen feet high. Against a skirmish, it might have posed some danger.

But this was the host that the karah had gathered, and they proved but a minor inconvenience. Hua-fire, hurled from beyond the range of bows by the giants, had set aflame first the walls, then the town. As the defenders were forced into the field, chariots rode forth, tearing down crops and hooting with bloodthirst. Those sons of nobility surrounded the Baegardians, and their arrows thinned their ranks before they could mount a charge. Only then did the chariots scatter, defying the resistance. Sehdra could almost hear the charioteers' laughter from the great distance as they fled with few casualties suffered.

At the orders of the new leader of the armies, Amon Baka, the mercenaries and infantry were sent in, the greenest among them forming the front ranks. "The herd will be culled," the general had explained to the karah, "and the strongest blooded." Hephystus, always delighting in despoiled innocence, had heartily agreed to the plan, and even ordered a woman be sent to the general's tent that night to warm his bed in his wife's absence. Amon, who struck Sehdra as a match for her brother in youthful arrogance, had bowed and smiled at this gift.

Sehdra did not speak against any of it. She kept to the shadows and held her tongue, watching, waiting.

Even before inexperienced soldiers, the savages did not last long. Their tactics proved deadly effective, huddling together so that their shields formed a wall before them that was difficult to penetrate. But they were only three hundred men, and while they felled twice their number, they were swallowed by Sypten spears, swords, and arrows. Even after the last man fell, the armies trampled over the bodies, perhaps in confusion, perhaps out of unsated fury, or maybe to sneak a bracer or two of precious metal from the fallen foes. Their captains tried to reinstate order for a long time afterward, a delay at which Amon frowned severely and promised rectification to the karah.

But nothing, it seemed, could dampen Physt's fair mood. He smiled as the giants rained down fire. He grinned as the chariotry advanced and dealt their damage. He chortled as the slaughter commenced. Even now, though the battle had long since ceased and the fiery orb of Hua teetered on the horizon, satisfaction radiated from him like heat from a hearth.

He was born for war. Sehdra had not thought her opinion of her brother could sink further, yet he proved her wrong once more.

"A glorious day, sister!" he said at one point, grinning at her, the smile slack with the wine he had imbibed all that morning and afternoon. "A glorious day in my name!"

She nodded and muttered her agreement, though "glorious" was the last attribute she would have assigned to the slaughter. And, with Oyaoan looming behind the provisional throne, she did not think Hephystus would be the name on the soldiers' lips.

"Are you well, Sehdra Ohkweht?" Teti murmured in her

ear. He had stood in silent vigil next to her, his presence offering a little comfort before the atrocities.

"Very well, thank you," Sehdra lied. She longed to close her eyes, to lose herself to oblivion and forget all she had seen. For a breath of air free of smoke and death. She wanted to scrub her skin and slough off her guilt.

But the karah had ordered her to remain in attendance, and not even the Royal Sister could defy a living god's will.

"Bring their leader to me," her brother ordered when the victory was complete. His lips curled with a private joke. "If he still lives."

The general bowed and did as he bade.

As they waited, Sehdra occupied her mind, longing to think of something other than battle. The ramifications of this attack would cascade throughout the mountain nation. If they had not already had reports of the People of Dust advancing with their armies, they would have them now. The Winter Holds would rally their warriors, send out their warships, and ready the great wooden machines that rained down death upon their heads. If they had not already done so, they would have the time; it would take weeks still to travel upriver to Petyrsholm.

But no amount of soldiers would be enough. The Duaat board was set, and all the figurines were on one side. What could stand against the huame and their god's weapons?

Fairglen's leader was escorted into the pavilion with hands tied behind his back. As he raised his head, Sehdra was surprised to find it was not a man, but a woman with a shorn head who led this town. The savage, though thrown to her knees, glared up with fire in her leaf-green eyes. Wounds puckered her scalp, and blood oozed down her pale skin, but she did not seem to notice. Her clothes were ashen and torn, yet she still held a quivering strength.

Sehdra found her respect for the captive growing apace with her pity.

"So," her brother began, "you sought to defy me. *Me*, the Karah of Ha-Sypt, with all the might of my armies before me. See what your arrogance has led to?"

An interpreter, a Baegardian slave brought in for this occasion, translated the Karah's words. Sehdra, who knew the Winter Holds tongue — as did Physt, though he chose not to use it — noticed the translation lacked the haughty dignity of her brother's utterance. If Physt noticed, he gave no sign.

The mountain woman was silent for a long moment. "We did not ask for your war," she replied finally. "Fairglen was a peaceful place before you came. It is not any arrogance of ours at fault, but your cruelty."

Sehdra struggled to hide her wince. The Baegardian leader was brave, but courage was a tainted currency before the karah. Vizier Zosar, standing next to Physt's throne, shook his head in exaggerated regret, but his low drama was nothing to the scene playing out before them.

The interpreter began to repeat the words in the People's tongue, but her brother was too impatient to let him finish. "Cruel, am I?" he mocked with a smile. "I will propose this to you, savage. Tell me what I wish to know, or each of your surviving kin will be shown how *cruel* I can be."

"Well said, Your Sanctity," Zosar flattered. "Quite merciful and wise."

The translator hesitated, as if reluctant to repeat what Hephystus had said. But he had been long enough a slave to know that resistance was futile in her brother's court, and he quickly rattled off the lines.

Fear spasmed across the Baegardian's features. Sehdra averted her eyes. Such despair as assaulted the woman, and the desperate strength with which she warded it off — it was almost as horrible to witness as the battle had been.

"No."

Even if she had not known the word, Sehdra would have understood. Almost disbelieving, she looked back at the leader. She wanted to shake her by the shoulders, to scream in her face, *Why? Why resist? Why throw away everything you have left — and for what?* And yet, she also found herself strangely ashamed. Were it her on her knees before her brother, she could never have defied him so.

Sehdra turned to her brother. The karah stood from his wooden throne, all but quivering with royal indignation. The goblet of wine tipped to spill some of the red liquid at his feet. *Like a foretelling*, she thought numbly.

"Take her head," Physt spoke, his throat so closed up with emotion it came out as a whisper.

The two closest guards glanced at each other, but before either could decide who would take the honor, the great shadow behind the throne moved, and a heavy footstep made the ground tremble. Sehdra barely breathed as Oyaoan showed herself before the Baegardian. The guards fell back a step at seeing the huamek revealed. Oyaoan turned her tusked head around, her beady eyes taking in every person among them, the karah included. Finally, they rested on the prisoner, tiny and trembling at her feet. The savage leader's chest heaved with panic as she stared up at the giantess. If she had seen her at all before, she must have thought her a statue with how still she held herself.

Oyaoan rumbled in her speech, and the Ibis stepped forward to interpret. Somehow, he did not tremble under Hephystus's molten glare.

"Great Oyaoan speaks! She has other plans for this one," he said, each word annunciated through his accent. "She commands that the female carry a messenger north, to tell those who would defy her of what happened here at Godanglan, at Fairglen. She commands that—"

"*Commands?*"

Sehdra retreated before her brother's shriek. Teti had placed a hand to her arm, as if he might pull her behind and protect her with his body. But she knew none of them were safe before this. The karah was red with fury now — red as wine, red as blood. There was no reason or mercy left within him.

"Oyaoan does not command here!" He strode forward, a drunken sway to his gait. His toe caught on a rug, provoking a furious kick before he lurched onward. Oyaoan watched impassively, as did the Ibis. The vizier's eyes wavered between hunger and fear.

Physt noticed none of it. He stalked past the huamek, past the Baegardian frozen at the giant's feet, to stand before the guards. Then, reaching forward, he ripped free one of their khopeshes from their belt, with some baffled assistance from the guard, spun on his heel, and marched back the other way. As he walked, he raised the blade overhead. His eyes were set on the back of the savage's head.

"Qa'a, no," Sehdra whispered as she realized his intentions. "Please, Gazabe, Bek, have mercy—"

But no Divine descended to stop him. Hephystus, with a furious scream, came behind the Baegardian and swung the sword with all his might. It was a clumsy strike, its owner impaired by wrath and wine, and at the warning, the woman threw herself forward, desperately trying to avoid the blow she must now know was coming. The blade nicked her shoulder, and the woman hissed in pain. She tried to scramble away, but instead sprawled on the ground with her hands tied behind her back. She could not right herself in time as Physt raised the sword again, bloodshot eyes open wide.

Prayers came to her lips. "Qa'a, Wise Scarab, mercy—"

Zosar half-raised a hand. "Your Sanctity, perhaps—"

"Ovvash drag you to the hells!" screamed the savage woman.

The sword slashed down.

The karah's royal robes were splattered with red, but he did not stop there. Again, he swung — and again — and again — until the white of his crown was stained in streaks, and his face was sprayed with scarlet. Long after the prisoner had gone silent, Physt finally stumbled back, his narrow chest heaving for breath. His teeth were bright in his red face as he grinned at Sehdra.

"There is the bitch's lesson, is it not, sister?"

She could not even pretend to play along. All her careful composure, a frozen mask woven over a lifetime, could not withstand this. *Did I ever know you?* she wondered as she stared at the monster wearing her brother's flesh. *Or were you always this way, even as the boy I chased through the halls, the boy I teased and dressed in women's clothes?*

She could scarcely remember that boy now. This man, if he could be called such, had killed him as thoroughly as the prisoner.

The smile slipped away. "Then be damned." His shoulders slumped, and the dripping khopesh fell from his limp hand. He made his way back to the throne and sagged into it. "Wine!" he snapped out, some measure of strength brought back by his irritation.

Sehdra scarcely bobbed a bow before she fled the pavilion. Outside, the sun was bright and the day warm. A fine spring day, comfortable unlike any they experienced in the deserts along the Nu. So at odds with all she had just witnessed.

Sehdra leaned over and sucked in deep gulps of air. She

did not care who saw her like this. She could not care. The horrors she had witnessed had pushed away all the propriety of her station.

"Sehdra, let us return to your tent." Teti pulled at her arm, his voice only just edged with panic. "We must not be near in case the karah notices your absence and wishes it otherwise. I fear for your life with his mood like this."

She nodded and found the strength to rise and walk next to him. Neither of them suggested turning around for the palanquin, which she had run past in her haste to escape. Every delay felt as if it might be the moment when her life became forfeit.

"She will kill him, Teti," Sehdra murmured.

"Oyaoan?"

She nodded, feeling as if she walked through a dream. "She will kill him for this defiance. And when she does, I will not shed a tear for him. Not one."

Yet the tears came then, leaking from the eye set in her cursed flesh. Sehdra did not hide them as they limped back to her shelter.

18. A CONSPIRACY OF WIVES

"For the man of middling stock, courage only lasts till heat touches his skin. Then, like a petal in the sun, it wilts."

- Yofam Dragontooth, Slayer of the wyvern Vardraith, First Drang of the Iron Band

The knock at the door startled Aelthena from her reverie.

Turning from her view out over her balcony, she glanced at Frey standing next to her. He nodded and moved into her quarters. A moment later, she heard the servant she had earlier requisitioned admit her guests.

It was time to weave her webs and hope they would hold, yet for a moment longer, she lingered on the balcony. Spring was blossoming. Branches hung heavy with flower buds and the beginnings of fruit, and bright green leaves covered their lengths. A mist shimmered down, saturating the earth and filtering away the filth from the gutters and streets. The fresh scent brought by the rain seemed to cleanse her spirit as well.

Baegard was beautiful. Holed up in the center of the city, she missed the reminders of it. Only the woman's voice behind her could draw her away.

Time to trigger the trap.

Rallying herself, Aelthena summoned what she hoped was a charming smile, then turned, the picture of the pleasant hostess. "Lady Iona," she greeted her. "How gracious of you to come."

"How could I refuse!" The Lady of Greenwuud wore her usual cheerful smile as she carried in her baby boy, Olle, in her arms. Yet behind her expression, Aelthena suspected more intelligence than Iona let on.

A huskarl came in a moment afterward, his gaze sweeping across the room. There was little to see. Her sitting room had been arranged for this meeting: the small table and chairs scooted closer to the fire, a bottle of Harrowmead uncorked and waiting by two painted cups. Given her quarters and finances, it was the best she could do.

The guard's gaze settled on Frey, and he gave the guardian a nod, which Frey returned. Aelthena breathed a little easier. It seemed the two knew each other.

Aelthena invited the Lady of Greenwuud to sit, and the thrall served them each honey wine. Aelthena ordinarily would have thanked the servant, but with a jarl's wife opposite her, she only spared the woman a brief glance.

Iona, having contented her babe with a rattle that jangled in Aelthena's ears, sipped at her goblet with a delighted expression. "By Skirsala's lips! What vintage is this, Skjold?"

"My own jarlheim, actually." Aelthena forced a smile. "Our river is named the Honeybrook for a reason."

"Indeed! I must requisition a few bottles for my Siward's enjoyment — and my own." Iona took a longer sip, and as she lowered it, Aelthena noted her glass was already half empty. She hid a smile. If Iona fell under the mead's influence, it could only help her cause. Aelthena only indulged mildly herself. She needed a clear head yet.

"It is actually of Lord Siward that I wished to speak, Iona — do you mind?"

The Lady of Greenwuud laughed and waved a hand. "Oh, do away with any formalities you please! Much more comfortable without them."

"Iona, then. I know you are not ignorant of our situation. It has only grown more dire since the unfortunate attack on your daughter — my deepest condolences for losing your man once again."

"Oh, you are too kind." Iona drained the entirety of her cup, though her mood sobered with every drop. "I am only glad no harm befell Helka. Oh, how she worried me!"

Aelthena leaned forward, waiting impatiently for the thrall to refill her goblet before speaking. "But do you not see what truly happened?"

Siward's wife did not startle as she expected, but considered her briefly before pushing away the rattle that flashed before her face. "Olle!" she reprimanded. The edge in her voice did not fade as her gaze shifted back across the table. "What is it I am supposed to see, Aelthena?"

"Who stands to gain the most from intimidating your husband? Who would know to threaten your daughter and not Lord Siward directly? Only one familiar with Baegard's politics could best aim the knife."

Iona's eyebrows raised. Gone was the veneer of politeness, and even with an infant in her lap, she appeared as domineering as any of the other jarls' wives. "Who better than our eternal enemies?"

"But they would be hard pressed to strike so accurately. Please, Iona. I think you know who I mean."

Iona considered her for a long moment as she bounced her son on her lap. Her eyes flickered up to Frey behind Aelthena's shoulder, then fell back to her.

"I do," she replied. "But I cannot say I agree, nor approve of your saying so. Unless you have proof?"

Aelthena's jaw clenched before she could loosen it. Proof had ever been in short supply, and she felt it now when she needed it most of all.

"None more than my inferences and oaths. But I assure you, if we follow the threads together—"

She cut off as a knock came at the door. *Djur's black balls!* Aelthena's heart hammered in her chest as the servant moved to answer the door. Iona twisted in her seat, her son looking curiously with her. A moment later, the Lady of Greenwuud glanced back with a wry smile.

"Ah, Aelthena," she said softly. "You have planned an ambush of your own, haven't you?"

She did not reply, but rose and painted on another smile as the door admitted two other wives: Sigrid Of'Harald and Nanna Of'Alrik. They had arrived too soon, before she had convinced Iona to take up her cause as her own. But it had been a necessary risk. Had she waited for another meeting later, Iona might have time to change her mind, or for Ragnar and Bastor to change it for her. But too soon could be the unraveling of the entire endeavor as well.

Yet Aelthena had not clawed her way to authority to surrender it now.

She made her way over to the newcomers. "Lady Sigrid, Lady Nanna! Thank you both for coming."

The women returned her greetings with varying degrees of warmth. Sigrid's dark eyes scrutinized Aelthena's sitting room, while Nanna glowed with her usual motherliness, pressing both Aelthena's hands in her moist grip. Formalities satisfied, they took the chairs that Frey brought in from the bedroom, then accepted their own goblets of mead.

The women looked at each for a moment before Sigrid spoke. "So," she said in her usual straightforward manner, "you have deceived us, Aelthena."

Aelthena's smile, though strained, was genuine. "Yes. The time for pleasantries is at an end. We women must make our decisions, and the right ones, before the men take Baegard down the wrong path."

Nanna's gaiety faded with every word. "You are not asking us to betray our husbands, surely?"

"Of course not," Aelthena hastened to say. "I ask the very opposite. The jarls respond to the incentives before them. Perhaps some, like Lord Hother and Lord Petyr, harbor ambitions to be the Arkjarl, but they lack the support to attain it, as I am sure they know. In the end, they will fold to another's influence. We all know of whom I speak."

Olle exclaimed into the silence, but none of the women so much as smiled. "Lord Ragnar," Iona supplied.

Aelthena nodded. "Iona, your husband remains the most viable candidate to oppose Lord Ragnar's ambition. He cannot fold to intimidation. Can you not see what path he'll lead us down? How he'll doom Baegard?"

She cut off, for the women's stares told her she sounded too shrill. *Control. You must seem in control.* It was the last thing she felt as she sensed her plans teetering on the edge of collapse, yet she reached for it all the same.

"What I mean is," Aelthena continued, deliberately slowing her speech, "Lord Siward must be the Arkjarl, and we four are the ones who must accomplish it. If the majority are in favor of Siward's election, Hother and Petyr might be swayed as well, and even Ragnar would be forced to yield."

"Perhaps," Sigrid broke in. "Or perhaps our opposition

would lead to no Arkjarl being chosen at all, and Baegard lacking a leader."

"Aelthena," Nanna said, her broad brow knitting together, "I am afraid I must agree. When Ragnar has such support, who are we to sow dissent?"

Aelthena tried to ignore the frantic racing of her heart as she looked at Iona. "And you? Do you feel the same?"

Iona's gaze flickered to the other two, then she turned a small smile back to Aelthena. "I am sorry to disappoint you, Aelthena. But I cannot think Ragnar's leadership will be as disastrous as you claim. The Arkjarl does not wield supreme authority; he is only the first among equals. Baegard will endure this war and thrive once more, never fear. I more than anyone wish this!"

Despair made her head ache. She wanted to cry. *Will it be enough?* No telling until she tried. *I'm sorry, Bastor.* If she could have convinced them without breaking her oath to him, she would have. But now, there was no other choice.

She spread a smile over her lips. "I think I have information that will convince you otherwise."

The women had grown meek with their apologies. At this announcement, however, each perked up with interest.

"Well?" Sigrid said impatiently. "Don't keep us dangling from the hook."

Aelthena met the woman's dark eyes. "What I am about to say must not leave this room. Only tell your husbands. Do you agree?"

Sigrid was the first to nod. Iona followed next, eyes bright with eagerness. Nanna frowned, but sighed and said, "If it must be so."

"Thank you." Aelthena leaned forward slightly, drawing their attention even tighter to her. "Now then. You know of the dragonfire that took my home?"

The women murmured their affirmations.

"It seems Ragnar has been keeping secrets from us. For he possesses the very substance behind that sorcery."

At once, the jarls' wives burst out in exclamations.

"Dragonfire!" Iona's hand strayed to her mouth. "Can such sorcery be controlled?"

"A substance..." Nanna shook her head. "I do not understand, Aelthena."

Sigrid was most insistent of all. "You can't be saying what I think you are. That Ragnar attacked Oakharrow."

Aelthena held up her hands. Her heart hammered against her ribs at the volume of their words. "Please, my dear ladies, we must speak softly. I am not saying Ragnar attacked Oakharrow with dragonfire." *Though that would not be far wrong,* she thought, but kept the words silent. It would be difficult enough for them to believe what she said without throwing treachery into the mix. "What I am saying is he has kept an important tool for our defense secret for his own ambitions. With firesand, as he calls this substance, we can protect ourselves against the Syptens and the Jotun. Even with inferior numbers, this sorcery will even the odds."

Sigrid crossed her arms and sat back in her chair, her frown never leaving. "He means to hold Baegard hostage."

She glowed with the words, especially as Nanna and Iona seemed to seize upon them. "It is criminal!" Iona cried, bobbing her son vigorously in her excitement. "Or close to it!"

"It is," Aelthena affirmed, dropping her voice so the others had to quiet to hear her. "And he must not be allowed to get away with it."

"Where did you hear this, Aelthena?" Sigrid asked. "I imagine Ragnar himself did not volunteer it."

Aelthena inclined her head toward the Lady of Skjold. "From one who would know: Ragnar's heir, Alabastor."

Nanna muttered what sounded like a prayer under her breath. Iona shook her head, while Sigrid smiled.

"You believe him? I know you traveled with him from Oakharrow, but he never seemed a trustworthy man."

Aelthena paused, considering how to answer that. *Trustworthy* hardly seemed the right word for Bastor, though he came closer to it than appearances would have led her to believe.

"I trust him in this," she said at last. "He told me it in confidence to convince me to support his father. And I do not think he would lie to me besides."

They were bending to her will; she could see it in their faltering expressions. *It's working.* Aelthena had to fight hard to ward away a smile.

"I will tell you all I know," she said after a moment's pause. "But before I continue, I must ask: do I have your support? Will you speak to your husbands about voting for Lord Siward?"

Aelthena looked at them, and one by one, they spoke their agreement. Now she afforded herself a small smile. *Four. That's four on our side.* The balance was shifting. Once the truth was revealed to the others, they would fall to her plans.

Soon, the right man would wear the Iron Circle. And she would be the one to have placed it.

Once the jarls' wives were gone, Aelthena thanked and dismissed the thrall who had attended them, then returned to the balcony. The day held a crisp beauty, yet a heaviness grew in her limbs, souring it. She leaned on the railing and frowned as she squinted against the sunlight.

"Ah, what the poets would say of your expression just now."

She had sensed Frey standing by her for the past minute, yet Aelthena had chosen to ignore him. She yearned for solitude, yet her tongue refused to make the request.

She finally looked at him and took in his features. Petyrsholm was not treating him well. His eyes were more sunken, his skin sallower, and the crow's feet more pronounced in the corners of his eyes. His hair resembled straw rather than sunlight. The chainmail and gambeson he wore was leftover from the Elkhorn, and though he had polished it, rusted metal could only shine so brightly.

Yet for all that, when she looked into his eyes, she found them as bright and alluring as she ever had.

"You'll tell me to smile now, won't you?" she murmured.

One of Frey's eyebrows shot up. "And why would I do that, when your frowns might inspire songs? No, m'lady — your sadness is to me as happiness might be to another man."

His impishness finally infected her. With a rueful laugh, she turned from the balcony and faced him. He stood only feet away, yet even that felt too far. She ached to close the distance between them.

"I suppose I am acting forlorn."

A smile claimed half his mouth. "A bit. Especially since it's for a man I despise."

"It's just..." She turned her head aside, trying to hide the tears suddenly welling in her eyes. "I have broken too many promises as it is, Frey. It's not about Bastor. It's..."

"I know."

Then he was there, taking her into his arms, though anyone might look up at them and see it. And she let him. Aelthena folded into his embrace, ignoring the hardness of his armor and how the polish would rub off on her dress. She needed him, needed him pressed against her, like he were an anchor and she a ship in a storm. She clung to him, and though the waves did not stop hammering against her, she could endure them.

"Aelthena," he whispered into her hair. His hand brushed down her spine.

It was enough to send her back to that moment. That night in the forest.

She had left camp, ignoring the questions of her companions, drowning in the depths of her failures. She stumbled through the dark trees, panic rising in her, an implacable flood that she could keep at bay no longer. Always, she had sought to claim control of the world, but at every turn, it belittled her efforts.

Then he appeared.

Frey took her into his arms. When she clung to him, he kissed the top of her head. But it was *she* who turned her head up and pressed her lips against his, she who pushed him against the tree, she whose hands traveled over his clothes, under them.

That night, she had claimed back some control. Frey had offered something she desired deeply, and she had taken it. It had been the gift she needed. She never regretted it, even as she later pretended it had not happened.

But she had never forgotten.

Now, that same stirring began in her belly. Aelthena moved her hands up Frey's back and into his hair, fingers grasping a hold. She turned her head up and pressed her lips against his. Their kiss grew more insistent, their bodies moving together with it. She imagined dragging him over to the bedchamber, so close by, and claiming once more—

She released him.

Frey's hands loosened, his brow knitting together.

Aelthena stepped back and turned her head aside. She saw the hurt in his expression before he hid it.

"Aelthena?" was all he said.

"We can't." There was more to say. To explain. But it took all her strength just to deny him. "Please, Frey. Let me have a moment."

He did not depart immediately, but stared at her, perhaps wondering at her abrupt changes in mood. She hoped he could forgive her. It wasn't fair; none of this was fair. But it was the way it had to be. Asborn remained her betrothed, her ally, her friend. She could not compromise that.

Even if it meant robbing herself of the one good thing remaining to her.

In the end, he left without a word. It was for the best. No words could make things right. Aelthena sagged against the railing and sighed out to the wind, wishing it could carry her or her worries away.

19. THE PATH FORWARD

"But if we endure... if, somehow, we prevail... there is sun still, there is light. Not all burns leave scars. Past the winter is life, a Honeyed Aeon, and it shall last so long as we remember it might end."

- Torvald Geirson, the Last King of Baegard

During some of his free afternoons after his lessons with Mother Sign, Bjorn wandered the lengths of Heim Numen.

Ordinarily, he would have gone to the library under the pretense of researching more of the Witterland Prophecy and the writings surrounding it. But after his glimpse of Tyra in the baths, he had become shier. Every time he saw her, the memory flashed back into his mind, and the shame rose with it. So he had taken to avoiding her. After all, nothing could ever happen between them.

Yet it did not stop him from longing to see her.

But there was always something of interest occurring on

the grounds. In the courtyard, off-duty sentries sparred and kept their skills sharp. He could often find Loridi and Seskef there, though Bjorn observed them chatting as frequently as they swung the wooden wasters used for practice.

Other times, he visited the stables and took Clap out for a jaunt. Though the wind was still bitterly cold on his face, it seemed to numb the thoughts in his mind, and the gelding enjoyed them, tossing his head and prancing in the remaining snow. Each time he went for a ride, the sentries at the town's entrances warned him to remain wary. Men's tracks had been seen in the area, and they did not belong to Sprallmen or gothi. Bjorn wondered if they belonged to the Jotun's men or the Skyardi, or perhaps another tribe he did not know. Either way, he saw no signs of strangers while he was out, and it only heightened the thrill of the rides.

In the buildings, a different sort of instruction occurred. Huddled in a cloister off the back of the dining hall, Bjorn heard a gothi telling young acolytes of the history of the Inscribed. Other enclosed places boasted more advanced classes. In steam chambers, priests and ascetics meditated, some in preparation for their vision quests, others to commune with the gods. These places, Bjorn avoided. He had enough exposure to *khnuum* without suffering further doses.

At the Etching Wall, newly inducted priests added their contributions to the foot of Yewung. Bjorn wandered up and down it, admiring the artistry of some and smiling at the clumsy efforts of others. The more skillful carvings were identifiable at a glance. Djur, half-morphed into a snarling greatbear. Nuvvog, with the face of a man but the slitted eyes and forked tongue of a dragon. Baltur wielded his quill, Volkur her spear, and Mostur his forge hammer.

He wondered what the Inscribed thought of the state of their world now, and if they prepared for the coming war in their own way. If it was the Eternal Night falling, as Bjorn was beginning to suspect, then surely even the gods would fight. Yet he had seen no sign of them.

They work through their servants, he reminded himself. *They will not kill the Jotun for you.*

Still, he wished it could be so. How they would kill the giant was beyond his knowing.

He moved on. As in any community, there were the ordinary and necessary goings-on: the preparation of food, the caretaking of livestock, the repair of leaking roofs and decrepit walls. But behind Heim Numen's fences, roles lacked their usual gender assignments. Women chopped wood, and men scrubbed laundry. All was done according to need.

Bjorn looked around at it all and breathed it in: the hay and the musk, the steam and the scents of cooking. He imagined what it would be like to smell that concoction every day. Would it always bring him joy, as it did then?

Could I belong here?

All his childhood, all his life, he had never felt he belonged anywhere. Something in him differed from others, like the stalks of their souls stood straight while his was bent. Now, he had a small glimpse of what that difference was, with his being *Volur*, but knowledge could only carry him so far. He wanted to be part of a community that knew him and accepted him. He wondered if here, among the priests and the people who assisted them, he could at last find that.

"Bjorn."

He startled and spun, feeling foolish, yet a little less as he recognized who stood behind him. Yonik grinned sheepishly at him from beneath his greatbear hood, and Bjorn returned it.

"Ever thought to walk louder, for others' sakes?" he asked the priest.

Yonik shrugged. "As many a drunkard will tell you, habits are hard to break. But come; there is something I'd like to show you."

Bjorn eyed the man, his gaze drawn to the satchels he clutched in both hands. One of them bulged with what looked like sticks, while the other one might have contained stones. After a moment, he only nodded and followed the priest. Once, the mysterious invitation might have spooked him. But Yonik had guided him this far; he would not doubt him now.

His resolve did waver, however, as Yonik led him past the Etching Wall and beyond the boundaries of Heim Numen to trek through the thick drifts of snow surrounding Eildursprall. Bjorn paused before the trees and eyed the trampled path before posing his question.

"Where are we headed, old wolf?"

The gothi turned back with a wry smile. "I wondered how long it would take you to ask. Sometimes, I think you ought to be less trusting, Bjorn. Even of me."

"An odd thing to say when you're leading me into gloomy woods."

Yonik laughed, then turned back to the path. "It's not far. We go with purpose, I can tell you that. And it is an ambush of sorts, though only a slight one."

More perplexed than ever, Bjorn trailed behind the priest once again. The going was hard, each step requiring him to lift his leg above his knees only to sink down into more snow. His boots and pants grew wet and cold, and the wool rubbed in the beginning of blisters. But he did not complain; he'd endured far worse.

At last, as they came to a cliff adjacent to Yewung's domineering face, the priest stopped. "In here," he said, then ducked beneath a large stone archway into the shadows beyond.

Bjorn studied the alcove as he slowly entered. It was a shallow cave, a crook in the cliff where it leaned over enough to provide shelter. Yonik crouched in the far corner of it before a blackened circle of stones. He wondered to what purpose a fire pit would be here, so close to town.

Then he remembered that night in the mountains, when they had sought the Jotun and his encampment, and instinctual fear struck through him.

"You wish me to use the Sight." Bjorn stated it as fact, certain of his conclusion.

Yonik glanced up from arranging sticks into a conical structure. "Yes. I do."

"But I train with it every day. Mother Sign has warned against Seeing too often. How some doors, once opened, won't close again."

"And she is wise to warn of it."

Yonik finished arranging the bonfire and struck his flint onto his firesteel. It was not long before the tinder caught and merry flames expanded across the kindling.

Bjorn drew no closer, but only watched the mesmerizing spread of the fire. "I trust you, Yonik. But I don't want to trust you blindly right now."

"Nor would I expect you to." Yonik straightened and approached. Reaching into his second satchel, he brought out two round objects. "Recognize these?"

Bjorn took the smooth stones in hand and tried not to wince as he looked at the shapes inscribed on their faces. "Runestones. *Forsja* and *gramur* — Mend and Frenzy."

"Yes. They are the two runestones most useful for our cause."

Bjorn raised his head to meet Yonik's gaze. "How do you have these? If I know Mother Sign, she wouldn't give them up willingly. Not for this."

The gothi flashed that wide smile in which peril always prowled. "I have my ways."

"Stealing?"

Yonik's grin faded. "I know it must seem odd, perhaps even wrong. But Bjorn, we cannot do everything as they wish us to. Even Mother Sign, zealous in her own right, moves too slowly in your training. If we are to influence the future, then you must be adept, truly capable, in the Sight. Trust me in this."

Blood pounded in Bjorn's skull. *Defying the Silvers. Walking the Hall of Doors on my own.* He had yearned to do that very thing as he lay on his cot at night, staring at the dark ceiling and recalling his lessons. In the month she mentored him in *seidar*, Mother Sign had not progressed him beyond practicing Heartfire. It was tedious work, though not without its rewards, for he could now hold his door steady for nearly an hour. She had even taught him to open the Silver's door through their shared connection of the magic, a thing he had not realized was possible.

And Yonik was right: from all he had learned of these two runes, Frenzy and Mend would be helpful indeed when it came time to leave Eildursprall. With a lifetime of training behind him, Frenzy might make him into the warrior he had glimpsed in Chasm Valley, removing all the doubts and fears that slowed his strikes and befuddled his focus. And to heal from his wounds — that such a thing was possible still astounded Bjorn to his bones.

But though the impulsive part of him wanted to seize hold of the stones and use them then and there, the cautious part hesitated. Bjorn tried to hide his conflicted feelings behind raised eyebrows.

"I thought I was too trusting of you."

Yonik's smile returned. "I did say that. But maybe, just this once, you can make an exception."

Bjorn knew there could be only one answer. He had seized upon his quest of vengeance, pursuing the Jotun into the Teeth. Though it had mostly proven to be folly, killing Keld and Summer and so many others, it had led him to where he was now, where he might change the fate of his jarlheim. Once more, he had to leap and hope the gods would catch him.

He nodded. "Fine. We'll do it."

Some of the tension left Yonik's face. "Good. I'll finish the preparations, then we'll begin."

The priest did not take long. Yonik stoked the flames hotter and higher and heated the drascale ore he placed among them. While he waited, Bjorn recalled all he knew of runelore. When the gothi motioned him over, Bjorn tried to ignore his churning stomach and stepped up next to him. The evening's golden glow emanated through the pine needles, but was beginning to fade, and the dancing orange light illuminated Yonik's face.

The priest gestured to the ground opposite him, his expression grim. "Best that you sit. No telling how you might fall otherwise."

Bjorn complied, tucking his legs under him and trying to ignore the wetness seeping through his pants. A bit more discomfort was the least of his concerns now.

"Which one should we start with?"

The gothi glanced up from prying the ore free of the flames. "Which do you think?"

A moment's contemplation gave him the answer. "Mend."

Yonik nodded. Bjorn hoped the priest did not realize

that conclusion had largely come from fear. The effects that Frenzy was supposed to confer scared him as much as they intrigued him. How much presence of mind would he keep? He had lost control once and nearly killed a man innocent of any crime but performing his duties. Would he strike at Yonik under its influence? Could he stop himself?

But it was not the time to find out. He set the stone to one side and cradled the Mend runestone in both hands.

"As it will heal," Yonik said, "I suggest you focus on fixing that cut Mother Sign gave you."

Bjorn twisted his arm to glance at his injury. It was scabbed over, for it had been days since he nearly stepped through Heartfire's door. It seemed a simple enough wound to fix.

"Alright," he said as he raised his gaze. "Best get on with it."

The priest raised the flask of water he carried on his hip and tilted it over the hot stone. With a hiss, steam erupted from it. Bjorn closed his eyes and leaned in, then breathed deeply of it. The hot vapor seemed to pop on his skin as it washed over and through him.

I'm ready, he thought as he opened his eyes and gazed upon the rune with its piercing touch. *As ready as I'll ever be. Forsja. Forsja. Mend. Mend.*

A key seemed to turn in his mind. All at once, Bjorn stood once more in the shadowy Hall of Doors.

He stared at the door, rippling like the surface of the water. The rune inscribed upon its face arrested him for a long moment before he reached for the handle. He pulled. The door resisted his efforts, stubbornly remaining closed. He pulled harder, and this time, it relented, opening a crack. From it poured so many sensations that Bjorn could barely keep track of them. Fresh scents curled his nose:

juniper, mint, winterlily. A cooling feeling swept through him, raising his skin in gooseflesh. Realizing that the Seeing was taking effect, Bjorn focused on the itching remainder of his wound, willing the energy sweeping through him toward it.

Forsja, he thought again. *Mend. Mend my wound.*

At once, his will was obeyed. The power coalesced at the point of his scab, and another host of strange sensations greeted him there: numbing and itching, burning and cooling.

Abruptly, they ceased.

Bjorn's eyes were lost to the Hall, but his sense of touch remained. He felt the skin along his forearm and felt nothing of the wound. No scab, no scar — nothing.

He smiled. *I healed.*

The effects of Mend still washed through him. Part of him longed for it to never end. Yet Bjorn had learned more self-control than to relent to that. With a shove, he pressed the door closed.

Bjorn closed his eyes and focused on his other senses, grounding him in the real world. When he opened his eyes, he sat before the fire again, Yonik leaning toward him with an eager expression.

"Did it work?" The priest's eyes had gathered the luminescence of a wolf's, as they sometimes did. "Did you mend?"

Bjorn's answer was to pull up his sleeve and turn over his arm. There, plain even by the flickering firelight, his skin was unblemished.

A grin split through Yonik's generous beard. "By Skoll, Bjorn. I had hoped it would be true, but until now..." He reached across the fire and took Bjorn's arm in hand, examining his skin as if the restoration might be a trick of the light. "Think of the good that might be done with such power."

Bjorn, however, was having trouble attending to the priest's words. A wave of vertigo rushed over him.

The world toppled.

"Bjorn. Bjorn! Damn my enthusiasm... are you well?"

He was staring at the fire, but it moved sideways rather than up. Abruptly, it was corrected as Yonik gripped his shoulders and brought him upright. Bjorn blinked through a rush of blood from his head. He thought he might faint, but the priest kept him straight until the sensation subsided. When he could see again, he met the priest's gaze and nodded, and Yonik released him.

"What happened?"

Bjorn shook his head. "Just a head rush, that's all. And I..." He placed a hand to his stomach as it audibly growled. "I think I'm hungry."

"Hm." Yonik peered into Bjorn's eyes, one at a time. "It appears Mend drains one's resources to speed up the healing process. I suppose it only makes sense, though it limits the application. If that is your reaction with a minor cut, how much greater would it be for a mortal wound?"

Without waiting for an answer, Yonik rose and paced behind the fire. Bjorn let him mull over it and stared into the flames. Though the hunger remained, the dizziness swiftly dissipated. As it did, excitement bubbled up, and he peered again at where his injury had been.

I healed myself. I used the Sight on my own.

He was one of the few *Volur* alive, and he was only just seeing what that meant. It was not only glimpses of the future; it was unlocking human potential in every way.

What else am I capable of?

Once, he had not thought he had the potential for anything notable. Now, he could perform miracles. He needed to know more. He needed to master this, the risks be damned.

If not for the good it might do, then for himself.

Bjorn spoke into the silence that had fallen upon their shallow cave. "Maybe it only happened because it's my first time. Maybe, with practice, I can manage it better."

Yonik paused as he turned again, staring down at him. "Maybe."

"We'll try it again." Bjorn reached down to his waist and tugged free his belt knife, then set it to the spot he had just healed. "See how I react the second time—"

"Bjorn, wait!"

Yonik's tone gave him pause. His brow crinkling, Bjorn looked up at the priest and startled at the alarm in his expression. "What?" he demanded. "What is it?"

"Are you truly well? You just collapsed. Perhaps we should attempt this another time."

Bjorn was shaking his head before the gothi finished speaking. "No, Yonik. It's just as you said — there's no time for hesitation. So I almost fainted and am a bit famished. It's far from killing me, or even harming me. Right?"

The priest seemed to consider his words. "True," he admitted.

Bjorn pressed the knife to his skin again, warm with triumph. "Then I'll try it again." A smile twisted his lips. "Just be ready to catch me."

Even as Yonik snorted a laugh, Bjorn cut the blade across his skin. Blood, dark in the gloom, bubbled up from the small gash at once, and pain accompanied it. He had to fight the urge to stem the flow of it as it beaded down the side of his arm, instead setting down the knife and picking up the runestone. Yonik was already pouring water over the still-hot drascale ore, and Bjorn leaned in for another breath of *khnuum* steam.

Forsja. Mend.

The Hall of Doors came more easily the second time. Bjorn glanced up and down the murky hall, then focused on the door that again appeared before him. Hauling at it, he found it took only a small tug to open, and he accidentally opened it wider than he meant to. The chill washed over him twice as strong as before, and the scents filled his head so he could barely think. But he had trained for this. Bjorn fixated his mind on his purpose, channeling the power that poured through him toward his fresh wound. The process stretched longer, the itching protracted, yet it still took only moments before the signs of healing faded.

Bjorn closed the door again and dismissed the Hall of Doors, then blinked through his hazy vision to peer at his arm. Blood was still wet upon it, but as he wiped at it with his gloved hand, he saw it was only from the before.

The injury had entirely healed, leaving not a seam or scratch behind.

A grin spread across his face even as his balance again pitched him sideways. Through the nauseating sea of it, Bjorn took comfort in what he'd accomplished. Only moments passed before the weakness receded and he sat back up.

Yonik kneeled next to him, a steadying hand on his shoulder. His eyes studied him carefully. "You're well?"

Bjorn nodded, still not trusting his dinner would not come up if he opened his mouth. At the same time, hunger kicked him in the gut, nearly doubling him over with its urgency.

"Food," he grunted.

"Right you are — only I didn't bring any with me. Just give me a moment, then we can go track some down."

Bjorn was content to watch the priest clean up evidence of their camp, kicking dirt onto the fire and packing up the runestones and drascale ore. This last proved difficult to do, yet with a stick and his sack, Yonik hauled it back into his bag. When all was ready, he moved back to Bjorn and offered his free hand. Bjorn took it, and his body felt light as a cloud as he came to his feet. Yet his spirit was lighter still.

Whatever came next, he walked the right path.

20. TEETERING TOWERS

"Thralls are the sorriest bastards in this blasted land, and that's coming from me!"

- Erik the Fist to his band, the Red Berserkers

When he tired of drinking alone in his room, Bastor ventured to the kitchens.

He could have easily summoned a thrall to serve him. As a jarl's heir, every servant in Lord Petyr's employ was at his disposal. Yet, unless at a feast or other event where it was not possible, Bastor avoided their use.

But he did not shirk their company.

He nodded to the huskarls along the way and ignored their knowing smirks; it was not the first time he had fetched libations that day. Bastor almost maintained an air of dignity while walking the stone corridors. It was only after three highborn daughters giggled to each other that he thought to examine himself. There, in the center of his chest, blossomed a wide yellow stain, courtesy of the cask of mead he had finished earlier that morning.

His lips twisted. *Truly a man of precision. It's a wonder I managed to kill that man.*

At the thought, his stomach bucked. Bastor swallowed hard and managed a queasy smile at a disapproving highborn woman passing him by. *Lady Audhild,* he realized belatedly. It would have been best to greet her, especially as her husband was one of his father's captains.

Only then did he entertain the possibility that he was drunker than he'd first thought.

Yet as he pushed through the kitchen door, he checked and was glad he had remembered the most important part of his errand. His parcel clanked softly together in his coat pocket, its bulk a comforting weight.

No matter how rumpled and stained his clothes, this would be the key to what he sought.

The din of the kitchens washed over him as he entered. Bastor paused and took in the bustle with a bemused smile. Junior servants hauled wood and stoked fires, fetched ingredients, and chopped vegetables and fruits. Cooks, a rung up on the ladder, prepared chicken and mutton with skillful precision, carving meat from bones and dicing it for stew. Over all, though nearly the shortest among them, was positioned the head cook, Pyhia. She barked commands like a general on the field of battle, and her staff obeyed as if they truly were soldiers.

As swiftly as Bastor's amusement came, it faded. The runes branded into their faces were a stark reminder for whose comfort these thralls toiled.

Those closest to him flinched at the sight of highborn clothes in their domain, but as their eyes flickered to his face, smiles replaced the fear. Many nodded or called greetings to him, and Bastor felt a slackening in his shoulders and a grin spreading over his lips.

To his peers, the approval of the kitchen staff was never a consideration. To him, it was all.

"Ah, you're back. Another refill?"

Bastor turned to find Pyhia with her hands propped on her generous hips, her usual scowl claiming her countenance as her gaze drifted to the stain on his shirt. "You" was about as much of a name as he could eke from her once he insisted she stop with the "m'lords." *Still, I'll take what I can.*

He was more surprised to find Uljana next to her. The jarl's attendant had her usual wariness gathered about her like a cloak as she looked at him. Though he wished he could crack her icy walls, he had long ago given up that battle.

"Not this time, Pyhia Faa." Bastor jerked his head toward a curtained-off section in the back of the kitchens. "Here on a different errand."

The cook's scowl grew more pronounced. "They'll begin to reek with how you spoil them!"

"They could use some spoiling."

That softened Pyhia some. For all her hard manners, she had a soft spot for children. Uljana almost seemed less distant as well, though he knew it could well be his imagination.

He summoned a fresh grin. "I'll be about it then. And while I'm here, ease off the salt, would you? I'm getting sores in my mouth."

Pyhia threatened him with a hand, and Bastor laughed and skirted away, hands held up. Before sliding off, he nodded to Uljana and greeted her by name. He expected no response, so when she did, he stumbled to a halt.

"Semat."

His eloquence failed him then. "Pardon?"

The attendant had a fierce look in her expression then. "My birth name is not Uljana. It is Semat."

Semat. Of course. All this time, he had neglected to wonder if a Djurian name like "Uljana" truly belonged to her. He had assumed she had been born in Baegard. That she admitted she had an older, truer name to him spoke volumes.

He bowed his head to her. "It is good to meet you at last."

A fraction of a smile curled the corners of her lips, then Semat turned her head aside. Pyhia looked between them.

"Odd couple, you two." The head cook shooed him. "But off with you! Kitchen doesn't run itself."

Bastor gave her a mutinous smile. "But you haven't given me the latest filth."

Though he had primarily cultivated his friendships down here for his own pleasure, Bastor had never done much for just one reason. A castle's staff heard far more than any highborn suspected, and in a life otherwise full of tedium, gossip spread fire-quick. Things he had learned down here had been critical in his intimidation attempt, and might be useful in the future.

But Pyhia only waved her hands. "Not now, not now — I must be about my duties, and you your errand."

Bastor had to relent to that. With a last farewell, he slipped through the bustle until he reached the pantry. There, he pulled aside the curtain and found the sight he'd been expecting. Three young children, two boys and one girl, sat in a huddle on the stone floor. They seemed to be arguing over something, and a sackcloth doll was being tugged to pieces between them.

"Hold on one moment!" Bastor boomed as he loomed over them, hands on his hips. "Gray gods, but what's happening here?"

The children, none older than six, were cowed at once, yet he noted none of them released the toy.

"Bastor Faa!" the girl piped up. "They're hurting my Pawura!" Bennu had her hair drawn up in twin tails that erupted from her head like a woolith's horns. Her face was small and round, while the gaps from her missing teeth were large.

He barely repressed a smile. An inexplicable warmth spread through his chest every time the children referred to him as they might an uncle. Instead, he pretended to be disapproving and raised an eyebrow. "Last I remember, that doll was named Gazabe, and it belonged to Neith."

Bennu scowled, while his support bolstered the courage of the boys.

"Listen to your elders, Bennu," the second boy, Soben, said with smug triumph. "Give it back!"

"But you said I could—" the girl protested, but Neith spoke over her.

"The Divine burn liars — *alive.* Do you want to burn, Bennu?"

"Enough." Bastor took a step farther into the room and glowered down at the children. To his amusement, they proved only slightly cowed. In the weeks that he'd been visiting their little sanctuary, they had grown to understand neither his size nor deep voice held any genuine threat.

Before they could resurrect their argument, he continued. "No one's burning for fibs. Liars, however, would get five whacks in the rear from Kiya Faa were she to hear of this."

The three children stiffened. The so-called grandmother of the young thrall was not known for holding back when disciplining with a wooden ladle. All of them stared up at him, wide-eyed, awaiting their condemnation.

Bastor smiled, and the corners of his mouth tugged wider still when their narrow shoulders relaxed. "I think I have a better solution. Bennu, release the doll and come here. Boys, mind you don't play anymore tricks on her, or a spoon awaits your backsides."

The boys bobbed their heads and retreated with their prize. Soon, they returned to giggling and whispering confidentially as they passed the ragged plaything back and forth.

He looked down at a tug on his coat. "Uncle? Why'd you make me give up Pawura?" asked Bennu, hope bubbling from every word.

Bastor crouched before the girl. "Because I have something better for you. Something I've made myself."

Her eyes went wide as he rustled in his pocket and began producing one piece after another. Blocks, wooden and rectangular, collected in a messy pile before him, each the same in size and smooth on their edges. Soon, there were two score mounded between them. Bennu stared, her hands hovering above them, but not daring to reach out.

"When I was your age," he said, "a man from the fields gave me a set of blocks like these. I spent many hours and days stacking them, and they brought me joy and comfort." He settled a hand on the back of the girl's head, and his chest sang when she did not flinch from his touch. "I hope these might do the same for you, Bennu."

The boys stared, jealousy aflame in their eyes. The girl's delight grew with their envy, and she scooped them up between her legs to lift and examine them.

"They're mine?" she asked tentatively, hardly daring to believe such a thing could be true. A thrall child had very few possessions.

He nodded. "All yours."

"Why does she get blocks and we don't?" Neith protested.

Soben shook the doll. "All we have is this old thing!"

Bastor raised his eyebrows at the boys. "But I thought you wanted it bad enough to lie for?"

As the lads grew sulky, he loosed his grin. "None of that, boys. You'll have your own sets soon enough — but only if you leave Bennu's blocks be. Understood?"

They remained reluctant. "When?" ventured Neith.

Bastor pretended to look disapproving, though he doubted it was convincing with a smile quirking his lips. "I've snuck you both plenty of sweetmoons, haven't I? I'm good for my word!"

At that, the boys relented, both bobbing their heads. Bastor reached out and rubbed their hair roughly, provoking laughing objections from them. He glanced at Bennu and found her smiling as well.

Peace had been restored to the pantry. *Isn't it a wonder that I forged it?* It was more good than he'd expected to bring to Petyrsholm.

"Lord Heir? A moment, if you please."

At the address, his fleeting escape shattered. Bastor slowly stood and turned around, comporting himself as the man expected by the courier. Gone was the generous block-carver the children called uncle. Gone was the highborn bastard who walked among the thralls and was welcomed into their fold.

The Heir to Ragnarsglade had returned. A part of Bastor hated himself for it.

"Yes?" he all but snapped. "What is it?"

The poor man, a Sypten thrall like so many of the servants, did not flinch at the unfair treatment. His face was glass-smooth as he spoke. "Lady Heir Aelthena Of'Bor wishes you to attend her chambers at your earliest convenience."

At any other time, he would have been intrigued by the summons. Yet chagrin had joined his self-loathing at his rudeness, and highborn politics were the last thing he wished to attend to.

But a jarl's heir did not apologize to servants. And now he saw that pretending to be anything else was futile. The kitchen staff was darting looks at him, their backs stiff and their eyes downcast. In one moment, all the trust he had worked so hard to gain had dissipated. Bastor glanced behind at the children in the pantry and found their reactions much the same. His only comfort was that Bennu still clutched his set of blocks to her chest. That, at least, had done some good.

It was not enough. Bastor closed his eyes and tried to still the swimming of his vision. He had wallowed in delusion for long enough. Sypten blood ran through his veins, but his pedigree was true. He could never belong among the servants.

He had killed a man, but he had killed many before. That this one had been in cold blood made no difference.

What's done is done, he told himself, and tried to believe it. He needed to erase the past to survive what was coming. He had to play the highborn games and forget about blocks burned to ashes long ago. It was time to take his place among his peers.

Bastor drew himself up to his full, imposing height and looked down on the courier. "If the Lady Heir wishes to see me, she can find me in my room."

With that, he strode away, not sparing a backward glance. He had ale and mead to spare in his chambers, and Aelthena would not take long in coming to visit. *I hope,* he thought with a bitter smile as he swept from the kitchens, wondering if he would ever return.

21. A THROW OF BONES

The bonewomen of the barbarian tribes claim to see all likely futures in their castings. That a throw of knuckle-bones will land in significant constellations, mirroring the stars whose meanings are clear only to them.

Though most claims must be held in suspicion, I do not doubt there are true seers among them. For just as Volur are born among Djurians, so might they exist in these savage peoples.

- The Seven Jarlheims of Baegard, by Sister Torhild Of'Yusala

Aelthena drew in a breath as she and Asborn came abreast of the door.

"Are you ready?" he murmured, settling a hand on her shoulder.

She immediately regretted her show of weakness and straightened. "Of course."

Asborn frowned slightly at that, but he only rapped lightly on the wood.

A servant answered moments later, a wan girl who looked no older than Bjorn. She silently prayed to the Fates that he was still alive as they stepped within. Aelthena glanced back at Frey, who had accompanied them as he always did, and muttered to him, "Remain at the door, if you would."

He nodded, eyes bright with understanding. With Bastor loose in the castle, and perhaps other assassins among them, every trip outside the room carried its risks, as the guardian well knew.

She turned back and, ignoring Asborn's glance, stepped up next to him into the chambers. There was no forgetting the jarl was known as the Black Ram in here. Every bit of cloth displayed his insignia: the drapes, the arrases, even the tablecloth. She suspected that was Iona's doing; Siward didn't seem a man to care for finery or finesse.

"Lady Heir Aelthena, Thane Asborn." Siward rose to greet them. He wore much the same garb as usual, his arms rattling with gold and silver, his gambeson and chainmail both as dark as his name. His blunt face did not shift into friendliness, but remained hard and lined as he regarded them.

"Lord Siward," Aelthena replied with more graciousness. "Thank you for accepting our invitation." She gave the room a brief, significant glance. "Is Lady Iona not joining us?"

"She is not. The young one is occupying her attention today." The Jarl of Greenwuud sat without first inviting them to, as would have been proper, then stared at them in silence.

Aelthena tried to ignore the inauspicious signs as she sat and Asborn followed suit. This was her chance to make sure things proceeded smoothly. Neither she nor Baegard could afford a slip now.

"Lord Siward," she began, "I understand that you're having some hesitancy about keeping in the running for the Iron Circle."

Siward only continued to stare at her with baleful eyes. It took all her self-restraint to wait with her hands tucked in her lap.

"Yes," the jarl responded at length. "My wife told you, I suppose."

She summoned a bracing smile. "She did. We women are concerned about the fate of our nation. I hope it is not too late to sway you to my way of thinking."

"No doubt." Siward might have been commenting on the movements of the clouds for all his interest.

Still, she persisted. "You're the best candidate for the position, Lord Siward. You have experience as a battle commander. You have faced the Syptens over a wall of bronze spear tips. And you are respected up and down the valley for your prideful heart and unfailing courage."

A laugh broke free of the Jarl of Greenwuud as he turned to stare into the flames. Aelthena watched him, the knot of worry in her stomach growing tighter. She had known from Iona that Siward was having some hesitations about still striving to be the Arkjarl. But she had not known the depths of those doubts.

"Did I say something amusing?" she asked lightly.

Siward swiveled his gaze back toward her. "My pride. They say my pride is as strong and unbending as iron. Yet here I am, casting it aside."

She wanted to shake the man by the shoulders. It seemed as likely as any platitude to break the man loose of his fears. Yet Aelthena remained in her seat, letting the silence be the hook and line that drew the stolid man out.

Siward chuckled again, the sound full of anything but amusement. His eyes stared, unblinking, into hers. "You are a well-informed woman, Lady Heir Aelthena. So I am sure you have heard of the threats to my daughter, Helka."

She nodded slowly. "I have. But if that is what gives you pause—"

"My children are everything to me," he interrupted, his voice choked. He swallowed hard and looked back into the fireplace. "Next to my daughters, pride is worth less than an empty sack of grain. Even so, I would cling to it if not for the morning's report."

She had to resist fidgeting with her braid. "Report? What report?"

"We heard nothing before we came," Asborn added.

Lord Siward looked up again, his eyebrows raised. "You do not know? The Sypten army is here, in the valley. Fairglen has fallen."

Fallen. Aelthena had only seen Fairglen as a small dot on a map, yet it had often been mentioned because of its strategic importance. Fairglen was the first major outpost along the Whiterun leading into the Baegardian valley. It was supposed to house a generous garrison of three hundred shields. If it had fallen, it meant Ha-Sypt had come with far more than a raiding party.

She shook her head, trying to reorient her thoughts. Everything had changed, but her priorities remained the same. "This makes it even more vital that you wear the Iron Circle. Baegard needs you at its head, Lord Siward. Now more than ever."

"The Arkjarl must be elected by a unanimous vote," Lord Siward said in his grating voice. "All seven jarls — or their representatives — must pledge their sword to one man. And Lord Ragnar has his eyes set on it."

Her hands betrayed her as they clenched into fists. The jarl's eyes flickered to her lap, and Aelthena pressed them flat against her thighs, pretending to smooth her dress.

Aware of Asborn shifting nervously next to her, she kept her voice even and her temper under a tight leash.

"Lady Iona has told you what Lord Ragnar hid from you, hid from all of us. He has dragonfire, Lord Siward. A weapon we desperately need, that can save us. Yet he keeps it for his own purposes. Have you not asked yourself why?"

"Do not insult me, Lady Heir Aelthena." The jarl's patience was fraying as well. "I know who and what Ragnar is."

"Then stand up to him." She leaned forward in her chair. "Hold the line as you did at the Sack of Qal-Nu. Be the Black Ram I came here expecting you to be and not cowering at the first sign of a threat."

He had said he was a prideful man. Now Lord Siward proved it as he stood and towered over her, his face a thundercloud, the bangles on his arms jangling with the movement. Asborn stood as well, though he looked far less threatening. The jarl scarcely seemed to notice him, his dark eyes set on her. Aelthena only sat back in her chair and crossed her legs and arms, waiting for his outburst.

His words were quiet. "I will not be goaded by women into taking the Circle. First Iona, now you... Do you think me a sheep to be misled so easily?"

It is in your name. But provocation would win her nothing further. Now, she needed to placate.

"No, Lord Siward, I do not. You are a shepherd, not a sheep. But I need you to protect more than your kin. All of Baegard requires your stout shield." She kept her chin high while her words fell softer. "It is your duty, yours alone. Lord Ragnar will lead us astray; his actions have shown it. And once his deception is unveiled, when he lacks all support, even he will uphold your election. Baegard will be united — united behind you."

The Jarl of Greenwuud observed her in silence. She

heard the cry of his young son from one of the adjoining rooms. The news he had shared and all that must be done spun around her head, but Aelthena held his gaze steadily and waited for him to speak first.

"You are brash," he said at last. "Contemptuous even. But I cannot deny you speak wisdom. I will do it, Lady Heir. Not for you, but for the Seven Jarlheims. I will accept the Iron Circle if my peers support my bid."

She stared a moment longer before the truth sunk in. *I did it. I convinced him.* Elation swept through her so strongly she felt dizzy with it.

But composure had long been hammered into her, so Aelthena shared nothing but a slight nod as she stood from her chair. "I am glad to hear it, Lord Siward. I look forward to your election soon."

With a glance at Asborn, she led her betrothed from the room.

A short while later, Aelthena pounded on a different stout door.

"I think he's heard you, if he's there at all," Frey noted from her shoulder. As always, he accompanied her through the hallways of the Elkhorn. Asborn had earlier parted ways with her to head for the Jarlmoot, though he left with profuse apologies. The meeting had been called early as reports of Fairglen's fall spread throughout the castle.

Aelthena ignored him as she stared at the door. Her plans were succeeding. She should still feel elated as she had not an hour before in Siward's quarter. Yet a nervous energy coursed through her now. She waited, but not patiently, her hands twitching, her legs vibrating.

"Be in there, Djur burn you..."

Just as the guardian looked about to speak again, the door unlatched and swung inward. A waft of unwashed air pressed out through the opening, but it was the least that bothered her as she stared up at the large man in the doorway.

Bastor gave her a ghastly grin as he looked down at her with hooded eyes. His room was dark, the curtains drawn over the room's window, and he wore only trousers and a stained tunic. The stench of sour alcohol washed out from his breath, though the sun had risen only a short time before.

"Lady Heir Aelthena," he said, his tone mocking the formality. "I wasn't expecting you to visit."

"Obviously," Frey said, packing all of his disdain into the word.

"Since you ignored my invitation, I had to invite myself." She nodded toward the room beyond. "May we?"

Bastor shrugged his slumped shoulders, then stepped aside. "Your grave."

Bracing herself, Aelthena strode into the room. She immediately headed for the window and thrust aside the curtains, casting the chamber in pale light. Turning, she noticed the strewn clothes, the litter of mugs and plates, and the tapped casks. Impossible as it first seemed, the least offensive thing in the room was its owner. Bastor watched her with an inscrutable expression while Frey closed the door behind them, his nose wrinkling as he stared about.

As soon as the latch clicked closed, Aelthena spoke. "I'll do it."

The tall heir went still, all mockery vanishing. "You'll throw your weight behind Ragnar?"

She projected all the anxiety she felt, though not for the reasons he believed. Grinding her teeth, as if it pained her to speak the words, she said, "Yes. I will do all in my power to make sure he is elected this very day."

Bastor glanced over his shoulder at Frey, as if suspecting a trap. The guardian put on a good show of looking shocked. *Though a tad bit exaggerated.*

Bastor turned back to her. "What's changed?"

"The karah and his forces have arrived in the valley. They took Fairglen." The tremble that coursed through her was not pretended; imagining the army darkening the land beyond the city's walls was sufficient to strike terror deep inside her. "If they march for Petyrsholm, and I cannot help but think they will, they may be here before the spring rains come in full."

The tall man was silent for a long moment. He seemed to have straightened, as if the revelation put some measure of resolve back in him. Bastor nodded as if to an inner thought, then met her eyes again.

"Now you understand," he said. "That we must unite. That it must be behind my father."

"You left me with no choice."

Though she would soon secure her victory, unexpected fury flared within her. *You should have worked with me,* she railed against him silently. *Then I would not have to deceive you.*

As if hearing her silent reprimand, or perhaps seeing it in her eyes, Bastor looked aside. "It is the right decision," he mumbled, sounding as if he were convincing himself rather than her.

She ignored the trite comment. "I do have one condition."

Bastor's eyes sharpened. He almost seemed eager. "Name it."

She lifted her chin. "You must swear an oath to me, on whatever you hold most holy, that, when all this is over, when Ha-Sypt and the monsters they have awoken are driven back, you will undo the ills you have done. You will help me bring your father to justice."

The irony of what she asked did not escape her, but she meant every word. Even if she would soon thwart Ragnar's ambitions for the Iron Circle, she needed to make sure he would pay for all he'd done. *For Mother. Annar. Yof. For Bjorn, whether he's fallen or still stands.*

The Heir of Ragnarsglade was silent for a long moment as he returned her stare. Behind him, Frey shifted his hand to settle on his sword. Aelthena did not flinch from him, even as he drew to his full height head and shoulders above her and hardened his expression.

"I hold nothing holy." Not a trace of a smile graced his lips. "But I will swear to what you ask on my word and honor, whatever is left of them."

Little enough, she thought, and Frey's expression betrayed a similar judgment. But for a man like Bastor, it was the best she could hope for. *Better than I gave him.* She nodded, then extended her arm. Bastor only stared for a moment, then accepted it, gripping her by the forearm in the men's way of agreement.

She nodded again as they withdrew their hands, the weight of their accord heavy in her chest. "Then I suppose we have work to do."

"I suppose we do." Bastor glanced down at himself. "Some of us more than others."

Aelthena cast him a last rueful smile as she navigated around him, then left the room. Frey closed the door behind them.

"Will he keep his word after he discovers how you treated yours?" he muttered as he followed her down the hall.

She could only shrug. "I suppose we'll find out soon."

22. MURMURS OF THE SANDS

The Words in the Sand — the Holy Words passed graciously down to us by the Divine — are the foundation for all life, and they are precious. To these, we may add further revelations observed by the priests through the many forms of divination — the scarab beetle in the sand, leaves in a cup of water...

- Revelations, by Kheti, High Chanter to Qa'a

Sehdra searched for refuge among the stars.

Refuge was in short supply on the war trail. The stink of the camp had grown familiar, but the sensations beneath it had not. The sweet, piney scent of the trees. The fragrance of blooming flowers. The birds and chattering animals, constant sounds in the night. The trees were sentinels: accusatory, truculent. The shadows between them stirred with malice.

She could not fault their hostility.

So she yearned for that which she had left behind. The desert's silence but for the sigh of the wind. The dry smell of dust and heat. Sky so clear every speck of starlight glimmered, and Gazabe's Headdress sprawled wool-white behind them.

The stars, at least, she could still claim a part of, though they were seen through a haze of smoke that lingered in the air wherever they traveled. When she looked at them, the stories her mother had once told her played across the sky, like the silhouettes on a sheet in a shadow play.

"Do you believe the gods speak to us in the stars?" she asked of Teti, who stood next to her. She reclined in a chair outside her pavilion. Out in the open, exposed to those few still milling about the war camp, he refused to sit next to her, insisting that appearances must be maintained.

"Of course, Royal Sister. The Divine speak to us through all the natural world. Bek communicates in fire, while Gazabe chooses entrails and flies."

"And Qa'a opts for scat?" she quipped.

"Even so, Sehdra Ohkweht."

Her fey mood goaded her on, so she pretended further ignorance. "And who wrote the Words in the Sand, the rules by which we People of Dust compose our lives? Did all the gods speak together? None of the stories I have heard show the deities to be proficient at compromise."

"Then you have not heard of Unity?" Teti had relaxed enough to tease her back. "They chose the karah to rule on earth as their brethren."

"So the Words have said."

But Sehdra had seen what sort of god Physt was. Even if his personal shortcomings had not instilled doubts in her, his deficiencies compared to the giantess standing behind him would have.

The teachings of old declare him a god. But if he is not... then are any of the Words true?

Teti, less comfortable with this line of thought, pivoted

the conversation. "But you asked about the stars. I have heard it said the stories are written there by all the gods, to serve as reminders of the lessons they wish to impart upon us." He pointed. "There — see the coil of Aya, wrapped around the Dreaming Antelope? It is to remind us of the value of patience, and that a hunter must strike at the right time."

Sehdra stared at the stars, contemplating his words. "The hunter's patience," she murmured. She had always identified with Qa'a because of her cursed flesh. But what if she were not the Scarab, but the Cobra in disguise, lying in tall grass for her chance to hunt?

She was jolted from her thoughts by the pattering of feet up the muddy path that cut through the camp. Teti tensed, glancing toward the guard posted outside her tent, who put a hand to his sickle sword. But as the torchlight caught on the runner's copper collar, she relaxed back into her chair. No assassins had come for her yet.

"A message for you, Sehdra Ohkweht," the slave said as he kneeled before her, panting. He held up a small scroll case over his bowed head.

At her nod, Teti stepped forward and retrieved the message, then popped open the case. Unfurling the papyrus, he frowned down at the glyphs.

"Thank you for bringing it," Sehdra said to the messenger before looking up at her friend. "What does it say, Teti?"

"A summons, Royal Sister. From Oyaoan."

Familiar dread rose in her. "Now? And from the Great One herself?"

"It appears so." Teti offered the missive to her, but Sehdra waved it away. Her thoughts were too full of what might be to come.

"It appears I will need my palanquin, my friend."

He gave a slight bow, then cast her one last worried glance before hurrying off to arrange for her transportation.

If I am a cobra, she thought as she rose and limped inside her pavilion, *then I am one without fangs.*

As Oyaoan's tent was not far, it took longer to prepare and mount the palanquin than to travel there. Yet, though the weariness of the day's travels dragged at her, Sehdra found they arrived too soon.

With Teti's help, she dismounted and approached the pavilion's entrance. In the months of the march, Sehdra had often seen the huamek's tent in passing, but never had occasion to visit. It smelled as foreign as it looked. In the air hung not only the sulfurous stench of the huamek, but spices for which she knew no names. Beads and bones dangled in equal measure, and gilded skulls were mounted on spears. The tent was as red as the strife Oyaoan had brought to Enea.

But she could not delay for long, not unless she wished to evoke the huamek's wrath. Though she often chose not to show it, Sehdra knew it to be an emotion for which Oyaoan had great capacity; the slave she had killed and the war she provoked proved that.

Still, Sehdra would not chance it. She wore her mask of Bek, red as the Divine's name, a curved tusk arcing from it in warning. Drawing in a breath, she limped forward.

Inside, the aromas inundated her senses. Smoke and steam filled the air, provoking a cough. The interior decorations were simple, the necessity of travel restricting even the huamek's gaudiness, but each one strange. Two braziers roared, and from them issued forth steam from a ring of water around their edges. In the center of the space, sand had been poured over a rug, and on this scuttled several black beetles. Sehdra watched as they collated small balls of dung, all the while watched over by a pair of Suncoaster slaves.

Oyaoan sat in the middle of it all. Her immense chair was made of as thick of trunks as existed along the Nu. She seemed more at repose than Sehdra had yet seen her, leaning on one arm of her chair, cradling her broad, tusked head in her hand. Her black eyes, lost but for a reflected gleam from the braziers' flames, seemed to watch the beetles as they wove through the sand. Sehdra wondered what she had walked in on. It had the atmosphere of a religious ritual, one whose purpose she did not know.

Sehdra blinked, trying to clear the fogginess from her vision. The heady air made her head swim. Almost, she thought she glimpsed shapes moving in the shadowed corners of the pavilion.

You're imagining things.

The Ibis stepped forward and spoke. "Great Oyaoan thanks you for attending her, Royal Sister. She has deemed you have many topics on which discussion may be productive."

Sehdra felt the urge to look to Teti, to feel his support, but to do so would be to betray weakness. She kept her stare on Oyaoan herself. Long ago, her mother had taught her that translators were to be ignored. With the huamek's pride as towering as her stature, she assumed the rule of court applied doubly here. But the sable eyes were hard to meet, even as the giant continued to ignore her.

"Thank you for the invitation, Great Oyaoan." Sehdra gave as deep of a bow as her crippled leg would allow. She had to speak through gritted teeth as she came back upright, her flesh weaker this night than normal. "I am honored you would speak to me." She hesitated, then dared to add, "But I must confess, I am curious which topics you wish us to discuss. Particularly not in the presence of His Divinity."

If the giantess heard her, she gave no sign, but only reached down a massive arm to trace a finger in the scattered sand. The scarabs fled before her intrusion, and for several long moments, the slaves were kept very busy herding the beetles back onto the carpet.

The Ibis's toothy smile brought her attention back, though she only observed him from the corner of her eye. "Great Oyaoan has many concerns she must weigh. You factor into several of these, Sehdra Ohkweht."

"In what way, First of Hua? If I may be so forward," she added a moment later, hoping offense had not been given.

Finally, Oyaoan let out a rumble that might have been a grunt or a word in her guttural language. The Ibis seemed to listen for a long while after the sound faded before he moved. He gestured to one of the servants on the peripheries of the tent, who shuffled forward with a large, golden bowl filled with sediment that shimmered as it caught the light of the flames. It took an effort not to furrow her brow as the bowl was brought first to the Ibis, who accepted it and bore it over to the giantess. Kneeling, the translator held it above his head and bowed forth.

Oyaoan's attention was finally drawn from the beetles and the sand, and her great horned head swiveled to settle black, beady eyes on the bowl. Emotions did not show readily on the huamek's gray, leathery skin, but Sehdra felt something radiating from her as she reached a large hand and, as gently as a mother handling her newborn, scooped out some of the shimmering dust onto her fingers, then lifted it to her mouth. Sehdra glimpsed two rows of flat, yellowed teeth before her mouth closed again, all but sucking the substance from her fingers. Her double-lidded eyelids pressed closed, and Sehdra could not help but think it a showing of ecstasy.

She wondered desperately what this substance was that could provoke such a reaction in the giantess. *A nostrum? An intoxicant?* She wished she had a clear head for a moment so she might puzzle it out. But between the steam and the smoke, there seemed little chance of that occurring.

His mistress apathetic for the moment, the Ibis rose with a litheness befitting a younger man, handed the dust back to the slave, then turned to face Sehdra. "Great Oyaoan wishes to know what you think of Hua's Strife."

The query caught her wrong-footed. All she could think to give was a banal response. "It progresses well, Red One. We have claimed a fine victory at Fairglen. The armies close in on Petyrsholm. Triumph over the mountain savages is inevitable."

"Inevitable?" The Ibis almost seemed to respond with his own mind as he shook his head. "It is not for the minds of humans to know what is inevitable, Royal Sister. That is best left to Great Oyaoan."

Sehdra bowed her head, accepting the chastisement for her clumsy wording. "Of course. My apologies, First of Hua."

"Great Oyaoan," the Ibis continued without acknowledgment, "wishes for a more detailed answer. Perhaps I shall rephrase my question. If you were leading the armies, and not your brother, would you proceed the same as he has?"

Icy fear blew inside her, like the nightly wind off the Nu. It was a deadly question, a test — though of what, she could not say. *Loyalty? Competence?* The Suncoaster knew the stakes as well from his coy smile. More than ever, she wished she could look to Teti, to feel some measure of reassurance. But her father had often said, *When in the jaws of a lion, do not stare into its throat — thrust a spear down it.*

She had to be bold now; bold, and wise. She wore the mask of Bek, but it was Qa'a who must guide her words. Sehdra prayed to both gods as she opened her mouth to speak.

"I would not, Great Oyaoan. The karah has made several decisions for which I would have chosen differently. Dismissing Nekau Baka, for one — particularly when he made a prudent decision in following your orders."

The words struck even her ears as cloyingly sycophantic. Hiding a wince, Sehdra pressed on.

"And the leader of Fairglen — I would have discovered all we could from her of this country, of their troops and their movements, not needlessly butchered her. For all of our might and reach, we have had precious few reports of our enemy — that I have been privy to, at least. We must be sure not to underestimate them lest we find, to our folly, they have hidden strength we have not expected."

She fell silent then, hoping she had struck the balance between daring and prudence. But for all her worry, Oyaoan did not show she had heard a word. The giantess reached into the sand again and, more deftly than Sehdra would have imagined possible, she plucked up a beetle. She let it scurry across her thick fingers, observing its progress. Almost, to her eyes, the scarab seemed to leave a dark trail in its wake, like its shadow were coming apart from it and dying the air. Like the head of a serpent entwined the giantess's hand...

Sehdra blinked and stumbled a step. Her senses felt too sharp, her mind too foggy. She felt Teti at her arm and realized he was the only thing keeping her from pitching over entirely.

"Are you well, Royal Sister?" he murmured urgently.

"Yes." She blinked and tightened her muscles. Though the smoke still felt as if it curled within her own hand, a measure of her control was returning. She gently extricated herself from her friend's grasp. "Thank you, Teti. Just a moment of weakness, that is all."

Teti nodded and stepped back, though she sensed his lingering gaze.

The Ibis watched the exchange, lips pursed, while his fingers played over the white tattoos that spiraled down his arms, their forms suggesting a line of elephants. He glanced up at his mistress, then nodded.

"Do you then criticize your karah, Sehdra Ohkweht?"

She clenched her teeth together. If she had feared before, now she knew true terror. He had positioned her over a pit with that question. Yet after all she had witnessed of the dynamics between Oyaoan and her brother, she thought she had the measure of it.

She hoped, then took the leap.

"I only answer you honestly and fairly, Great One. If my words contradict my brother's actions, then it is for you to judge."

The translator grinned outright. "Great Oyaoan thanks you, Royal Sister. You have been quite... *illuminating* in your answers. My mistress would like to offer one more piece of wisdom before you depart."

At the indication that the interview might be at an end, Sehdra felt her balance giving way again. But she could still falter. If she were to avoid a sharp end, she had to keep her wits close.

Sehdra bowed her head and fought to keep upright as the world pitched about her. "I would be delighted to have it, First of Hua."

"She bids you go to the disgraced general, Nekau. He remains with the camp at Great Oyaoan's bidding, and may be found among the mercenaries. She would remind you that soil which lays fallow will soon be fertile again, and sowing your seeds where you may is wise planning — for who knows what future is inevitable?"

Mind turning over this cryptic advice, Sehdra bowed deeper. "Thank you, Great Oyaoan," she spoke to her feet. "You honor me greatly."

Anticipating her rush of dizziness, Teti was at her arm as she rose, balance pitching like a fishing vessel on the flooded Nu. Still, she endeavored to raise her head to the giantess and found, for the first time, Oyaoan's gaze upon her.

The huamek lowered her hand to the sand, allowing the scarab to scamper free, then rumbled in her foreign language. It sounded like the dirge of a burial procession. The sounds carried on for several long moments before Oyaoan finished and fell silent again. Her dark eyes wandered from Sehdra to drift back down to the beetles and the sand.

"Great Oyaoan dismisses you, Royal Sister," was all the Ibis said. The translator's eyes were on his mistress, absorbed by her every movement.

With Teti supporting her, Sehdra left the huamek's tent. Hidden currents moved here, but she did not know how to touch them. Of only one thing was she certain now.

"We must visit the former general, Nekau, at his tent tomorrow, before the army moves," she whispered to Teti. "Time constricts."

It was not only to do as the giantess had commanded. If her plans came to fruition, she would need a general loyal to her first. Honorable as Nekau had proven to be in the past, the aged general could prove fertile ground indeed.

An image interrupted her scheming: that of the beetle-snake winding around Oyaoan's hand. She only noticed she had ceased walking when Teti tugged at her arm.

"Of course," her friend assured her. "But for now, you must rest."

Sehdra nodded. Even with her head befuddled, she heard the wisdom in his words. She leaned on Teti as he helped her back into the palanquin, then relaxed into the cushions as she was borne back to her quarters.

23. A TIME FOR SECRETS

"Ah, but to join a shield wall — that is to be alive, brothers!"

- Erik the Fist to his band, the Red Berserkers

D o not be timid, bear cub. Pick it up and look."

Bjorn had barely had time to enter the hut before Mother Sign set to her usual harassment. Repressing a sigh, he shed his coat, folded onto the wooden floor in front of the fire, and picked up the runestone set before him. He had come alone that day, for Yonik was again preoccupied by other interests.

Peering at the lines etched into the smooth stone's face from his peripherals, Bjorn recognized it at once. This was the rune he had first seen, back in the mountains, when Yonik had roughly carved it for him to use. *Vidasuum,* he knew its name to be now; Farsight, in the modern tongue.

He looked up at his teacher's sightless eyes, stomach stirring with nerves and excitement. It was the first time she had allowed him to practice a new rune. "You want me to See with it? To augur?"

Mother Sign cackled. "Oh, no! I wish you to admire its dun qualities! Yes, cub — or what else are we doing here?"

Bjorn rolled his eyes openly, glad she could not see his exasperation. He had to fight hard to keep it from his voice. "I did not visit the Hall of Doors the last time I used it. Will it come now?"

"As I said before, that was because of Brother Yonik's remarkably inept rendering of the rune. There are few runes that do not take you to the Hall, and all of them are exceptionally dangerous. But there is a difference: instead of simply opening it, you are to peer through and examine what lies inside." Her hand snapped up, fingers crooked in warning. "Do not enter! Never do that! Only look and remain in the corridor. Understood?"

His throat had gone dry. "Yes, Mother Sign."

"Good. Now, if you will fetch the ore...?"

With Bjorn's help, the Silver prepared the ritual. It was not long until he sat again before the fire, the drascale ore lying at his feet, its silver veins glowing orange and radiating heat. He braced himself, then heaved the boiling cauldron of water and poured it over the top.

Khnuum steam rushed over and through him, flooding his senses.

Once he set down the pot, Mother Sign's cold fingers found his arm, then worked under his glove to grip his wrist. It had been a while since she had taken such a precaution, but she could not know he had already succeeded in Seeing with new runes.

"Look, cub," she murmured. "Tell me what you See."

Bjorn turned his head down and stared fully at the runestone. At once, the world fell away, and another materialized before his eyes.

The Hall of Doors. It was around him in its usual shadowy shades. Adjusting to the disorientation quickly, Bjorn peered at the rune-inscribed door before him and recognized it. *Farsight.* He remembered his first visions, and for a moment, he hesitated to open it.

But he was not a helpless boy now. Bjorn firmed his jaw, reached for the handle, and pulled the door open a crack, then leaned forward to peer through.

The world beyond was too bright to distinguish at first, but slowly, the light faded. *Flames,* he recognized, as they danced and swayed. The flames spread over what looked to be the remnants of buildings, the same way they had curled over the shelters of the Jotun's encampment around the Chasm. The same as had burned on the Harrowhall for hours after the attack.

Don't lose yourself. Focus.

Bjorn rested his face on the edge of the door as he peered closer. The orange light receded a fraction more, and now he could detect something moving among the flames. He thought them men, though he could see only shadows. But as they came closer and the light illuminated their features, he recognized them for what they were.

Jotunmen.

Animal fear struck through him. He had killed their kind before, but he had no weapon now. The bestial men seemed to be heading toward him. Their hands, layered with thick, brown fur, reached forward, as if to seize him.

What would they want with me?

The answer was not a far stretch. The Jotun had taken Oakharrow; that much news had come to Eildursprall. Though he could rule by strength and cruelty, the giant was likely clever enough to realize his rule would never be absolute while any of the ruling family survived. He would kill

Bjorn if he caught him, just as he had slain the rest of his kin.

The jotunmen were half a dozen paces from him. Soon, they could grab him. Would they pull him through the door? Bjorn wrenched himself away. He needed to know more. Which town or city would burn? Oakharrow? Eildursprall? Or some other jarlheim, still to be conquered? Would the jotunmen catch him or not?

But as the giant's servants lunged forward, his fear won out. Bjorn slammed the door shut and leaped back as it rattled with the impact. His thudding heart seemed to make the corridor tremble as he waited for the men to break through.

The door went still and silent. He breathed out a sigh. He was safe.

"Bjorn, come back..."

Hearing Mother Sign, he was all too willing to obey. Bjorn let go of the Hall of Doors, then opened his eyes back into the fire-lit hut.

As he raised his gaze to the Silver, she seemed to sense his return and released his wrist. "What did you See?" she asked sharply.

Bjorn recounted the scene. It seemed too meager now that it did not consume him. But as he fell silent, and Mother Sign shared in his quiet, a buried memory suddenly surfaced. The vision took on an uncomfortable new light.

"I think I've had this vision before," he said slowly.

The Silver did not react immediately, her eyes narrowed at the ceiling. "When?"

"When I first looked down on Eildursprall from the ridge above. It wasn't exactly the same, but... I saw the town burning." He shrugged. "There weren't jotunmen, but it could have been the same."

Mother Sign shrugged, the thick furs layered over her

almost hiding it. "Many towns will burn soon, I fear. But that you saw Eildursprall in flames..." She felt silent, her eyes falling to the fire. "I must think on this. That will be all for today."

Glad for the dismissal, Bjorn rose to his feet. He swayed for a moment, his balance pitching from the exposure to *khnuum,* then shook his head free of it. He was nearly to the door when the Silver spoke again.

"You did well, bear cub. You should be proud."

He found himself lost for words. Bjorn only nodded, though he knew she could not see it, then pushed out the door.

———

Not long after, Bjorn worked his muscles loose in the training yard.

It came as a surprise to be drawn there. As a boy forced to learn to fight, he had hated every moment spent on the yard. The place only held ridicule for him, where he had endured failure again and again, and in a discipline he did not much care for. It had been the place where his father and brothers most often frowned at him, seeing him for the coward he was.

Then he had fought and killed, and its role in his life changed.

The yard in Heim Numen had begun to feel different over the weeks he had spent there. The sword was not something he feared, but valued, and the shield doubly so. They, and his skill in using them, had kept him alive. They had shown him he was not the coward he'd always feared himself to be. He admired the dark edge of Harrowsteel now, its glimmer as it cleaved through the air. He had even gained a quiet respect for the snarling bear molded into the pommel. The weight of the shield was a reassurance, a bastion between him and all who sought to kill him. As he moved through the forms Blademaster Raldof had drilled into him throughout his boyhood, the heat of movement warmed him through, body and soul. And going through those exercises with Loridi and Seskef, even teaching them some, for they had received much less formal training than Bjorn, bound him closer together with the two merry men, giving him a taste of the comradeship ever spoken of between brothers-at-arms.

But that afternoon, it was not comradeship he sought. He had seen jotunmen in his vision and been freshly reminded that they were still out there, waiting to spill his blood. Though *seidar* could produce miracles, he knew he would find far better protection from the sword and the shield than magic could ever provide.

Bjorn was drawn from his thoughts when a knot of the Sprallmen approached him, Loridi, and Seskef. Abruptly, the yard shifted back to how he had always seen it. It took all his willpower not to shuffle his feet.

"Loridi, Seskef, Bjorn of Oakharrow."

Flint had spoken, acknowledging him and his companions with a nod that they returned. Two of the other barbar warriors who guarded Eildursprall had dressed in padded clothes and carried wooden wasters and shields as they stood on the edge of the yard.

"Flint!" Loridi called cheerily to the Sprallman. "Fair weather we have today, eh?"

Bjorn glanced up. Gray clouds hung thick overhead, promising a sleeting rain soon, and a cold gale had whipped up in their wake. Only by the jester's standards could it be considered "fair."

Flint, apparently thinking the same thing, only grunted

before his eyes slid back to Bjorn. "You've shown skill. Show it to me now."

Bjorn exchanged a look with Seskef, who looked as skeptical as he felt. "You want to spar?" he guessed.

The barbar gestured, his broad hand resembled a bear's paw in its glove. "You three against us. Harrowmen to Sprallmen." A sudden grin erupted from his generous beard, though his eye remained dark. "Let us see who proves the stronger."

Bjorn liked this idea even less. As one of the jarl's sons, he had been instructed in the techniques of fighting next to other men, including the shield wall which their ancestors had employed effectively against their enemies for generations. But at this, he had fared even more poorly than sparring on his own. Somehow, when he had to account for the movements of other men as well as his own, his mind went to tatters.

But it seemed he would not have a say in the matter, for Loridi had brightened at the suggestion. "A fine notion! But if you expect any other result than lying flat in the snow — then, my friend, you shall be disappointed. I am not called Lord Sword for nothing!"

"No?" Seskef observed, rolling his shoulders and stepping up next to his accomplice, waster and shield in hand. "And here I thought 'nothing' was exactly what the title meant."

Bjorn swallowed and tried to smile along with his companions as he closed the gap between them. "If you want to."

Flint nodded, then led his fellows to take up position on the other half of the yard. These two Sprallmen were potent foes, Bjorn had learned in his time observing the sparring contests. One, a Yewling called Wuldof, had an even shaggier mane than Yonik and stood nearly as tall as Loridi, though with more girth than either of them. He was strong and quicker than he looked, and Bjorn had never seen him smile.

The other, a Djurian named Dagar, was the shortest among them, and perhaps the slightest as well. His hair was shorn close around the sides and back of his head, leaving only braids laced with beads atop his skull. His speed often made up for his lack of reach and brawn.

Flint, however, was the most dangerous of the three. He was not especially strong or quick, nor tall or broad. But he moved with purpose, and possessed an eerie sense of how his opponent would behave, always anticipating where the next strike would fall. Even Yonik and Hoarfrost, two of the finest fighters Bjorn had ever seen, struggled to best the Eildursprall drang.

"On a three count," the Sprallman called hoarsely across the snow. "One..."

"Keep our shields up and our shoulders close," muttered Seskef. "Let them make the mistakes."

"Two..."

"Counting won't stop the clobbering you're in for, inbreeds!" shouted Loridi.

"Three!"

Flint and his men moved as one, round shields rising in a line. They seemed to have the same idea as Seskef, for they advanced slowly, their weapons held at the ready behind their small shield wall.

Bjorn raised his shield at the same time as Loridi and Seskef. He tried to shove down the doubts filling him from his boots to his skull as they shuffled forward. *You've been in battle,* he reminded himself, as he had a hundred times on the yard. *You've fought for your life and survived. This is nothing compared to that.* Yet somehow, these contests always seemed to have just as dire of stakes, though of a different sort.

They were a dozen feet off, then half that. As the two units came within striking distance of each other, Flint spoke a grunted word in the Yewling tongue, and as one, the Sprallmen surged forward, shields thrusting against theirs. Bjorn barely had time to register the attack before they crashed into him.

Wasters darted over the rims. Bjorn, straining with all his might, dodged the probe of one before he felt another smack against his knee. Pain shot up his leg, and his stance faltered. The snow, always hard for his boots to grip, seemed to turn slicker still. Flint, against whom he had lined up, suddenly gave a stronger shove than he had before, and Bjorn went stumbling back, breaking the Harrow line.

Flailing as if he had been thrown into a river rather than the ice-crusted snow, Bjorn fought to gain his feet as the Sprallman bore down on him. From the corner of his eyes, he saw Loridi and Seskef square off with Wuldof and Dagar.

Then Flint was on him. Bjorn threw up his shield, the boss catching his waster to deflect the blow. Never one to be caught off guard, the barbar shoved Bjorn back with another blow of his shield, preventing retaliation.

He tried to set his footing and take a swing, but Flint got there first, cutting in low under his shield for another shot at the leg. Bjorn was tempted to catch the blow with his shield, but remembered just in time to skip back instead. Sure enough, the shield-strike that Flint followed up with, which would have caught Bjorn in the jaw, was blocked instead.

Bjorn found a grin stretching his cracked lips wide as they faced off again. The coals of training had flared back to flame fire, burning away his doubts. He had caught the rhythm now, and it sang in his limbs as he edged forward—

Flint suddenly spun and ran the few steps back toward the fight. Just as Bjorn thought to follow, the Sprallman's waster smacked first into Loridi's back, then Seskef's. Bjorn's companions howled with pain as they tried to face their opponents on either side. But Flint was already roaring, "Enough!"

Bjorn skidded to a halt, shield lowering. His face flushed with more than just the exertion.

"Had enough already?" Loridi asked, his mockery spoiled by a wince as he pressed a hand to his side.

Flint stared at Bjorn, drawing his gaze. "You let the shield wall break," the drang said. "You let me strike down your fellows."

Bjorn tightened his jaw. Resentment rose, trying to contend with the shame and anger for supremacy. "I saw."

Wuldof snorted and spat to the side. "Seems to me Sprallmen are strong, and Harrowmen weak."

"I wouldn't go that far," Loridi protested, though the look he gave Seskef seemed uncertain.

Flint had not shifted his gaze from Bjorn. "Stand with your fellows, and you will stand strong. Understand?"

He had understood since the moment it had happened. But all he answered was a sulky "Yes."

The Drang nodded, then turned back. "Come. We go again."

Part of Bjorn wanted nothing more than to flee the yard. But a greater part of him needed redemption. He had made a mistake and learned a lesson. He wanted to show he could stand strong in a shield wall. He wanted to show he was not afraid.

He stood between Loridi and Seskef once more. The bigger man leaned in close.

"Want me to take the middle?"

Bjorn shook his head. Perhaps he was only being stubborn. But if he could not stand up to Flint, how could he have a hope of prevailing against the Jotun?

"No. I have to."

He raised his shield, and beside him, the former Hunters in the White did the same. Bjorn set his teeth in a grimace as he watched the Sprallmen mirror them, then advance. He had always been more of a scholar than a warrior, and possessed courage in like.

But, by Volkur's spear, I don't need to fight like one.

Bjorn roared with the others as the shields clashed once again.

The icy rain fell by the time Yonik put a stop to their contests.

Bruised and battered, sore down to his bones, and with the tangy taste of blood lingering in his mouth, Bjorn felt a distinct satisfaction over the yard's proceedings. Though the Harrowmen and Sprallmen had moments before been slamming shield and waster into one another again and again, they parted ways with gripped forearms and grins all around. Bjorn thought he might have smiled the widest of them all. This experience, male companionship on the yard, had always eluded him. He was glad to have claimed a sliver of it as a man.

But as he turned to see the gothi leaning against the fence marking the end of the yard, the smile slipped away. Yonik had rarely worn so grave an expression. His greatbear hood was pulled over his head, the long incisor that extended before his face dripping as ice melted down it. His shadowy features looked washed out in the gloomy day. His bushy mess of a beard was white tinged and glistening with moisture and frost.

But his eyes — they burned with a fire that startled Bjorn.

"The weather looks to have put our priest in a foul mood," Loridi noted as he wiped at his nose, dripping rain, snot, and blood.

"Yonik never minded the snow before." Seskef worked his shield arm in a wide circle, wincing as he hit a kink, then sighing as he pushed past it.

Bjorn felt a heaviness settling over him that had nothing to do with the water-weight gathering in his clothes. "Guess we should go see."

They ambled over to the fence where the priest leaned. As they neared, Yonik straightened and fixed on a smile. The result was an expression even more ghastly than before.

"Alright, priest — out with it." Loridi leaned on the fence. "What's on your mind?"

A genuine smile stole over Yonik's lips now. "Nothing to fill your empty head with, *Lord Sword*." His eyes slid over to Bjorn. "Just need to steal this one for a bit."

"More witchery?" Seskef crossed his arms across his broad chest.

The gothi seemed to consider this, then shrugged. "Not in the way you're thinking — but yes, I suppose *seidar* is involved."

Bjorn could not decipher the cryptic clues. "Always with the riddles, old wolf."

The corners of Yonik's eyes crinkled. "Have to keep things interesting, don't I?" He waved a hand at the other two Hunters. "Don't let me keep you from your baths — Wild Wives know you need them."

With cheery farewells, their companions parted ways. Bjorn followed the priest as he led them from the yard.

"Don't suppose I have time to change?" Bjorn asked hopefully.

Yonik shook his head. His cheerfulness had dissipated, leaving behind the same smoldering drive Bjorn had glimpsed before. "I'm sorry, Bjorn. This must be dealt with immediately."

Impatience rose in him. Here he was, trudging through the winter-bit rain instead of heading for the hot baths, and Yonik would not even deign to tell him why.

"What are you talking about, Yonik?" he demanded. "Tell me plainly."

The priest ran a hand through his beard, scattering droplets and small shards of ice. "I have only suspicions," he answered finally. "Vague indications of something that may be of great aid to us. But the Silvers will resist revealing its truth, I think."

Bjorn pressed his lips tightly together. It had not escaped him that the priest had, once again, evaded his question.

"It will make more sense soon," Yonik offered belatedly. But Bjorn only turned his head aside and kept pace next to him.

As they entered the longhouse, dripping onto the bearskin splayed across the entrance, the last of their companions stepped away from the wall and approached.

"Hoarfrost," Bjorn greeted her. He immediately shed his sulky attitude. Before her, the last thing he wished to appear was childish.

The Skyardi gave him a tight smile, then looked to Yonik. "They claim to be occupied."

The gothi swept the hood back from his head and wiped the moisture from his face. "Then we'll force ours upon them," he said grimly.

Desperately curious, Bjorn followed as they strode through the longhouse to the chamber at the opposite end. Yonik had always been respectful of the leaders of the priesthood; whatever had changed that was important, and he could think of only one thing that would qualify. But if this related to the Jotun and the Witterland Prophecy, where had the priest learned it? Bjorn had spent just as much time as he in the library, though not as much of late. Yet Yonik had often searched in different places. Still, if the priest had discovered something, Tyra should have been privy to it and let him know.

Tyra. Bjorn shook away the image of her rising from the baths. That was a distraction he could not afford.

As they reached the door, Yonik immediately opened it without knocking. Hoarfrost glanced at Bjorn, then jerked her head toward the entrance. He preceded her after a moment's hesitation and stepped into the gloomy chamber.

"What is this intrusion?" Father Temperance was objecting as Bjorn entered and stood next to the gothi. Hoarfrost closed the door and remained beside it, as if guarding against escape.

Mother Iron glared her disapproval at the three of them, though Yonik bore the brunt of it. "Brother Yonik," she said tightly, "you were told to await our availability to discuss this matter. You do not have the authority or right to barge into our conferences unannounced."

Mother Sign's blind eyes wandered over their heads, a sudden grin splayed across her aged face. "Are we so old and set in our ways that we chastise a minor interruption?" she mocked. "Come, Brother Yonik: tell your Silvers what has your beard in a tangle."

Yonik did not catch any of her glee, but glowered at each of the Silvers. Bjorn held his breath, waiting for the explanation behind such behavior from the mild-mannered man.

Finally, the gothi spoke, his voice as low and dangerous as a wolf's growl. "Why have you kept Torvald Geirson a secret all these long years?"

Bjorn stared at Yonik. *Torvald Geirson.* It took him a moment to connect that name with the more popular moniker ascribed to him. *The King of Ice? What does he have to do with this?*

But the Silvers' reactions told him there was something to the claim. Mother Iron defiantly met Yonik's eyes. Father Temperance's gaze wandered over to the wall, as if hoping this might all go away if he ignored it. Mother Sign's smile faded, replaced by a wistful look.

"At the end," she murmured into the silence, "all veils will be shorn."

Yonik looked from one Silver to the next. "Tell me," he said, his voice quieter, but no less demanding. "We must know all you can tell."

Mother Iron turned her glare to the other two Silvers. Father Temperance only tentatively met it, while Mother Sign remained oblivious. Finally, her bristling manner faltered, and her head fell a fraction.

"Very well," Mother Iron said, a great weariness in her words. "It seems the time for secrets is over. We will tell you all."

24. A TIME FOR TRUTH

ᚺ

And Skaldi spoke unto them:

In the final hours, all veils shall be shorn
All lies shall be skinned
All blades shall be broken

In the final hours, all men shall know:
This is the night of which I have spoken

- The Saga of Skaldi, translated by Alfin the
Scribe

Bjorn's attention was unwavering as Mother Iron drew in a breath.

"Torvald Geirson," she began, "the King of Ice, the Last King of Baegard — he came to us after wandering the Teeth for many years. So claim our records, which you seem to have uncovered, Brother Yonik. The Silvers of the time were surprised that King Torvald had survived for so long. Yet it had come at a cost, for he acted as one sprite-touched. The foremost seeress of that time, Sister Thera, listened to him long after the others had abandoned their attempts to pry reason from the fallen sovereign and wrote down what he said. In him, she saw something that warned that these were no mere ravings. Studying his words, she divined patterns among them, glimpses of things corroborated by other prophecies. And thus Sister Thyra began to believe that the king was not mad at all, but a seer such as the world had rarely seen before, if ever. That his visions illustrated the future as starkly as it had yet been depicted."

Bjorn's scholar's courage came alive, drawing the scenes that Mother Iron spoke of. Yet even imagining them, Bjorn had trouble believing. That the King of Ice was not a mere story, but a man in truth, and that his lonely sojourn into the mountains had not only happened, but been recorded... It felt as if he stood on the edge of a pit of which the walls were crumbling, inexorably swallowing him down.

But don't we all now live in a myth, with jotunar and dragonfire on the rise? This was only one more impossibility he had to accept.

"With time," Mother Iron continued, "and much patience, Sister Thera formed a prophecy from Torvald's disjointed sentences. It was a horrid telling, by report: of fires rising from the land itself to swallow half of all life, and ice blowing down from the mountains to choke out the rest of it. Death, the sovereign claimed, was coming for all — and, by the turning of the world, it would come soon."

Yonik, who had been listening with head bowed and eyes closed, finally stirred. "Where is this prophecy?"

"Lost!" Mother Sign suddenly screeched, and there was a great sadness in her cry that clawed through Bjorn's chest. "All lost," she repeated softer.

Mother Iron frowned at her peer. "Yes. The pages burned in a fire after Torvald had gone and Sister Thera had joined the sprites of earth and water. No one remained who had a firsthand account of the Last King's Prophecy."

"Then nothing remains. This Torvald does not matter, for his visions were lost."

It was Hoarfrost who had spoken. The Skyardi had listened with her arms crossed over her chest, as erect as any Harrow warrior. Her glacial eyes betrayed no sign of what she thought of the impossible tale.

Father Temperance's gaze slid over to Mother Iron, who scowled once more. Bjorn felt a glimmer of something there, an acknowledgment — though of what, he could hardly say. Mother Sign, however, was not content with subtle communications.

"Oh, the King of Ice still matters." She smiled off toward the doorway.

"He does."

Bjorn was surprised to see Yonik's stance: arms by his sides, hands clenched into fists. *Like a boy before a bully,* he thought, the sight and feeling familiar.

He could not remain silent any longer. "How?" Bjorn pressed. "How could he matter when nothing remains of him?"

Yonik turned to him. A tress of tangled hair had fallen before his eyes so that they seemed the eyes of a predator, stalking through the brush.

"Because Torvald Geirson never died."

Bjorn blinked, sure he had misheard. A smile came to his lips, assuming this must be some twisted joke of the priest's.

"Of course he died." When Yonik did not look at him or respond, Bjorn turned to the Silvers. "He lived two hundred years ago. He had to have been middle-aged when he ascended into the Teeth. He was seen here. He died."

But Father Temperance had lifted his head, as if

beseeching the sprites of air to lift him away from the room. Mother Iron met Yonik's stare with a hard one of her own. Mother Sign cackled.

Am I the one who is sprite-touched? Bjorn wondered as he looked around the room for a scrap of sanity. *Or are they?* His vexation shredded his timidity.

"Will someone answer me?" he demanded of everyone and no one.

"Well, Iron?" Mother Sign leaned close to Father Temperance to cast a leer in her peer's direction. "Will you tell them, or shall I? We both know the Honored Father will not deign to."

"Such secrets are not within the purview of a mere gothi, much less the seer boy and the Skyardi." The aged man kept his eyes downcast though, his protests meek.

Mother Iron bared her teeth as she met Bjorn's gaze. "Dark days require dire measures. Baltur preserve us all, but I suppose I must speak. Better I explain than you, Sign."

Yonik's smile was just as sharp. "Then you will answer our questions?"

Mother Iron's lips twisted in a sour pucker, but she nodded.

"Is he alive still, as the priest implies?" asked Hoarfrost, blunt as ever. "This King of Ice?"

"Yes."

Bjorn still could not banish the thought that he had somehow stumbled into a *khnuum* influenced dream, where nothing could be believed. "How?" he objected. "It doesn't make sense."

Mother Iron's steely gaze slid over to him. "Because he's a powerful *Volur*, Bjorn Borson. More powerful, as I have said, than any we have known."

That she had used his full name, admitting the Silvers

knew exactly who he was, barely registered in Bjorn's mind. "But two hundred years...?" he objected weakly.

"There are many things you do not know of the Sight, bear cub." Mother Sign's mouth still smiled, but her eyes, which drifted to his chest, had narrowed. "*Seidar* may unlock doors in our bodies and our minds, for they are inextricably connected. The secrets of longevity are lost to us now, but Torvald explored depths that were forbidden to the priesthood. He discovered capabilities we had only theorized possible from the tales of the past."

Bjorn shook his head. Already, his imagination raced down the remembered Hall of Doors, speculating about what lay behind each rune.

If seidar *can defy death, what is it not capable of?*

But Yonik's thoughts went down different paths. "If he is alive, then we must speak with him."

Mother Sign cackled. "You may find that difficult."

The gothi frowned. "And why's that? The records of his keeper's visits clued me into Torvald's existence. It seems one Sister Embla visited him just days before my companions and I arrived."

The old seeress was lost to her mirth, so it fell to Mother Iron to answer. "Visiting him is difficult enough. But speaking is altogether another thing. It has been over a century since any heard Torvald speak. I would be surprised if he were still able."

Yonik's scowl spread across his face. "Can he write then?"

"If you could put a quill in his hand, perhaps!" Mother Sign japed.

"So he cannot communicate," Hoarfrost surmised. "What good is this old king?"

The seeress pointed to her eyes. "He can *See*, my dour

Skyardi — far more clearly than any of us. Myself included!"

Bjorn understood at once. "The Sight. Can he somehow pass on knowledge of his Seeings then?"

"We believe so." A sigh escaped Mother Iron. "It has been generations since anyone attempted it, for there have not been dire enough circumstances to warrant the risks. The last endeavor ended with a priestess drooling on the cave floor, never to recover her wits. But there are records of success as well."

Yonik's lips pressed tight. "How is it done, this sharing?"

"By performing a—" Mother Sign began, but her peer cut her off.

"That is not relevant." Mother Iron's eyes brooked no argument. "Because we will not risk it now, either."

Bjorn had taken a step forward before he realized it. Blood pounded in his head, and his thoughts pressed out through his lips. "We have no other choice. Don't you see? The jotunar are returning. The Eternal Night is falling. We must risk everything!"

The aged woman did not flinch. "It may addle or kill the one who shares his visions, Bjorn. It may kill Torvald himself. He has weakened during my time as a Silver. I do not think he can endure another Seeing."

"Then we must go to him while there's still time." Bjorn looked to Yonik, and the priest stared back. After a long moment, he nodded.

"Bjorn is right. We must go to him, despite the risks. We must know his visions. With so much unknown about our enemy and their movements, anything we can discover could prove invaluable."

"He is not ready." Mother Sign leaned forward on thin arms, hands folded under her chin like wilted flowers. "He is too inexperienced. If Bjorn attempts to See with the King of Ice, he will die."

A phantom hand grabbed hold of his chest and squeezed. As Bjorn struggled for a breath, Hoarfrost spoke. "Then another will perform this task. A priest — or you."

The aged seeress tilted her head to the side, and her eyes fell closed, as if she had just nodded off to sleep. She spoke from that strange position. "No other has the potential to go in Bjorn's place. Except I — but I would not reach him."

"Why?" Yonik spoke. "Where is he?"

"Enough." Father Temperance straightened in his chair and smoothed the front of his robes. "We have said you will not go to Torvald Geirson. The matter is settled. Do not pester us any longer with this request."

The chamber fell silent. Bjorn listened to the murmur of the longhouse through the door as thoughts circled in his head. He tried to picture the King of Ice, and what a Seeing with him would be like. But he had too little knowledge to understand.

I might die. But he could die any day now. There was an old saying, oft-repeated before companies embarked on green hunts: *Death and its hounds stalk the shadows.* With war coming to Baegard — or already arrived — countless things might put him at risk.

At least in this, he had a choice. At least here, he might make a difference.

Bjorn raised his head to stare at Mother Sign. "I know I still have a lot to learn. I know it's not the right time. But it's the *only* time. I must go to Torvald Geirson, Mother Sign. I must see what he has to show me. If I die..." His throat swelled closed for a moment before he fought the rest of the words through. "If I die, then I die. But it would be far worse not to try."

Courage was not a quality he had ever claimed to possess. But in this act, at least, he knew his family would not be displeased.

All in the room stared at him. He kept his eyes on the aged seeress. Slowly, Mother Sign straightened. Her clouded eyes nearly found his, and a small smile grew on her lips.

"Before such an impassioned speech, what else can we say?" She slapped both of her hands on the table, making Father Temperance jump, to his frowning displeasure. "I change my mind. Let them go to him."

"Sign, are you certain?" Mother Iron frowned at Bjorn, looking him up and down like he were a horse she had been thinking of buying, but now reconsidered. "He is young."

"Too young," Mother Sign agreed. "And long have I looked for one of his talent. But this is *war*, my dear Silvers — a war for all our lives and freedoms. A war worthy of songs and stories for generations to come! You would not deny a young man his part in it?"

"I, for one, still counsel against it." Father Temperance sniffed. "I was a young man once and am glad to have outlived it."

"We all know you were born old," jeered Mother Sign. "And you, Iron?"

The Silver was now looking between Yonik and Hoarfrost, then she sighed and slumped. "Very well. You may go to him."

Bjorn struggled to work out how he felt about this victory. Before he could decide, Yonik took a step forward to loom over the elders. "And where is he?"

"Up!" Mother Sign pointed to the ceiling.

"The sky?" Hoarfrost asked drily.

"The mountain," Mother Iron answered. "He lies in a cave high atop Yewung."

Yewung. Bjorn had often seen the legendary mountain from the town at its foot. Most times, its apex was lost in clouds, but he'd had the fortune to glimpse it one day. It had shone with reflected sunlight, its far-off, snow-capped peak defiant of any attempts to melt it. Blue veins traveled down its bluff sides; glaciers, Tyra had informed him, when they had both ventured outside of the library to observe the phenomenon. It looked impossible to ascend.

Yet that was where they had to go.

Yonik looked at him, and Bjorn, not trusting his voice, gave him a nod. The priest managed a small smile in return.

"We will begin our preparations at once," he said, his resolve quiet but firm. "And if Sister Embla might be our guide...?"

"We have agreed thus far, haven't we?" Mother Iron waved a hand. "Outfit yourselves as you can. Beware of avalanches — it is the wrong time of year to ascend, for they will be frequent. But try to come back alive."

"And not kill Torvald while you're up there," Father Temperance noted with annoyance.

"We will do what we must, Silver." Hoarfrost glanced at Bjorn and gave him a thin smile. "So you lead us again into peril, Bjorn, Son of Bor."

Bjorn now felt a thrill run through him at being named. "So it seems," he muttered.

Though he meant to face death, he hoped he would come back alive. With Tyra's face rooted in his mind, he was not yet ready to die.

25. A FATHER'S LOVE

Those enthralled become the property of the man who has taken them. Thralls must obey in all respects or receive reprimand. Yet as a beast of burden is cared for, so must a man care for his thrall. Neither man nor beast, they remain of value and serve best when provided sustenance and shelter.

- The Inscribed Beliefs; Verse the Fourth, Line the Thirty-first

Bastor pulled at his collar and grimaced as he approached the huskarls outside his father's door. He had consented, for once, to dress as a jarl's heir should, and resented every stitch. The clothes had supposedly been tailored for his broad frame, yet the tunic and coat pulled at his shoulders, while the trousers hung loose in all the wrong places. With his brutish stature, he knew he must look ridiculous. *Like a bear in costume.*

Yet it was past time he tried to look respectable. His father would soon be the Arkjarl, placing Bastor under ever more scrutiny. And while he loved to embarrass Ragnar, he had a greater game to play.

"Wouldn't go in there, Lord Heir, if I were you."

Bastor stopped short and glanced at the guard who had spoken. He wore a conical helm, thinning black hair hanging in braids below it. That and the faint wrinkles around his eyes showed him to be middle-aged. His beard, in contrast to the hair atop his head, enveloped the lower half of his face. His eyes were set close together, and they held a hunger in them Bastor knew well from his childhood. He had not always been bigger than the other boys, and bastards were easy to bully.

"And why's that?" he asked, emphasizing each word.

While his fellow glanced skeptically at the black-bearded man, the huskarl appeared unfazed. His lips twitched from within the wiry hair in the beginnings of a smirk.

"The jarl would appreciate privacy, s'all."

"He can have some space when he's in the ground. What's your name, man?"

"Endre, Lord Heir. Endre Kettilson."

"Well, Endre, let's leave the thinking to better minds, shall we? What do you say to that?"

At last, a tightening around the eyes. "Yes, Lord Heir."

The tone was as mutinous as before, but Bastor was satisfied. He did not much like lording his position over others, even when the situation called for it.

Not wasting another moment on the man, he reached for the door handle and wrenched it open, speaking as he did. "Father, it seems I have—"

He stopped short at the sight before him. There, in the middle of the sitting room, stood his father, trousers unbelted and fallen halfway down his legs. His manhood was scarcely hidden beneath the hem of his tunic. A young

Sypten woman scurried to her feet from where she had been kneeling on the carpet and pulled her undone clothes about her, hiding her bosom and belly. She stared with wide eyes at Bastor, the white showing around the brown edges of her irises, and he saw she recognized him even as he knew her.

Ipu.

He could barely speak. His body trembled with the fury that poured through him. "Dress yourself, then leave us," he all but barked at her. He regretted his harshness, but could not rein it in.

Ipu darted a glance at the jarl, and when he did not contradict the order, she swiftly obeyed. Bastor gave her whatever decency might remain to her by turning his head aside. He remembered all their interactions before, the shyness with which she carried herself, and burned all the hotter with each memory. She was not one of those who would willingly do this. Only a command would have put Ipu on her knees.

"And you as well, Father," he spoke toward the wall, not caring how his words sounded to the huskarls outside.

Lord Ragnar stood unmoving a moment longer, as if in defiance of his son's command. But even the Jarl of Ragnars-glade had difficulty seeming imposing with his trews about his ankles. At length, Bastor observed from the corner of his eye as he bent over and pulled his trousers back up to cover himself. Ipu was already scrambling from the room, ties only half-done. He caught the sparkle of tears in her eyes before she slipped through the doorway.

Bastor slammed the door after her, then paused, attempting to seize back some measure of composure before facing his father again. As he turned, however, all he saw was a blur of motion.

Bastor reacted on instinct. He caught his father's

swinging arm and twisted it so that Ragnar was forced to turn away or let it break. The pained gasps that escaped his father's lips made something stir in Bastor's chest. He wrapped an arm around his neck from behind so that the jarl was entirely helpless in his grasp.

They stood in a grunting standstill for several moments, during which Bastor listened for any sign of the guards entering to protect their jarl. The door remained closed. Bastor twisted his father's arm further behind his back, and suddenly Ragnar's resistance petered.

"Release me, son," he grunted through Bastor's choke-hold. "Now."

He held on. Fantasies flitted through his mind, dreams he had never come so close to fulfilling. *Twist his neck,* a voice within him whispered. *Break him like he's broken you. Leave him like a toppled tower of blocks on the floor.*

His muscles twitched. His temples pounded.

Bastor released his grip and stumbled back. All the fight left him as swiftly as it had come. How close he had come to killing him, to patricide. How much he still yearned to do it.

He half-expected his father to take another swing. Instead, Ragnar slowly turned around and eyed him. If his father had been another man, Bastor might have almost thought it an expression of pride.

"You do have a spine," the jarl said at length.

Bastor did not answer, suspecting a trick. He crossed his arms to hide his shaking hands.

Ragnar rolled the shoulder that Bastor had savaged. "Well?" he said, impatience edging back in. "Did you only come here to attack your father?"

"Not only." Bastor returned the cutting smile he had long ago learned from his father. "I come with good news."

"An odd way of delivering it." Ragnar adjusted his

trousers, which were still only haphazardly secured. "Well, out with it. I don't have all afternoon."

Bastor waited several more breaths. It was rare he could lord something over his father, and he wanted to savor the moment. But when he remembered how short their time was, all childish vindication faded.

"Call the election," Bastor said in a low rumble, "and you will be made the Arkjarl."

All the creases lining his father's face smoothed, and a ravenous look replaced it. "How did you do it?"

Bastor only shrugged.

The Jarl of Ragnarsglade, traitor to his country, stared for a moment longer at his son. But though he had always pressed for an answer before, now Lord Ragnar only nodded and strode to the window, where the curtains were drawn, and threw them open. The light was still pale, and a spring shower had begun, but may as well have been a glorious flood of sunshine for how proudly his father stood before it.

Bastor's lips twisted. *As if he wasn't assaulting Ipu just minutes before.* He wondered if he could push his father through the glass in a single shove, if he would bleed out from lacerations before he hit the ground.

It's not too late, a part of him whispered. *You can still stop this.*

"You've made the right decision, son."

Bastor roused from his red thoughts. "You would think so, wouldn't you?"

"Not for me." His father halfway turned back, the sunlight limning his profile and casting his face in deeper shadow. "For Baegard."

"Yes, Father. Because you're our Djur-burned savior."

Even his sarcasm could not deflate the jarl's elation. "I have in my possession a weapon. A weapon that our enemies will not expect. A weapon that will turn the tide of this Summer War. With the Iron Circle upon my brow and the hidden advantage at my disposal, Baegard will be saved."

At what cost?

But his thoughts had caught on a question. Bastor stared hard at his father's visible eye, glimmering yellow with reflected fire from the hearth.

"Then you succeeded?" he finally asked. "You made it into a weapon?"

Lord Ragnar's lips pulled back in a familiar smile: part teasing, part mocking, mostly self-satisfaction. "Wait until I am elected, my heir. Then I will explain all."

Bastor crossed his arms, the seams of his overtunic straining at the elbows. He understood then that his father suspected the trail down which his thoughts often wondered. Control of the weapon, and the secrets of its refinement, was his security against Bastor's knife in his back.

But also... *My heir.*

When was the last time his father had called him that? Not since Ragnar the Younger had been born, surely. The claiming of him sent shivering fingers clawing over his skin. As much as he wanted to deny it, he had longed for it.

Longed with all his soul.

Bastor bared his teeth. "Then I suppose we'd best elect an Arkjarl today."

His father turned slowly back to the window. "Yes," he said, the word swollen with desire. "We will."

26. THE IRON CIRCLE

Though the stairs were many and the climb long, Aelthena still brimmed with nervous energy by the time she reached the top of Antler Tower.

She did not arrive alone. Other than Frey, Asborn had come, his forehead wrinkled over the coming election, as well as her father. Lord Bor stumbled up the tower's many stairs, surly as a tired child. He became more intractable to Uljana's urgings with each floor ascended, yet now that the soporific was settling in, his feet dragged and his eyelids sagged. Aelthena found it almost unbearable to look at him, torn between conflicting emotions. She wondered how all these events might have gone differently had her father been in sound health.

Would Oakharrow have fallen? Would he have been elected Arkjarl in Siward's place?

But her father was sprite-touched; that was the way

things stood. And if she were to dream of a different world, it would be one where she was elected Arkjarl, not him.

That was all it was, though, a dream. She released it and focused back on the world as it was.

Her resolution was a tight knot within her. Her plans would succeed. She would see them through to the end. Not even Ragnar and Bastor could unwind them now.

Her eyes wandered to Frey then. The guardian, wary as a wolf, gave her a small smile, a ghost of his former mischievousness still glimmering there. A smile came to her own lips, at least until she noticed Asborn's gaze on them. While he did not quite frown, the lines in his forehead grew more pronounced.

Aelthena turned away and, focusing back on the task at hand, approached the huskarls at the bottom of the final stairwell. They were different men than had stood guard previously, and she hoped they would have different sentiments than their predecessors.

"I come escorting Lord Bor, the Jarl of Oakharrow, and Thane Asborn. Do we have admittance?"

The older of the two guards, a man with a patchy gray beard, nodded at once. "You do, Lady Heir Aelthena. Lord Petyr has issued you permission."

Aelthena wondered if Lady Olga had been whispering in her husband's ear for such a dramatic change of heart. *Behind every good man, indeed,* she thought. *Or at least every man with a wife.*

"Good." Glancing over her shoulder, she met Frey's eyes, and he nodded at her. He would stay below, as was proper. With Asborn's gaze upon her, she did not linger, but set up the stairs.

As she opened the door to the tower's top, a chill wind greeted her, the scent of rain riding upon it. Aelthena repressed a shiver as she took in those in attendance. All the other jarls had already arrived. Petyr, neatly manicured, watched her with his mouth smiling and his eyes grave. Hother no longer sported his circlet, at last acknowledging the futility of the accessory. Siward stared at her, fire seeming to have returned to his eyes. She did not acknowledge him, but trusted he was a man of his word. He would do as he had said.

Alrik and Harald stood by a window, their heads close together in conference. They turned and met her gaze, something searching in their expressions. But she could not unveil the deception yet, so she gave them as little as she had Siward.

She met Ragnar's gaze last of all. The traitor smiled as her eyes alighted on him. Though she knew she had him beat, Aelthena wondered how it would feel to put a knife into one of those lake-blue eyes. The thought lingered longer than she expected. But though she kept a blade hidden under the folds of her dress, she kept it sheathed.

Your time will come, she promised him silently. First, she had an election to win.

Her gaze lifted to the one other present, looming behind Ragnar's chair. Bastor had shaved and dressed according to his rank for once. He seemed awkward in the stiff-collared tunic and jacket, yet startlingly handsome. Despite the shadows around his eyes, she found the garb suited him better than she had thought possible. As he returned her stare, Aelthena looked away, somehow afraid he would see her plans in her eyes.

"Good; all are present." Without rising, Lord Petyr gestured to one of the empty chairs around the map table. "Please, Lord Bor, sit and be welcome."

The jarls watched her father as Uljana escorted him to his chair. Lord Bor slumped heavily into it, his chin almost falling to his chest before his head jerked back up.

Aelthena's muscles went as hard as iron. With an effort, she forced herself to relax. She longed to flee the pitying eyes and furtive smirks as they observed what the mighty Bor the Bear had become.

Let them laugh, her father had once told her. *It is all the power they will know.* She had been young at the time, perhaps nine winters old, and had just slipped and fallen in the mud. The other children in the Harrowhall's yard had fled giggling upon Lord Bor's entrance. Her father had helped her stand. He did not pull her into an embrace, but kept a hand on her shoulder. She had thought then it was to keep her muddy clothes from touching his. Now, she saw the truth: he had let her stand on her own. Even then, though she doubted he realized it, he had been grooming her to take up his mantle.

I cannot protect you, Father, she thought as she looked down at his disheveled hair. *No more than you could protect me then.* Somehow, the thought brought her a measure of relief.

As Harald and Alrik sat, the Jarl of Petyrsholm continued. "We will not mince words. A thing lies before us, a thing we have long put off, but cannot any longer. Today, we choose who among us will lead Baegard's armies in the war against Ha-Sypt."

The narrow-faced man turned his gaze around at the attendees, most of whom were nodding to his words. Aelthena, standing behind her father next to Asborn, was now ignored, for she was of no consequence to him. Her father's past advice held close, she let the slight pass.

"Unless there are objections, we will hold the election for the Arkjarl." Petyr paused, and when none were voiced, continued. "Very well. Would any put themselves forward, or nominate another, for consideration?"

Siward, who had bowed his head, now raised it. His

eyes flickered toward her, but settled on Asborn. She slowly looked around at her betrothed, and the gazes of all other attending followed.

Asborn blanched under their gazes, but maintained his composure as he spoke. "I nominate Lord Siward Jonson," he said in a carrying voice.

Petyr's eyebrows shot upward, while Hother darted a glance at Ragnar. The Jarl of Ragnarsglade did not seem to see anything amiss, for he still wore that infuriating smile of his. Alrik rumbled his approval and leaned his elbows onto the table, while Harald held his silence.

"Very well," Petyr said, a touch of annoyance in his voice. Perhaps he had hoped against reason for the honor of a nomination. "Lord Siward is to be considered. Any others?"

Aelthena looked again over the other jarls. Hother seemed the most likely to put himself forward for such a distinction, but even he was no fool. Mouth pinched, he squinted at Ragnar for a long moment, then said, "I would have Lord Ragnar considered for it."

Part of her had hoped no one would volunteer his name. *But things could never be that easy.*

"Very well," Petyr said. "Lord Ragnar will be considered as well. If there are no others, would anyone speak before the voting?"

Her time had come at last. *To bury Ragnar's dreams.* She stepped forward, her dress brushing against the table, and all eyes in the room drew toward her. Bastor's seemed to burn into her, intent and questioning. She ignored him and looked around at the jarls seated before her. He would find out soon enough how she truly felt about the matter.

"My lords," she began, "and others gathered, before the votes are cast, there is something you must know about one of those considered. About the secrets Lord Ragnar has kept from you."

Alrik, never subtle at the best of times, openly grinned. Harald dared a shy smile. Siward only looked grim, and Asborn anxious. Bastor frowned, and the muscles in his arms seemed to bunch under his fine shirt.

But it was the other three jarls with whom her attention was occupied. Petyr seemed bemused; Hother, more perplexed. He glanced at Ragnar as if for reassurance, and she followed his gaze. The Jarl of Ragnarsglade seemed calm, his expression placid, his brow uncreased. As if he had expected this very ambush.

The first stirrings of doubt coursed through her. *Don't question it now*, she told herself. *You will prevail. You must. All Baegard will pay the price if you do not.*

Aelthena drew in a breath and continued, her voice more certain than she felt. "You have discovered a weapon, have you not, Lord Ragnar? Firesand, I believe you call it."

Ragnar gave her a slight smile. "Yes. I do."

"And this weapon — when introduced to a flame, it produces an effect miraculously similar to dragonfire, does it not? The same dragonfire that consumed my home and led to Oakharrow's downfall?"

The jarl's smile widened. "I did not see the conflagration, so I cannot say."

The others muttered now. Even Alrik and Harald seemed troubled by the implications. Knowing treachery would be a step too far, Aelthena drew herself back in.

"Do not mistake me — I am not claiming you are behind that attack. No one would question your loyalty to Baegard." A scowl tried to assert itself, but she fought it back down. "What I am saying is that you possess the very sorcery that our enemies employed against us, yet have not mentioned it. What reason would you have for that, Lord Ragnar? I have a guess."

"Do you?" Ragnar gestured expansively. "By all means, do tell."

He was far too willing. *Is this my trap?* she asked herself. *Or his?* Perhaps she had not been the first to break her oath. Aelthena's eyes flickered to Bastor, then away. No — the hurt in his gaze was too real to be feigned.

"Here is what I think. You, Lord Ragnar, want to wear the Iron Circle, and you judged it easiest to do by making your fellow jarls see you as their only salvation. By withholding knowledge of firesand, you portrayed this war as unwinnable, hoping they would be desperate enough to make you their leader."

She paused, judging how her words were being received. Hother and Petyr were looking at each other now. *Good.* They were having doubts. So long as the election was held soon, she could exploit those to put the Iron Circle on Siward's head.

But Ragnar still seemed too calm by half. "Is that all?" he all but drawled, his cold eyes steady on hers.

Aelthena gave him a tight smile. "Holding our nation hostage is not enough?"

"Then let me say my piece." The Jarl of Ragnarsglade stood, drawing himself up to his full height, not an ounce of shame in his appearance. Aelthena stepped back, feeling as if she waited for a lawspeaker's sword to fall on her neck.

Ragnar gazed upon each of the jarls for a moment, then spoke in a slow, carrying voice. "I did not deceive you. Until just days before, I was uncertain firesand could be used as a weapon. It is a volatile and dangerous substance, liable to ignite at the slightest mistake. The containers used, the mechanisms for lighting it..." He waved a hand before him.

"Many factors must be considered, and I have had little time in which to consider them."

To Aelthena's horror, Hother and Petyr nodded at his words. Siward's expression darkened, and his bangles rattled as he sat back and crossed his arms. She tried to catch his eye, but he only stared at Ragnar, waiting for him to continue.

Then she felt Ragnar looking at her, and she slowly met his gaze. *Like the eyes of a snake,* she thought, and did not bother to hide her fury.

"One quality a leader must possess is knowing when to divulge information," Ragnar said, almost seeming to lecture her. "Speak too soon, and you risk awakening false hope and undermining your authority." His eyes slid away from her to the others gathered. "I did not hold back what I had learned of firesand to deceive you, my lords. This very day, this very meeting, I intended to announce it, no matter who was made Arkjarl. For there are far more important matters to consider than personal ambition. Do you not agree, Lady Heir?"

For a moment, she was speechless. Somehow, he had made her accusations bolster his reputation, not undermine it. Siward had drawn into himself, while Harald and Alrik shared a look rife with doubt. Even Asborn was staring at her, seeking confirmation that their course was correct, though he knew of Ragnar's treachery as well as she did.

But there was only one thing she could say, one phrase that rang uncomfortably true in that moment. How much of electing Siward over Ragnar had been for her ambition rather than the good of all?

Ragnar's a Djur-burned traitor! part of her railed. *He'll ruin us all!* Yet Bastor believed in him as the best man for the job, even still. Whatever else Ragnar's heir was, she had never thought him a fool.

The silence had stretched too long. She raised her chin and spoke the words. "I do."

Ragnar nodded gravely, though cruel amusement gleamed in his eyes. "If that matter is settled, I think we should move to the vote. Lord Petyr?"

"Wait."

Aelthena's stomach dropped. Siward, whose gruff voice had spoken, stood then. His posture was bowed, but his dark eyes were steady with resolve.

Ragnar smiled as he sat. "Please, Lord Siward. Speak your piece."

Siward nodded sharply toward him. "The Arkjarl must be elected by a unanimous vote. Baegard must be united behind one shield. I would not further divide us now with the enemy at our doorstep." He bowed his head for a moment, then raised it, looking balefully out from under his bristling eyebrows. "I withdraw myself from consideration."

The room erupted into fresh mutters. Aelthena barely heard them. She stared at Siward as he slumped into his chair again. For all his words, he seemed a defeated man.

You are, she thought, as if he might hear her words. *We have both failed.*

"Very well," Petyr said with a sigh, as if weary of the proceedings. "Then we shall consider Lord Ragnar as the exclusive candidate. Unless anyone else has something to say..."

He looked around the room, and those gathered fell silent. Only Aelthena's father continued to speak, but his mutters were for himself alone.

Petyr nodded. "All in favor of Lord Ragnar's election?"

The jarls looked at one another. No one moved to speak. Her breath caught. She dared to hope no one would.

Then Siward's hand rose. His eyes remained firmly on the map in front of him, but his arm never wavered.

Hother's followed a moment afterward, then Petyr's. Glancing to her right, she found Asborn's raised as well. As their eyes met, she was glad for the first time that he represented Oakharrow and not her. Had it been otherwise, she was not sure she could have raised her hand, even knowing it was the only choice they now had.

Oakharrow's vote seemed the final straw for the two holdouts. Alrik followed with another noisy sigh, and Harald raised his hand last of all. For all his timorousness, he wore his displeasure openly. She wondered if that would haunt him. Ragnar did not seem the forgiving kind.

Petyr spoke again, drawing her attention back to him. "Assuming you vote for yourself, Lord Ragnar, it appears we are decided. Lord Hother, if you would."

The pompous jarl nodded, then stood and took something from his lap. Aelthena stared at the circle of dull metal as the Jarl of Djurshand held it up in his hands and moved stately around the table to stand behind Ragnar.

The Iron Circle was not a thing of beauty. It lacked the delicate metalworking that the crowns in books always showed: the gemstones, the frivolities, the filigree. But as Hother lowered it over Ragnar's blonde hair, she saw it was never meant to be that kind of diadem. It was a blade, a weapon to aid in the bloody work of the one who wielded it.

As the metal ring settled on the jarl's brow, the wind bayed, gusting in through the cracked windows higher up the chamber and swirling through the clothes of the witnesses. Aelthena imagined it to be the very valley itself protesting Ragnar's appointment. But its objections would do as little good as hers had.

"Before, you were Ragnar Torbenson, Jarl of Ragnarsglade," Hother intoned. "Now, you rise as Highlord Ragnar, Arkjarl of Baegard. Go forth and lead our warriors to victory."

Ragnar, who had sat utterly still while Hother crowned him, now stood. He looked over the others, his features made of stone. Though she would never admit it aloud, the Iron Circle suited him, magnifying the poise and power he naturally possessed. He looked regal.

"Thank you, my lords." Ragnar smiled and lifted his hands. "I will not betray the trust and responsibility you have placed before me."

Traitor! she longed to spit at him. *Nuvvog damn you to the red hells!* Instead, she clenched her jaw until it ached. For all her scheming, she had lost; no amount of fury would change that. And Baegard needed to be united, now more than ever. Even if it was behind this repulsive man, it was better that than her homeland being razed by Syptens.

She exhaled, and a bit of the tension left her.

Ragnar's hands dropped, and his smile disappeared. "We have delayed overlong while our enemies caper through our lands. The so-called 'King of Barbars' has taken our sister city of Oakharrow." Here, Ragnar nodded toward Aelthena's father, though his head was tilted back against the chair in slumber, as well as to Asborn. Though his eyes flitted over her, he did not extend her the same courtesy.

She lifted her chin a fraction higher. She may have accepted his reign, but she would not let him see her despair yawning beneath her, threatening to swallow her down. She would stay strong, even now, when her ambitions crumbled around her, and her enemies seized greater power still. For now, she would be patient and remain in the shadows.

"Our age-old foes, Ha-Sypt, march up from the south," the Arkjarl continued. "Already, they have taken Fairglen, and soon will sweep up other outposts and towns in their wake." Ragnar suddenly slammed a fist onto the table, tumbling the pieces scattered across the map. "Here, we will turn them back! We will meet them with sword, spear, and fire!"

The jarls gave grunts of agreement.

Ragnar came upright, smoothing back a stray hair. "All signs of their movements point to them coming to Petyrsholm. The karah wishes to secure the Whiterun so that his ships may move freely up and down the river, simplifying their supply lines and splitting the jarlheims in two. We cannot let that happen — nor will we."

To Aelthena's surprise, it was Harald who spoke first among the gathered. "And what of their dragonfire?" the young man asked quietly. "And their numbers — they are twice what we can hope to muster."

"And the beasts at their call!" Alrik boomed. "You know, the big gray things?"

"Elephants," Petyr supplied with a thin smile.

"Them ones. They's as big as two houses together, from the way I've heard tell. What in Ovvash's hells can we do about that?"

The Arkjarl only nodded, the picture of graciousness. He seemed to revel in their confidence. "Of course, these are pressing concerns, and we will meet to hone our plans. Before that, however, we must issue the call to gather our men to us."

Alrik thumped his chest. "Aelford should be on the march within the day, Highlord."

The other jarls gave similar assents.

Ragnar smiled. "Wisely done, my lords. Ragnarsglade, too, marches for Petyrsholm and is due to arrive a week before the Sypten forerunners. But we will discuss the formation of troops when we have a full account of our numbers. For now, Lord Harald, I will answer your first question. For I do not doubt that what befell Oakharrow and its castle weigh heavily on many minds."

The Arkjarl paused and looked down at the map, drawing out the suspense until it was as tight as a noose embracing a criminal's neck. Aelthena pressed her arms tighter around her middle, trying to hold in the acid disappointment that threatened to spill forth at any moment. *Stand tall,* she reminded herself. *Don't let them see your pain.*

Finally, Ragnar looked up to the window to stare over the long valley. "Let me tell you more of firesand. In a gulley near Ragnarsglade, a shepherd discovered a pit of a curious nature. It steamed like a hot spring, but was filled with a shimmering powder. Around its edges lay black rocks veined with silver."

"Drascale ore?" Asborn queried, his brow drawn.

"Yes. The stone was drascale ore, previously only known to exist in the mines of Oakharrow."

This revelation was greeted by a round of murmurs from the jarls. Aelthena wondered what to make of that fact.

The Arkjarl clasped his hands behind his back. "But the true marvel is what lays within the pit. This sediment, firesand, has useful properties. You know of its hidden fire, but there are other things. Too much exposure might ruin a man entirely, causing him to grow hair and other grotesque attributes. But once harvested, a single handful can burn down a house."

Ragnar smiled, baring his teeth, and she saw where his son had learned his feral grin. "With it, we will bring the Dragon's flames to our enemy now. Elephants will fall. Chariots will burn. Men will falter and flee."

Aelthena raised her gaze to Bastor, who still leaned against the wall behind his father. The heir slowly met her eyes. She looked away first. His stare was too difficult to hold now.

Alrik stood, slapped a hand on the table, and roared, "We'll turn the bastards back!"

The other jarls grunted assents. Alrik grinned, then clasped Harald on the shoulder, causing the younger man to wince.

"So we will," Ragnar agreed.

Aelthena sighed. Despite her failure, despite the man who now led them, she felt a curious feeling growing inside her. For the first time in a long while, she had hope. They would survive. Though legends rose and old enemies burned the land, they would survive.

But who will come out the other side?

She looked at Asborn and found his eyes bright with hope, his expression mirrored in the other men. It made her want to sigh again. She should have expected nothing else; after all, the best thing he and the jarls could do was cooperate.

She just prayed she had only lost the battle and not the war.

PART II
FURY

"When a real battle starts, you'll always find that there is no bravest man."
— Jackson Crawford, *The Poetic Edda: Stories of the Norse Gods and Heroes*

27. GODS' BLESSINGS

All who swear oaths stray, and the same must be said of those of our order.

As we know, love — or lust, depending on its manifestation — is forbidden. When a man or woman becomes an acolyte, they promise to forgo all physical and emotional affection but for the Inscribed. But one may ask why this is necessary.

The logic is simple: love of one turns the mortal mind away from communal and spiritual matters. A gothi cannot serve their community first if they give their lover primacy. Thus, it is simpler to never make exception.

But as I have said, no oath is kept entirely whole. Mortality is compromise; we would be fools to believe otherwise. When one of our order strays, they are to be accepted back into the pack, though of course with penance to be done.

But as love comes down to us from Yusala herself, it cannot be an evil thing. And so, when it rears, it must be forgiven. Just be sure the punishment is severe enough that such an error is not repeated.

- Counsel on the Inscribed Beliefs, by Mother Vigilance

They rose before dawn to begin their ascent.

Despite the early hour, Bjorn jangled with nerves. It was not only for what — or who — they hoped to find high upon Yewung's bluff sides. Often, he had looked up at the mountain's towering heights, both from afar in Oakharrow and throughout their journey through the Teeth, and it had seemed like the sky — distant, beautiful, untouchable. He felt it would always stay at a distance, even as they hiked to its feet.

And now he meant to climb it.

The venture involved more equipment than their passage through the Teeth. As he had arranged his bloated pack next to Yonik, Loridi, and Seskef the night before, he stared at all arrayed before him with both fascination and horror. Ice axes. Iron-ridged clogs, contraptions that provided traction for one's boots. Heavy ropes that could take a man's weight. It was so much gear Bjorn thought he would tip over when he put it on and began scrambling up the side of the cliffs.

Yonik, with a sparkle in his eye, had tried to console him. "I have climbed several mountains before, so trust me, Bjorn — when you're hanging off the side of a cliff, you try your damndest not to fall."

"Whatever you say, old wolf." Despite his nerves, Bjorn had grinned at the priest, and Yonik had returned it.

He clung to that assurance as he shrugged on the pack and tottered under its weight. He had not been idle since reaching Eildursprall, but no amount of training in the yard could prepare him to wear a heavy pack once more — and this one weightier than the one he'd carried before, for Clap had been there to assist him. Fumbling the ties with fingers made clumsy by the cold, he cursed under his breath.

"You ready?"

Bjorn nodded toward Seskef's silhouette as he came near him. "Ready as ever."

"I, for one, am looking forward to this," Loridi said as he joined them in the middle of their bedchamber.

"Where's the priest?" Bjorn had noticed Yonik's bed was empty that morning and his pack disappeared with him.

"Probably gone for one last wallop through the snow." Loridi shook his head, just visible in the darkness. "That man is unnatural, no mistaking it."

With no more reason to delay, they headed out of the lodge. The sky was clear and light gray, the sun still shy below the horizon. A heavy chill draped over Bjorn as he stepped outside, like he walked through a translucent curtain. Fighting down a shiver, he led the other two men through the quiet compound to the Etching Wall, where they had agreed to meet.

There, Yonik and Hoarfrost awaited them, their packs leaning against the rock face. A third rucksack and three more people stood with them. Bjorn had only met Sister Embla the night before, when she had given their party brief instructions on the equipment they would use for their ascent. She seemed much like Hoarfrost in her toughness and abilities, though with a lighter sense of humor. She took every opportunity to rib the Skyardi, and though Bjorn had not thought the barbar woman amenable to it, Hoarfrost smiled and made small japes in return. They stood now together, their heads bent toward one another like leaning rocks.

"So that's still happening, is it?" Loridi groaned.

Before Bjorn could ask what he meant, the last two figures pulled back their hoods. He had wondered if it was Mother Sign waiting with them, but could not think why she would. Even more surprising was the one who stood next to her. Tyra's face was serious, but her green eyes were bright even in the gloom. He guessed the acolyte had volunteered to lead the Silver that morning.

But why?

His stomach did flips as Bjorn untied and deposited his pack next to the others, then tottered over to stand before them. Though he longed to say something to Tyra, no words came. After a prolonged glance, he looked instead at the Silver.

"Mother Sign, I'm afraid I won't be making my lessons this morning."

The Silver cracked a wide grin. "The cub finally found his sense of humor, did he? I'm not here for lessons; I'm here for your graduation."

Bjorn's mind turned over that. "But if all goes well, we'll be back within three days. Sister Embla said it was two days' climb up to the cave and one back down."

"Much can happen in a short amount of time. And who's to say you'll stay once you return?"

He only shrugged, then glanced again at Tyra. Her face held only more questions. Before Bjorn could speak, Mother Sign held up a small satchel, weighted with several clunky items. Taking it, Bjorn pried open the ties and peered inside. He knew by the foreign touch on his mind what they were even before his eyes registered the familiar lines on the smooth rocks.

He looked back into the Silver's clouded eyes. "Runestones? What for?"

An enigmatic smile curled her lips. "Do you forget I am a *Volur* myself, cub? I give them to you because I have seen that I must!" The aged woman waggled her gloved fingers as if teasing a young child.

Bjorn frowned down into the bag. Reaching in, he

shifted the five runestones about, accounting for each. *Heartfire. Mend. Farsight. Wolf Eyes. Frenzy.*

At the last, he jerked his head back. It felt as if a brand had touched the inside of his skull. Bjorn tried to hide his wince as he closed the bag and looked up into the Silver's sightless eyes. He felt Tyra's gaze intently upon him.

"I haven't practiced most of these," he said. "And you've said they're dangerous. Farsight, Frenzy — even Mend and Heartfire have their pitfalls. Are you sure I should take them?"

"You are already in peril." Mother Sign patted down his arm until she found his hand. In a rare show of affection, she squeezed it. "Do not misunderstand me, Bjorn — they *are* deadly, and must only be used in the direst of circumstances. But you are *Volur*, a trueborn seer. Using the runestones, fraught as it may be, is what you were born to do."

He had not imagined himself born to do anything but serve as the lawspeaker and walk in his brothers' shadows. Now Annar and Yof were gone, and Bjorn was in exile. Oakharrow was under the Jotun's thumb, and the best he could hope for Aelthena was that she had escaped. He had tried to act as the jarl's heir, but had led his company to ruin, and gotten Keld, the only person in all of Enea who had looked up to him, killed.

In all the upturning of his world, he was glad to have at least one purpose to which he could cling.

Bjorn squeezed Mother Sign's hand back. Even through the gloves, he felt comfort from it. "Thank you," he murmured, lowering his gaze. He hoped Tyra didn't detect the moisture that pricked his eyes.

By the Silver's smile, she heard it in his voice. "There, there," Mother Sign said, words dripping with sarcasm. "You're not off to your death, and neither am I. But mind that you take care of those — they're worth more than any green hunt bounty."

"I will."

With that, Tyra led Mother Sign over to Yonik. The Silver conferred with him and Hoarfrost while the acolyte's gaze drifted back to Bjorn. Wiping his eyes covertly, he edged toward her. It seemed to take an agonizingly long time, but Tyra sighed and unwrapped her arm from the Silver's to walk toward him. The eyes of the other three followed them for a moment, but they were tactful enough to look away. Bjorn was glad for the darkness to hide his flush. He hoped they had not guessed at his feelings for the acolyte.

Tyra stopped before him. For a long moment, they stood in silence. Bjorn desperately tried to think of something clever, but his mind came up blank. He was relieved when Tyra spoke until her words sunk in.

"You've been avoiding me."

His cheeks burned hotter. "I haven't," he said at once. But his nature was too honest to lie for long. "That is... I've been busy."

Her flat look told him she knew the truth. "Why? I thought we were friends."

"We are friends."

Tyra had always been even-tempered. Now, he saw the first glimmers of anger, and he feared them all the more for their first appearance.

"Bjorn..."

As if his name were an incantation, he found his lips unlocked, and all he had tried to hold back poured out. "We're friends, of course we're friends. But I... You're training to be a priestess, and I'm to be..." But he couldn't tell her what he was, because he did not know himself. *The jarl's heir? A seer? Or some other unknowable fate?*

He tried again. "We can't..."

She'll slap me. I deserve to be slapped. That he would insinuate a relationship between them likely offended her to a degree that they could never be friends afterwards.

So he was shocked as she leaned closer and pressed her lips lightly to his cheek. They left behind a moist impression that burned cold with the wind's touch.

"My mother left Heim Numen to be with my father," Tyra murmured. "Or there are other ways. I know you're a seer, Bjorn. But even you can't see the whole future."

With a fleeting smile, the acolyte turned from him, her gloved hand lingering on his for a moment. Then she was striding back over toward Mother Sign.

Dazed, Bjorn stood there, wondering at all that had just happened. When he came back to himself, he figured he'd better not look more foolish than he already did, and so joined the other knot, where Loridi was teasing Sister Embla. He was too much in his thoughts to even be surprised when he found it was actually the other way around, with the priestess giving the joker a hard time.

"You look as if that pack will snap you in two," Sister Embla was saying as she ran a critical eye over the tall, spare man. She herself did not appear thickset, though it was difficult to tell with the number of furs draped over each of them.

Loridi pretended outrage. "I, Lord Sword, famed blademaster and adventurer, take offense at that!"

"He moans about his back every night," Seskef whispered to the gothi loud enough for all to hear.

As Sister Embla barked a laugh, Yonik and Hoarfrost rejoined them. Bjorn glanced back to see Mother Sign and Tyra making their slow way back through the snow. His gaze lingered on the acolyte's back until Embla clearing her throat drew his attention.

Their guide looked around at their party with narrowed eyes, her earlier amusement fading. "Well, if we're all set, we'd best be off. Yewung makes her own storms, and they come without warning or care for who clings to her sides. And that still doesn't account for the Djur-burned clear skies we have today."

As Bjorn tried to hide his surprise at hearing a gothi curse, Loridi ventured, "Surely we'd prefer the sun warming our way?"

"Not so," Hoarfrost interjected. "Sun will melt the snow and make avalanches more likely. Not to mention blind us."

Embla nodded and gave the Skyardi a tight smile. "Right. To be safe, we'll make our first camp just past noon, though sooner is better."

With that, the priestess began issuing orders like a drang to his company, and they strapped on their packs once more and set for the path. The way up Yewung began little steeper than it had been when they first hiked into the Teeth. Even as the straps of his rucksack dug through his furs and into his shoulders, Bjorn found himself warming to the exercise. His body seemed to remember the challenge and, in defiance of reason, rejoiced at it. Air whistling through his teeth, he grinned as he labored up the hill after Embla and Hoarfrost. Yonik plodded next to him, as little winded by the exercise as usual, while Loridi and Seskef took up the rear.

The elation of the endeavor quickly faded. As the sun rose, the world around them brightened. Ascending on the western face of Yewung, they were left in shadow for the first few hours, but their reprieve was fleeting. Soon, sweat poured down his face and froze in his hair and on his burgeoning scruff. Bjorn squinted against the blinding glare. He sought some relief by pulling on his snow mask, a cloth hood with only a slit to see through. While this blocked out much of the brightness, the narrowing of his vision was terrifying on such precarious terrain. He reeked of his own fear inside the mask, and his limbs trembled with it.

But despite the strain and stress, as he looked out west over the Baegardian valley, slowly unveiled from behind the lesser mountains of the Teeth, he discovered a peacefulness upon Yewung's sides unlike anything he had felt before. Only the wind breathed up here with their company. All the rest of the world laid out below them, spread in splendid glory. Immediately below, he saw the razor-edged peaks for which the mountain range was named sawing out the borders of the vale. Beyond the gray-and-white tors lay Baegard in spring. The distant meadows and forests glowed green in the morning sunlight, softened by a faint mist. The Whiterun slithered through the green like a vast, pale serpent, from the Torn Hills in the north to branch into the Sypten rivers, Qal and Nu, in the south.

Bjorn looked upon it and stretched his cold-chapped lips wide. This was his home, the place he fought to protect. This beauty and bounty, which sustained his people, and they cared for in return. He remembered his vision of fire burning through it, leaving little but ashes and blackened bones in its wake. But this — *this* was what he resolved to recall should he ever lose his way.

His attention was drawn back to the climb as Embla halted their company at a place with no way forward. Then she pointed up, and Bjorn's spirits settled heavy in his boots.

"Now we climb!" the priestess shouted, her voice muffled by her snow mask and the ever-present wind.

Embla had them tie a long, heavy rope to their waists, a task that reminded Bjorn too much of his company's descent into Chasm Valley. She then instructed that they secure their iron clogs to their boots, take out their ice axes, and follow her lead. With no more orientation than that, she turned and set to the climb.

Bjorn watched her, then Hoarfrost, proceed up the sheer wall of ice. They moved in a deliberate repetition, striking with one pick, then the other, before hauling themselves up to strike in their spiked boots.

As the slack in the rope tightened, it came to his turn. Stepping up to the base of the cliff, he struck the ice face with one of his ice axes. When it bounced loose, he tried again, and this time, it held. Cutting in the second pick, Bjorn tested his weight and was surprised when he could drag himself up. As he kicked his boots into the ice and found his footing, exhilaration coursed through him. Though he was mere feet off the ground, he distinctly felt that nothing lay below him.

"Not going to get up it just by looking at it!" Loridi called at his back.

Grimacing, Bjorn craned his neck and saw the tall stretch of ice still before him. *Long way to go,* he thought grimly.

Working loose one of his picks, he reached up for his next hold.

He inched his way up the cliff. Loridi came behind, and finally Seskef and Yonik. Bjorn could not spare a glance down to watch their progress. It was not long before his arms and legs burned, and his heavy pack threatened to pitch him backward. He kept himself pressed as close to the cliff face as he could, but it was never close enough. Setting his picks once more, he moved up to his next foothold.

His foot slipped.

As he lost traction on one boot, then the other, Bjorn clung to his ice axes. His arms screamed, threatening to give way. Chest heaving, head spinning, Bjorn scrabbled to get a foothold. Yells called from above and below, but he could not hear their words through the blood roaring in his ears. He kicked at the ice and felt it shatter under the iron ridges. Panic set in. He could not hold on. He would let go, and fall into Loridi, and all of them would fall—

His foot hit the cliff again, and this time, it stuck.

Bjorn could do nothing but suck in air for several long moments. As the din in his ears faded, he registered what the others were saying.

"...alright, Bjorn?" Hoarfrost shouted down.

"Fine!" He squeezed the word from his throat. "I'm fine!"

To his surprise, he was. *Frightened, but fine.* He had slipped and had not fallen. He survived.

I can do this.

Though he should have been more afraid, Bjorn found his confidence had grown instead. With a wide grin, he set his feet higher, then worked his picks free for fresh holds.

He kept climbing.

Bjorn collapsed at the top of the cliff. Loridi groaned as he sloughed off his pack and fell down next to him. Seskef panted and bowed forward over his splayed legs. When they'd caught their breath, the men clapped Bjorn on the back and shook him until he was grinning against the fabric of his snow mask.

"If anyone should have slipped, it was me," Loridi insisted, a hand pressed to his gut. "I think I'm carrying a bit more weight than I should."

"I could use some relief, too." Bjorn shook his head. "Nearly pissed myself just then."

As the jester guffawed, Embla plodded over to stand before the company. The gothi seemed tireless, outmatching even Yonik and Hoarfrost's endurance in the climb, and she remained straight-backed as she scanned her masked face over them.

"We'll reach a glacier up ahead," she said, just loud enough for all to hear. "There, we can take care of any necessities, if you men will deign to look away."

Though Bjorn expected Loridi to seize the opportunity for a ribald joke, he only waved a hand.

"Just off the glacier," the priestess continued, "we'll stop at our night's shelter, a shallow cave the ice has carved out."

Bjorn nodded with the others. During the preparations the day before, Yonik had informed him it was imperative to give plenty of time for their bodies to acclimate to mountain heights. *Push too hard*, the priest warned, *and your blood grows thin*. Bjorn had worried over the possibility all throughout the ascent, and was glad to be nearing the day's end.

The glacier proved no more challenging than the initial hike, and they soon reached Embla's cave. Bjorn put down his pack and set to making camp with the others. They had to conserve the little fuel they had brought for communing with the King of Ice, so their meal of smoked caribou and hardtack was warmed by nothing more than their body heat.

He expected the evening to drag long and dull, wits and tongues dulled by the day's march. But despite their exhaustion and the sound of avalanches rumbling in the distance, Bjorn found the company to be in high spirits. Embla and Hoarfrost often held their own conversations separate from the others. Among the men, Loridi stoked the embers of dialogue every time they cooled. At the jester's insistence, each member of the company went around and told an anecdote, most amusing.

Loridi began, recounting a tale Bjorn had heard on their initial journey into the Teeth, a convoluted plot that involved an adopted vixen, a jilted lover, and a feud that ended in a harmonious feast between rivals. After the dubious story's conclusion, the jester convinced Embla to speak next. Bjorn was shocked at her raunchy tale of a nude rendezvous with a lover in the mountain springs of her tribe's summer grounds. He noticed her eyes flickered over to Hoarfrost often during the telling, and the Skyardi did not seem to object to the attentions.

As he puzzled through this, Yonik leaned in next to him and spoke in a hushed voice, "So you finally noticed."

Bjorn glanced around, but Loridi and Seskef were bent together, while Hoarfrost and Embla had returned to their own dialogue. "Noticed what?" he asked cautiously.

The priest wore a half-cocked smile. "I trust you know the old stories of the Inscribed from your readings?"

Bjorn shrugged. "And from attending the temple."

"Then you will have heard of the romance between Volkur and Ovvash."

"I suppose so." The tales held it that the Goddess of War and the Maiden of the Dead were enamored with a passion born of their neighboring dominions. It was claimed that they went to every battle with hands held, for death and glory were never far apart in a fight.

"Passion exists not only between men and women. Just as the gods have shown us, desire lies among the sexes as well — women with women, men with men."

At once, he realized what he meant. In a way, it was not surprising. But his last words spawned a different notion.

Men with men...

Slowly, he looked over at his stalwart companions huddled in the back of the shallow cave. It was true that Seskef and Loridi were inseparable.

But can they be...?

"So I suspect," Yonik murmured, speaking to Bjorn's

thoughts, which must have been plain in his gaze. "But I hope it will not color your impression of them. They have as much right to it as any, and are smiled upon by the gods."

Bjorn nodded. The thought was a bit unsettling, but more for its unfamiliarity than the idea itself. *Doesn't everyone deserve love?* His thoughts flitted to Tyra: his glimpse of her in the baths, her kiss on his cheek. He was glad his cheeks were already flushed from the cold.

If Embla can be with Hoarfrost, then can Tyra...?

He didn't dare voice the thought aloud. The hope was too precious.

The priest pressed his shoulder and smiled through his beard, dripping with melting frost. "I thought you would understand. You've an open mind, Bjorn, and an open heart. I have long admired that in you."

He looked over, surprised out of his daydreams. It was a strange thought, Yonik admiring him.

"Thank you," was all he could think to say.

The gothi pressed his shoulder once more before releasing him. And though the cold pressed in closer as darkness fell, Bjorn found the praise kept him a bit warmer.

28. A RECKONING

When treating with the Winter Holds before a siege, the wise general sends an expendable emissary, for they are as likely to be returned a head as an accord.

- Sieging the Winter Holds, by Paser Baka, general to Holy Karah Khufu

The bluff walls of the enemy city had only just come into view when the karah summoned her.

As she bobbed with the movement of the slaves bearing her palanquin, Sehdra looked out across the valley toward Petyrsholm. The sun shone merrily in a periwinkle sky, only a few wisps of clouds adding texture to it. The mountains, tall and white-capped, lined the horizon to the east, west, and the distant north, majestic in their lofty heights. Within the valley, spring had blossomed. Flowers were everywhere, some even remaining as yet untrampled between the tents of the army. They grew so wild and free that she imagined she had momentarily slipped into the Jackal's Delight. The trees were dyed various shades of green, some wreathed in new leaves, while the pines had brightened with the return of life. The upper Qal — or Whiterun, as Baegardians named the river — ran clear and strong with the snowmelt, glittering in the noon sun.

It was as arresting a sight as she had ever witnessed. It inspired awe and wonder at all the world could hold.

And we come to destroy it.

A heavy weight pressed down on her breast, and Sehdra sank back into her pillows. Already, the valley was ruined by their passage. Hooves and elephantine feet and tens of thousands of muddy boots trampled the flowers. Chariot wheels cut through the fields. The trees had begun to fall as soon as the army halted, fortifications and siege weapons swiftly constructed from their trunks. Everywhere she looked, the valley was being consumed, as if they were a swarm of locusts.

Who is to say we are not?

She arrived at the karah's pavilion and dismounted with Teti's aid. His expression was drawn, dark smears under his eyes like he had wiped mud over his skin. She had often awoken the past several nights to find him out of his cot, and knew sleep had evaded him as well as her.

Not wanting him to worry, she smiled at him; though, with her masks forbidden to her, she wondered how reas-suring she looked.

"He just wants to keep an eye on me," she said. "Nothing is going to happen."

Teti smiled in return, though it was strained and small. "Of course, Royal Sister."

There was nothing more to say, and no time to say it, for they were stepping beneath the raised flaps of the grand tent.

Within, the aromas overwhelmed her senses. Smoke and incense filled the air, thick and cloying. Sehdra fought down a cough and peered through watering eyes at her brother's throne. As usual, the karah lounged in it, a cup of wine lolling from one hand, a smoking vase cradled in the other. He was surrounded by people — advisors, generals, Vizier Zosar, and other sycophants — yet paid little attention to any of them.

And, as always, a deeper shadow loomed beyond him, presiding over the menagerie.

Physt's bored expression sharpened as she entered. Any hopes of avoiding notice faded as he straightened and called through curling lips, "Sister! At last, you join us. Come — I have fine news to share."

Trying to hide her limp, Sehdra waved Teti back and strode forward. Her brother would not harm her directly, not severely at least, but Teti was always vulnerable. The further he stood from her when Physt's attention was upon her, the better for both of them.

As his court parted to stare at her with thinly veiled disdain, Sehdra labored to bow. "You humble me with your summons, Divine One."

"Yes, yes, everyone is always humbled." Hephystus gestured impatiently, and Sehdra rose from her prostrations with a wince. "I have more amusing things to attend to than your adulation. Fine news indeed, sister. Or have you already heard?"

Uneasiness was a caged lion within her. "I am afraid I do not know what you speak of, Your Sanctity."

"No? And here I thought you had spies seeded among my council." He gave a careless wave over the gathered notables, who turned their gazes upon each other, no doubt wondering whom the karah could mean. Only the vizier kept his eyes on her, an imperious smile making his features even crueler than usual.

"Fine news," Physt repeated, and he took a long pull of

his wine before leaning forward. "I have a singular privilege to bestow upon you. You, dear sister, are to be my emissary in our initial negotiations with the savages."

The ramifications of the announcement pounded in her head. She suddenly felt a caged beast, the karah's flatterers watching in open mockery. They, like her, knew what this meant.

Sehdra sought for calm as she spoke. Only years of practice kept her voice from shaking. "You honor me, Divine One."

Physt's lips curled, and he leaned back. Next to his makeshift throne, Vizier Zosar scowled. That, at least, gave her a glimmer of satisfaction.

"We will see if you feel that way when you arrive," her brother said. "A messenger has been sent. You are to meet them midway in three days at dawn. Be sure to make your prayers and sacrifices before then."

"Of course, Divine One." She bowed lower still. "Deference to the gods is ever important."

"Yes, yes, of course." He waved a lazy hand. "Oh, and when you meet the savages, you are to demand their complete and unconditional surrender."

Her throat went even drier than before. Such terms were untenable; they were a blatant insult. And such an offense would be sure to rouse the Baegardians' wrath, which they would take out on the most convenient victim. Physt's smile grew as he saw her dawning realization.

He meant to kill her. Her own brother played with her life as easily as he played with the others.

If he is not a god, then he has a god's callous heart.

Her bitterness surprised her. It was no less than she should have expected from him. Yet somewhere deep within her, she had always harbored hope that he cared for her, at least a sliver.

So swiftly, he squashed that hope.

Sehdra raised her eyes to the shadowed monolith behind the throne. But if Oyaoan cared of what had befallen her, the huamek gave no sign of it. Sehdra had begun to believe the giantess had plans for her, plans that would defy Hephystus, and perhaps even grant her a measure of her own power. But it had been foolish to expect protection.

I am a tool to them. For amusement or for convenience, she would be cast away at the first sign of a flaw.

She had carefully pruned her emotions over the long years spent in the karah's court. She had schooled herself through the tutelage of her mother and the hard lessons of her appearance to repress her true feelings and keep a level head. But now, something beat within her like a second heart. She had so little indulged it she almost did not recognize it.

She had not realized she could still feel fury such as this.

"Well, sister?" Physt openly grinned. "Do you have no thanks to give your karah?"

His amusement was mirrored in the expressions of his retinue. Vizier Zosar bared his bright teeth along with his master like a trained Suncoaster monkey.

As Sehdra smiled back, she imagined herself a leopard, teeth sharp and claws ready. "You have my sincerest gratitude, Divine One, as you must always know."

She bowed low, so low she got down on both knees and folded herself over them. It was a slave's posture, a shocking way for the Royal Sister to show herself, and she heard the murmurs in response. Sehdra remained there for several long breaths before she labored back upright. Her anger blocked out the pain of rising.

Physt had lost his smile. His eyes promised punishment.

Taut silence fell upon the pavilion. She did not quiver or yield. What worse could he offer her than disdain and death?

"Leave us," her brother all but hissed at her.

Without delay, Sehdra turned and limped from the tent.

Though she wanted nothing more than to climb back into her palanquin and rest her aching leg, Teti clung to her hand and arm as he came by her side to assist her up.

"Sehdra," he whispered. Even if she had not seen it in his eyes, his fear would have been plain in his lack of formality. "You must find some way out of this duty. They will kill you for the insult you deal them. Do you not remember the fates of our emissaries in the previous Summer Wars?"

She met his eyes. The tranquility that had evaded her in her brother's pavilion had returned, like the calm within a storm. "All too well. But do not fear, my dear Teti. I am the Scarab, and beetles are hard to kill."

Her friend fell short of a smile. "You are. But it is better still if that is never tested."

She squeezed his hand. "I know. But there must be a reckoning, Teti. Between me and my brother. Between us and Oyaoan."

"Sehdra..."

She pulled away. She loved him as she wished to love her brother by blood. But love could not stop her now from doing what she must.

"I will face this," she told him. "And I will survive. Then we will sort out the rest."

She spoke with finality, forcing Teti to accept it and nod. Sehdra tottered into her palanquin, then was borne back through the valley her brother would soon destroy.

29. FORSWORN

Should a marriage oath be revoked or broken, the woman betrothed shall be seen as undesirable and her family as shunned. For if a man does not remain committed, the fault must lie with the woman.

- The Inscribed Beliefs; Verse the Second, Line the Thirty-second

I s there no end to them?" Asborn murmured.

Aelthena had no response. He gave voice to the despair that weighed on her own chest, heavy as if a moon had fallen upon it. She listened to the horde below and looked out from her balcony over the gathered enemy forces. They seemed as vast and indomitable as the Treacherous Sea was said to be. Baegard could not hope to match them.

Yet we must.

The morning, as if in defiance of the pervading sense of calamity, was bright and cheery. Birds chirped in awakening songs in the trees below the balcony, and squirrels chattered

307

challenges to each other from across the branches. High clouds caught the sun's first rays and painted them scarlet. *Red as blood,* she thought, though she knew it was her mind straining to find omens in the weather.

Though there was to be a truce and parley between their emissaries — a mission to be carried by none other than Bastor himself — the karah's forces had come out in a full show of strength. Their infantrymen stood in neat ranks, spear tips glinting in the rising sun like candle flames. There was a stark difference between them and their mercenaries, both in look and organization. The sellswords, reportedly hailing from the Sumerland, knotted together in jagged lines. They carried a motley assortment of armor and weapons, none of it matching. But their sheer numbers were enough to drive fear deep within her.

Beyond this mass of humanity waited other factions. Chariots, each pulled by two horses, were arranged in neat rows. If her studies had informed her accurately, the carts held one driver and one archer. The fields surrounding Petyrsholm were flat enough to allow for easy navigation.

Behind the chariots loomed behemoths she had only seen drawn in books. *Elephants.* Each was nearly as large as the Jotun, or so it seemed at the distance. Pavilions were erected upon their backs, crawling with half a dozen archers and spearmen.

Beyond that, the forest was slowly being gnawed away by a colony of workers, trees toppled and built into the rising fortifications and siege machines. It grated on her that they must witness their enemies entrenching themselves into their own land, making use of their resources to do so.

Though this was a diplomatic mission, the Sypten king's intentions in displaying his forces were clear: *Yield, or die.* Aelthena was beginning to believe the choice might be as simple as that. Though with Bastor as the emissary, she would not be surprised if he returned with heads swinging from his saddle.

But Baegard was not without its own weapons.

Ever since the election of Highlord Ragnar, Petyrsholm had come alive. The meandering preparations for war increased tenfold, and every able man was conscripted and made to dig, build, and train. Women and children were put to work as well, sewing, laundering, and supplying soldiers in their endless need to eat. Some even fletched arrows and put together rudimentary armor for those who had none. A steady stream of warriors from the other jarlheims had poured into the city's walls, packing the crowded city even tighter. And though they suffered some losses from the poor conditions of the camps, at the last estimate she had heard, their forces neared seven thousand.

Seven thousand. Their enemy looked to have thrice that, if not more. Yet they had the walls, and they had their secret defenses. She clutched her sputtering hope close and prayed it would be enough.

"Have the sentries called an estimate of their forces?" asked Aelthena.

"Perhaps twenty thousand in the main host, from what I last heard." Asborn gnawed his lip. "Far more than we can hope to muster."

"We have the walls." It sounded a feebler defense when spoken aloud. She tried asserting her faith more strongly. "And we are defending our homeland. We won't yield it to foreign invaders, no matter how many."

Despite her better judgment, she glanced over her shoulder. Frey stood behind them next to the keeper who tailed Asborn that day. As her eyes met the guardian's, he flashed her a tight smile. She wished she could linger upon those bright eyes. *Like a lime-kissed river.* The thought startled her enough to turn back around. She had never been moved to poetry before when staring at a man. She was not sure what to make of the experience.

Aelthena noticed then that Asborn was staring at her. His expression had tightened in a different way than usual.

"Guardian Frey," he said. "Keeper Latham. Please leave us for a moment."

Aelthena looked back as the keeper nodded and turned toward the exit. Frey did not move until Aelthena inclined her head, and even then he went slowly.

When the men had disappeared behind the door, Asborn looked at her and spoke in a rush. "Let us swear our oaths to one another. I cannot wait any longer, Aelthena. I wish to be bonded to you."

She repeated the words in her head. It took an effort to comprehend their meaning. "You wish to marry?" Her tone was as even as she could manage, which amounted to the tottering footsteps of a toddler. "Now? As an army knocks on our walls?"

"Yes, *now*." Asborn took her hands in his. She allowed them to rest limply in his grasp. "This may be our last chance. We might die tomorrow at the hands of Syptens, or the Jotun and his barbars could come down from Oakharrow to trap us from behind. Any number of things might end our lives at any moment, and I don't want to risk my thread running up before you are my wife, and I your husband."

It was as impassioned of a speech as she had ever heard from him, yet Aelthena could not smile. Dread seeped through her, more rising with every word.

A choice. She had to make a choice. And whichever way she swayed would change everything between them.

They had sworn to marry after the season's turning and before the harvest. But with usurpation and war and legends coming to life, she had pushed the promise from mind, an irrelevant personal concern. Yet now, it suddenly reared, demanding a decision.

He's right. We might die at any moment. It was more true for him than her. A thane and a young man, he was honor bound to battle Ha-Sypt when the negotiations inevitably failed. She wondered how that might change her decision. If it was better for Asborn to go to his death believing a comforting lie.

"Aelthena?" His voice was pleading, his face scrunched. Asborn looked as if he might weep at the slightest provocation, a waterskin set to split at the seams.

She thought the sight of him, so nearly broken, would push her toward mercy. How could a man fight when he was robbed of love? How could she send him out to die in her defense after driving a knife through his heart? Aelthena opened her mouth. The words were on her tongue, the biting acid of deceit.

But midway through forming the first word, she halted. A memory, long forgotten, suddenly bubbled to the surface of her mind. She saw Bjorn, no older than seven winters, standing before her and looking up with his worried amber eyes. Aelthena had just wormed the truth of a misdeed from him: that he had indeed spilled ink on their mother's dress. But instead of scolding him, she had been perplexed.

Why didn't you just lie? she had asked.

Lies hurt to keep, Bjorn had answered. *If I lied, how would you ever know me for me?*

She had forgotten it, but now it struck her anew. She might spare her betrothed pain now if he died. But it would not change that it was a festering wound.

Asborn deserved the truth.

Frey deserved the truth.

Gray bloody gods, I deserve the truth.

Aelthena stepped inside, away from the balcony and

any prying eyes not settled on the army on the horizon, and pulled him with her. Asborn's steps were slow, cautious. Drawing in a long shaky breath, she met his eyes and tried not to flinch at the desperation shining from them.

"I'm sorry, Asborn," she murmured. "So, so sorry. But if you're asking me to marry you, here and now... then it's no."

She forced herself to hold his gaze, even as his expression crumpled. Tears trailed down his cheeks, but Asborn did not seem to notice. His eyes flickered back and forth between hers. His hands slipped free to fall by his sides. His color grew even paler than before as he opened his quivering lips to speak.

"I-is this something to do with Frey?"

She could not hide her surprise. "The guardian?" She tried to scoff. "No, of course not."

But even to her own ears, the denial rang hollow.

Asborn's expression shifted. He barely seemed to breathe as he stared at her, silent and unmoving as a tree in winter.

She made another stumbling attempt. "It's just that we've grown apart, Asborn. We're different people. And I... you love me in a way I cannot hope to match. You deserve someone who can."

Despite her resolution, her thin reasoning was riddled with half-truths. *That night in the forest with Frey,* part of her taunted. *Was that you "growing apart" from Asborn, too?*

She pushed the thoughts away. She did not want to remember that, not now. She had confessed as much of the truth as she could. Say more, and Asborn might not only be angry with her — he might never forgive her.

And, though she believed he would never stoop to it, he would have the legal grounds to have her stoned to death.

"Did you use me?"

She startled back to the moment. "Use you? What do you mean?"

Asborn's jaw twitched as he struggled to find words — or perhaps to hold them in.

"As an ally," he finally said. "Did you pretend you would keep our oaths so you had a voice in the Jarlmoot? Did you use me for your political maneuvering? And before, when I allowed you use of Vigil Keep — did you already feel this way, and just kept me on for my resources and influence?"

His voice rose with each new accusation, while Aelthena's heart pounded quicker. She thought of calling for Frey, but she dismissed the notion at once. His appearance could only worsen the situation. No; she could handle this on her own.

"Of course not, Asborn. I loved you once — truly, I did. We did not spend those nights—"

"Don't." Asborn turned his head aside, a hand upraised. She wondered if part of him longed to hit her just then. She only just resisted the urge to step back.

"That is not why I took our oaths, for political gain," Aelthena said instead, softening her voice. "Nor why I kept them. And if it must break our ties now, I understand. But I had to be honest with you. How could we truly know each other otherwise?"

He surprised her with a sudden laugh. "Oh, I know you now. Know you all too well." He almost sneered the words. "Forsworn is what you are. What you always have been."

In the unveiling of that hate, Aelthena saw Asborn's father. Eirik Bloodaxe had passed on more than his red hair to his son.

Staggering as if drunk, the thane turned and made for the door. As he rested a hand on the handle, however, he paused and looked over his shoulder.

"Don't—" he started, then cut off. The next moment,

Asborn heaved open the door and strode out into the hall, slamming it shut behind.

Aelthena still stared at where he had disappeared when the portal opened again. Frey's face appeared through the crack in the doorway. "Aelthena? Are you alright?"

She looked away. "I'm fine, Frey. Just leave me be."

With his usual temerity, Frey slipped inside anyway. He walked slowly across the chamber to stand several paces away, regarding her in silence for a long moment.

"I won't speak," he said at last. "I'll just stand by you. But leaving you be — that is one thing I cannot do."

Aelthena turned back to the balcony, and the striking day outside, and the oncoming clash. Even as she looked, she saw the pinprick dots of horses trotting from Petyrsholm's gates to the tent erected in the vast open area between the two opposing factions. Their emissary, errant as he may be, was going to meet the Sypten envoy.

Gods help us all, she thought. *Bastor will need all of Baltur's wisdom and Skirsala's patience if this is to have any hope of success.*

Though the Inscribed intervening seemed as likely as Ragnar's son preaching peace.

But despite the hopeless situation below, despite all the pain she had just caused one she had long cared for as a friend, despite all the pitfalls of whatever lay between her and Frey, Aelthena found comfort in Frey's words.

"Good," she murmured. "Then come stand next to me and watch the end begin."

30. FINAL ASCENT

*Yewung, the tallest mountain in Enea, held significance
for our ancestors as it does for us. It has always been a
place close to the Inscribed, elevated among the sprites of
ice and air. I do not believe this to be only due to its domineering height, but because mountain apexes were held to
be holy in the Witterland. This seems to me a superstition,
for no climber I have met has been holier than myself, who
has never braved such slopes...*

- Commentary on Djurian Culture, by Alfjin the Scribe

Bjorn awoke before the others the next morning.
Staring into the gloom outside the cave mouth,
where clouds had gathered over Yewung's sides, he
thought over what the day would hold.

This day, if the Silvers spoke true, he would lay eyes
upon Torvald Geirson, the Last King of Baegard. The King
of Ice, of whom he had heard so many tales. He could still
scarcely believe it was possible. That a man could survive,

not only for centuries past his thread's length, but up so high upon such an imposing mountain.

What does he eat? Or drink? How does he keep warm? It seemed impossible that *seidar* might provide all that.

Mother Sign had said Torvald knew things of witchery that none alive did. That he opened doors no other dared touch. But *seidar* was a magic of the mind; it tapped human potential and released it. Did that mean immortality was within any *Volur's* grasp, the secret merely locked away? Could he himself survive without food and water, survive the cold and aging, if he opened the right door? His scholar's courage balked at the prospect.

Such things — they are the providence of the Inscribed. It felt sacrilegious to even contemplate them. Yet, in the privacy of his mind, Bjorn did not deny his intrigue.

He was entranced by the ideas until the others roused. Setting his mind instead to the hike ahead, Bjorn packed up camp and stuffed his share back into his rucksack. As soon as all were ready, Sister Embla led them back out into the frigid dawn and began ascending the glacier.

The sky brightened as they walked, and the wind, never-ceasing, picked up in ferocity. The clouds were scoured away, and Bjorn's skin felt as if it would do the same, even with the protection of the snow mask and his thick furs.

There was nothing for it but to continue forward, roped to one another as they were, plodding with one foot in front of the other. Their journey that day mostly followed the glacier up into the clouds hovering around Yewung's peak, then along a ridge to the cave.

The glacier, however, was not always as forgiving as it had been during the first stretch. Several times, where the slope grew too steep, they were forced to stop and climb with ice axes and iron clogs once more. Each rise took far longer to ascend than the distance seemed to warrant and left Bjorn wheezing in the thin air. Yet compared to the scare of the first ascent, these proceeded with barely a hitch.

When they reached the final ridge, Bjorn had lingering stars in his vision that had nothing to do with the bright snow. Blinking furiously, he tried to see clearly through them to follow the narrow path. Yonik walked just ahead of him, and he kept his eyes on the priest's boots, resolving to stay in a straight line as his balance pitched and tumbled like a ship in a storm.

"Halt!"

Bjorn continued forward two steps before Embla's shout registered. His head felt in a thick fog, like the one that surrounded them. He guessed it to be mid-afternoon, though it was impossible to tell from within the clouds. He looked up and tried to detect what had brought about the delay.

Only then did he see the ridge had widened, and the cliff side opened up before them.

The cave mouth rose as high as two men standing atop each other. Icicles hung down from the rim like the teeth of a wyvern. The ice shone dully in the matte light, yet kept a rich turquoise unmatched by anything he had seen before. The ice continued into the tunnel within, ridged in waves, like the water had frozen midway through rushing down it. The floor itself was like a great tongue, ridges showing where liquid water had once flowed. Bjorn wondered if he had seen anything so mystifying in all his life. The cave seemed to breathe secrets of a world of which he knew nothing.

When he finally tore his eyes away, he looked at his companions and judged their reactions to be much the same as his, even behind their snow masks. Embla watched them, her emerald eyes squinting.

"Once you've recovered your wits," the gothi taunted, "Torvald awaits. We'll shed our gear at the entrance, where we'll make camp tonight, then go in."

Bjorn found himself at once impatient and reluctant. He stepped under the icicles and felt a weight settle over him that had nothing to do with the surrounding ice and stone. Almost, it felt like an omen's coming, like the wind whispering of death before Nuvvog's Rage, or the one that spoke of fire above Eildursprall. But no words reached his ears, only chilly breath, like a sprite of ice haunted them. He shivered and pushed the thoughts from his mind as he shed his pack, pulled off his snow mask, and untied the rope from around his waist.

They lit the two torches they had hauled up the mountain with them, Embla holding one, Yonik the other, then their party pressed forward. Bjorn watched how the firelight danced across the ice. No one spoke, not even Loridi, for even the jester seemed to feel the sleeping solemnity.

Just as Bjorn resolved to break the silence to ask how much farther it was, the ceiling and walls opened up around them. Their labored breathing gathered a faint echo in the large space. Their torches were not the only light; above, a natural flue allowed in a circle of light on the stone floor. Under it, a small mound of ice and snow had accumulated.

Bjorn's gaze traveled beyond it as the opposite wall came into clearer detail.

At first, he detected the unusual formation only by the strange shadows it cast. As their party drew closer, he saw its details. The ice thrust forward here as if water had dripped sideways from the wall as it froze. Each spear seemed sharp enough to impale a man thrust upon it. They bristled from a central point like quills from a porcupine.

Bjorn followed them to their base, where the ice turned darker. In place of the brilliant blue, something obscured the light's passage. Yonik raised his torch, and the firelight reached through the protective ice.

Then he saw him.

No. His thoughts went limp with shock. *It cannot be.*

"King of Ice" was no trivial title. Torvald Geirson was trapped within his cold cage. Only his head was exposed above the ice, and this just barely. Hair, once black, was silvered with rime. His eyes were as gray and occluded as the clouds outside. His skin was a dusky violet, a hue unnatural to any living man. His beard glimmered in the light with the frozen jewels adorning it. A crown, as much ice as iron, sat upon his brow.

Bjorn stopped and stared at the legendary man. He could not detect any movement from him. Despair welled up inside him. *He's dead, if he was ever alive.* They had come all this way for nothing.

The others continued forward, leaving Bjorn in the darkness. Though he remained reticent to approach, he feared the gloom more, and so hurried to keep within the twin pools of light.

Embla stopped at the circle of light cast down from the flue. Bjorn gathered around her with the others. His breaths were shallow as he looked first at the priestess, then at the ice-bound man, waiting for something to happen.

Finally, Embla spoke. "Torvald Geirson, Last King of Baegard. Your Grace, we have need of your counsel once more. Will you wake from your dreams and speak with us?"

The echoes of her words died down. No one stirred. Bjorn's hands fidgeted with his cloak as he watched and waited.

The King of Ice did not move.

Loridi leaned close to Seskef, but spoke in a whisper

loud enough for all to hear. "Is he talking yet? Can I not yet hear him?"

Bjorn wished he would stop. His heart thundered. His lips pulled back, and his teeth ground together. The wait turned from suspense to agony.

"Torvald!" Embla spoke again. "Answer me!"

Yonik took a step nearer to the priestess. "Is there perhaps—?"

But before the gothi could finish speaking, a creaking welled up from deep within the cave.

Bjorn braced himself against Seskef and Loridi as the ominous sound surrounded them. It seemed to come from everywhere and nowhere at once. He imagined the walls cracking and caving in, burying them all in ice, the shards spearing them through as the light was forever blocked away.

But the walls did not collapse. Instead, something moved among the shadowed spires.

The King of Ice's head had been tilted back, resting. Now, it slowly came upright until his blind gaze settled upon them. Bjorn froze. Something terrible and unknowable looked out from those eyes, something mortals should never know.

Then Torvald's jaw moved, crumbling gossamer threads of ice as it did. A voice like the final throes of an avalanche issued forth, deep yet shallow-breathed, and flooded the cavern with whispers. For a moment, Bjorn did not hear the sounds as words, not until he recognized them as Old Djurian.

"*I have... been waiting. Waiting a long... long time.*"

"Of course, Your Majesty. We are sorry to keep you." Embla gave Torvald deference as if he still reigned as king.

And does he not? Bjorn's tattered mind could make no conclusion.

If Torvald heard her, he gave no indication. His head moved with all the speed of a frozen river until his blind gaze settled on Bjorn.

"*I have... been waiting,*" the King of Ice repeated, "*all this time... for you... Stoneseer.*"

31. A MEETING OF MINDS

"Cut off the Sypten envoy's head; their tongue won't say anything worth hearing."

- Highlord Carr Gunnarson, Fifth Arkjarl of Baegard

Bastor's smile was wide as he rode across the field to the distant tent.

The first tentative sunbeams crept over the Teeth. The air was crisp as a ripened apple, and redolent with the perfume of war — smoke, dust, fear, rage. His gelding moved at a nervous canter, but seemed grateful to be out of its cramped stall. The Whiterun glittered as if it were not a river, but the gargantuan, sinuous body of Lavaethun, the Sea Serpent said to encircle the world. Each fish darting to the surface was like a scale as it caught the light. Before him spread a sea of Syptens eager to spill his blood. Behind, men lined the gray walls of Petyrsholm, spears and bows in hand, ballistas and catapults interspersed between them. The ground he had covered had been uprooted, and only mounded lines of dirt remained, concealing the weapon they would use to win the coming battle.

He reveled in it all.

"What a day!" he all but sang, head buzzing with the honey wine he'd imbibed that morning. "What a glorious day!"

The two men that rode beside him exchanged looks, but Bastor was immune to their scorn. They were his father's men, and one of them the sour-faced Endre. No doubt they were eager to abandon him at the first sign of treachery; not an unlikely scenario, considering what they rode to. His father had not made him an emissary as an honor; half the time, they came back with their heads separated from their shoulders. No, this was his punishment for divulging the secret of firesand to Aelthena before the jarl was ready to reveal it; that was plain enough.

Bastor paused, his smile stiffening. If he died here, what of it? He was one man, one pinprick of life, of little significance to the world. There were worse ways to go than serving his country.

Yet his wild abandon flailed at the prospect. He was not afraid of death; he had stared Ovvash in the eyes enough to know that. But he could not give his father the satisfaction of ceding his claim to the Gnarled Chair of Ragnarsglade through his untimely demise. Not when his father had just donned the Iron Circle and drew nearer to his ultimate desire. Not when his younger brother was at least as evil as their father, though half as clever.

Volkur, hear me, he prayed. *Save me now, and I will make a glorious sacrifice on the battlefield to you — be sure of that!*

He rarely beseeched the gods; he hardly knew if he believed in them. But if there was a day to plead for aid, it was this one. He needed every scrap of help, divine or otherwise, that he could get to survive.

He settled his gaze back on his destination. The tent had grown closer as Bastor observed his surroundings. Now, it rose half and again his height, so as he dismounted and handed his reins to Endre, he did not even have to duck as he sauntered inside.

Ignoring the people sitting before him, he looked around the tent. There was little to see; despite the showy display of his army, the karah apparently did not care to make a pretense of diplomacy. The only nod toward decency was that the fabric had not been left undyed, but was striped with red, black, and white, the colors the Sypten ruler favored for his three primary gods. There was no furniture but for one chair, and this occupied by a curious noblewoman. Behind her stood two men, one of middling years, the other young and from the Sumerland, telling by his ebon skin and features.

Bastor studied the woman from the corner of his eye as he pretended to look at the guards standing on either end of the tent. The woman wore a mask that only covered the right half of her face and had the look of something black and shelled. *The scarab beetle,* he recalled from his long ago studies. The uncovered side of her face struck him as homely and spare beneath her paints. Her skin was the deep brown of water-soaked sand. Stoles draped over her neck, the last the pelt of a lioness. Silver and gold jangled on her arms. She held herself erect, almost rigid, as if hiding some pain or discomfort. A glimpse of her sandaled left foot, the skin red and scaled, told him the reason. *Burns, perhaps, or a flaw in the womb.*

He finally settled his gaze directly on her. The karah's emissary was dressed like a queen, but like himself, she had been sent out here because she was expendable. They were two puppets dancing to strings for the entertainment of no one.

But what if the dolls were cut free? He tucked the thought away as he bowed and touched both hands delicately to his forehead.

"Emissary to Karah Hephystus the Third. Blessings of the Red, Black, and White upon you. I am Alabastor, Son of Ragnar, Heir to Ragnarsglade. You grace me and those I represent with your presence." He spoke in Sypten, though of a low-status dialect, as he had learned from those taken as thralls. The gesture and words, at least, he was sure were respectful in their culture.

The envoy's eyes widened, but she quickly stifled her surprise. "Blessings to you as well, Lord Heir Alabastor Ragnarson," she spoke in mildly accented Djurian. "I am Sehdra Ohkweht, Royal Sister to the Holy Karah."

Bastor grinned as he came fully upright again. The very sister of the karah sat before him. *What kind of bastard sends his own blood into the wolf's jaws?*

Yet he suspected he knew the answer. The same sort as who sent their firstborn son.

"Whichever slave taught you our tongue did well," he said, stubbornly continuing in her people's language. "You're almost fluent."

"Almost?" Her visible eyebrow quirked, though the rest of her face remained smooth and impassive. Like him, she continued to use his speech rather than her own. "I have been told I might pass for one of you, were our skin of a match. Though yours and mine are not so different as I expected."

"Your tutor is a liar as well as talented, Royal Sister."

Sehdra Ohkweht only smiled with the visible half of her lips. "I wish I could say the same for you, Lord Heir Alabastor. But your tutor has instructed you only in the speech of laborers and farmers. You would be greatly embarrassed in my people's courts and manors."

Bastor shrugged. "The humblest speech is the most honest, I've found. And those folks I learned from were the best-hearted I know."

"Slaves?"

"Friends, Royal Sister."

They matched stares for a long moment before she smiled again. Bastor returned it. Mortal enemies they might be, but he was beginning to like this sister to the Sypten king.

As swiftly as it came, her amusement disappeared, and a frigid veneer stretched over her expression once more. "But we have not come to exchange clever words. His Sanctity has commanded that I give you his terms."

Bastor did not quite let his smile curdle. "Alright then, Royal Sister. Let's hear them."

"As you can see, Lord Heir Alabastor, you are severely outnumbered. You have no more than half our host, if you have even mustered that much. You will soon be cut off from the other Winter Holds. Walled within your city, you will starve, and you will not prevail if you take to the field. And we are not the only enemies facing you. The people of the mountains you name Nuvvog's Teeth have taken Oakharrow and will not be content with only that. You cannot stand against a war on two fronts."

Bastor puffed up his cheeks and blew out the air slowly. When he had fully exhaled, he responded. "Why now, Royal Sister?"

Sehdra Ohkweht seemed taken aback. "Why has His Sanctity come to Baegard?"

He shrugged. "I know there's the old excuse — that my ancestors took the land from yours centuries ago, and every karah since has vowed to take it back. But it seems to me your brother has reignited the conflict for no reason. Is it just that he is young and eager for blood? Can that alone be enough to end thousands of lives?"

Bastor knew the answer; men had died for less on the whims of kings. *Crowns corrupt the brows they sit on,* he mused. He wondered how much worse his father might become.

His Sypten counterpart, however, seemed at a loss for words. *Almost as if she had never considered the question.*

"I..." she started to speak in Sypten, then abruptly reverted back to stiff Djurian. "The Holy Karah's will is not to be questioned. His reasons are his own."

Bastor shook his head. "A woefully unsatisfactory answer for my father and the others jarls, I'm afraid. You see, Sehdra Ohkweht, the reason for this war is integral to why we must bring it to a swift conclusion. Are we to negotiate with madness? So tell me — why has King Hephystus come to our peaceful valley? What has pulled him here — or rather, what drives him forward?"

Sehdra stared up at the strange Baegardian and wondered if he knew more than she had first suspected.

He speaks as if he knows of Oyaoan. How the savages could know of the giants, she could only speculate. Of course, Ha-Sypt had spies among the jarlheims; it only stood to reason that Baegard had seeded some of their own. And the huamek had hardly made a secret of herself and her followers in the past season.

But if he knew of the First of Hua, did he also know the karah was her pawn?

Too many lines drawn in sand. She felt as if she waded deeper into the flooded Nu with every passing moment. She was Ha-Sypt's emissary, yet she only understood less than half of her own nation's part in the conflict. Why had Oyaoan sought war with Baegard? What did this valley hold for her? Sehdra had seen enough of the giantess to know she did little without reason. Even her visit the other night to her pavilion, when the huamek had seemed adrift and watched the beetles scuttle across the sand, had to have some explanation.

But that central question, the crux of this entire war, evaded Sehdra's comprehension.

Why? She wanted to shout the word, decorum be damned. *Tell me why!* Her expression remained smooth, unblemished by her roiling emotions. The proper words — stiff, enigmatic phrases that would say nothing and mean less — filled her mouth so she knew she must say them. Yet she kept her jaw clamped shut.

Something was shifting in her. The meekness which she had so long adopted was shuddering away, revealing something beneath she barely dared look at, something hard and dark and full of deep-rooted resolve.

She did not know what it was, this new layer of her. But she desperately needed to know.

Though she was painfully aware of Oyaoan's representative at her shoulder, she spoke with unrepressed honesty. "I do not know why we go to war, Lord Heir Alabastor. I do not know what drives my brother, nor have I for the entirety of his life. But I know this: no one can stop this conflict. I came here not to sue for peace, but to bring terms of surrender that I knew you could not accept. I was sent here to insult you, then die by your sword for it."

As she spoke the words, she felt her body grow numb and distant, as if Gazabe stretched forth a clawed hand to claim it. She did not know this savage, not truly, even if she felt she did. Perhaps this bout of truth might be what led to her death. She could almost feel Teti's fear for her like the bitter touch of the Nu's nightly gusts.

But, for once in her life, she had spoken truthfully and trusted blindly. She prayed to Wise Qa'a that she had not acted foolishly.

Alabastor Ragnarson, heir to a jarlheim, yet sent here as if he were as expendable as she, watched her in silence. His eyes were like the storm clouds farmers blessed when they burst over the Nu in a torrent of rain. His jaw was strong, and he stood as tall and broad as the mountain savages were always rumored to be. His skin, warm and familiar as any of her people, was a contrast to the shock of blonde hair falling in thick braids from his head and covering his chin. She found herself stirred by his gaze in a way men had rarely moved her. Under that blue-eyed stare, she warmed, and not entirely from discomfort.

Finally, he nodded, a slow and thoughtful gesture. "I appreciate you telling the truth, though I suspect we both knew it." She liked the way he spoke her people's tongue, crude as his accent might be. "You are not at risk from me," he continued, his voice falling softer. "I have seen enough men dead not to give Ovvash — or Gazabe, rather — more spirits than I must."

It took an effort to keep as ice before the warmth flooding her face. She hid behind politeness. "Thank you, Lord Heir Alabastor. I appreciate your understanding."

The savage snorted a laugh and glanced at the guards standing behind him. They seemed wary of the jarl's heir; a strange characteristic for those who meant to be his protectors.

"I suppose we go to war then, for Highlord Ragnar will not surrender. I should wish you dead." Alabastor flashed her a rueful smile. "But I don't. If we both wind up alive after this, and in different circumstances...

perhaps we can find a way to negotiate other than sharp metal."

Words of peace. They were hardly what she expected from this brute of a man. But she suspected there was much more to Alabastor Ragnarson than his appearance betrayed.

She nodded. "Under different circumstances... yes, I hope we would."

The Winter Holds emissary stared at her for a moment longer, turning away just as her exposed cheek flushed anew. "Farewell, Sehdra Ohkweht," he called over his shoulder before taking the reins to his horse, mounting it, and riding off in a cloud of dust.

Teti was kneeling by her as soon as the savages had gone. "Are you well, Royal Sister?"

"Fine, Teti. Fine." She rose from the chair and swayed, her withered leg trembling beneath her. She took his arm to gain her balance. "As fine as any of us can be."

32. THE KING OF ICE

...And yet, because of these superstitions, many have ascended Yewung seeking enlightenment, and few ever return.

- Commentary on Djurian Culture, by Alfjin the Scribe

Bjorn felt his party looking at him. Torvald Geirson's words had faded, yet their meaning clouded the cave. Yet he stood mute, his emotions twisting into his throat and choking him to silence.

He spoke. He speaks. He called me Stoneseer. What the name meant, he could not say. But though he had never heard it before, it echoed in his mind like a memory forgotten.

"Bjorn," Yonik murmured, "I believe he means you. You should be the one to respond."

"With deference," Embla added, an edge to her words.

Bjorn cleared his throat. Even as it still like felt a sizeable rock lodged in it, he croaked out, "Do you mean me, ah" — he fumbled for the correct address — "Y-your Grace?"

King Torvald continued to stare at him, unseeing, for a moment that stretched into several heartbeats, then a dozen. As his companions shifted around him, Bjorn opened his mouth to respond. Then a noise rose like the cave itself breathed.

"*Yes... You are... the Stoneseer...*" The whispering voice faded to hissing, like steam leaked from the stones.

Bjorn waited another breath before a nod from Yonik provoked him from silence. "What does that mean, Your Grace? That I am this Stoneseer?"

The King of Ice answered with the same ponderous pace as before. "*You are... the one foretold... foreseen. The ice... it was thinner... when first I... began to wait.*"

Bjorn hesitated, then leaned close to Yonik to murmur, "Should I tell him?"

The priest nodded again, his eyes remaining on the cave's occupant.

Clearing his throat, Bjorn tried to speak as Annar had taught him, as if he knew with certainty that what he said was fact. "Your Grace, it has been two hundred years since you entered this cave. You were the final monarch to rule Baegard. We have been the Seven Jarlheims since, each hold reigning over itself."

He paused, waiting for a response. The King of Ice seemed to consider this for a long time. Only a susurrus like the movement of underground water gave any sign he was alive and listening.

Sister Embla had sidled closer to whisper in Bjorn's ear. "I was forbidden from telling him before, unless he asked. This may be a great shock to him."

There was a hint of reproach in her words, but Bjorn shrugged it off. He was realizing that, even with all her visits up to this cave, the priestess had as little conception of how to proceed as any of them did. They all ran blindly forward in the darkness, like the night Bjorn and the Hunters in the White fled Jünsden.

Finally, King Torvald stirred, and the cave resonated with his inhalation. *"It has... preserved me. The doors... they are open... all open..."*

A chill prickled Bjorn's spine. He had undergone enough lessons with Mother Sign to know what he referenced. *The doors are all open* — what could that feel like? The Hall of Doors had been endless to his Sight. He had barely endured opening the Heartfire and Mend doors too wide. How could he survive even a second door opening, much less all of them?

"I could not live as you have been forced to, Your Grace." The thought sprang from him. "It must have been torture for you, living this way, waiting this long."

The cave sighed, and the air seemed to grow colder still. *"Yes..."* the ancient man murmured, even softer than before. *"Torture to wait..."*

Yonik's hand pressed Bjorn's shoulder, a reminder of his purpose. As much as he might sympathize with the old king's plight, he could not lead him down a path toward despair and darkness. Not when they still desperately needed him.

"If you have waited for me, Your Grace, then I am here. But why have you waited? Was there something you wished to pass on to me? There is—" Bjorn cut off, wondering how to convey the events that were occurring in the world below. "War is coming, one like we've never seen before. Jotunar are real — or one is, at least. My home, Oakharrow, has been taken." He felt a squeeze in his throat as he thought of Aelthena, and his father, and all the others likely suffering at the Jotun's hands. Stubbornly, he pressed on. "You are a seer, Your Grace, a great one. It is written that you have predicted what is to come. We must know what you have seen so we can prepare. Please, Your Grace: tell us, if you can."

His words reverberated a moment longer, then died away. No sooner had they faded than did the King of Ice respond.

"Seidar... *it came upon me... late in life... its pull, irresistible... its duty, all-consuming... It came before... all others... even to Baegard... even to... my people...*" Torvald's head dipped slightly. "*I, as you... must care after... not one nation... but all... all of humanity...*"

Bjorn strung together the wheezing speech. *All of humanity.* He could not imagine how such a burden must weigh. Though it seemed the king wished him to bear it.

"My apologies, Your Grace. But I don't understand how this relates to me."

"*You are... the Stoneseer... I have seen... many things... countless things... but you see... I cannot act... upon them.*"

It took Bjorn several long moments to wonder if Torvald Geirson had just made an attempt at humor. He smiled uncertainly, but the ancient man's face remained as stiff as the ice that bound him.

"*These things... I have seen... they must not... die with me...*" King Torvald's gaze lowered, slow as the movement of the moons and stars, to stare down through the spires of ice erupting from him. "*The runes... we must See... See together... with them...*"

Bjorn's jaw clenched tight at that. *A Seeing.* From the discussion with the Silvers before, he had suspected it would come to this. Fear and exhilaration swirled inside him. If he sat to a Seeing now, there would be no Mother Sign monitoring him. Yonik might have some minor affinity for the Sight, but he had never been able to protect him before. Bjorn would be on his own, to succeed or fail by his own will.

He had not wanted the responsibility of even a single jarlheim. How could he take on the fate of all humanity?

You have the wrong man, he wanted to cry out. *I'm not enough. Strong enough. Brave enough. Clever enough. I'll break. I'll shatter, like thin ice.*

But as he stared at the ancient king above him, a realization came to him. Perhaps he *would* shatter; what of it? It was no more than Torvald Geirson had done a hundred times over. So broken was he that he barely qualified as human. And yet he still served his purpose.

Bjorn was not the right man for this task — but he was the *only* one for it. None of his companions could take his place. Mother Sign could not ascend the mountain, and King Torvald could not descend it. There was only him.

Only me.

If the King of Ice noticed his long silence, he did not mention it. Nor did Bjorn's companions, he finally realized. They waited for him to come to terms with this on his own. They deferred to him, giving him the right to decide.

My decision.

He breathed in and found, to his wonder, that his chest moved easily. Something had finally been freed. With acceptance came an easing of doubt. Despite his weariness, despite the uncertain circumstances and all that depended upon his success, here and now, Bjorn smiled.

He stared at Torvald Geirson's bowed head. "I will See with you, Your Grace. I will learn all that you have to show me. As much as I am able."

A humming filled the air, something both haunting and uplifting in its resonance.

"Yes... you are Stoneseer... you must know... the path forward... the chest... open it... the stones... they await..."

Bjorn hesitated a moment, then strode toward the dark shape nestled at the feet of the frozen throne. He heard his companions drifting after him, like phantoms in the night, but kept his eyes set on a strongbox as the torches lifted the darkness around it.

Bjorn kneeled before it and ran his gloved hands over the chest. It was not large, barely the width of his shoulders and half as tall, yet sturdily made. Hauling it all this way up the mountain must have been an arduous effort, and not one made by a man who thought to make a return journey. After its long rest, the bottom half of it had been swallowed by the ice of the cave floor.

He tried unfastening it, but the latch stuck. The lid was frozen shut.

"Here."

Bjorn turned to see Yonik holding out his ice axe, handle first. Bjorn accepted it with a nod. The priest's eyes flashed as he stood, the torchlight catching on them. If Bjorn had not believed he was on his own before, he knew it now.

Working carefully, he swung the pick at the clasp and the edges of the lid. The layer of ice fell tinkling to the cave floor. As he completed his circuit, Bjorn set the ice axe aside and tried opening it again. This time, though it still resisted, the lid gave way to unveil a deeper darkness within.

"Light," he requested softly, and both of the torches grew near enough that he could see inside.

Four gray stones lay on the bed of the chest. As firelight touched their faces, the etched lines came into view, and shadows rose from the recesses of Bjorn's mind. They teased with sensory fragments: the stench of smoke; blistering heat on his skin; visions of great beasts rising from among the rocks...

Bjorn jerked his head back up and swallowed hard. As with other runestones, they affected him even before he had breathed in *khnuum*. But these had touched him more powerfully than even the Frenzy rune had. He dreaded to think what their Seeings would be like.

Never shy away from a hard thing. A saying his father used to tell him, and often with a scowl. Bjorn had often done just the opposite of that. He had avoided the usual boyhood contests. Even in Eildursprall, for the first several weeks, he had not engaged with Flint and the other guards, but only sparred with those with whom he was comfortable.

But it turned out he had followed his father's advice after all. He had ventured into the Teeth, knowing he and all his men might die. He had carried on when it would have been easier to collapse, especially after the greatbear stole Keld away. He had embraced the Sight and thrown himself into unknown. He had sparred with Flint. He had ascended Yewung, a mountain whose peak scraped the belly of the sky.

I have done so much. I can do this. For a wonder, he believed it.

Bjorn glanced over his shoulder. "Please prepare a fire," he said, quiet but firm. "Heat the drascale ore and a pot of water."

As his companions did as he bade — a marvel in itself — Bjorn looked back up between the jagged icicles projecting from Torvald's throne.

"Tell me what to do, Your Grace. I am ready."

33. PROMISE OF BLOOD

"In the moments before a battle, the land holds its breath."

- Lion Ankhu, Paragon of Pawura's Sorrow in the 171st Flood of Gazabe

The advance began at dawn.

Sehdra balanced on her hale leg as she watched the might of Ha-Sypt pour onto the fields. Grass, newly come alive, died beneath the feet of thousands of men, each bearing spears and shields and reeking with the thrill of the nearing contest. The stench of the camp lingered, but lessened as the tents emptied and horses and elephants stomped toward their destination. The gray walls of Petyrsholm loomed in the distance, faintly catching the orange glow of the rising sun like a prophecy of flames. The masts of the feluccas bristled above the water as they sailed toward the opposing dragon-ships.

She wondered if she should feel a failure. Sehdra had been the Sypten emissary, the only one who could negotiate peace with their age-long enemies. But she knew the truth without Teti, ever by her side, telling her: it had been a doomed mission from the start. Her strange counterpart, Alabastor Ragnarson, had acknowledged it as well as she.

With the First of Hua at our head, blood was promised.

Sehdra watched ruin's encroachment from her brother's war pavilion. All the usual company was present. Physt leaned forward on his wooden throne, eyes bright amid his war paint as he watched for glory. The true ruler of Ha-Sypt stood over him, half-shadowed, like a silhouetted mountain peak. The Ibis was near at hand, as was Vizier Zosar, though he kept drifting away to meddle in the war plans.

Less idle was Amon Baka, who had erected a war table in the front half of the tent and was orchestrating the war from it. There was a savage delight in him, apparent through his forceful words and proud posture. His decorated bronze armor shone like a second sun. The general seemed a queen of bees as messengers buzzed around the tent, bearing tidings and orders back and forth from the captains on the field. Every word spoken up here would be conveyed down to the specks of figures below, no larger than ants in the distance. Men were pieces on a Duaat board, though less compliant than the players preferred.

A separate stream of Suncoaster runners moved to the back of the tent to consult with the Ibis. The giantess's translator spoke softly to each before they scurried back to only the Divine knew where. The karah frowned at this, his contentment spoiled, yet his temper failed to rear. For everyone's sake, Sehdra hoped he would remain tame. Enough blood would be spilled without his intervention.

As if her thought had drawn his attention, Physt's voice called over the hubbub. "Sister! Attend me at once!"

Sehdra glanced at Teti before turning and bowing to her brother. Her leg trembled as she stood back upright and limped toward the throne. Her friend hovered at her side, ready to catch her should her strength fail.

The karah's lips curled as she stood before him. Physt's face was painted to match the Ascendant crown. Black, red, and white lines transformed his face into something unworldly and feral — *divine,* he would have put it. He stared at her cursed flesh and curled his upper lip.

"Qa'a's shit, but you are ugly, sister. I would not believe a woman could be born so unsightly had I not grown with you."

Sehdra remained impassive. Though his insults stung, the stakes here were far too high to rise to low goads.

"I apologize if my appearance offends you, Divine One," she said. "Were the use of a mask allowed, I might avoid such affront."

Only as the words slipped out did Sehdra realize she had not leashed her temper after all.

Physt bared his teeth. "It might. But I have forbidden it, and the word of a living god is firmer than any drawn in the sand."

From another man's tongue, it would have been sacrilege. But Karah Hephystus the Third was no mere man. He was a god.

Yet what kind of god can be killed?

She wondered if this slight would lead to an encounter, but Physt only waved a hand and turned away. "I tire of such prattling; this day holds grand things for me. Look below, sister! Do I not host the deadliest army you have ever seen? Do not the mountain savages stand little chance before them? The chariots! The feluccas! The behemoths from the south! And thousands of men with spear and sword and bow, all ready to kill and die for me."

He sounded drunk, and on more than wine and smoke. Sehdra felt her chest further constrict with every utterance, while her brother's exuberance waxed. *Perhaps he is a god,* she thought. *He is not human.*

"Yes, Divine One," she replied, tone stripped of emotion. "It is a glorious sight."

"And it will become more glorious still! The battle here will be sung for ages to come, will be written in the books and painted onto palace walls. My descendants will remember me and say, 'There lived the greatest karah ever known!'" Physt shrieked with sudden laughter. It sounded strangely empty without his usual hangers-on echoing it.

"Of course, Divine One. The greatest in all the world."

His hysterics cut off as he looked down with narrowed eyes. "What? You do not believe it will be true? Just see, sister. Just wait and see."

Sehdra only bowed her head. She did not show her eyes. Especially in the one surrounded by cursed flesh, she doubted she could hide her horror and disgust.

She startled as the Ibis suddenly called out, his manner strange and foreign. Physt, too, jerked in his chair to stare wide-eyed at the Suncoaster. But as the karah demanded an explanation, his words were drowned out.

The world trembled.

Sehdra leaned, her balance upset, but Teti steadied her before she could fall. She flashed him a grateful glance before turning back to see what could make even the earth shake. Each moment, the pounding grew more pronounced. Hephystus shouted, Amon roared, and servants and heralds alike scrambled about in confusion and fear.

The huame marched past the entrance of the pavilion, and Sehdra forgot all else.

The giants were so tall that their heads rose above the war tent's entrance. They were clad in armor of a dark gray metal that shone in scales from their chests and around their legs in skirts. Around their broad waists were secured the largest belts she had ever seen, and they sagged with the heavy sacks tied to them. Across their backs were lashed weapons twice as large as a man: hammers, axes, even a square-headed sword.

As they rumbled by, a fresh trembling began behind Sehdra. She spun to see Oyaoan throw back her head and bellow with the might of a hundred horns. Sehdra clasped her hands to her ears, knowing she would soon go deaf under the blaring. Pain bloated her head so it felt it would rupture. She squeezed her eyes shut and leaned into Teti's grasp.

At last, the giantess ceased her call. Through the ringing in her dulled ears, Sehdra heard the strains of her brother's screaming. She pried open her eyelids and squinted at the chaotic scene in the war tent. The largest movement drew her attention first as the Red One turned away from the karah and the throne and reached out a broad hand. With ease, she wrenched up the tent cloth until the brightening daylight filtered in, then strode out. The pavilion threatened to collapse around them, but only just held. The Ibis followed his master, only casting a black-eyed look back at Sehdra before slinking out of sight.

"The Children of Hua march," she murmured, so softly she could only hear the words in her mind.

***

"Gray bloody gods," Frey muttered as they watched the rising tide of enemies.

Aelthena prided herself on having a clever tongue, and rare was the occasion when she was at a loss for words. But as she witnessed the creatures who marched from the Sypten camp down to the trampled fields, she found all her thoughts leeched away, leaving only a numbing, overwhelming dread.

Giants.

Even at a distance, they were gargantuan. A dozen in number, they rose as high as the shoulders of the elephants that stood at the back of the Sypten army — no, higher, she realized, as they came abreast of the behemoths and eclipsed their great height twice over. Scaled armor, dark as volcanic rock, gleamed with their every stride, and helms of the same metal sat atop their heads. Almost, it seemed to be Harrowsteel from the way the faint light glittered upon it.

Impossible. Even if Silverfang, owner of most of the drascale mines, had taken his betrayal so far, such trade would have been noticed by someone. This had to be a new metal that had gained Ha-Sypt's favor. She hoped it did not prove as potent as their own.

Stranger still were the bags that hung from the belts of the massive creatures. Aelthena squinted at them, but could not understand what they might wish to bear. All she could imagine were the severed heads of Baegardian men, slowly staining the burlap red.

She had suspected the Jotun was in league with Ha-Sypt, but he was not the only giant to ally with them. These were different in appearance. Whereas shaggy brown hair had covered the Jotun's body, the bared skin on their arms and legs was as gray as the elephants they stood beside. They were not beings adapted to the cold and snow, but lands of sun and sand.

Surtunar.

She had scarcely believed the jotunar existed. That their counterparts might be real as well stretched her mind to its limits. Laughter bubbled up in her, and she could not stop from shaking with it.

She felt Frey's gaze on her. "It seems you're taking my old advice too much to heart," the guardian noted. "Now's hardly the time to laugh."

Aelthena made a wide gesture out over the battlefield. "Ragnar cannot fight those... *myths*. The battle is lost before it's begun, Frey. This entire Djur-burned war is over. Baegard will be..."

She trailed off, unwilling to entirely admit their fate. Frey cocked his head and stared at her until he drew her reluctant gaze.

"You never give in to despair, Aelthena. It's one thing I admire about you. Even when the task before you seems impossible, you press on." He took her hand, ignoring the impropriety of it, and squeezed it. "Don't change that now."

She clutched his hand back, glad he had been permitted to remain behind as her guard. Considering what they faced, she was not sure any of their warriors would survive.

"I can't help it, Frey. Even with all our preparations, even with Nuvvog's Rage at our disposal, how can we defeat them? And who knows if even dragonfire can harm giants?"

Inwardly, her turmoil took a different turn, the questions plaguing her too private even to share with Frey. *Did I give up my rightful place as the jarl's heir for nothing? Did I doom Baegard instead of give it a chance by electing Ragnar to be the Arkjarl? What if he surrenders? What if he does not, and we all die anyway?*

Futile questions. She was no warrior. She had not trained with her brothers in the Harrowhall's yard. She had attended their mother and learned all a woman should know — sewing, cooking, tending to the castle. And when she had been able to sneak away, she learned all she could of being a leader — politics, geography, governorship. But in combat, beyond a passing knowledge of military strategy, she was woefully inadequate.

War was upon them, and Aelthena was useless to her nation. She could do nothing but watch as Asborn, and Bastor, and thousands of other good Baegardian men marched to their deaths.

She was squeezing Frey's hand hard enough to grind his bones together, and as he grunted, she abruptly released him. The guardian only let his gloved hand fall back to his side.

"It's alright to be afraid," he murmured. "Volkur knows I am. So is every man down there, whether or not he admits it."

A heavy sigh escaped her. "It's not the fear I cannot stand. It's that there's nothing to do with it."

A quiet descended upon their balcony, interrupted only by the sounds of the tumultuous city below, and the distant cries of the army swelling within the streets of Petyrsholm. Warriors of every jarlheim and clan were armed and crowded together. Tempers were running as high as their fear from the many tussles that broke out. She looked to the main gate, where she assumed Asborn would be with the cavalry. She wondered if he had forgiven her, or if he would die hating her. She wondered if she hoped for Bastor to stay alive, or if they would all be better off if he found his own end.

"This won't be the end," Frey spoke into the silence.

Aelthena did not reply. They both heard the false ring in the promise.

The wall drang chewed for a long time over his words before he spoke them. "S'not looking good, Lord Heir."

Bastor flashed him a wild smile. Bloody gods, but he felt alive! His heart pounded. His blood flowed like fire in his veins. His head spun with his allotment of liquid courage.

He was ready to run. He was ready to *fight*. Though he had not vacated his guts in two days, he felt as light as a feather, light enough that he could leap off the wall and soar instead of fall.

But beneath the battle elation, a colder part of him held the reins. Though his muscles shivered with the need to act, his words were even and deep, his baritone still a commander's rather than a boy on his first green hunt.

"I'm sure many a woman has said the same of you, Drang Yerrik — yet here you remain." Bastor clapped the man on the shoulder and gave him a friendly shake. "Just remember, looks aren't everything. We didn't dig all those ditches for nothing."

"Volkur's tits, but I hope not."

Bastor jerked his head back toward the city. "And would my father be out here if he expected us to fail?"

Highlord Ragnar was easy to spot, even among the crowded soldiers. Both he and the purebred he rode were adorned in golden armor that shone in the pale light. He looked over at Bastor's glance, but he was too distant for Bastor to see if their eyes met. Near him congregated the other jarls taking to the field. Siward, in armor as black as his name. Harald, seeming to have ants in his chainmail, judging by how he twitched. And last of all, Alrik, the man grinning as madly as Bastor. Petyr and Hother had remained behind in the castle, neither man pretending to be warriors.

Yerrik frowned. "But he's the Arkjarl, en't he? Supposed to command us. Where else would he be?"

Cowering and preserving his life. But though he wanted to believe his father a coward, he knew better. His father valued his life above all others, to be sure, but he wasn't one to back away from a daring gamble.

Somehow, the wall drang seemed cheered by their talk, standing up a margin straighter. "Best do him proud. Or at least not draw his ire."

"Wise enough words."

Bastor turned his gaze back over the wall to the field ugly with enemies. Tens of thousands of the bastards had marched the farms surrounding Petyrsholm into mud. Half were Syptens, while the other half appeared to be mercenaries from the Sumerland and a few other nations. Their armor and weapons were lacking, with more skin on display than a man should want when meeting an adversary's sharp edge. But what they lacked in gear, they more than made up for in numbers.

But sellswords run when the fighting gets hot. His lips curled. *And I mean it to be as hot as Nuvvog's own burning breath.*

The infantrymen would be taken care of, he had little doubt of that. But there were many more to face besides them. The Sypten ships, their feluccas — they rowed up the Whiterun with few signs of slowing.

Behind the sea of bristling spears, chariot horses pawed at the ground, ready to pull thousands of noble whoresons around to swarm and harass their troops with little fear of repercussion.

There were the siege machines, built over the past two weeks from the surrounding forest and now loaded and ready to rain stone and fire upon the city. Ordinary ammunition would not be used, not when Nuvvog's Rage was in their possession. Under such an assault, there would be no lengthy siege. By the day's end, either Petyrsholm would stand, or the karah's standard would wave in the ruins of the Elkhorn.

And then there were the giants.

They had caused quite a stir when they had first marched down from the camp. How their scouts and sentries had not seen them before, Bastor could only speculate, for they were each as large as the Jotun. But they saw them now, even with an army and a field waiting for blood in between them. Each was as tall as a tree, as broad as a cliff, and wearing enough armor to fill a smithy. The men around Bastor had quavered, and he'd had a doubt or two himself. Surely, no feat of trickery or courage could stand up to such foes.

But, odd as it seemed, he trusted his father, or his shrewdness and foresight, at least. He believed in the measures they had taken for Petyrsholm's defense. Bastor had witnessed the power held within Nuvvog's Rage, within the firesand that produced it. With it at their disposal, and with the enemy ignorant of it, they just might stand a chance.

Here you go, believing in your father like he's a god. A laugh tried to work free of his throat.

He turned his gaze to the man standing on his other side. Thane Asborn Eirikson was as pale as the stars at the best of times; now, his face had gone as white as the froth before the prows of the ships cruising the Whiterun's waters. He had brought his own armor to the Jarlmoot to prepare for just such an event, and it shone golden and more brilliant than any borrowed set could. Seax and sword were belted at his hip, and a shield strapped over his back.

Even dressed as he was, Bastor found it difficult to imagine the thane killing a man. *Too soft. Too gentle.* Qualities a man could admire, and women even more so, but hardly suited to facing down a relentless swell of enemies.

He glanced down at himself. His armor was as polished and finely made as the thane's, though it lacked its filigree. A dark shirt of scales hung midway down his thighs, padded with a gambeson. The scale armor appeared similar to the metal the giants wore, though his was Harrowsteel forged, obtained at great expense by his father. Ragnar had deemed it worth the expenditure to ensure his heir was properly outfitted, less for Bastor's protection than to glorify his own name. He'd also fitted a metal cap to his head, a necessary nuisance, and one he wished he could discard. He had most often used a knife for his killings, but now he wore a war-axe and a seax, paired with a round shield painted with the violet lynx. A sword was fine for sparring in the yard, but when it came to butchery, he preferred an axe in hand.

Bastor reached out and clapped Asborn on the shoulder, as familiar as if they were old friends. "Hope you know how to use those blades."

The thane looked around and seemed not to comprehend his words for a long moment. Finally, he nodded. "We ride together," he answered, so softly the words were almost swallowed in the tumult of the men on the wall and below.

Little reassured in the man's prowess — to say nothing of mental acuity — Bastor gave him one last friendly shake before releasing.

"Best head down. The men will wonder if we've abandoned them; you know what tykes they can be. And the sign to charge will come soon enough."

"The sign." A ghost of a smile curved the thane's lips. "A small word for a big thing."

Bastor shrugged. "Small or big, I doubt there's a word adequate for the job."

With a farewell and last jape for the wall drang, Bastor led the thane down the stairs toward the waiting cavalry. Endre held the reins to his spirited roan, and at Bastor's approach, he offered them back, though not without an added sneer. "Spinners' fortune out there, Lord Heir."

Bastor grinned back, too elated to feel much annoyed. "May Volkur guide your spear and sword. Kill a score of the bastards, will you?"

Endre seemed surprised by the comaraderie and returned a thin-lipped smile. With an inward laugh, Bastor mounted his horse and settled in. The gelding had gathered some armor of his own, covering his head and flank in bright steel. The lynx adorned the metal wherever his father's armorer had been able to place it. He leaned down and stroked the steed's neck.

"There'll be fire out there," he murmured in its ear. "Enough violence and anger for a storm, and blood will spray in a fine mist. But you just follow me, and I'll lead you through it."

Empty promises, but all that mattered was his soothing tone. The roan stamped the ground, as if to say he was ready, so long as they did not wait any longer.

The mounted men knotted around him — *My company,* Bastor supposed — seemed as eager to be off. "Lord Heir!" one of them cried, a fresh-faced young fellow with a bush of curly red hair that poked out from under his helmet. "When are we cutting down the Djur-burned devils?"

The surrounding men let out a cheer, and Bastor grinned. News of the giants' appearance had spread like wildfire through the gathered warriors, yet none blanched before it. He wondered if they thought them mere rumor, or if the hearts of Baegardians were stouter than he knew.

When the cheer quieted, Bastor raised his voice in answer. "The better part of battle is waiting, lads, and we have some time to wait still. But never fear! As soon as the signal comes, we're through the gates!"

"What's the signal?" another asked, unseen among the others.

Bastor barked a laugh and glanced at Asborn, who had come astride him on his own steed. The thane gave him a nod, his back erect, his hands only slightly trembling.

"Even if your ears are plugged," he answered the man, "you won't miss it."

34. FIRE AND FURY

The tides of war obey no man — and perhaps not even the Divine themselves.

- Sieging the Winter Holds, by Paser Baka, general to Holy Karah Khufu

The infantry marched on land, while the feluccas kept pace through the water.

After the drama of the giants' passage, Sehdra had taken up a position outside the pavilion entrance. Teti had found her a chair in which to sit and ease her throbbing leg. She felt strangely like a spectator at a gladiatorial ring as she watched the battle unfold. Sehdra slipped out a mask and secured it to her face; the sun did not stop shining for the terrors of men, and her cursed flesh was sensitive to its burning touch. She wore Red Bek's aspect, the god being suited to the day.

"So it begins," Teti murmured from beside her. "I wonder how quickly it will end."

"It cannot come soon enough," she replied softly.

The feluccas struck first. They were at every disadvantage; they had to row to move upstream, while the dragonships had the current to carry them forward, leaving more men to carry shields and weapons. But the karah's navy was the greater, almost twice the number of drakkars. The flaming arrows were visible even at the distance, and from the number of ships aflame, the mountain savages were losing the water.

The infantryman, with their long, wavering lines, took longer to come within range of the defenders' bows. Mounted upon the walls, they had more than a hundred paces to shoot safely down on the Sypten army. Soldiers fell in heaps under the deadly dark clouds, but the men behind simply marched over the bodies, always pressing forward.

In addition to spears and bows, the front lines carried hooked ladders for mounting the walls. Sehdra wondered if even that much would be necessary. The infantry served as the distraction; the huame with their sorcerous fire would be the ones to turn the tide.

As the majority of the footmen came within range of the wall, archers halted and, protected by a line of shields, returned fire to the defenders. The roar of battle cascaded up the hills to where she watched. Sehdra shifted in her seat, uncomfortable at the sound. Contained in it were the last gasps of dying men, violence dealt and received. She gazed upon something horrid and primeval, a world she wished she had never known.

The chariotry and elephants advanced behind the mass of men, though they remained out of harm's reach. They would not be effective until the enemy took the field. They would, however, defend the catapults that had been set and loaded behind their line. As the first of these became ready, they flung flaming boulders above the walls and into the city beyond. Sehdra mostly detected the damage by the plumes of smoke rising from within the walls, yet she knew soldiers would be the least of the day's casualties once the fires spread.

On the river, a few of the feluccas had broken through the dragon-ships, rowing as swiftly as they could for the shores beyond. Sehdra frowned, wondering at their mission. But Teti's incredulous exclamation brought her attention back to the battle below.

"What are they doing?"

Sehdra looked back. "What do you mean?"

Her friend pointed. "The archers on the walls. Our infantry are raising their ladders, but they're largely ignored. The savages just keep shooting into the middle of the army — incendiary arrows, no less."

She saw what he meant. Streaks of flames arced through the air to land amid the Sypten army. It made no sense; the arrowhead was far more lethal than the fire, and there was little the flames could spread to. Such mild fires would be easy to stamp out. But this was not madness; with all their lives at stake, it could not be. There was a plot here that she could not understand.

The giants, however, appeared undeterred. Their line, a dozen strong, advanced. Oyaoan remained behind, a colossal statue watching her underlings march forward. The gold, jewels, and bones she usually wore had doubled. Her armor was not of scales, but solid plate, and the dark iron was lined with silver and gold. Her helmet spanned the whole of her massive head and had the image of a sun engraved upon it. She was as terrifying a warrior as any human had beheld, yet she seemed content to command from the back lines.

Just as any queen would.

Suddenly, the giantess threw back her head and bellowed. Even with her halfway down the hill, the sound was near deafening, and Sehdra had to fight the urge to cover her ears, still smarting from the first occasion. The other huame called back, and they increased their pace, whole swaths of trampled ground traveled with a single step. They quickly approached the last ranks of the mercenaries and infantrymen, then halted. The giants reached into the large sacks at their hips, and into their hands appeared large, round objects that gleamed like metal. She wondered how such a thing could cause all that she suspected it was.

Oyaoan bugled again, a short burst this time, and the giants moved into the position a man might when throwing a spear. At another call from their leader, they whipped their long arms forward, and the objects in their hands flew through the air, winking with their passage as the light caught their metallic sides. Sehdra watched them arc over the walls, as easily as the catapults managed, then disappear over the side.

Fire blossomed from within the city in a dozen plumes, and the ground trembled beneath her chair.

Teti gripped her shoulder, and she reached up to grasp his hand. Such a conflagration would be deadly in a wooden city such as theirs. Civilians and soldiers alike would burn, newborn babes just the same as old veterans. She had witnessed the Hua-fire the giants possessed. Yet she still had not believed this possible.

What have we done?

One of the huame's missiles had fallen shorter than the others and clipped the wall. Where it had, the stone shattered halfway down, leaving a ruin behind that belched black smoke. The Sypten army swarmed toward it, seeing their passage within.

Victory was coming soon.

The defenders still did not stop shooting their flaming arrows among them. Sehdra shook her head. Whoever led them had failed. If they thought the People of Dust afraid of fire, they had been sorely misinformed. This war would be the last between them. The savages would be made into slaves destined for the huame's pit, from which there was no return.

The world split open.

Sehdra was thrown from her chair as the ground bucked. Gasping, Teti clutching her arm, she staggered upright. The battlefield had turned black. Everywhere she looked, smoke and ash claimed the land. *Bright Hua has come to the battle*. It seemed as likely an explanation as any. Yet the sun had been blotted out, casting the scene in an orangish glow.

A scalding wind suddenly blew over the hill, and Sehdra gagged on the stench. Her mind went back to that night when Oyaoan had summoned her to the pavilion, to the aroma that had filled the tent. Like a heap of food rotting for weeks on end.

Teti was shouting something, and it was only then she realized she had been robbed of her hearing. Her ears hummed like beetles burrowed into them. She clung to her friend as her mind tried to understand what had happened.

An inferno had taken the army. Covered by smoke, they were blind on their hill. Yet Sehdra knew one thing.

The tides of war had abruptly reversed.

Aelthena could scarcely look away from the hellscape. It was as if Nuvvog himself breathed his sulfurous breath onto the land and smote it in one fell sweep. The wind that had swept up to her balcony had smelled just the same as the dragonfire that had taken the Harrowhall, only ten times as foul. The land had split apart in a riot of flames and smoke and swallowed all the men, chariots, and elephants in its wake.

"It worked," she muttered. "Ragnar's plan actually worked."

She had not believed in it until then. When the Arkjarl had ordered the ditches dug and the caskets of strange, silvery powder buried within them, she had thought him mad. From all she had learned of the sorcerous substance, it required a flame to ignite it, and no flame could reach it below the dirt.

But Ragnar had an idea. "We will make channels down to the barrels," he explained during one of the war councils. "Into these we will place a rope of oil-soaked cloth, to be drenched again each night under cover of darkness. When the enemy is positioned over the firesand, every archer will let fly flaming arrows. Only one must ignite; the others will react to it."

Highlord Ragnar had spoken with such supreme confidence that she immediately dismissed the scheme. It was too far-fetched and relied upon too uncertain a material. What did they truly know of this firesand? Perhaps it needed more than a flame. Perhaps it sometimes failed to ignite — if, say, the substance became wet, as the spring rains often threatened.

Yet, facing an enemy of superior numbers, organization, and with Nuvvog's Rage no doubt at their disposal as well, the jarls had little choice but to trust the man to whom they had given the Iron Circle. As she had when she orchestrated Ragnar's raising, Aelthena swallowed her words and pride and allowed the man to lead all of Baegard further down the path to ruin.

But she had been wrong. His gamble had succeeded. And now the conquerors were quickly becoming the conquered.

"It worked." Frey shook his head in disbelief. "But the battle is not yet won. Not while any giant still stands."

Whether any did remained to be seen, for the wall of smoke hid the Sypten army from view. Meanwhile, the gates to Petyrsholm opened, and the Baegardian warriors behind them pushed through. She thought of Asborn and Bastor and found herself murmuring a prayer, or as close to one as she could manage.

"Djur, Volkur, Ovvash — hells, Nuvvog, if you're listening. Keep them alive, hear me? *Keep them alive.*"

"That's the bloody signal!" Bastor roared as he thrust his axe into the rotten air.

Men whooped, horses stamped, shields and weapons clashed together. It was all just noise to him. In his mind, Bastor already charged through the smoke and cinders to cut through the enemy ranks. *This* was the stuff that the epics were composed of, that inspired bards to song and scribes to pen. No — it went deeper. This was the core of man, the raw animal kept caged by the trappings of tradition and expectation, ever clawing to escape.

Bastor grinned toward the black sky. Now, it would finally be free.

The gates cranked open — slowly, too slowly. "Come on..." he muttered under his breath, shifting in his saddle.

His roan, riled by the explosions, stepped forward and back, forward and back.

"Come on..."

The gap opened wide enough for one rider, but Bastor was not positioned to push through. He pulled the reins tighter in his left hand, his right clutching his axe like it was a neck he meant to wring. Asborn's bright armor flashed in the corner of his eye as the thane's horse danced.

"Nuvvog's bloody ashes, *come on!*"

The gates came fully open.

The first of the men flew through, and Bastor surged after them. Sounds ripped from his throat that were no longer words. What did words matter in this? Hot wind scratched at his face; his mount strained in a gallop beneath him; the taste of metal filled his mouth. All artifice — of language, of manners, of damned respectability — was gone as swiftly as the Syptens had been swallowed by sorcery.

When everything else had burned away, only fire and fury remained.

The ground was cracked and shifting beneath his roan's hooves. Though it grated on him, Bastor slowed. He would never get to fight if he broke his neck trying to reach the enemy. As he navigated the uncertain ground, he saw men around him doing the same. The world had become like something out of a nightmare, the earth spewing flames and smoke around them. His throat was raw with it, his lungs burning, his eyes tearing.

"Where are you?" he rasped as he squinted into the murk, trying to detect silhouettes among it. He heard the battle everywhere around him, the muffled cries, just loud enough to indicate they were near. Bastor finally glanced behind him, the colder part of him recognizing he should not charge into the fray alone. Two score horsemen followed, half with bows in hand. He turned back with a wide smile. They were enough to press on.

A shadow moved among the smoke. Heart leaping, Bastor charged forward, closing the distance between them and swinging his axe. He caught only a glimpse of the soldier's soot-smeared face before the axe head thudded into his chest and knocked him to the ground in a red spray.

They began appearing all around him then, ghosts in the haze. Bastor made for them and, one by one, sent them to their graves. At first, the Syptens did not seem to understand what was happening, lost among the smoke. But after his weapon found the flesh of a fourth man, the soldiers finally formed up. Spears lowered toward Bastor, forming a sharp wall his roan could not hope to survive.

Snarling, Bastor turned aside from them and rode away, seeking easier prey. His men's horses churned the earth as they followed.

As he pressed on, he found the smoke thinning and the day brightening. Heaving for air, Bastor ran an arm across his brow, trying to keep his eyes clean, but he only smeared the blood splattered up his axe arm across his forehead. The gelding carried him forward, and his visibility became clearer. Then he saw their true quarry.

Giants.

They stood there, their line unbroken, yet wavering with uncertainty. All twelve survived; Bastor had hoped at least one would be caught in the explosion. But his chest swelled at the sight all the same.

Time to rectify that error.

"There they are!" Bastor roared, pointing his axe toward the gargantuan creatures and looking over his shoulder. Some of his regiment had been lost, either falling to Sypten spears or wandering among the smoke, but a score remained. At his call, they formed up behind him, some semblance of their training returning.

"Archers! Light your gods-damned arrows!"

Those with bows did as commanded, while the other riders formed up around them. They would be the shields, both with wood and flesh, as they escorted the archers forward.

As his men struck with flint and steel at the resin-soaked tows on their arrows, Bastor glanced again at the giants. He had known of their existence, but had not realized they would be different than the Jotun, with leathery gray skin that resembled the elephants of the Sypten army.

Surtunar? He almost laughed at the thought. *Legends are sprouting faster than weeds!*

The giants had caught sight of them now, and their black eyes, sheltered beneath their heavy brows, kept a careful watch. They looked like beasts, yet those eyes held the intelligence of men. It scarcely mattered. They would end up scorched meat either way, if he had anything to say for it.

Finally, the arrows were aflame. "Ready, Lord Heir!" one archer shouted, and a brief cheer went up.

Bastor grinned and wheeled his roan around. "Then let's damn well break them!"

Though he led the charge, Bastor had never felt so powerless in his life. He was a brute compared to most, halfway a giant by some men's reckonings; yet compared to these behemoths, he was little more than a doll. His axe would do nothing against their hides and armor. Yet he was the head of the arrow; without him, the men behind would splinter and break off. Only his mad courage kept them surging toward impossible odds.

The giants suddenly seemed to realize the contest was not entirely uneven. One took a stumbling step backward, and the concession broke the line. Suddenly, the world trembled with stampeding giants, all fleeing before the small knot of horsemen. The bellows of the behemoths filled the air.

"Fire!" Bastor screamed, thrusting his axe into the air. "Fire for the sacks!"

Behind him, flaming arrows arced toward their quarry. Most fell short or went wide, the distance and wild ride conspiring against the marksmen, and half of them extinguished midair. But one lone arrow found a giant and lodged into the sack at his hip. The surtun did not look around as it continued charging back up the hill.

Bastor was grinning so wide he could barely speak. "Fall back, men! Fall back—"

Wildfire roared down the hill.

A wave of heat pummeled him. His roan screamed and reared, and Bastor lost his grip. Suddenly, he was flying, weightless, the strangest bird ever seen—

The ground clobbered him into darkness.

Another blaze burst through the smoke.

"What was that?" Aelthena held the stone railing before her so tightly it felt as if it must shatter. That, or her teeth soon would.

"Sounded like another Nuvvog's Rage." Frey seemed little interested by it, for he glanced back into the room with a frown.

"Is there something more interesting back there?" she snapped.

"Not sure." His hand fell to his sword. "I'm going to check."

A shiver ran through her. "What do you—?"

She never finished her question. Without warning, the lock shattered, and the door to her chambers flew open. Aelthena whirled, clutching at the railing for support, as Frey drew his blade and positioned himself in front of her. The intruders, three in number, were armed and armored. Their garb and looks betrayed who they were.

Syptens had infiltrated the Elkhorn.

35. OMENS AND SHADOWS

True seidar manifests in a Volur's use of the runes.

Runes of the Witterland, carved into stone, appear to have an effect on the seer's mind such as to evoke a vision — or "open a door," as they say. It is said many doors might open, but only those related to the Seeing of future events are used, and few have the talent for it. The danger, I have been told, lies in their potency, as well as the fear of a door opening and never again closing...

- Commentary on Djurian Culture, by Alfjin the Scribe

The time had arrived.

The preparations were complete. The fire, composed of the wood they had hauled up from Eildursprall, had been coaxed into a crackling blaze. The fist of drascale ore Yonik produced from his pack had been placed amid the flames, and its silver veins glowed orange with heat. A small pot of water tucked next to the fire bubbled, steam curling off its roiling surface.

Bjorn cradled the first of Torvald Geirson's runestones in his hands.

He did not look at it. The experience had been painful enough to sort through the four stones and select the one the King of Ice indicated. Even before inhaling the *khnuum* steam, images evoked by the runes leaped up at the barest glance, and the Hall of Doors trembled, the doors fluttering like a powerful gust blew through the corridor. A knot of fear tightened in his belly with each minute they spent preparing for the Seeing, despite his best efforts to untie it through Yonik's quiet counsel to *Breathe, slow and steady, like the deep sigh of the mountains.*

Nothing, he suspected, could prepare him for what came next.

"The carving... of these runes... nearly slew me... many years ago," King Torvald had informed him as Bjorn and his small company made the arrangements. *"They contain truths... truths that defy... man's comprehension."*

"Then how am I to understand them, Your Grace?" Bjorn dared to ask.

A sound welled up through the cave like a gurgling spring just broken through stone. *"You are... the Stoneseer,"* the ice-locked man said. Almost, there seemed a trace of amusement in his weary tone. *"If you cannot... none can."*

And what about you? he had wanted to ask. But a suspicion stilled his tongue. If Torvald felt the need to pass on his hard-won knowledge, it meant he would not be long to this world. And that this man, who knew so much of what was to come, might soon perish and leave Bjorn the sole possessor of that knowledge — the weight of the responsibility terrified him.

But this is my duty. The one thing I have the courage to accomplish. Whereas Vedgif, renowned warrior and respected elder, had blanched before his Seeing in the wilderness, Bjorn had embraced it. He was *Volur*; he could touch *seidar*. The Last King of Baegard, a man who had preserved himself through hundreds of years and killing conditions, named him "Stoneseer" and entrusted to him all his life's work.

He would not break. Not yet.

Bjorn turned and looked up at his companions from his seat before the fire. Sister Embla stood near Hoarfrost, the gothi's arms crossed under her breasts, a frown etched into her cold-flushed face. The Skyardi leader leaned on her spear, hard eyes barely blinking as they bore into Bjorn, like a navigator testing the thickness of a patch of ice.

Yonik and Seskef idled on the other side of the cave, while Loridi waited at the cavern's mouth, out of sight and earshot. Bjorn suspected the priest had not only sent away the jester to keep watch, but to give them all a moment's peace. As anxiety pressed in deeper, the self-proclaimed Lord Sword had grown more animated and shrill, and no amount of Seskef's scolding could temper his humor. Loridi himself had seemed relieved when Yonik finally ordered him out.

Bjorn took comfort in the presence of the remaining two men. Seskef had always radiated a steady calmness as he watched over him like a sentinel. The stout man nodded at his glance and smiled through his dark beard, which had grown unruly during their time in the Teeth. Bjorn returned the gesture and finally met the priest's eyes. Yonik's chin was lowered, but the dancing fire snuck under his greatbear hood to illuminate his face. Strange shadows danced upon his spare features. His jaw was clenched, and his hands were buried within his cloak, as if he clutched a talisman or weapon before an encroaching dispute. The gothi tried to smile, but Bjorn could not help but see his fear shining through.

Phantom fingers crept along his skin. *If Yonik is afraid, how much more should I be?*

Nevertheless, that his companions surrounded him gave Bjorn the strength to face the frozen throne. Though his blood was chilled to ice, and the runestone in his hands had all the weight of a gravestone, he would do his duty.

I'm a Bear, after all. The thought evoked a rueful smile. He hoped that, somewhere among the sprites of fire and air, his brothers were watching him, and Keld as well. He wondered if he would have finally impressed Bor the Bear and made his father proud.

Bjorn lifted his chin to meet Torvald's dark gaze high above. "We have completed the arrangements, Your Grace. I am ready."

The King of Ice had lapsed into silence over the past several minutes, so much so it seemed as if he had already slipped into Ovvash's grasp. But at Bjorn's words, he stirred, and the ice creaked as he moved and spoke.

"Good... good... Then we See... See together, Stoneseer."

Bjorn clutched his gloved hands tighter around the rock, then called softly over his shoulder. "Yonik, if you would..."

The gothi pressed Bjorn's shoulder as he passed. Drawing one of his long knives, he rolled the glowing ore out of the flames and positioned it before Bjorn's crossed legs. The ice, which had already melted around the fire, now protested the presence of hot stone, hissing as it changed into vapor. A waft of the steam found Bjorn's nostrils, and it smelled of many things that did not belong in a mountainside cave. Freshly picked winterlilies. Pungent, seared meat. Honey unharvested in combs.

Shaking his head, he found Yonik had lifted the boiling pot in one gloved hand by its handle, but paused before pouring it.

"You sure you're ready?" the gothi murmured, soft

enough that the others would not hear. "We can wait if you need time."

Bjorn looked up in astonishment. Yonik had never been harsh, but he had always pushed Bjorn to do what had to be done. He was a man carved of the mountain wilderness, both in body and spirit. Yet some gentler side of him had been unveiled. Almost, he could see the man he'd been as a father, before his family was ripped away.

Bjorn smiled with cracked lips. "Growing soft on me, old wolf?"

Yonik returned a shamefaced grin. "I wouldn't go that far."

His chest warmer, Bjorn gestured toward the glowing rock. "Best do it quickly, before the ore cools."

The priest hesitated a moment longer, then nodded. With a last glance, he tilted the pot of hot water and poured a thin, steady stream over the stone's surface. Bjorn leaned forward into the cloud that rose from it, the heat nearly blistering his face, and breathed in.

His senses distorted. His vision grew sharp, slicing his eyes. His hearing swelled like a waterskin filled too full. A hundred needles stabbed into his skin again and again.

Clenching his teeth, Bjorn forced himself to look up at the swimming face of Torvald Geirson. "I've inhaled the *khnuum* steam," he said, his voice grating in his ears. "Should I look at the runestone?" He noticed too late he had left off the proper honorifics, but with his senses rebelling against him, he found it difficult to care.

The cave breathed once more. But instead of the fatigued voice welling up from the cavern's depths, a clear, vigorous one spoke inside Bjorn's head.

Behold the First Shadow, Stoneseer. I will shelter and guide you.

No time for wonder. Bjorn pushed away his fear,

breathed in the steam once more, and bent his head to the item in his hand. As his gaze drifted to the stone's surface, the carved lines set hooks in him and anchored his vision to them. His eyes darted along them, tracing the rune, even as scenes unfolded from it. The flames seemed to swirl and form into a twister above the small bonfire.

The fire leaped forward and enveloped him.

Bjorn waved his arms and dispersed the blaze, gasping for a breath. To his surprise, the flames faded, leaving a dark, wet night beyond them. Bjorn looked around, perplexed. Damp earth sucked at his boots, its rich scent filling his nose. Rain pattered against his face and dribbled down his unkempt hair. The darkness pressed in like a smothering quilt. Despite the wetness, he tasted smoke on the air.

They come, the King of Ice spoke in his mind. *Mount the sentries. Toll the bells. They come, fire and hounds at their call.*

The gloom lifted enough for Bjorn to perceive more of the scene. *A city* — it was all walls and crowded buildings illuminated by the twin light of Skoll and Lavaethun. *What city?* he wondered. *And who will come?*

They sail over frozen waters, in boats bent from trees aeons grown. Torvald continued as if he could not hear Bjorn's queries. Almost, it seemed the words were part of the runestone rather than coming from the ancient man directly.

Still, he shouted into the void. *Who, Djur take you! Who comes?* But even as he asked, he suspected the answer.

The dark city was suddenly illuminated. An inferno blossomed in its center, like the eruption of a volcano. *Like the breath of Nuvvog.* It rolled over the buildings, swallowing all in its wake, before reaching the walls and crashing against them. By the wash of light, Bjorn saw he was not the lone sentinel in the dark.

The silhouettes were man-shaped, though distorted. Their legs were too thick, their arms too long, their heads too round. But it was their size that alerted him to the truth of their nature.

Jotunar. Giants, seven in total, ringed the city.

Torvald again rumbled in his head. *The youngest comes as the herald. The rest are mightier still. They will tear down the works of men, stone for stone. None may now stand against them.*

Bjorn trembled like a fawn in its first storm. *What can we do?* he cried out, but his voice made no sound. *Please, tell me!*

His neck craned back to stare up at the ancient foes, and his knees gave way. But as he fell to the squelching earth, the night was torn away, like a curtain pulled back from a window, and a different scene greeted his dazzled eyes.

Sunlight beat against his skin, the heat as heavy and blunt as a shield blow on the training yard. Bjorn threw up an arm against the glare and squinted as beams struck knives through his eyes. The moisture in the air had been stripped away, replaced by a dry heat that parched his skin and tongue. Where mud had been, there was only sand of a golden quality he had never witnessed. Bjorn dipped a gloved hand into it and watched it pour through his fingers, unimaginably fine-grained. Raising his head, he stared around him and saw miles upon miles of the same: golden fields of sand, ending in a line of blue sky.

Where am I? he thought, dazed and afraid.

They come, Torvald spoke again. *Light the torches. Man the outposts. They come with fire and beasts at hand.*

Stumbling to his feet, he saw them then. They emerged above one of the countless dunes, their forms hazy in the rippling heat. They walked steadily toward him, a line of silhouettes with the sun at their backs. In this land of nothing, he lacked perspective, yet from how they rose from the landscape, he suspected they were as tall as many of Oakharrow's pines.

They come over accursed wastes, with slaves ruled for aeons long.

Surtunar. He knew them with sudden intuition, and with the revelation, he saw the features that led him to it: the tusks jutting from their heads, the upright posture like that of a man, the unreality of their size. *Giants of Fire as well as Frost. They're coming to Enea — if they're not already here.*

Torvald's voice carried on. *The oldest among them comes as the queen. The rest obey and follow. They will yoke all the races of men, one by one. None may now stand against them.*

The stifling heat suddenly seemed to choke him. Bjorn fell again to his knees. He willed the distant enemy to disappear, to be nothing more than a sun-made delusion. But he blinked, again and again, and they remained.

The giants were coming, just as the Witterland Runestone had long ago predicted. The rest of its prophecy must also soon be fulfilled.

The Eternal Night — it is falling, it is falling — it will smother all humanity — none will survive, none can stand — why can't I stand?

Even as he fought to gain his feet, the world was again torn away. He kneeled now in what appeared to be a crude, hide-covered building. Though large, the logs were not trimmed or seasoned, and the pelts that stretched above reeked with inadequate curing. Bjorn glanced down at his hands and found them covered in oily soot. He raised his head, and only then saw he was not alone.

A gargantuan silhouette rose above the rest.

The Jotun. He knew him even before he recognized the Oakstone at his feet, blackened and deformed from Nuvvog's Rage. *The Jotun ruling Oakharrow.* He should have felt furious. Part of him did, distantly. But the greater half cowered.

The King of Ice spoke once more. *He rises, the King of Mountain and Snow. Go to him. They come, yet he watches, and waits, and prepares.*

Go to him? Bjorn struggled to comprehend. Why would he go to the enemy who stole everything from him? The only way he would return to Oakharrow was to kill the giant.

But the vision had not finished. *The secrets of his kin and humankind are known to him. He holds the key to every door.*

Bjorn clutched his hands to his head, heedless of the ash he smeared over himself. *The key, the key...* Was Torvald saying what he suspected?

The final words fell like killing blows.

The smallest among them is your shield. Knowledge is your sharpest sword. He may save all the races of men, should he wish. None but him may stand against them.

Bjorn closed his eyes. *No. No, no, no...*

He could not seek the Jotun as an ally. He had burned his home, killed his brothers and mother. He had seized his city and forced him to enter the deadly wintry mountains.

He would never go to the Jotun. Even if it meant letting the world burn.

Bjorn opened his eyes, but the darkness did not relent. He was caught in it, helpless, airless. He could not breathe! He tried to inhale the darkness, but stone filled him, and he sank down, down into the murk—

You cannot rest, Stoneseer. The king's voice rumbled like

a quake through his mind. *Wake. Rise. Reach for the light. The cost will be dear. But blood has always been the price for peace.*

He felt himself wrenched from his tomb by invisible hands. Sensations rushed through him. He was rising, rising up—

"Bjorn! Come back!"

Stone. It was not inside him now, but pressing against his cheek. Bjorn blinked, and the world reappeared before his eyes. Ice stretched around him, the runestone fallen upon it. A fire flickered, orange and yellow, shadows dancing around the cave. Someone leaned over him, a bare hand pressed to his neck, the flesh cold. But as he stirred and tried to sit up, it abruptly pulled away.

"He survived," he heard a woman say, one he struggled to identify for a moment. *Embla*, his fragmented mind supplied.

"He is stronger than he seems." Hoarfrost now, replying to the gothi.

"Bjorn? Are you with us, lad?"

He looked around and saw Yonik's face swimming before his eyes, mere inches away. Behind him, Seskef leaned close, his broad face scrunched in worry.

As the priest's words settled in, Bjorn nodded. "I'm here," he said aloud. His voice sounded distant and tinny to his ears.

Yonik smiled, and though the wrinkles around his eyes eased, the worry did not. "What did you witness? What vision did Torvald pass to you?"

Before Bjorn could respond, a rattling, like the shaking of many chains, welled up from around them.

Even through the haze of the *khnuum* steam and Seeing, he knew its source at once. Bjorn jerked his head up and stared at the figure mounted above them.

"Your Grace!" Bjorn croaked, pushing away Yonik's hands and tottering to his feet. "My king!"

The King of Ice had thrown his head back, skull grinding against the ice nestled behind him. His silvered crown tilted sideways, barely clinging to his head. Though it was difficult to tell, he thought the ancient man's eyes had rolled up in their sockets, for he saw only glimmers of white within his purpled skin. The jangling grew louder still. Bjorn had never heard such a sound before, but other men had spoken of it: *Ovvash's bells*, a sign that the Maiden of Death was coming to claim the spirit.

But he could not die yet.

"Torvald Geirson!"

Hardly knowing what he did, Bjorn threw himself onto the throne. He climbed the icicles projecting from the dying man like they were the branches of the trees he had scrambled up in his youth. He ignored the shouts of his companions below, even as one of the icy spines snapped underfoot and almost pitched him to the hard floor below. He managed to keep his grip. The Last King of Baegard drew ever closer, shaking with the last vestiges of life.

"You can't die!" The words ripped free of Bjorn as he closed the final distance between them. "Damn you, Torvald, *you can't die!*"

He was close, so close, then he reached toward him. His glove had come off, or perhaps he had pulled it off, and it was his bare fingertips that brushed the face of the King of Ice. He was hard, hard as his name, and so very cold. Nothing could live within that husk. He was gone.

Then his faint voice spoke in Bjorn's mind.

Heed me, Stoneseer. I have shown what I can, protected you in this first vision. I cannot help you travel the other Shadows. You must take them, and when the time comes, pry open their secrets. Look too soon, before you know you are ready, and you will perish. Yet still, you must look. They are my prophecies and contain all I know of the Runewar to come. They will guide you in my absence.

Bjorn's mind, still turned inside out, struggled to follow the wisps of thoughts. "What is the Runewar?" he asked. "Is it the Eternal Night? The fight against the giants?"

But the rattling, which had grown louder throughout his climb, suddenly ceased. Only an echo remained, filling the chamber before fleeing down the tunnel. Bjorn did not move, but kept his fingers to the frigid flesh. He stared into the unmoving eyes of the ancient seer and king.

"Your Grace?" he whispered.

His hand quavered, and even the slight movement seemed too much. The crown, precariously clinging to the ancient king's head, came loose and rattled down the spires of the frozen throne. Bjorn twisted around in time to see it shatter upon the ice below.

He knew it then with certainty. Torvald Geirson, at long last, was dead.

Bjorn slowly retracted his hand. He barely even noticed the cold gnawing at his bare skin. All he had seen and all he had learned pounded through his head. The epiphanies had come so quickly, so forcefully, that he had trouble believing any were real.

What have I stumbled into? Despair welled up in him like a cold, dark pool threatening to suck him into its depths. *What does any of this mean?*

Before he could move or speak, footsteps reverberated up the tunnel, rapid and growing louder. Bjorn looked around again to see Loridi sprinting into the cavern, only to slip on the ice and flop to the ground. Though the spill looked painful, the man did not spare it more than a groan before he blurted forth.

"Fire! There's fire in the valley! Eildursprall burns!"

36. ASH AND IRON

"There are two aims in battle. The first: survive. The second: kill. For best results, keep to that order."

- Yofam Dragontooth, Slayer of the wyvern Vardraith, First Drang of the Iron Band

The assailants stalked them, silent as specters. Frey edged forth, securing his position before Aelthena. Blood pounded in her ears as she reached down and pulled free the knife she kept strapped to her leg. But seeing their swords, the short blade seemed little more than a toy.

"Stay back," her guardian commanded over his shoulder, voice faint through the din in her head. "Run as soon as there's an opening."

Her emotions were too knotted to make sense of. Her limbs trembled with their battle for supremacy.

"I won't let you die," she warned him, though she scarcely knew what she could do to prevent it.

Frey barked a laugh as the first Sypten attacked. In

addition to a small, bronze buckler, the man bore a sword that curved halfway up its length like a sickle. *A khopesh,* she remembered from her erstwhile studies. The khopesh whistled toward Frey, but only found air. She had known the guardian was quick, had even witnessed it before, but she still could scarcely believe he avoided such a blow. Frey stabbed in retaliation, but was thwarted by a wild swing of the man's buckler, and only scored a shallow cut along his arm.

The other two Syptens attacked then. One slid around to the guardian's flank and swung at Frey's back. A hiss escaped Aelthena's lips as she anticipated the blade chopping into his spine, but again, the guardian twisted out of the way. He was as slippery as a river eel, but even his skill could not save him for long.

Do something, damn you! a part of her screamed.

She had her knife, but she would never reach them before they cut her down. So she lurched toward the first other object in sight: a ceramic oil lamp. Aelthena lifted it and, positioning herself like she would throw a packed ball of snow, she hurled the lamp at the closest assailant.

The Sypten stumbled forward as the crockery shattered over the back of his head. Oil splattered over his head and shoulders, and lines of red appeared along his scalp where the shards cut. The man whirled around, gaze baleful as it fell upon her. He was far from dead.

"Damn!" Aelthena dropped her useless knife and lunged for the next thing in reach, a copper serving platter from her morning meal. She positioned it in front of her like a shield in time to catch the khopesh stabbing toward her. The platter was not meant for battle; the blade cut through the metal, lodging at the notch where the curve went straight and stopping just shy of her belly.

Terror pounded like blood through her, lending her

strength. Aelthena twisted the platter, trying to dislodge the weapon from her opponent's hand. The Sypten did not resist, but struck forward with his bronze buckler instead to catch her on the shoulder. Pain blossomed down her arm and up into her skull as she staggered. Gasping, Aelthena kept her grip on the impaled platter and wrenched the sword back the other way. This time, she disarmed the man — or so she thought, until she realized he had let go on purpose. Now he clutched a knife, straight-edged and sharp. His eyes, wide and edged with white, held equal measures of resolve and reluctance. As he hesitated a moment, she dared to believe he might not kill her.

The Sypten lurched forward.

Aelthena screamed as she swung the platter around. Movement blurred behind the man, but she could register nothing but his knife headed for her gut. Even with her unwieldy weapon, she caught her opponent on the temple. He went down at once, groaning, and she stumbled back a step in surprise. Only then did she see her blow had not been the killing one. A red line spread across his spine where a sword had cut through.

Frey's agonized cry brought her back to her senses.

She looked up to see the guardian spin down to one knee, a hand clutching his left side. Blood seeped through his fingers. *No.* She denied the wound even as her eyes knew the truth. It was bleeding too furiously to be a shallow cut, and Frey was having difficulty keeping his sword raised.

She acted by instinct. Turning the platter around, she seized the khopesh by the hilt and dashed forward. Her dress, still heavy against the spring chill, flapped between her legs, and she nearly tripped on the fallen Sypten. Only one assailant still stood, Frey having apparently felled another, but even one was too many. He knocked the sword from Frey's nerveless hand and swung his blade back around to finish the guardian.

With a wordless shriek, Aelthena crashed into him.

She fell in a confusion of limbs. The Sypten grunted beneath her, then gurgled. *Where was his sword?* Only after did she feel the blade sawing into her thigh. Hissing with pain, Aelthena tried to lever herself up. Her hands still gripped the khopesh, but something made it difficult to move. Then she saw red liquid seeping through the rent in the platter.

She had stabbed the man through.

Stumbling away, Aelthena gained her feet and stared down at the man. The sword had gone through his side; by the sound of his wet breathing, it had punctured at least one of his lungs. He was dying.

I killed him.

She shoved the thought down and set her mind to the only thing that mattered now. *Frey.* Keeping her distance from the dying enemies, she staggered toward the kneeling guardian.

"Frey." Her voice came out in a strangled whisper. She made herself speak louder. "Frey!"

He gave a noncommittal grunt. His head was bowed, and his hand still clutched at the wound in his side. Blood stained his gambeson and tunic.

"We have to get out of here. We cannot stay." The last thing she wanted was to leave this room. Terrible as it would be to remain with the dead, it was almost preferable to venturing out into the corridors where enemies lurked. But she knew they had no other choice. Frey needed help at once, and if more Syptens came and found her and Frey here, they would die anyway.

The guardian raised his head and met her gaze through

sweaty blonde curls. His eyes scrunched with pain, he whispered, "Help me up. And take my sword."

Complying, she grasped the sword's hilt. Despite having just killed with a blade, she felt awkward holding the weapon, afraid she might accidentally cut herself or Frey with it. But there was nothing else for it. Returning to the guardian, she dragged his free arm over her shoulders and hauled him upright. Frey moaned, but he supported most of his own weight.

Only then did Aelthena wonder where they should go.

"We have to check on my father." The thought came of its own accord, the frost-bent part of her mind rising as she faltered. "His quarters are near the rest of the jarls. That's where the resistance will be."

And the hottest fighting.

But if Frey thought the same thing, she could not tell, for he only nodded and shuffled forward at her step.

They made their limping way out into the corridor.

If she had not already understood the result of the battle, Sehdra knew as soon as the huame stampeded past the karah's pavilion.

Teti practically dragged her up the hill to shelter there, yet she scarcely felt safer. The giants charged through the camp, indiscriminate of the tents or humans in their way. Two collided near her, nearly tumbling to the ground before shoving apart, snarling and bellowing at each other before continuing to run on. Even in her mindless daze, Sehdra counted how many of the huame passed her. *Ten.* The mountain savages had killed two of Oyaoan's followers and injured many more.

She had not thought it possible. But unless she had miscounted, the evidence loomed before her eyes.

Someone sprinted from the tent and stopped short of the road, then shouted in a thin, reedy voice.

"I did not order a retreat!" the Karah of Ha-Sypt screamed after them. "Turn around, Gazabe blight you! I *command* you to turn around!"

Sehdra looked at Teti and saw the same knowledge in his eyes. *Madness.* Madness to think such beings would ever obey a human, even a living god and powerful king. She had thought her brother knew that. Yet here he stood, trying to exert his paltry influence over them.

From the dust and smoke sprinted a lone figure, diminutive after the giants' passage. Only then did Sehdra realize that, at any moment, Winter Holds soldiers might ride through. Their army had been routed; no place was safe now. She glanced around at the score of guards that remained around the tent and the slaves milling about. *Too few.* Especially if the servants opted for a chance for freedom — and who could blame them if they did?

But the approaching man was not one of the mountain warriors, but the Ibis. Gray ash peppered his sable skin, and though he had always seemed a spry man, his breathing was labored as he halted before the karah. Physt ignored the Suncoaster, still staring after the huame and heaving with barely contained wrath.

"Great Oyaoan instructs to sound the retreat," croaked the Ibis, his accent more pronounced with his weariness. "The pale men have claimed this day."

At last, he provoked Hephystus into action. With a swiftness and force that shocked Sehdra, the karah struck the translator across the face with the back of his hand, then leaned forward to spit at him.

"*I will not retreat!* I am the Holy Karah, the god of Ha-

Sypt! I lead the greatest army ever to be fielded. I summon the flames of Hua and command giants. I cannot lose!" Physt grabbed the Ibis by the back of the neck and dragged him closer. "*Oyaoan does not command me.* She does not *own* me. I have lent her my authority because she has brought the huame. But see how they flee! What is their sorcery worth now? They are nothing to me. Your 'Great One' can run after her craven beasts and take comfort in them!"

Her brother flung the translator back, and the Ibis sprawled before scrambling back to his feet. Though he touched a hand to his jaw, the Suncoaster looked far from cowed. A calmness that belied the violence struck a deeper fear in Sehdra. Her muscles felt they must snap, like rope put under too much strain.

The translator stared a moment longer at Physt, then turned to Amon, who had been speechless as he watched the exchange. At his raised hand, half a dozen messengers anxiously dallied, and more joined them with every passing moment.

"Amon Baka," the Ibis addressed him. "In the absence of the karah's reason, Great Oyaoan's command falls to you. Order the retreat, general. This battle is over."

Physt spun around, glaring first at the Ibis, then the general. He adjusted the crown on his head. The paint had begun to run down his face. "Remember, Amon Baka: you owe all you are to me. Do not listen to this foreigner. Guards!" The karah whipped his head around to look at the closest men. "Seize this interloper!"

Two of the guards obeyed, hands folding around the thin arms of the Ibis. The translator remained unperturbed, as fearless of death as he was of giants and kings. Sehdra did not know whether she found the display admirable or terrifying.

Amon cleared his throat. He leaned over the table where his map lay ruined by spilled ink and tumbled pieces from the giants' flight.

"Divine One," he said, his rich baritone broken with strain, "I beg you to reconsider. We cannot know the depth of our losses in this smoke. At minimum, I should marshal our forces, take stock of what troops remain. If there is enough, we may attempt a second assault."

Physt's hands twitched at his sides. "Did I ask for your opinion?" he hissed through clenched teeth. "Send the orders, general. Or your successor will."

Amon's mouth fell open, but no answer came out. *What reply could he make?* Sehdra knew of none that could change the outcome.

The vizier finally edged forward, self-preservation bringing him out of the shadows. His eyes were wide with repressed fear.

"Your Sanctity," Zosar wheedled, "perhaps it is best to heed…"

He trailed off as Physt's blistering gaze fell upon him. The man had always had as much of a spine as the cobra he worshipped.

Then, for no reason that Sehdra could determine, Amon's eyes flickered to her. She startled back to herself. *What can I do?* Physt had made his opinion clear. Defy him now, and he might as easily take off her head with the rest of theirs. She was being practical, realistic.

She was afraid.

It could only end in disaster. It would not change the course of the day. *But if not me, then who? If not now, when?* Her brother would kill every last man and woman in this camp before he bent his pride. Her choice was not to live or die; it was die here and now, or die when the northern savages brought their sunfire to the camp.

She had a chance to save her people's lives — and the man she loved as a brother.

Sehdra brushed off Teti's grip. Only after he released her did he realize what she intended. Teti lunged and caught her hand again, disregarding formality for once.

"Don't, Sehdra." His voice was a whisper. "It will do nothing!"

She looked back and gave him a small smile. She doubted she hid her fear well. It felt as if the world trembled around her. She suspected it was her twisted leg giving way.

But I am strong enough.

Sehdra pried away Teti's hand, then stepped forward and looked back to her brother. Physt was watching her, eyes wide, a wild smile twisting his lips.

"So the cursed bitch wants to mewl as well!" he mocked, then burst out with a laugh. "Well then, *Royal Sister*. Let's hear your pleas!"

Sehdra stood before all that unwanted attention. Sweat beaded behind her mask, the heat of the fires having long ago rolled over the camp. She tried to spin words that would not be entirely futile.

"You should not challenge Oyaoan, Divine One. Please."

Another laugh ripped from her brother's throat. He stepped forward as a horrid smile claimed his features.

"Should I not, sister?" he jeered. "Do you fear for your brother?"

"I fear for Ha-Sypt. And yes — I fear for you."

Despite all the terrible things she had seen him do or heard tell of, despite the tyrannical ruler he had turned out to be, it was true. Part of her still remembered the young boy who had pulled at his elder sister's hand and begged her to play in the fountains and sand gardens. Whatever he was now, she could not help but believe a kernel of her younger brother — sometimes sweet, sometimes joyful, always full of vigor — still remained.

But at her words, the smile disappeared, and his eyes narrowed. Physt stepped close enough she could smell the sour cloud of his wine-tainted breath.

"Liar!" he hissed. "You have wished me dead a thousand times! I have seen it in your eyes. You believe you would be a better karah, don't you? *Don't you?*" His voice rose with these last words.

Sehdra opened her mouth, not knowing what to say, but knowing she must try to calm him. "Physt, I—"

Agony splintered through her skull.

She hit the ground hard, her cursed leg capitulating at once. Her arms and shoulders smarted from the fall, but her head hurt worse. The eye where he had struck her — the eye set in her cursed flesh — throbbed. She suspected only her mask had saved her from more severe damage.

No sooner had she looked up than a second blow doubled her over. Nauseating pain spread through her gut. Sehdra rolled, desperate to escape. Tears stung her eyes.

"Mercy, Divine One," she gasped as she crawled away. "Have mercy."

Hephystus stalked her, always a few strides behind. "Mercy? For one who has conspired against me since the day I was born? No, dear sister. I have tolerated your repulsive features long enough."

No one moved to intervene. How could they? Her brother would order any of them executed without cause. He could beat her to death, and there was nothing anyone could do to stop it.

Physt raised a sandaled foot, his face alight with delight, ready to bring it down on her cursed leg. Sehdra tried to wriggle out of the way. A scream built up behind her teeth.

Movement blurred behind her brother, and suddenly he

was flailing to the ground. Only as he fell did she see who his assailant was.

Teti!

Shouting filled the tent. Guards swarmed upon them. Her brother's frenzied shrieks filled the pavilion.

"Kill him! *Kill him!*"

Desperation lent Sehdra a surge of strength. Her jaw clenched against the pain wracking her body, she rose and threw up her arms against the guards. They collided with her, pushing her off-balance, but she was caught among them.

"*No!*" she screamed. "*Stop! I order you to stop!*"

A few did. The rest pressed forward, khopeshes drawn. Only his entanglement with the karah preserved Teti's life as the guards tried to pry him loose.

A bone-shaking roar brought the melee to a halt.

Sehdra, supported by the men she struggled against, stared behind their heads at the source of the sound. But she could not deny it. There was nothing in the world like a huamek's bellow.

Oyaoan stood at the entrance to the pavilion. A hand pried back the fabric to stare down at the tangle of men. Her eyes were as black as a cavern, black as Gazabe's dominion. Her leathery skin crinkled in a furious snarl.

Oyaoan had come.

Ash and iron were all he could taste.

Bastor's head jerked up just before the coughs claimed him. He leaned on his arms as his lungs tried to squeeze out of his throat. Gray gods, but he felt weak, weaker than he ever had in his thirty winters. Agony ran like chains of fire through his limbs to wind tightly around his skull. He spat, straightened his tilted helmet, and through blurry vision, saw his spittle come out red on the blackened ground.

Yet the sounds grating in his dull ears spurred him upright. *Screaming. Clashing metal. Roaring flames.* Bastor worked his knees under him, then pushed himself onto his feet. He nearly fell on his rear, but managed to pull himself upright.

Axe. Where's my bloody axe?

He staggered like a man so far into his cups he barely knew who he was anymore. His vision was poor enough for it, clouds swirling behind his eyes. Bent halfway over, he scrabbled in the mud until his fingers burned. He cursed, realizing too late he'd touched a sharp edge.

"Djur burn you," he muttered as he seized his axe and straightened.

Only then did he properly look around him. He was alone in the smoky wasteland. His warriors had either abandoned him or been slain. *Or both,* he thought as he saw the dark mounds scattered across the ground. Perhaps the blast had killed them as it nearly had him. Perhaps the giants had turned and paid their assault back in like. Or maybe the Sypten army had stormed back through and routed those Baegardians who had broken through.

Any way he looked at it, he was damned lucky to be alive.

Bastor staggered blindly in one direction, aiming downhill. The Sypten camp had been been atop a slope. He could only hope he had chosen right, or he might find himself surrounded by an enemy none-too-pleased to see him.

But there was no end to the blighted land. The ground rose in rifts, the firesand having distorted the terrain. His feet dragged, then his axe, the head plowing the ashy dirt. It was difficult to keep his head up. He almost prayed for Volkur to take him now, a glorious death be damned.

He jerked back to awareness as a silhouette came running toward him through the smoke.

Bastor jerked back a step, axe raised and clutched in both hands. His arms felt as if anvils were strapped to them; it took all his effort just to keep them there. The specter came close enough that even with his unreliable eyesight, he could make him out as a Sypten. He had a boy's slenderness, and the soot smeared over his skin made him seem a shadow. His eyes were wide and bright by contrast. He carried a spear upright, but it lowered as he noticed Bastor. His limbs seemed to tremble, though it could have just been his wavering vision.

Bastor showed him a silent snarl. He knew he should strike before the boy could take his measure. *Bait the spear. Hook it out of the way. Cut him down.* If the youth was as green as he looked, he could probably manage it.

But he did not move forward, and neither did the Sypten. They stood opposite of each other, wheezing in the contaminated air, endeavoring just to keep their weapons leveled.

A laugh worked free of his tortured lungs, and Bastor let the axe head drop to the dirt.

"Go, boy," he said in the Sypten tongue. "Go back to your camp. Enough have died today."

The Sypten youth did not move. He wondered if he had spoken incorrectly, if his head was more muddled than he thought, and the wrong words had come out.

Then the spear raised, and the boy bobbed his head. "Qa'a bless you," he muttered, the words trembling.

The spearman moved away. Bastor watched him limp off, using his weapon like a staff. *He'll make it.* The boy would likely remain a soldier. Odds were he did not have a choice in the matter. If he remained alive, he would kill Baegardians in subsequent conflicts.

Only fools claim to know the future, his father was fond of saying. And though he agreed with little his father had said over the years, Bastor found wisdom in those words. He could not know the young man's path. All he knew was, after all the threads he had severed that day, at least he had preserved one.

Bastor had just turned back to look the other way when hoofbeats sounded from the smoke.

Bastor tensed, his axe rising again as he squinted toward the clamor. A split moment after he made out the shapes, they burst past him, two riders surging forward at full tilt. One of them cried to the other as they passed on either side of him, and for a moment, he thought they would cut him down where he stood. Instead, they continued past him. Only as Bastor turned did he see where they headed.

He let out a strangled roar. *"No!"*

The Sypten youth barely had time to turn before one of the rider's weapons pounded into the space between his shoulders. He went down limply, the force of the blow enough to break his spine. *Dead.*

Bastor swayed, blinked rapidly, and forced himself to straighten. His axe sprang up in his hands again. A measure of strength returned with the anger that beat through him, more flooding his muscles with every heartbeat.

The riders wheeled around and trotted up to him. He could just make out their faces in the gloom. Baegardians, by their garb and skin color. His fury grew as he recognized them.

Endre, his father's huskarl, smirked down at him. Ash spotted his black beard. "So you're still clinging to life, eh, Lord Heir?"

Bastor resented the breath he had to waste on the exchange. "Go back," he panted. "I'll find my own way."

The warrior shook his head. His heels pressed in lightly, and his mount edged closer.

"We were just coming to retrieve your body for your father. Wouldn't want to disappoint him."

Bastor was quickly rallying. "'Fraid you'll have to." He gestured with his axe. "Volkur would have already taken me if I was dying this day. Seems she has other plans."

"Guess we'll see who she favors, won't we?" Endre nodded at his companion, a second of his father's huskarls.

Then, with twin calls, their horses surged forward.

37. THE FLAMES BELOW

Concerning the use of the runes, there are some doors best left locked. The berserkers have shown the dangers of flouting such warnings, for when the fighting ceases, still they shed blood...

- Counsel on the Inscribed Beliefs, by Mother Vigilance

Bjorn stepped free of the frozen cavern and into the scouring winds. His skin, feverish in the aftermath of the Seeing, now burned with cold as it clawed through his furs and closed talons around his bones.

But it was the sight below that struck the deepest chill through him.

Fire. Eildursprall was a distant smudge of orange and red through the clouds, yet bright enough to know it was no trick of the light.

Fire in the valley. Just as the wind had warned him upon first arriving at the town. Just as he had seen using Farsight in Mother Sign's hut.

Could I have prevented this? Bjorn did not know where

to turn for answers. He had already known he was *Volur*, had seen his prophecies come true. Yet, still unsure of himself, he had first pushed the omen to the back of his mind and willfully forgotten it, then failed to insist that Mother Sign act on it immediately.

I let them burn.

Embla stepped to the front of the party, eyes narrowed as she stared over the sheer drop at the town below. "We may reach it just after nightfall," she called over the keening winds, "if we cast aside caution!"

Bjorn judged the others' reactions. Hoarfrost nodded, her expression tough as leather. Loridi and Seskef bobbed their heads as well, their usual joviality replaced by furrowed brows and worried eyes. Yonik was more reserved in his reaction, only frowning and staring down.

The priestess stared hard at her fellow gothi for a long moment, then turned to Bjorn. "Will you risk the descent now?"

He startled at being addressed. Stoneseer he had been within the cave, and he had been exposed as the exiled Heir of Oakharrow. But out here on a narrow ledge, at the mercy of the capricious gusts and snows, his opinion seemed of little import. Especially when his decision had led to this.

No. I cannot doubt. I cannot break. He drew in a shaky breath to answer.

"Yes. I have to. We all do."

The priestess gave him a tight smile, while Yonik glanced sidelong at him.

"But is it our highest duty, Bjorn?" the gothi murmured, low enough that Embla would not hear.

He met Yonik's gaze. Bjorn had not yet passed on all he had seen to the others. *That's why they look to me,* he realized. *They think I know the path. They think Torvald Geirson naming me Stoneseer gives me insights into the future.* They did not know just how little he understood. And that none of it related to the predicament before them.

It was not *seidar* or visions that guided his decisions now, but an influence far more powerful. *Tyra. Mother Sign. Flint, and Mother Iron, and Father Temperance, and everyone else in Heim Numen.* They were down there, subject to fires that he had let spread. Even now, they fought for their homes and lives, be the flames accidental or brought by enemies.

He swallowed hard. He had never been a brave man. But he had abandoned his friends once, and Keld had paid the price. He would not do it again. Even his cowardice had limits.

"It is our duty," he said at last.

From the furrowing of the priest's brow, the distinction was not lost on him. He nodded all the same. "Then we go with all haste, and pray for the Wild God's mercy."

Embla had already sprung into action, handing out the rope for each to wind around their waists. "Follow where I tread and nowhere else," she instructed as they secured themselves to the line. "I cannot stop and explain why and where I go. You must watch and trust me."

Bjorn found his throat horribly dry. His vision, never quite clear following the Seeing, grew murkier for a moment. He shook his head, trying to clear it. Instead, it only seemed to make it worse. Without conscious thought, the Hall of Doors appeared in his mind. *Khnuum* steam still clouded his mind, and his emotions were fraught. His lessons with Mother Sign had lessened his susceptibility to errant visions following exposure to *khnuum,* but they could not fully protect him.

"Bjorn?"

He looked over to see Loridi standing nearby. The tall

man put an arm across his shoulders and gave them a small squeeze.

"Just keep your eyes on Yonik and you'll be fine," the jester said, perfectly serious for once. "You know he won't step amiss. Like a snowcat, he is."

"Or a wolf," Bjorn countered softly.

Loridi only smiled, then set off as the others plodded down the narrow trail.

He had thought ascending the mountain would be the tricky part, yet going down proved thornier still.

Snow conspired to slip under their feet at every moment. Even deadlier was the ice, hiding on rocks and under snow. It was liable to make even their clogs ineffective. More than once, Bjorn and the others fell hard to the ground, sliding a little way before they could gain their feet again. Each time Bjorn was sure they would be carried off the steep sides to a death far below.

Yet urgency still scorched his chest, and the rest of his company were filled with the same fire. No matter how many times they stumbled, no matter how perilous the descent, they did not slow. And as they went below Yewung's bank of clouds, the fires plaguing Eildursprall came into clearer view.

He tried not to imagine what was happening down there, tried not to picture the fates of those he had come to care about. But once again, his scholar's courage had different plans. He saw faceless marauders kicking into the *Volur* hut, Mother Sign cowering defenseless before them. He saw the library door chopped down, then Tyra screaming as men chased and caught her in a dark corner.

Bjorn clenched his jaw tight. Were they visions or mere

nightmares? *Khnuum* still touched his mind; he could feel it in the strangeness of his senses. But he remembered his fateful stagger through Oakharrow's streets, the world turning to fire and frost around him. He was not so far gone as that now. He was still sane.

Yet the wind mocked him with its whispers. *Fire in the valley*, it sighed, again and again.

They went down the long glacier and past the cave where they had spent the previous night, making it in half the time it had taken to rise. Yet though they carried on with treacherous swiftness, it was not quick enough. Bjorn wanted to throw himself down the mountain rather than carefully pick his way from foothold to foothold to the ground below. The painful cold in his fingers and toes was nothing compared to the wretchedness lodged tight in his chest.

Are they still alive? Are we too late?

He could not contemplate the questions overlong. They sapped at his strength, and paltry as it already was, he did not doubt there would be precious little to fight fires at the end.

With interminable slowness, the final stretch curved before them. The sky above had cleared, and the bruised glow of dusk claimed it as the sun fell behind the western peaks. Embla, who led their party, spun back, and Bjorn and the others plodded over wearily to stand before her.

"Some fires still burn," she said, her voice hushed as if afraid of being overheard. "If there was a battle, we might not be too late. Best be prepared."

They started by untying themselves, prying at the thick rope with clumsy, gloved fingers. Bjorn wondered what he could possibly do to prepare for this fight. A fire still raged in him, but his body cried out for rest. Could he still swing a sword or raise a shield after all this?

But as he thought again of the friends that might have fallen prey to the flames, an idea sprang to mind.

"Wait!"

The others had already worked free of the rope and turned to continue the descent. At his cry, they turned back. Embla scowled and Hoarfrost frowned, but Yonik approached with his brow creased.

"What is it, Bjorn? Can you continue?"

"Yes — it's not that," he answered quickly. Even as he spoke, he untied his heavy pack and slung it down to the snowy ground with a grunt. "I thought of something."

"We need to go!" Embla hissed. "Or there won't be anyone left to save."

"Just a moment." Bjorn ripped open the top of his pack and rummaged through it. It was not long before he came up with a satchel in hand, its contents dully clinking together.

"What's that supposed to be?" Loridi asked, incredulous. "Dragonfire?"

Bjorn ignored him and looked up at the gothi. "Mother Sign gave me these before we went up. One of them is a Frenzy runestone."

The priest's expression twitched, then went flat. "Are you still affected enough for *seidar*?"

Bjorn reached for the Hall of Doors, and a faint image of it materialized before his eyes. He nodded. "Barely. But yes."

"Bjorn." Hoarfrost gave him a warning glance.

"A moment more." Bjorn looked back into Yonik's shadowed eyes and swallowed. "We don't have a choice. Do we?"

The priest hesitated, then shook his head. "Wait until we see if there are enemies, at least. It only takes a moment to open a door."

Bjorn nodded.

"Then you do not want that one ajar before the red hour arrives." Yonik flashed a mirthless smile.

Relieved to put off the moment a little longer, Bjorn opened the satchel and peered inside. As his eyes strayed over the faint outlines of the runes carved on the five stones nestled within, doors rattled in his mind. He gritted his teeth and sifted through them, resisting the efforts of each to claim his mind until he finally found the one he sought.

As soon as the Frenzy runestone was in hand, he closed his eyes and held it up. "Hold this for me."

A pressure left his hand as Yonik accepted it, and Bjorn closed the satchel and returned it to his pack. Then he rose to his feet, shrugged on the heavy burden once again, and looked down the path. Embla had watched him pull the runestone out, and she alone seemed to understand what the delay had been about now. A stony expression had stolen over her face. Hoarfrost only watched with her usual placidity, then followed the priestess as she set down the trail.

Yonik pressed the runestone back into his hand. "Just remember what you've learned. And remember yourself."

Bjorn swallowed and nodded.

As the priest started after the others, Bjorn shouldered his pack and followed in his footsteps. Loridi and Seskef came up on either side of him. Loridi was bent forward like a pine under a heavy snow, while Seskef panted like the bellows of a forge.

"More of your witchery, I suppose?" Loridi noted, eyeing the stone clutched in his hand.

"Yes." His voice felt raw, and not only for the hard hike down. He wondered what it would be like when that door opened. Frenzy was one that he had never practiced, and he had to think it was for good reason.

But Mother Sign gave me the stone. She had to think I was ready.

"Careful... Lord Heir," Seskef advised between pants. "Magic... cuts both ways... as my father... always said."

He gripped the runestone tighter still. Truer words had never been spoken. *But what choice do I have?*

His heart beat faster, his breath came quicker, his chest pressed tighter — and the glow of the fires came nearer. Smoke bit at the inside of his nostrils, and he tried not to imagine the gothi and Silvers burning alive in the longhouse.

Baltur, if there is any justice in this world, let them be alive, he thought, increasing their pace. *Volkur, preserve them; they were never meant to die to battle.*

At last, the descent leveled out ahead. The periphery of Heim Numen lay a hundred paces farther. Against the glow of the fires, he saw their three other companions huddled together, and he and the former Hunters hurried over. When he reached them, all three had removed their packs and drawn weapons. Embla only held a blade somewhere between seax and knife. Hoarfrost carried her spear, and the sheaths of two knives hung from her belt. Yonik's long daggers glimmered orange in the darkness. His gut twisting in agony, Bjorn followed their lead, drawing his sword and untying his shield to settle at his feet. Loridi and Seskef were silent for once as they followed suit.

"Strangers move in Eildursprall," Yonik informed them quietly as they prepared. "Clad in barbar furs. It is difficult to tell, but they have the features of jotunmen to my eye."

Jotunmen. Only one could have sent those fiends. Bjorn had hoped they were out of the reach of their enemy, but he had known it a fruitless hope as soon as he glimpsed them in his vision with Mother Sign. Yet why had the Jotun attacked now? Was it because of the mountains thawing, a natural expansion of his territory? Or was there another reason Eildursprall was targeted?

He had no answers, nor could they make a difference now. They did not change what needed to be done.

"We've seen a dozen so far, moving in groups of two or three," the gothi continued. "They appear to be camping near where the longhouse used to stand."

Used to. So much was said in those words. Bjorn found the worry fueling another feeling now. Even without the stone's help, anger was taking hold.

Hoarfrost, who had been staring over the ruins, turned toward them. "We will strike, silent and swift, at the far end of the compound — as near to the *Volur* hut as we can. Kill each group we encounter and press closer to town. If Jün favors us, this dozen will be all we face."

"And if the Wild God does not favor us?" Loridi asked, weak humor in his words.

No one even smiled.

Bjorn felt Yonik's gaze and turned to meet it. "If you mean to use the stone," the priest said, "you should do it now."

He clung to his resolve as he cradled the runestone in both hands and slowly looked down. Even in the gloom, his eyes latched onto the carved lines at once. He felt his vision narrowing, all else seeming to fade away. His mind cleared of all but the Hall of Doors, and he flew through them until he stood before one, the others shrouded in shadow.

Bjorn stared at the door and the iron handle set in it. *Open,* he thought, and the door rattled, like something wished to get out. *Open.* It pushed outward again, its hinges straining. *Open, damn you!*

Bjorn reached out and yanked it wide.

As soon as it was free of the latch, the Frenzy door blew open. The corridor remained in the periphery of his mind, but Bjorn was abruptly grounded in his body. All the pains and ills of the day slunk away, and a terrible strength blazed in his limbs.

He grinned into the night, filled with a savage delight, a berserker's bliss. His doubts crumbled away like the Harrowhall in Nuvvog's Rage, leaving only a cleansing fire. He could do anything, anything he wished, and nothing could stand in his way.

And underneath, fueling all else, was a blood-pumping, muscle-clenching rage.

"I'll kill them." The words growled in his throat as Bjorn leaned down and seized his shield and sword. He felt a strange calm settle over his mind, like standing under the shelter of a roof while a storm lashed the world outside. He accepted the resolve without question. *"I'll kill every last burning one."*

He ran. The people around him — *My companions,* some distant part recalled — called after him, but their voices were soft and weak. They were afraid of what the night held, afraid of those who moved about the flames.

He knew no fear.

Laughter gurgled in his throat as Bjorn pressed faster, faster, boots churning the snow. Two silhouetted figures ambled through the compound's main path, but they paused and turned toward him at his approach. He did not care.

He wanted them to see him coming.

He hungered for their shock.

He craved their fear.

Bjorn charged between two smoldering buildings and, with a bellow, fell upon the jotunmen.

38. ASCENSION

When the Karah passes unto death
To reunite with Our Divine
The Crown must not be left bereft
A successor you must find

In royal blood, the wise do search
In blood Our Splinters hide
A new Karah, from the loins of the First
Hua's reign shall ever survive

- Words in the Sand, refrain 12;213-214

When you strike an enemy, his father had counseled him early in his training, *hit them so they won't rise again. Hit them hard where it most hurts.*

Bastor had always had strength and speed. But it was the instinct of knowing where and when to use it that made him deadly.

The huskarls bore down on him, trying to pin him between

their pounding mounts. Bastor dropped below the reach of their weapons and swung as he ducked. His axe hooked the foot of the second huskarl, and he clung to it, though his shoulder screamed with the effort. He was dragged for a short distance before the gamble paid off. The huskarl, caught between the momentum of his horse and the man attached to his foot, was finally pulled to the ground, where he crumpled in a pile.

Bastor snarled as he gained his feet and freed his weapon, then whirled around to where Endre turned for another pass. He had no time to finish the downed man before the warhorse charged. Bastor knew he could not execute the same trick twice.

Time for another.

He moved in front of the horse and swung his axe in a wide arc before him. The sharp head cut through the horse's chest just as Bastor threw himself to one side. Pounding hooves and shrieking whinnies filled the air behind him.

Muddy ground pummeled him again. His fury nearly fled before the abuse to his tortured body. Air hissed through his clenched teeth as Bastor levered himself upright with the axe and looked around.

The horse fled into the smoke, its rider lost. But Endre pulled himself up, a steady stream of curses confirming he lived on. Bastor could guess what had happened: the straps of the saddle had severed under his axe's sharp edge, and the horse, frenzied with pain, had reared and thrown the huskarl.

All was just as he had intended.

Bastor limped toward the rising man and risked a glance over his shoulder. The other huskarl lay motionless now. With any luck, he was knocked out, or perhaps dead. *Volkur does smile on me today.* He turned his gaze forward again and met Endre's shadowed eyes.

"You couldn't just burning die, could you, bastard?" The huskarl spat, though his eyes wandered as if dazed.

Bastor never gave up an advantage to bandy words. He forced himself into a run and charged. Endre brought up his own weapon, an axe to match Bastor's. The shafts clacked together, and as Bastor pressed, the curved heads locked. He grabbed ahold of his adversary's weapon and forced it down, then drove his head forward. They had both lost their helmets, but the bone of his skull was enough to send the huskarl lurching back.

Bastor kicked him and sent Endre falling, arse first, to the ground. The huskarl struggled to keep his weapon before him as he rose, but succeeded at neither. Bastor looked down at him. His body begged for rest. He gave it no more quarter than he intended to give his adversary.

But Endre spoke, clearly playing for time as he recovered. "Don't you want to know why?" he wheedled. "Why your own father wants you dead?"

Bastor edged around him. He felt as if a millstone were strapped around his neck, dragging him toward the ground. Even standing was an effort.

So he sucked in air and responded. "I know why. I've always known why. My crime was to be born."

Bastor moved before he finished speaking. Endre had expected it, but he was too slow and too weak. Bastor's axe crashed against his again, but he pressed past it so that the axe head lodged into his skull. *Like chopping wood,* a stray thought bubbled up as the huskarl fell nervelessly to the ground.

Bastor released his weapon as he went, too tired even to hold on any longer. He slumped to his knees. Only instinct compelled him to check again that the other huskarl remained down. Then he bowed his head as if to pray, and his hair, pulled free of its braids, felling in a ragged, dirty curtain about his face.

It was a long time before he rose.

Aelthena rarely wept. When she fell as a child, she more often shouted than cried. She had always despised the tears of other girls. What use were they? They changed nothing, and only made a girl into a sniveling, pathetic mess.

But as she hauled Frey through the corridors of the invaded Elkhorn, the unfamiliar grip of the sword in her trembling hand, tears streamed down her face. At last, she understood there was comfort in acknowledging her helplessness.

She blinked rapidly and tried to keep her vision clear. At each corner, more Syptens could emerge and attack. Signs of their passage littered the hallways: doors caved in; curtains and paintings torn apart; crockery shattered; bodies of servants, guards, and invaders lying in dark pools. Strains of distant fighting sometimes echoed along the stone. Always, she turned away from it to continue her and Frey's limping progress in safer directions.

Yet one of the Inscribed seemed to heed their plight, for no more enemies found them. Only as they rose to the floor that housed the jarls and advanced toward her father's room did their luck run out.

Aelthena paused, breath hissing through her throat, and tried to listen for where the fighting came from. Frey leaned heavier upon her. His head often lolled back, and he sagged until she shook him back awake. She feared it would not be long before he could not rise again.

They were only a couple dozen paces away from her father's quarters. The door was open, but she was not sure it was the source of the conflict. Then she heard a man's reverberant roar. She clutched tighter at Frey as she recognized the voice.

Father!

She wanted to cry out to him, but she did not dare. Instead, Aelthena dragged the half-conscious guardian to an alcove a few feet ahead. "I'm sorry, Frey," she muttered as she settled him against the wall. She moved him rougher than intended, and as his head knocked against the stone, Aelthena winced. Yet there was nothing she could do for him now.

She could not let her father die alone.

Aelthena rose and wiped a sleeve across her eyes, then gripped the sword with both hands. She knew little of combat and less of wielding a sword. But she could swing it. If her enemy was caught by surprise, that might be enough.

Her nose was stuffy, so she breathed through her mouth, as shallowly as she could. She pushed away the doubts and fears that assailed her and focused on the sounds from within the chamber. Lord Bor shouted again, a wordless and enraged sound, and a babble of men's voices responded. Aelthena clenched her teeth until they ached and advanced the last steps. One more, and she spun inside the entrance, lifting the sword—

And stopped short, dumbfounded.

They were not Syptens surrounding her father, but Elkhorn guards, their weapons sheathed and their empty hands raised. Lord Bor wielded a chair like a shield. A dozen cuts layered his body, but none seemed to bleed badly. Around them lay Sypten bodies and smashed furniture. The walls were painted red. Behind the jarl crouched Uljana, an ugly cut across her forehead that leaked blood into her eyes. The thrall ignored the wound as she stared at the huskarls with wide eyes, a knife clutched in her hand.

At Aelthena's entrance, the guards looked around. "Lady Heir!" one of them greeted her, relief evident in his voice. He was an older man with a lined face beneath his helm and no evidence of hair, telling of his being a veteran of the Sack of Qal-Nu. "Look here, Lord Bor. Your daughter has come."

"And armed," a younger guard observed wryly with a glance at her blade.

She had no time for embarrassment. "I was attacked. Frey — that is, my huskarl has been injured. Is there anywhere safe now?"

Despair crept into her voice, and she had to wipe her eyes as tears leaked from them once more.

The younger guard winced, while the veteran seemed unaffected by her display. "You're to go to Antler Tower," the older huskarl told her. "Lord Petyr has secured it from the invaders." He jerked a thumb back at her father. "It's where we're trying to take Lord Bor as well. Can you calm him?"

Impatience was plain in the huskarl's manner. Anger flared in her for a moment, but it faltered as she remembered Frey's plight. Still, as she spoke, a bit of her old iron returned.

"Yes. One of you take my man to Antler Tower and find him a healer at once. You need to stem the bleeding in his side. He may have other wounds as well."

The three guards exchanged a look before the veteran jerked his head at the one who had been silent thus far. "Do as she says."

The man passed with a nervous glance her way, then disappeared out of the door. Her hands felt clammy. She hoped they were not too late.

You've done all you can. She turned her attention back to the task at hand. Stepping between the remaining huskarls, she stared into her father's eyes. They were blood-shot around the amber irises, and his leathery face was rippled into furious creases. His hair fell in wild tangles about his face. He looked as sprite-touched as he ever had.

Yet he was her father. Though she had failed to sway him before, she had to try.

"Father," she said in a low voice. She bent to place the sword gently at her feet, then held up her empty hands. "Father, it's me. Aelthena."

The jarl gave no sign of recognition, but growled and brandished the chair to ward her away.

She knew he might attack. She took a step forward anyway.

"I wouldn't go near him, m'lady," the younger guard said from behind her. "He might be your father, but he killed two of those Syptens with the furniture alone. Give him the chance, and he'll do the same to you."

She ignored him. "Father, please. You're safe now. You protected us. But you must put down the chair. We have to go to a safe place. Will you do that for me? Put the chair down?"

He seemed not to hear a single word. The chair did not lower, and the rage did not lessen. Though she thought she had long ago buried the part of her that could be hurt by her father, the moment proved her wrong. As if a leak had sprung in her that could not be repaired, tears prickled her eyes again.

Aelthena turned to the woman behind her father. "Uljana. Please, will you help me? He listens to you."

The thrall met her gaze. Only then did Aelthena realize she must have fought to defend her father. She was his thrall, a slave for all of two decades. She had been captured and brought back to Oakharrow in the Sack of Qal-Nu. She was a Sypten, an enemy.

Why would she protect him?

Uljana nodded and set down her knife. "M'lord," the thrall murmured as she rose from her crouch and approached cautiously. "Dear Bor, do not upset anyone. They're nice people, don't you see?"

Aelthena blinked, realizing how little she had heard her father's servant speak before. She spoke to him as a mother to a child. Is that how she thought of him? Why she defended him rather than run for her freedom? It made Aelthena uneasy. If their places were reversed, she doubted she would show such loyalty.

Uljana's hands pressed on the jarl's arm, and Aelthena braced herself for the inevitable lash. But though her father startled, he only looked around at the thrall. His face crinkled, confused now rather than angry. Uljana smiled at him and came a step closer.

"There, m'lord, there. Now, the chair?"

Obedient to her gentle urging, Aelthena's father slowly lowered the broken furniture, then reluctantly released it. It clattered over, one of its legs broken from earlier use, and Aelthena flinched. But the jarl did not startle, but only stared at it with his head cocked to one side.

"We are going to walk now, m'lord," Uljana told him, pressing him a step forward.

Aelthena moved out of their way as the jarl and the thrall walked toward the entrance. She tried to tamp down the jealousy rearing in her chest. *He heeds his slave, but does not know his own daughter.* She felt the eyes of the Elkhorn's guards watching her, their silent judgment as loud as if spoken. She wished she could dash the superiority from their expressions.

Instead, she only bent over, picked up Frey's sword, and followed them to Antler Tower.

Everyone in the pavilion stared at the First of Hua as she took a step closer and trumpeted in her bullish tongue. Though she and Teti still teetered on a precipice, liable to tip either toward life or death, Sehdra stilled and listened with the others.

"Great Oyaoan speaks!" the Ibis called into the midst of the huamek's clamor, his words made nasal by his bloody nose. "Karah Hephystus the Third, you have believed yourself a god, immune to the harsh realities around you. But you are not!"

Sehdra stared at the translator in mute horror. The words were sacrilege; worse, they could only provoke one reaction. Her eyes slid over to her brother, who had been extricated from Teti's grasp by his guards. Physt trembled with repressed emotion, but he did not interrupt as the Ibis continued.

"Everyone pays tribute to a higher power — even you, Hephystus. Kneel, then. Kneel, as you ought to have all along. Kneel to the Red Empress of the South!"

As Sehdra had known it must, the ultimatum went too far.

"Red Empress?" The karah's voice was strident and mocking as he stepped forward. Behind, his guards shifted, but fell short of following their monarch.

"Red Empress?" Physt repeated, shriller still. "Empress of *what*, precisely? That — that *beast* only remains because I tolerate it. Because I allow her a sliver of my power! And what have I gained for it? *Not one gods-damned thing!* Her huame are cowards, the first to flee the battle! She herself remains here when she might kill a dozen at a stroke! *Red Empress. You rule nothing, beast, nothing — least of all my empire!*"

Throughout his speech, her brother slowly drifted forward, farther from his reticent guards. Sehdra thought he must turn around at any moment and notice. Perhaps the fear of his warriors might finally instill in him the self-preservation he so sorely lacked. Now he stood, defiant and alone, before the Ibis and the giantess.

Why should I care? She wiped at her lip, throbbing with the blow he had dealt her. *Let him spit on the cobra and be damned.* She pushed unsteadily through the guards toward Teti, and they wilted before her, as if made paper by their monarch's madness. Teti, battered and bruised, gave her a small smile. And instead of him leaning on her as she intended, she found her friend accepting her weight.

"Let him go," Teti murmured in her ear. "He cannot be stopped."

Only then did she realize he intended not only to help her stand, but to restrain her. She shook her head and opened her mouth to agree. Yet she could not form the words.

"I'm sorry, Teti, dearest to my heart. But he's my brother."

As a strangled noise broke from his throat, Sehdra forcefully pulled away from Teti and, stiffening the muscles in her withered leg, stood before the others.

"Divine One. Brother. Physt. Please, look at me."

The karah whirled around, his eyes still crackling with passion. "You dare call me that now? Need I teach you another lesson?"

Sehdra fought down a spurt of anger. The wounds he had dealt her still smarted, yet she ignored them as well.

"Pause. Breathe. Think about what you are doing and saying. Is this the course you must take? You can remain upon the Radiant Throne. The Ascendant Crown can still sit upon your brow. But if you are to rule, brother, you must first kneel."

Physt's lips curled further with every word. "Spoken like one of the flock," he sneered. "I am not a *lamb*, sister. I am the crocodile, the lion, the leopard! I am the hunter and keeper of mortal bones. I am lord of the sands and oases. I am the highest general of this glorious army, with all the men at my command. Should I quaver before an animal, even a large one?" A wild laugh ripped from his throat, his eyes widening further still. "Never! I am the Holy Karah, the living Sliver of the Divine, and I—"

The monarch of Ha-Sypt turned back to face the one he defied, but Oyaoan's hand already closed over his head.

Sehdra could not breathe. Her lungs flattened against her ribs as the giantess's fingers, each as thick as the trunk of a young tree, pressed together. Hephystus's scream was muffled beneath the hand. Whether it was command or plea, Sehdra could not tell.

It did not matter; no one moved toward him. All knew it was already over.

The huamek's fist slowly tightened around the ruler's crowned head. The shriek twisted, rising higher and more pitiful. Sehdra squeezed her eyes shut. Her body trembled as if wracked with fever, and her stomach kicked. Hands seized her, supporting her. *Teti*. But even he could offer no comfort.

She did not see the moment it happened. But she heard the slight *crack* of the skull, and the squelch afterward.

It took every shred of court-bred dignity in her to remain upright. Slowly, Sehdra opened her eyes and stared at what had become of her brother. Oyaoan had released his body so that it fell in a crumpled heap on the carpeted ground. Blood poured from the ruined remains of his head. The reek of it made Sehdra's stomach turn.

She swallowed hard and raised her chin to meet the giantess's gaze, so far above, as the huamek rumbled.

"Heed this lesson, Sehdra Ohkweht," the Ibis spoke. "Learn from your brother's folly. Remember who Great Oyaoan is. A Child of Hua, a daughter of divinity. The Red Empress. No human karah should be so obsessed with their power as to forget that."

Her mind was still frozen, and the meaning of his words flitted just beyond her understanding. Still, she nodded and responded hoarsely, "I remember."

Oyaoan had spoken through the exchange. Not for the first time, Sehdra wondered how much of what the Ibis said was directly as the huamek said, and how much was his own invention. But as the Suncoaster spoke again, she knew that in this moment, they were one and the same.

"Advance toward your brother's corpse, Sehdra. Pry from his decaying spirit the symbol of your people's power. Take the Ascendant Crown."

She could barely look at him, barely stand to smell him. Approaching her brother's body felt beyond her.

You have no choice.

She wished she could cling to Teti's hand, to lean on his strength as she always had. But in this moment, she was on her own.

Sehdra took one tottering step forward. Then another, and another, until she stood over what remained of Physt. Trying not to look, not to think, not to *feel*, she crouched. Excruciating pain ran up her leg into the base of her skull, yet Sehdra was grateful for it. Pain was all that seemed right to feel just then.

Not gladness at her tormenter's demise. Not relief at being free of her brother at last.

She ignored the devilish thoughts and focused back on her task. The white cloth of the Ascendant Crown was stained dark with Physt's blood; the tongue of White Aya was as red as the ears representing Bek. Though crumpled in the giantess's fist, it still bore some resemblance to its former shape.

With trembling hands, Sehdra reached for the crown and took the wet ornament in hand. Then she stood and looked at Oyaoan.

"Place the crown upon your head, Royal Sister." The Ibis almost spoke in a purr. "Become who you were destined to be."

Destined. This was never what she had been destined for. She was the elder and wiser of their parents' children, but as the first son of the family and their father's namesake, Hephystus had always been meant to rule Ha-Sypt.

Yet had she not thought that should the rules have been different, she could do far better than he?

This is not a coronation, she reminded herself. *This is a shadow play. You are not the ruler, but a puppet that must play its part.*

She raised the bloody diadem and, with as little cere- mony as the moment deserved, placed the Ascendant Crown upon her head. The wetness pressed against her forehead and into her hair. A drip started down one temple.

The Ibis grinned wide, his teeth bright in his sable skin, and swept an arm toward her as he looked at their audience. "Hail! The new Holy Karah of Ha-Sypt!"

Sehdra turned to look at those who remained. The guards, the servants, the general and his messengers — all were hers to command now. She had ascended.

She had become a goddess. So long as Oyaoan deemed her worthy.

39. THE OPEN DOOR

"There is a kind of bravery in fury, but it is a coward's courage."

- Coppereye the Insurgent, First Drang to the Unchained Thanes

As the jotunmen roared and flinched away, Bjorn struck.

His sword, lined with ever-sharp Harrow-steel, chopped through the first's scant coverings to bite deep into his side. Like the chieftain of Jünsden, these ogreish men wore little in the way of armor or clothes beyond their thick, furry hides.

He would make them suffer for it.

As the jotunman staggered back, a hand clutched to his side, his companion retaliated. Half a head taller and far broader, he charged with his shield raised. Bjorn snapped his own shield up to catch his adversary's before spinning past and dealing a glancing blow to his calf. The jotunman took another step, then collapsed with a yowl. Bjorn judged he had cut through the tendon.

He wore a grin as he faced the first jotunman again. The man rushed forward, axe aloft, bestial face twisted with anger and alarm. Large and strong as he was, he feared Bjorn.

He nearly laughed at the sight.

Bjorn could not match the man for strength. Though he lifted his shield, he simultaneously stepped to the side. The blade hit the steel boss in the center of Bjorn's shield and careened away. The force of the blow jarred down his arm, but he barely felt it.

Seeing his opening, Bjorn lashed out with both sword and shield. His blade tangled with the axe as the jotunman swung it back around, desperately trying to ward him off, but the shield thudded into the man's side, bruising and breaking ribs.

Bjorn strained to fend off the axe. His enemy was forced into an awkward grip to keep hold of it. Bjorn took every advantage he could, slamming his shield into the barbar anywhere he could reach. His shoulder, his side, his leg — the iron boss was like a hammer pounding into the unprotected flesh.

The jotunman was not down yet. He shoved and kicked to win his weapon free, forcing Bjorn back. Bjorn knew he was sustaining injuries, but he felt none of them as he fell back a step. Amid the tempest roiling inside him, his mind was cold and focused. With that deadly detachment, he took in his enemy's condition. The jotunman hunched forward now, his wounds too great to hide. The hand held to his bleeding side kept slipping. The jotunman's strength was fading, and quickly.

He would give no quarter, spare no mercy. Just as they had given the gothi none.

Bjorn roared as he fought. He threw up his shield against the axe, felt the metal thud into the wood. His shoulder rattled, and sharp metal stopped inches from his face. Bjorn only snarled at it and thrust his sword into the jotunman's middle, then tore it free with a savage twist. His enemy groaned and gurgled. His hand slipped off his weapon as he bent over the gaping hole in his belly.

Axe still lodged in his shield, Bjorn turned to find the second jotunman lunging at him, swinging a club in one hand and raising a shield in the other. It was a clumsy attack, off-balance and desperate, but it was still a narrow miss as Bjorn dodged. Gaining his feet, he found the jotunman struggling to one knee, injured leg unable to support him. The bestial man snarled at him in a speech he could not understand, though his meaning was clear enough.

Bjorn laughed. "May Ovvash welcome you!" he mocked as he stepped forward.

Even downed, the jotunman was not to be underestimated. Bjorn pretended to swagger, taunting his opponent into another unbalanced attack, one which he easily knocked away with his shield. A kick to the barbar's shield knocked the assailant on his back. Even then, the ogre of a man did not relent, but swung the club wildly about him. Bjorn cut his arm, then went for the neck as he found the opening.

Catching his breath, Bjorn stepped away from the dying man and looked up. The town was orange with the lingering fires. Through it, he could see silhouettes running toward him, most in pairs, but altogether too many to face alone.

Caution should have sent him fleeing into the shadows. Instead, he planted his feet and yelled a challenge.

"Come to me, jotunmen! I've killed two of you bastards already — I'll enjoy putting down the rest!"

The first two invaders neared, a mere two score paces away. One bore a torch and an axe, while the other held a spear. Neither seemed to fear him.

Bjorn had never been feared in the yard. But he was no longer a boy, nor even a man. He was fire and fury, death cast in flesh, he was coming for them all.

He barked a laugh, raised his shield, and knocked aside the thrusting spear.

No sooner had he staggered back under the blow than the night roiled with others. The second jotunman spun and yelped as a sword and a hammer slammed into him. Loridi and Seskef appeared behind the weapons, uncharacteristic scowls on their countenances. The spearman kicked at Bjorn's shield to pry his weapon loose, but could not manage it before Hoarfrost's spear stabbed through his gut. The jotunman pawed at his waist as he sank to his knees, but only just pried his seax free before Yonik's long knives whipped across his throat.

Bjorn threw down his shield and picked up the fallen torch, then shared a wide grin with his companions. "Had to save some for you!" he called merrily as he jogged past.

"Bjorn!" Yonik called at his back, but he paid him no heed. Blood begged to be spilled.

The other jotunmen, seeing the fates of comrades, knotted together in a group of eight. Bjorn could not tell if more still lurked in the flickering darkness. He did not wait to find out. His fey amusement had faded as he passed the destruction and recognized the buildings that had been felled. *The* Volur *hut. The longhouse. The library.* Only the library somewhat stood, its stone walls difficult to dismantle. But books could still burn. He saw Tyra falling to the smoke and flames in his mind, and he screamed as molten rage heaved through his veins.

"I'll kill every gods-damned one of you!"

He charged, torch and sword swinging, embers flying from the cage. The world reeled under the uncertain light. Weapons struck back, but Bjorn twisted out of the way, taunting and luring them toward him.

But the jotunmen were no green fighters. They fanned out, surrounding him. Metal flashed in the firelight. Most attacks were feints, but a few nearly landed. Bjorn's weapons blurred as he parried. He was outnumbered, outmaneuvered, yet he knew no fear. He would fight them, all of them, and strike them down, no matter how long it took—

Steel stabbed into his thigh.

A spear had gotten through his defenses. It lodged in his leg, deep enough to bury the point. Bjorn glanced down at it to see the damage. He should have gasped in pain. His mind should have been shocked into numbness. Yet he felt nothing, nothing but a weakening of the flesh, and the irritation that it might slow him.

Bjorn snarled as he dropped his torch and took hold of the spear. Using his leg for a leverage point, he pried the weapon free of the stupefied jotunman's grip, then struck a glancing blow with his sword. The shaft of the spear, still lodged in his flesh, knocked into a second enemy's face, momentarily stunning him.

Even with the unnatural display, the other jotunmen closed in, but were rebuffed. Bjorn's companions fell upon them, and grunts and cries and the clashes of battle surged.

Bjorn yanked the spear free of his thigh. He tried to run forward, but fell instead. No matter how he tried to stand, the leg refused to cooperate.

Two jotunmen stalked him: the spearman, who had

drawn a long knife, and one wielding a crude sword and a scarred shield. Seeing their enemy downed, they closed in for the kill.

Bjorn bared his teeth at them, daring them to make the attempt. As they came within range, he surged up on his good leg and struck with his sword clutched in both hands. His blow knocked the jotunman's blade aside and provoked him backward. Bjorn continued the swing as the second enemy stabbed forward, seeking to take advantage. The knife cut through Bjorn's furs. If it found flesh, he could not feel it. His sword chopped between the bestial man's neck and shoulder, cleaving halfway through his body before lodging in the bones.

Knowing he could not pry it free soon enough, Bjorn rolled, grappled for his seax, and came up on his good knee with it held before him. The jotunman had not followed. The whites of his eyes were visible even in the scant light as he stared down at Bjorn, then around at the melee continuing behind him.

The barbar threw down his shield and fled into the night.

Bjorn tried rising to give chase, but his leg collapsed again. Cursing at it, he looked back at the rest of the battle to see if there were other enemies to hunt. Again, he was disappointed. His companions had cut down the rest or provoked them into fleeing. Three jotunmen sprinted after the first, while the rest lay dead around them.

He exhaled noisily, then noticed his companions regarding him warily. Bjorn bared his teeth in a smile.

"What?" he barked. "Bloody cowards, aren't they? I'd kill them if I could catch them!"

For a moment, no one responded. Then Yonik sheathed his knives and approached. Heedless of the gore and ashes, the priest kneeled with his empty hands upraised. "Bjorn.

Come back to us. Close the door; let go of the wrath. The jotunmen are dead. The battle is won."

For a moment, Bjorn wanted to strike the gothi. Who was he to mock him? But as he stared into Yonik's gleaming eyes, he saw the worry there, and a slumbering part of him roused.

The Hall of Doors glimmered into mind, as well as the faint outline of an open door. He reached for it and touched a hand to the handle. He did not want to close it. Why would he? He was powerful, invulnerable. Pain could not touch; enemies ran before him.

But Yonik had pleaded with him.

Let it go. Close the door? Now is your only chance. The voice belonged to him, he suspected, a part of him that had not ceded to rage. He did not trust it. He could not help but listen.

Or do you want it always open? Do you invite in madness, like your father?

He ground his teeth, but he could not dismiss the words. With a sudden shove, he slammed the door shut.

The shadowy corridor disappeared from sight. The blinding anger drained away.

In its vacuum, agony clawed its way back in.

Bjorn could feel nothing else. He might have screamed, but could not tell for the pounding of his heart and blood. He curled in on himself as pain rolled up and down his body.

He should not have listened. He had been filled with power, with strength. He had been protected.

Now he lay vulnerable and weak.

He reached for the door to Frenzy, but he could not find it. The Hall of Doors was gone. The door was closed.

Bjorn screwed his eyes shut and wept.

40. CORONATION

"This land has taken my sons — so let the kingdom return to the land. You will find a new king, if you need one. Or perhaps I will be the last."

- Torvald Geirson, the Last King of Baegard

Bastor was delayed at the gates. Though the mighty doors had been knocked askance by the enemy's dragonfire, that they remained at all seemed a wonder. But there was nothing left in him for wonder. He had wandered the smoke-wreathed battlefield for what seemed a lifetime until the air cleared enough to see the walls. As he approached the soldiers stationed there and joined the lines of soot-covered men filtering inside the city, he saw what he must look like in their miserable appearance.

Yet the exterior still fell short of the inner tempest.

Like shattered pieces of pottery held together by mud — that was all he was now. Weariness cut him to the bone. Worse still were the biting questions.

Why did the boy die while I live?
Why did fire reign and giants flee?
Why do I keep going?

Only one thing did he know: why his father's huskarls had attempted to assassinate him. That had been clear even before Endre had confessed it.

I'm the son you never wanted, he thought to his father. *The unnatural bastard you claimed because you so desired an heir.* He wondered how Ragnar would try to cast him aside now that his first attempt had failed. *Scandal and disownment? Poison? Or simply wait for war to do the job for him?*

He wished he had a horn of mead at hand.

Bastor barely noticed the press of men around him, even as they jostled him and aroused fresh agony from his wounds. He paid no heed to the black plumes rising from the city, where houses burned from the firesand the giants had flung over the walls. The battle had ended for him, but it raged on for those trying to save their homes. Yet he could do nothing for them.

Gods know I can do little enough for myself.

Only when a mounted man appeared beside him, gleaming dully in ashy armor, did Bastor raise his head. He was surprised to see the man alive.

"You survived." Asborn sounded dazed, or perhaps astonished. Survival must have seemed a far cry for any of them as they charged into those burning hells.

Bastor did not have a smile in him, but tried for one anyway. "So did you."

Oakharrow's thane looked to have seen his fair share of fighting. The golden armor was dented and bloodied. His horse bore more wounds, though it seemed hale enough as it carried him through the street. The deepest pain lay in the man's eyes, a haunted look with which Bastor was all too familiar.

Asborn was not one to crave battle. *Not like me.*

Their exchange was cut short as a larger retinue of horsemen came up from behind. Bastor moved off the street with the other weary soldiers to avoid being trampled. Only as he turned back did he recognize the foremost rider.

Highlord Ragnar Torbenson still raised his chin high. He had removed his golden helm to reveal his shock of golden hair, only slightly subdued by the smoke and ash. His armor bore fewer flaws than Asborn's, and Bastor wondered which corner of the battlefield his father had hidden in after his valiant charge into the fray.

His father seemed about to pass him by, but at the last moment, he glanced down. When his eyes fell on Bastor, he flinched before he claimed control of himself again.

A biting smile curled his lips. If he had clung to any doubts about his father's role, they had all been dispelled.

The Arkjarl halted next to him. "Alabastor. My son. I am glad you survived."

The smile spread until it enveloped all of Bastor's ashen face. Half of him felt like laughing; the other half wished to fall where he was and never rise again. But he had always had a defiant streak in him.

"I'm sure you are, Father." His mouth burned as if he had swallowed acid.

If Ragnar noticed the irony laced in the words, he gave no sign of it. "Come with me. There has been an attack on the Elkhorn. Lord Petyr claims to have secured it, but I may have need of your arm."

His father gestured to one man in his retinue, who swiftly dismounted. Bastor regarded the horse for a moment. *Does he mean to get rid of me now? Or is this something else?*

The Arkjarl brimmed with impatience. There was something he expected, something he had long looked forward to. Whatever it was did not bode well for Bastor or Baegard.

A large part of him wanted to refuse. Men watched from all around, curious about the quiet confrontation between father and son, jarl and heir. He could undermine confidence in his father's leadership through such a display. After all, if a man cannot even compel his son to obey, what chance has he with other men's sons?

But the cold, calculating part of Bastor still reigned. *Refuse him, and you give him another reason to disown you. Be like the snow-cat in the mountains: silent till it's time to strike.*

"Very well, Father," he said, as loud as his tortured throat could manage. "I'll go."

Accepting the reins from his father's huskarl, Bastor pulled his aching body into the saddle and once more fell in behind Ragnar. Only now, his dream of placing a knife between his father's shoulder blades was far from an idle reverie.

Though the jarls congregated in the chamber above, Aelthena remained by Frey until the Arkjarl arrived.

She raised her head as fresh footsteps echoed down the hall. Her hand closed over Frey's sword, still bared by her side, and did not set it back down until she recognized the men coming down the hall. They were soot-smeared to the last of them, though the man who strode at their front remained cleanest. Highlord Ragnar did not wear the Iron Circle at the moment, but his title was carved into his bearing. His cold eyes took in the impromptu infirmary at the base of Antler Tower, not seeming the least concerned with the injured guards' welfare. Aelthena stifled her sudden anger. Realizing one of her hands rested on Frey's arm, too intimate a gesture between a highborn and her guard, she quickly withdrew it.

Another familiar man strode at the Arkjarl's shoulder. If Ragnar had kept to the thinnest of the fighting, Bastor had dove into the thickest. His skin was nearly black from the ash and mud caked over it, while his eyes were bright and red-veined. Open cuts oozed from his face and through his ripped clothes. He limped, and his broad shoulders sagged, but he only seemed more dangerous for it.

With a last glance at Frey, for reassurance that he still breathed, Aelthena rose to her feet. "The battle? Highlord," she added belatedly.

The Arkjarl scowled, but only for a moment. "We won, Lady Heir."

With that, Ragnar swept past her and up the tower stairs. Bastor cast her a lingering glance and seemed about to move past her as well. She seized his arm, arresting him. Ignoring the filth that smeared across her hand, she kept hold of him until he looked around.

"What's happening?" she demanded. "Is Ha-Sypt driven back? Are we in further danger?"

The tall man eyed her, then shook his head. "You are safe here." His voice had been reduced to a whisper. "As safe as anywhere these days."

Aelthena released him. *Safe.* She looked back down at Frey. He had fallen unconscious after being administered the gothi's poppy tincture, but she suspected it was more from blood loss than the potion. She was loath to leave his side.

But the jarls — those that were left of them — were meeting above. She could not be excluded, not now.

Bastor stayed a moment after she released him, then

bared his teeth and turned up the stairs. She wondered what he had to smile about after a day like today, but gave up the question as soon as she thought of it. Some men could never be understood.

"Aelthena."

Despite his haggardness, she recognized his voice. She glanced at the doorway.

"Asborn."

He had fared well in the battle, though he was far from unmarred. His red hair was wild and untamed. His brow wrinkled in that familiar way, which she had so often run a hand across to smooth. He stank the same as Bastor: of smoke and sulfur, battle and blood. Of brutality received and given.

Asborn had never shown the affinity for fighting that his father, Eirik Bloodaxe, had. His was a gentle spirit, one forged for Baltur's peace rather than Volkur's wars. She wished she could have spared him this.

But no one chooses their path.

She had known it since she had been forced to a woman's duties, and understood it better still as she traveled the road from Oakharrow. All anyone could do was forge their own way, and pray better hopes lay ahead.

They regarded each other in silence before Asborn's eyes flickered down to Frey. He hardened then, and she saw a flicker of what he must have become on the battlefield, enough to wonder if he was his father's son after all.

His words, however, came as a surprise. "He protected you?"

She nodded. "Against three. They would have killed me."

Asborn met her eyes again, then looked away. "I'm glad they didn't."

"I know."

Silence fell again, only broken by the gothi's ministrations and the soldiers' groans. From the stairwell echoed Ragnar's voice.

"We should go," Asborn said at last.

Aelthena glanced down at Frey. Even though Asborn watched, she gently pressed his arm and murmured, "Stay strong."

Leaving the guardian's sword by his side, she rose to her feet, brushed her dress, as if that would smooth away the bloodstains, and approached the stairs. She did not look at Asborn, fearing he might see her feelings written across her features. The thane only followed her up the stairs, a ghost of the man he had once been.

After the terror of the invasion and frenzied flight through the Elkhorn, Aelthena dragged with weariness. But Asborn had experienced a yet more harrowing fight, so she kept her chin upright and her posture erect. She would not betray weakness before him, nor any of the jarls above. She would show them she was every bit the leaders they were, and hope it was enough to win her rightful seat at last.

Two of the Elkhorn's guards, both of whom looked to have fought the Sypten raiders, watched the landing at the top of the tower. One wore a blood-soaked bandage wrapped around his head, and he nodded respectfully to Asborn, but eyed Aelthena with distrust. She returned his gaze, chin raised. Even when she fought beside them, the men would not accept her. But she did not need the respect of huskarls. That they did not stop her passage was as much as she could ask for.

Mounting the final rise of stairs, Aelthena heard the jarls speaking animatedly. She could not tell if it was an argument or a celebration, and her shoulders drew tight in anticipation.

Asborn stepped into the tower room ahead of her, and

men hailed him in comradely praise. But as Aelthena entered, the smiles turned to frowns. She could not entirely hide her grimace as she looked at those present. Petyr had survived; she had already heard word of as much from his huskarls. Hother, too, had come through, and without seeing conflict, from the tidy state of his clothes. Siward had prevailed in the battle, though he looked much the worse for wear. Her father was present as well, earlier escorted up by Uljana after a healer tended to his wounds.

But two of the jarls were missing.

"Where are Lord Alrik and Lord Harald?" she demanded, not bothering with greetings.

Ragnar glowered at her from his usual chair. "If you must be here, Lady Heir Aelthena, sit and listen before asking questions."

She stood her ground. Skjold and Aelford were two of Oakharrow's staunchest allies. That they were both gone could not be just unlucky happenstance.

"Where are they?" she repeated.

"Dead." It was Siward who answered, his tone flat. "Fallen to Sypten spears. Saw the bodies myself."

Aelthena looked back at Ragnar and saw the Arkjarl studying her, his expression guarded. She took care to smooth hers. *Careful. Tread lightly.* She knew what the man was capable of. The two jarls had as likely fallen to knives in the back as their enemies' attacks. Yet she was sorely outnumbered and out of favor. Accusations would lead her nowhere.

Though the truth burned inside her, Aelthena kept her silence and took the seat that Alrik had once sat in.

Ragnar stared at her a moment longer before panning his gaze around the chamber. "Lord Petyr, please continue."

The Jarl of Petyrsholm nodded with a sly smile. "From what my men have gathered, the Syptens gained entrance to the castle by sailing their ships past the drakkars. They then scaled the northern walls, which were left with too few men to repel them. The Elkhorn, too, was vulnerable to their force, though we have ultimately repelled the invaders. All corridors have been cleared, and my men are checking every room for any attempting to hide."

Aelthena was hard-pressed not to frown. The story seemed too tidy. It was all she could do not to cast another accusatory stare in Ragnar's direction. Was this, too, a betrayal? She recounted who had been targeted. *Myself. My father.* The only other jarls who remained behind in the castle, Petyr and Hother, seemed not to have suffered any danger at all.

Was it too far even for Ragnar? No, it was not — she knew it with sudden intuition. How could it be when he had sacrificed her jarlheim for his own gain?

She looked again at the Arkjarl and held her chin high. *One day,* she promised him silently, *Baltur will judge your fate. And then you will know all the suffering of Ovvash's hells.* It was an oath sworn, even if it was just to herself. And this was one she meant to keep.

The Arkjarl nodded, seemingly oblivious to her stare. "Well done. If that matter is settled—"

"What of the battle?" Aelthena interrupted.

Ragnar seemed to struggle to master himself before he looked at her. Aelthena met his gaze with a hard one of her own. It was not only for the information that she dared to cut off the Arkjarl. She was finding it harder and harder to stay silent before the man's smugness.

"We won the battle, Lady Heir Aelthena." Ragnar spoke as if she were sprite-touched. "We routed the Sypten army and drove them back. Already, there are signs of their camp dispersing."

"And why did we not seize the advantage?" she pressed.

Anger glimmered in his eyes now. "I would not expect you to understand."

It was less his words and more the chuckles of the other jarls that grated on her nerves. Aelthena tightened her jaw and sucked in a steadying breath.

"I understand enough, Highlord Ragnar, that when your enemy is on the run, you cut them down so you will not have to face them again."

Bastor flashed her an amused smile, while Ragnar glared balefully. At length, the Arkjarl rose from where he had leaned over the table.

"Our warriors were scattered and weary, and smoke exposure such as that can kill a man. We are also unsure of how many of the enemy troops remain to resist. The worst thing we could have done was charge blindly into a battle we could easily lose."

His reasoning seemed sound as far as she knew. Placated for the moment, Aelthena folded her hands.

A corner of his lips curled as Ragnar looked at the other jarls. "But there is one thing about which Lady Heir Aelthena is correct. We have shown these southern invaders that neither their numbers, nor their surtunar, nor their fire-sand will break us. We have shown our men this is a war we can win. And win we must — for these Summer Wars are coming to a head. Mark my words, my lords: we must conquer Ha-Sypt, or they will kill and enslave us, down to the last babe."

The jarls were nodding to his words, all convinced of their truth. Asborn seemed to agree with them. Only Bastor, leaning against the tower wall with his head bowed and his arms crossed, gave no sign of assent. Aelthena sat with lips pressed tightly together. There was a fair chance he was correct; after all, such a concerted invasion had not occurred in over a hundred years. But she had thought in absolutes when she had inherited control of Oakharrow, and thus been blindsided by the Jotun. She did not intend to make that mistake again.

Ragnar leaned over the table once more. "I can prevent this," he said in a low rasp. "I can win this war as I have won this battle. I possess substantial quantities of firesand and know its secrets. I flatter myself to think I have earned your trust as the Arkjarl. But to take the measures necessary to win this war — to recruit the men, organize them, pay them — I must have greater authority still, my lords. *I must be king.*"

The ominous words hung suspended in the shocked silence. *I must be king.* The declaration, bold beyond any expected, rattled in her head. Aelthena looked around, half-expecting the men around her to laugh. How else could they react?

But no one cracked a smile, not even Bastor. All stared at Ragnar, expressions spasming with repressed emotion.

The Arkjarl pressed his knuckles against the map-table. "What will it be, my lords? Will you allow me to save our nation? Will you help me lead Baegard to victory?"

Ransom — he holds the jarlheims at ransom again. She saw it clearly then. Ragnar Torbenson was the rope tethering Baegard together. Without him, their army would splinter apart. And he was the only one who had firesand, the weapon that had saved them. Unless they wished to risk Ha-Sypt conquering them one by one, the other jarls were entirely at Ragnar's mercy.

She saw what would happen, saw it was inevitable. Still, she stood.

"No. You will not be crowned, Ragnar. Not while I'm my father's heir."

All eyes in the chamber turned toward her. Ragnar did

not seem offended by her objection, but somehow pleased. Unsettled, she still pressed forward.

"You have led us well as the Arkjarl, I'll admit. You have secured a great victory today. But Baegard has not had a king for two hundred years, and it does not need one now. Let you remain as the Arkjarl until the war is won. But of becoming king — there's no justification for it."

Ragnar straightened entirely now. His hands rested on the pommels of the blades at his sides. Aelthena read in the gesture the threat she knew he intended.

"I disagree, Lady Heir." His tone was cool, reasonable, where her words had been hot with fervor. "You may not know the machinations necessary for running a war, but I do. There are unpleasant measures that must be taken, ones that will be impossible without greater authority. And what of Aelford and Skjold? Will we allow their succession politics to interfere with their contributions? No, Heir of Oakharrow — only with a king may Baegard forge itself into a sword that won't shatter on the first strike."

Part of her wanted to scream in defiance, another to attack him as she once had Lawspeaker Yaethun. But Aelthena felt the currents beating against her. No one stood to speak in defiance. No one. Not even Asborn.

Only then did she know.

He won them over. All of them. Bribes for some, threats for others, she did not doubt. But she knew with certainty that all of this Ragnar had planned for months, likely years. His ambition burned even brighter than hers and outshone it. And there was nothing she could do.

Aelthena sat heavily back in her chair.

Ragnar let his hands fall away from his weapons to clasp behind his back. "I would hear it then, my lords. Lord Petyr — will you swear fealty?"

Aelthena looked at the gaunt jarl. His features pinched

together as he raised his dark eyes to meet Ragnar's blue gaze. After a moment, the Jarl of Petyrsholm stood, his chair legs producing a slight shriek. His hand fell to his belt knife, and for a moment, she dared to hope.

Lord Petyr drew the blade and, holding it parallel to the ground, bowed his head. "I swear Petyrsholm and my house to you, Your Grace."

Her hopes plummeted.

Ragnar practically shone with his victory. "Thank you, Lord Petyr. Your pledge is heard, and I will reward you for your faith. Lord Hother?"

The balding man, who had so often worn a circlet of his own, did not have one on his brow just then. He drew his dagger as well and followed Lord Petyr's lead, if with slightly less grandeur. "Djurshand and my house are yours, Your Grace. May your line be long and prosperous."

Ragnar did not bother hiding his smile now. "Lord Siward?"

She knew his response before he gave it. The veteran might be brave on the battlefield, but he was a coward in this arena. She had seen how he capitulated before the threat to his daughter's life. Ragnar had a hold on him he would not risk breaking, even for this.

"My sword and my jarlheim are pledged to you, Your Grace."

Ragnar's eyes had opened wide. "Thane Asborn?"

Aelthena startled from her stupor. "No, Highlord," she spoke before Asborn could. "*I* am the Heir of Oakharrow. Look to me in my father's place."

"And yet Thane Asborn has been the one to sit the Jarl-moot in your stead." As easily as that, Ragnar dismissed her, settling his focus again on Asborn. "I would hear your answer, Thane Asborn."

She stared at him, disbelieving. What could she say?

Her authority was not recognized here. But it would not matter. *Asborn won't pledge Oakharrow. He knows my stance. He would not contradict it.*

Her former betrothed glanced at her. His tongue moistened his lips. Then he stood and drew his sword.

"Oakharrow is yours, Your Grace."

She barely heard the words as he spoke them, as shocked as if he had thrust the blade through her. Her hands clenched into fists beneath the table. Tears threatened her eyes.

No. No, no, no—

"NO!"

Everyone jerked around, Asborn dangerously, for his sword was still drawn. But Lord Bor, who had roared the denial, paid them no heed. He stared at Ragnar, trembling with the bestial ferocity for which he had been named.

"The king is crowned in ice and sorrow!" Lord Bor spat. "The king is here and yet to rise. The last king dies as the first king comes. *There can be only one king of Baegard!"*

Aelthena stared in astonishment at her father. Almost, his words made sense, as if he responded to the events here, though he had seemed asleep only moments before. Perhaps he had heard this capitulation and it had roused his sleeping defiance.

But as quickly as the change came, it melted away. Lord Bor sat again in his chair, his eyes growing vacant.

"The king comes..." a final mutter escaped his lips.

Asborn hastily sheathed his sword, while Ragnar propped a fist on his hip. "Lord Bor's words are heard," he said curtly, his irony hidden well enough Aelthena was sure only she detected it. "But seeing as how Oakharrow itself has deemed him unfit for his responsibilities, I must take Asborn's fealty in lieu of the jarl's denial."

Aelthena stood and gestured to Uljana, who began

coaxing the jarl into standing. She did not look at Asborn. She could not stand the sight of him.

"Take his word if you must," she said to Ragnar. "But no matter what the thane says, Oakharrow will never be yours."

Ragnar smiled with his chin raised. "But neither is it yours. And I wonder — what is an heir without a jarlheim?"

She had said almost the same words to herself before. But now, she denied them.

"A woman who will win back what is rightfully hers."

Aelthena turned and led her father and his thrall from the tower chamber.

41. A DREAM OF HOME

"The best part of a journey is the return home."

*- Yofam Dragontooth, Slayer of the wyvern Vardraith, First
Drang of the Iron Band*

Bjorn came awake and immediately regretted it.

He moaned. Everywhere hurt; some as aches, others with sharper pain. Blinking, he tried to make sense of his surroundings. *A tent.* He was in one of the shelters they had used when traveling through the Teeth. *Light.* A glow came through the seams in the skins that told of daytime. For some reason, he thought it should still be dark.

Slowly, the pieces of his memories threaded themselves back together.

Darkness. Fire. Fury.

He remembered what had befallen Eildursprall. His body's agony paled before the deeper hurts that cut into him.

Tyra. Mother Sign. The Silvers. All the gothi and acolytes and Sprallfolk.

Bjorn forced himself upright and hissed as the pain spiked. He felt as if he had been mauled by a greatbear, like the one that had killed Keld. As he touched his leg, he felt the damp bandage and recalled vaguely the spear piercing through it. At the time, it had felt like little more than an inconvenience. Now, he trembled as he remembered how he had just kept fighting.

Was that in me all along, that anger, that rage? Just waiting to be released?

He had no time to wonder. Wheezing with the effort, Bjorn stood on his good foot, then grabbed his sheathed sword lying nearby. Using the blade as a crutch, he hopped free of the tent.

The sunlight dazzled him for a moment. A breeze, warm for so high up in the mountains, teased his scorched cheeks. A beautiful spring day, but for the lingering stench of smoke on the wind.

Bjorn scanned the surrounding town. Every building in sight had suffered from the fires, yet he recognizing the longhouse, though it was reduced to ashen walls that rose to half his height. Whoever had looked after him had set up his tent within Heim Numen. His shelter did not stand alone, but was nestled next to several others. He hoped all his companions had survived the night.

Anxiety lent him a measure of strength as he began limping through Eildursprall. In the middle of the compound's main road, someone had stacked the bodies of jotunmen, but left them unburned. Bjorn remembered how he had killed them and was surprised to find the memory tinged with satisfaction. Even now, a touch of Frenzy stirred in him. He had never reveled in killing before.

But, as Alfjin the Scribe had once written, *All seasons change; all mountains shake; all seas rise and fall.* Compared to those, a coward becoming a warrior and a seer was no great accomplishment.

Drawing his thoughts back to the task at hand, he turned toward the town proper to see several figures knotted together. His chest leaping, he began moving toward them as quickly as he could. He wondered who he would see. *Does Yonik live? Loridi and Seskef, Hoarfrost and Embla? What of Tyra and Mother Sign's fates?* He squinted, willing his vision to sharpen like he looked upon the Wolf Eyes runestone.

One of the group noticed him and jogged over. Bjorn was not surprised to find it was Yonik, just as spry as usual.

"You shouldn't be up," the priest said, his brow creased. "You've taken a grave wound, Bjorn. It will open again."

"It never closed," he grunted as Yonik put his arm across his back. He had to admit, though, it helped as the gothi took some of his weight. "Did everyone survive?" He stared at the group ahead through his swimming vision, but could only guess at who stood there.

"In our small company, yes. But certainly not in Eildursprall." The priest's voice was low and grim. "The Silvers... I'm sorry, but Mother Sign is gone."

He should have expected it. How could one blind, old woman hope to survive an attack that leveled the entire town? His knees buckled, and he only remained upright through Yonik's help.

"Steady, Bjorn," the gothi murmured in his ear. "Steady now."

"She was supposed to guide me." His vision went blurry. *Tears,* he realized. He hadn't known he had any in him. "There was still so much she knew that I don't. And... I never saw someone so happy."

"Me neither, lad. Me neither."

They were silent with their memories for a long

moment. Then Bjorn wiped at his eyes, drew in a ragged breath, and tried to stand more on his own.

"Tyra?" he dared to ask. "Did she...?"

Yonik exhaled. "Yes. She survived."

As quickly as his hopes had plummeted, they soared again. "She did? She's alive? Where is she?"

"Right over there. She saw you while you were unconscious, but I expect she'll be — Wait, Bjorn!"

Bjorn had torn free of the gothi's grip to hobble toward the knot of people ahead. He tried to make out Tyra's slight form among them, but could not find her. Instead, Loridi, Seskef, and Hoarfrost came into view.

"Well, look who finally decided to rise." Loridi grinned as he sauntered up to Bjorn.

"Where's Tyra?" He looked around at them in vain hope.

"I'm glad you survived as well," Hoarfrost said drily before she pointed behind him. "She's in the chapel with Embla — Sister Embla, that is." The Skyardi cleared her throat and looked aside.

"They're performing the burial rites," Yonik supplied from behind. "Even though she's an acolyte, there are too many for Embla alone to handle."

Bjorn felt the tide of sorrow at all that had been lost here rise in him again. He turned and glanced back at Yonik. "Take me to her?"

The priest gave a small smile, but he nodded.

Their small group followed as Bjorn and Yonik made for the small chapel, still standing by benefit of its stone walls.

"We've been searching the rubble for survivors," Loridi informed Bjorn. "Not too many, unfortunately. Though Embla thinks some fled."

"Not as many bones as expected," Seskef muttered in Bjorn's ear.

"There's a place they go in the hills. When we're finished here, we'll check for any who went there."

Bjorn nodded, though he could only focus on the news with part of his mind. The greater half reached forward faster than his body could comply, yearning for a glimpse of Tyra's face, for the confirmation that Yonik and the others had spoken true.

He found himself asking, "Why? Why did the jotunmen come? Why did they raid Eildursprall and...?" He broke off, words failing.

"Why did they attack?" Yonik glanced back at Hoarfrost. "We don't know exactly. Though Acolyte Tyra's story is telling."

"Her story?"

"We'll let her tell it," said Hoarfrost.

They arrived before the chapel. The door had been ripped off its hinges and lay shattered outside. Bjorn extricated himself from Loridi's helping arm and, his heart hammering, he entered within.

Then she was there.

Tyra stood and turned from where she had kneeled before the altar. He started forward, but she reached him first, throwing her arms about his middle and pressing his bruised ribs tightly. He gasped with the pain, but regretted it when she pulled away.

"I'm sorry," she whispered, wincing. "I... I'm so glad you're up."

"You survived." He reached out his free hand, though he hardly knew what to do with it. *Hold her hand? Touch her cheek? Draw her in close again?* Yet the sheer joy of her being alive banished any embarrassment. "How?"

Tyra saved him the trouble of deciding as she took his

hand in both of hers. Her luminous green eyes peered into his. *Like a bumblebee might a flower,* an errant thought blew through his mind.

"Luck," she admitted. "I was in the library when those horrid men broke in. I hid in the basement in the darkest corner I could find. They came down. I..." Her hands squeezed hard on his for a moment. "I was terrified, Bjorn. But I couldn't scream, couldn't make a sound, or they would catch me and—"

He swallowed hard and tried to dismiss the images his scholar's courage brought to mind. "But they didn't find you."

"No. They found what they were looking for first. I thought it must be one of the ancient writings, something that would interest their master. But it was the largest item we had."

Bjorn thought of it at once. "The Witterland Runestone."

Tyra nodded. "It took eight of them to haul it out of the library, and it occupied all their attention. Once they got it out, they left, and I bolted the door behind them. Others came later and banged on the door, and they set fire to the roof. I thought I would die inside. But I hid, and waited, thinking they would find me..." She suddenly smiled, wide and bright. "Then you came back. You saved me."

He had taken little pride in any of the fighting he had done. But those words, *You saved me,* and from her — that made every pain and ache worth it.

"He didn't do it alone," Loridi pointed out from behind.

His words broke the spell that had fallen over him. Bjorn withdrew his hand with an embarrassed smile, one that Tyra mirrored. But though the moment had passed, Bjorn thought he would not be the only one to cherish it.

"What now?"

Evening had fallen again, and they sat around a campfire eating what victuals remained. The invaders had stolen most of the supplies, but Bjorn's companions had discovered small stores in a few of the less-charred houses. Bjorn chewed through a tough, suspicious-tasting strip of mutton as he mulled over Loridi's question. His leg throbbed. As soon as he recovered his strength, he would try to heal it with the Mend runestone, but his mind had been too recently flayed by Frenzy to make the attempt.

Yonik answered. "First, we wait to see if Hoarfrost and Embla discover any survivors. Then, when they are settled in..." His gaze slid over to Bjorn. "We follow Torvald Geirson's guidance."

Bjorn looked away. He had told them what he had seen with the King of Ice, and what Torvald had told him: that they must align themselves with the Jotun. It had been a tough draught for all of them to swallow. Bjorn still was not sure he believed it himself. But though he doubted everything, he took comfort facing it with Tyra beside him.

"To Oakharrow?" Loridi shook his head. "It feels strange to return after so long."

"It's what Bjorn's vision says we must do," Seskef pointed out. "We must follow what he has foreseen."

But what if I interpreted it wrong? Bjorn wanted to cry out. *What if going to Oakharrow only means our deaths?*

But they all knew the stakes. With jotunar and surtunar not only real, but both coming to Enea, and the rapidly falling Eternal Night — or Runewar, in Torvald's interpretation — they had no other option but to travel the vision's path. Only if Bjorn dared to use the other three runestones, the Shadows, could he know for sure. But the king had said he would know when it was time to See them, and to do so before would risk his death. Perhaps it would come as a premonition, like the omens on the winds. If so, he had heard nothing yet, nor was he strong enough if he had. There would be time in the days it took to reach Oakharrow to change his mind.

Tyra's hand brushed lightly over his arm, almost awakening a shiver in him.

"They took the Witterland Runestone for a reason," she said. "I'm sure of it. Could it have something to do with your Seeing?"

Bjorn could only shrug. "It wasn't in the vision. But the Jotun is supposed to hold — what was it? — 'The key to every door.' I didn't realize it then, but maybe it relates to the Hall of Doors."

Loridi sighed. "More magic... Makes you wonder why the old kook couldn't just tell us straight, doesn't it?"

As Seskef grumbled his agreement, Yonik gave them a look. "Torvald Geirson was old beyond our comprehension. And if the Silvers tell true of the records, he may have been mad even before he isolated himself in that cave. We should be grateful we gleaned as much as we have, for all could have been lost."

Their small camp fell quiet at the priest's words. Bjorn's mind turned over the problem, but he knew it was fruitless. Yonik was right. All they had to follow were the glimmers of riddles that the King of Ice had passed to them. And until he could use the other runestones, that path led to the Jotun.

To Oakharrow.

He would finally return home, to the jarlheim he had failed — but not to conquer it. He meant to go to his enemy and beg or steal humanity's salvation from him.

The one who had stolen his city. His family. His life.

Bjorn clenched his hands into fists, but he raised his gaze to find the others looking at him. He exhaled noisily and decided.

"We go to Oakharrow."

As his companions nodded, the wind hummed mournfully in his ears.

42. THE LOYAL PRINCE

- Erik the Fist to Lord Vali Ulfson, Jarl of Aelford

Bastor followed the newly crowned king to his chambers.

He was nearly delirious with exhaustion. His armor, painted with the blood of Syptens and Baegardians alike, seemed to weigh heavier with each passing moment. His wounds ached and scratched and pulled. His muscles had grown stiff, and his tortured joints stiffer still.

Yet, like a loyal pup, still he trailed after his father.

He wondered if, in his deepest spirit, he was a coward. Aelthena had stood up to his father when she had everything to lose and nothing to gain. She had defied him because she knew it to be right. But though Bastor shared her sentiments, he had remained silent, telling himself to wait for the right moment to strike, that his hand would be steady and swift when it came.

But he had acted as the assassin before and knew he made a poor one.

His father was not one to indulge in excess, but as soon as he passed through the door, he strode to the cask of mead and poured himself a horn. Then he did something that surprised him: he offered it to Bastor.

"Drink with me, my son," he said, eyes bright. "Celebrate this victory as kin should."

Bastor accepted the drink, though he scarcely knew why. His father wore a smile as he served a second horn, then held it up. "Our first loyalty is to our blood, is it not?"

Bastor raised his honey wine with a smile of his own. "Right you are, Father. Our first loyalty."

As they drank, the spicy sweetness soothing his raw throat, Bastor wondered if this was the opportunity he had waited for. He and his father were alone; his father had commanded his huskarls to remain without. His sword and seax were belted at his waist. His father was heady with victory.

His father had ordered him killed.

Do it. End him. Just as you've always dreamed.

His hands twitched, itching to reach for the hilts. He clenched the horn so tightly he felt it must crack.

His father saw none of it, for he stared out the window. "Soon, I will drive the karah and his ilk from our borders. Already, there are signs of retreat, though I do not believe they will surrender. This Summer War is not yet over." His eyes slid over to hold Bastor's. "But while they are on the run, we will take care of the wolf at our backs."

"You mean to take back Oakharrow."

"Yes. This Jotun, whether a true giant or not—"

"He is," Bastor interrupted. "As I have told you."

Ragnar regarded him for a moment, some measure of his elation cooling, before continuing. "He has a barbar army at his command and city walls to protect him. But he will have to fight hard if he means to protect his eastern flank, seeing as the gate has been destroyed."

Bastor wondered what his father's aims were for Oakharrow. That he acted out of charity was laughable even to consider. If he took the jarlheim, it would not be for Lord Bor and Aelthena. But if he meant to keep it for himself, he would have difficulty convincing its people of his claim. *Even if he is a king now.*

His father drained the rest of his honey wine and clapped down the horn on a side table. "I will take it by summer's end," he declared, as if his word made it reality.

"It must be as you command," Bastor said softly. "For you are our king."

Ragnar squinted at him. "Yes. I am."

"But, as your son, you know what that makes me?"

The king did not answer, but waited with a watchful gaze.

Bastor spread his arms. "A prince. Can you imagine? A Sypten's bastard rising so high!" He let them fall back to his sides and shrugged. "But perhaps that is not as high as I will go. For if our king falls, who else but his prince should take up the crown?"

His heart pounded with his boldness. The threat could not be missed. Yet his father made no reaction. Bastor's breathing quickened. Even with fatigue wrapped tight around his bones, he could not help but look forward to the coming fight.

His father smiled, a glimmer of teeth showing between his lips. "You are truly my son, Alabastor. Ill-born you may be, but you have shown yourself to be worthy of our sigil." He took a step closer, his expression never shifting. "But you would do well to divert your ambition down different channels. Our first loyalty is to our blood. It is the rest of the world we must conquer."

Bastor turned his back on his father and king. "So you have always claimed, Father."

He strode from the room. He would not strike down his father — not today. But neither would he stand idly by. He would be like Aelthena and act boldly.

Even with all the world set against him.

Aelthena jerked upright from Frey's side at the knock at the door.

Once more, her hand fell to the guardian's sword. *You're safe*, she scolded herself as she released the hilt and rose to her feet. *As safe as you can ever be after defying a king.* Yet much of her behavior, she knew, came from guilt. She had instructed that Frey be moved to her bedchamber so she could keep a careful eye on him, but it had meant there was only one bed to lie down in. If she had lain by his side, what of it? When had she ever cared about propriety?

Still, she adjusted her plait into a slightly more presentable arrangement before she opened the door.

Bastor, as filthy as he had been in Antler Tower, stood beyond it. The stench of the battlefield — smoke, muck, gore — wafted over her, forcing her to breathe through her mouth.

"Alabastor," she greeted him coolly. "Or should I call you 'my prince'?"

The roguish man, now one of the most powerful men in Baegard, flashed a smirk, yet it lacked its usual vigor. "Bastor will do for you. Can I come in?"

She hesitated. Though Frey feared the man's intentions, Aelthena doubted she was in any physical danger from him.

Once, they had worked closely together, and even built a measure of trust.

Besides, she thought as she scrutinized him, *no one else is calling at my door.*

She stepped aside. "Make yourself comfortable. The furniture isn't mine, anyway."

With another amused glance, Bastor stepped within. He strode to the middle of the chamber and glanced at the doorway leading to the bedroom.

"The guardian is resting?" he asked without looking around.

Aelthena crossed her arms and did not answer.

Bastor turned and, seeing her expression, merely shrugged. "Just inquiring into an old comrade's health. I'm not always out for blood, Aelthena." He cocked his head. "Though, in a sense, I am right now."

Her skin prickled. "And whose blood would that be?"

The roguish prince took a step forward and spoke in almost a whisper. "I'm sure you've already thought of it. But with my father now king, in accordance with the Inscribed Beliefs, I stand to inherit all of Baegard. Upon Ragnar's death, whenever it should come, the crown passes to me."

An auspicious feeling sparked to life within her. "You've thought much on your father's demise."

"I have. But we cannot be rid of him yet, much as it pains me to say. He is the right man to repel the invasion, even to retake Oakharrow. And until we know more about his firesand, we cannot move against him." Bastor stared at the floor, his shoulders bowed. She wondered at all the weight on them now. *Our entire nation, in a way.* She grimaced, doubting he was up to the task, from all she had seen of him.

His gaze rose to meet hers. "But his reign will not be long. Though you broke your oath of silence, I will keep mine to you. Baltur will serve his justice for Oakharrow and your fallen kin. He'll get what he deserves. And when it's at an end, I'll return Baegard to the Seven Jarlheims. All will be as it was before, as it should be."

Despite the appeal of his words, Aelthena found she was shaking her head. "I want to believe you, Bastor. After all we've been through, I have to think there's hope that we can be allies. But you're his son and heir. How can I trust you in this?"

The prince laughed, low and bitter. "Perhaps we should discuss how I can trust you! Don't forget who last drove the knife into whose back. But still, I'm not sure you have much of a choice. What better chance do you have of recovering Oakharrow? Yet if it makes a difference..."

Bastor went quiet for a long moment before speaking again.

"When I was young, one of my father's thralls carved me a set of blocks from a tree he had felled in the fields. From childhood, the thrall adopted me as one of their own, on account of my mother, and perhaps the way I look. But this man — Khaba was his name — encouraged me to play with the blocks, and I took to it with abandon. My father would scold me when he caught me at it, thinking stacking blocks to be an unsuitable activity for his heir. So I hid my playing, spending time in the servants' quarters where no one minded me being underfoot. As I built, they taught me my mother's tongue, and I learned all the joys and hardships of their lives."

A wistful smile curled Bastor's lips at the reminiscing. Aelthena found it difficult to remain on her guard, as she knew she should, as he drew her deeper into his past.

"But all good things die. When I had seen thirteen winters, my father discovered me still toying with the blocks. Seeing as I was on the cusp of manhood, the childish activity made him furious, and he flew into a rage such as no one has seen outside of his household."

When the prince did not speak for a long while, Aelthena gently prompted him. "What happened?"

Bastor let out another laugh and turned his head aside. "He threw my blocks to the flames. Seeing them burn hurt worse than the beating he gave me. Worse still was what he did to the thralls. One by one, he brought them out and whipped them until he found out who had carved me the blocks in the first place. Then he whipped Khaba until I thought he would die. But thralls are too valuable of property to throw away needlessly. Khaba was ill for weeks afterward, but he eventually recovered and returned to work. Afterward, he took care to avoid me, and I let him. To do anything else would have gotten him killed."

Aelthena dug deep in herself for some kernel of comfort. "Asborn's father struck his mother so often and hard she can no longer stand straight. Cruel men are harshest toward those closest to them."

Bastor observed her from the corner of one eye. "True enough. But my father did not beat the defiance out of me. Oh, I did as he bade for many years after. I threw myself into riding and hunting and swordplay until I mastered all those manly activities. I took to avoiding the thralls. That pleased my father. He believed he had squashed out all my childhood oddities.

"But when I was eighteen, there was a boy among the thralls, only five winters. Khaba had passed away, and no one else made blocks. So I carved the boy a set. The joy on his face..." Bastor closed his eyes for a moment. "I remember that feeling. And I've tried to give it to every thrall child I can."

It was a small gesture, a little rebellion. But Aelthena saw what Bastor meant by it. "You'll always defy him," she murmured. "From childhood on, you knew you were not like him."

Bastor shook his head. "If it were only that. No, I am my father's son. But in this, it's a boon. Ragnar Torbenson never quailed at accomplishing anything he set his mind to. And neither will I."

The prince faced her and drew fully upright. "I have hated my father since he burned those blocks. That fire has not gone out in all the winters since. If you cannot trust me, Aelthena, trust in that."

Could she trust it? The man was too opaque, too diffi- cult for her to distinguish between his lies and truths. Yet whether or not his story was false, he was her only option. She had to believe in him, as she had before. As he believed in her.

She stuck out her arm. "Very well. I'm with you."

Bastor accepted her offer. His hand closed around the whole of her forearm, while hers barely encircled half of his. Yet she looked up into his face and did not quail.

Releasing the grip, the prince grinned. "I'll leave you to your guardian now. I'm sure he'll require much... minis- trations."

Unable to help a scowl, she shooed him from the room. Prince or no, a woman had to draw a line.

After she shut the door, Aelthena pressed her back against the wood, rested her head on it, and closed her eyes. If Bastor was sincere, her tattered plans could weave back together. The jarls' wives had proved only marginally useful before the stirrings of war, but she knew best how to use them now. And she would not stop there. Politics was said to be the arena of men. She would contend there also, in the manners they understood: coin and power.

It was a bone toss, this rebellion, a game in which all odds stacked against her. But she would succeed.

I must.

Aelthena opened her eyes and straightened, her resolve reforming and hardening. Outside, the orange light was failing. But her work was just beginning.

She would take back what was hers. She would defy her king.

EPILOGUE

All who attended the ramshackle hall flinched as the flaps that served as doors ripped open.

Egil hid a grimace as he watched the newcomers process in. Shame was becoming a familiar feeling in his new station in life, but he adjusted poorly to it. He was not one to bow and scrape and grovel. He was not a spineless boy like Bjorn Borson — or how the exiled heir had appeared until the battle at Chasm Valley.

Yet in the court of the Jotun, those who stood tallest were cut down first. Egil was too much like his father to spite survival.

He lowered his head before the entering jotunmen and examined their burden from the corner of his eye. Whatever it was seemed heavy, judging from the grunts of the six bestial men hauling it. It was hidden under a woolen cover and carried on a sturdy litter. The jotunmen marched down the aisle, little more than a pathway swept clean of rubble, as one of their kind babbled ahead of them in their growling speech. They continued all the way through the structure to the figure looming at the other end.

Hesitantly, furious at his reluctance, Egil looked up at the giant.

The Jotun — Kuljash, as his translator claimed his name to be — was too large for any ordinary chair, so it was almost a platform that had been erected to support his weight, and even then with many protests from the timber. The King of Chieftains paid it little heed. Even sitting, he towered as tall as four men. Tusks framed his broad jaw with square teeth that looked strong enough to crush stone. He leaned to one side, an elbow propped on one knee, while his fist ground into the groaning planks. His black eyes, small within his large skull, gazed unblinking on the procession. His face, covered in thick brown fur, obscured any expression written upon it.

But like the other hangers-on of the court of the Jotun, Egil had learned to guess the giant's moods. One wrong calculation could cost a man his life. He had a notion that whatever lay beneath the heavy cover was precious to Oakharrow's usurper.

Egil's father leaned in close. "Do not appear too interested," Yaethun Brashurson murmured. "We don't wish to attract unwanted attention."

I understand better than you, Egil wanted to snap in reply. But he only gave a tight nod and looked aside. Quarreling with his father yielded more trouble than it was worth, and as the former lawspeaker's efforts to ingratiate himself with Oakharrow's new ruler might be the only thing preserving both their lives, he would not willingly undermine him.

But even good sense had its limits. Egil felt he was quickly approaching his.

We must do more, he thought as he continued to watch the beast-men. *Are we sheep to bow our heads to the wolf? Am I?* He wondered how he had thought himself braver than the jarl's heir. Bjorn had been quiet and timid, yet he had rallied a company and ventured into the Teeth when winter still claimed them. He was not a man to inspire confidence like Vedgif, nor full of deadly competence like Yonik. Yet he had made himself a force to contend with, and struck a blow against their enemy that had, from all his father could glean, sent the Jotun into a killing rage when he discovered it.

How could he, Egil Yaethunson, do any less?

The procession halted a dozen paces before the usurper, and the jotunman at its head raised his hands and voice in what seemed a triumphant gesture. Then, with that brief ceremony, the speaker turned and ripped the drapery away.

Egil stared at the object as it was revealed. It appeared to be a slab of age-weathered stone; a gravestone, perhaps, though the grandest he had ever seen. *The marker of a monarch?* But why such an object would appeal to the Jotun, much less warrant such pageantry, defied Egil's comprehension.

He looked away again. But as the giant stood from his platform and lumbered toward the large stone, he saw his caution was for naught. Kuljash was absorbed with the grave marker. The giant reached out one gargantuan hand to caress its face, and Egil watched in open astonishment. After all of Kuljash's violence, tenderness was the last emotion he expected.

The Jotun withdrew his hand and drew himself up to his full towering height. Then he threw back his head and roared.

He was no coward, but Egil cowered with the others in the shabby court. And he doubted he was the only one dreading what it might portend.

An author's career isn't built by the writer alone. It takes every reader who has bet hours of their time on a cover, a blurb, and the hope that this will be the story that grips them and sweeps them away. A story that gives them something new.

Thank you, dear reader, for taking that risk on my book.

I hope *The Crown of Fire & Fury* has been everything you were looking for and more. If you did enjoy it, please consider leaving a rating or review, particularly on Amazon.

Most readers don't know the difference a review can make for a book. I know I never gave it a thought until I became an author myself. But here's the truth: it makes or breaks a book's success. By reviewing, you can help other readers determine if they'll like the book, and hopefully a virtuous cycle blooms.

I'd like to be doing this till I have one foot in the grave. I wrote my first (terrible) book at twelve, and I don't intend on stopping now.

So if you're feeling generous and want to help an author

out, look up *The Crown of Fire & Fury* on Amazon to leave a review. You'll have my infinite gratitude!

APPENDIX I

THE WORLD

COUNTRIES AND CONTINENTS

The Witterland - An ever-frozen continent to the north from which Djurians, the ancestors of Baegard and Benwold, are said to have long ago migrated.

The Sumerland - An eternally hot continent to the south from which Zakai, the ancestors of Zakowa and North and South Vinaxi, are said to have migrated. Known as "the Suncoast" to Syptens.

Enea, or The Middle Land - A continent positioned between the Witterland and the Sumerland where the events of the story take place.

Baegard, or The Seven Jarlheims - A nation founded among the mountains and the wide valley cradled among them. The jarlheims are city-states within Baegard that share similar cultures and unite for the purposes of common defense. Known as "the Winter Holds" to Syptens.

Ha-Sypt - A nation that has long been the antagonist of Baegard. It is a land of deserts and oases, founded primarily along the rivers Nu and Qal. It is ruled by a monarch held to be a god, the Karah. Syptens are descended from Eneans, the native people of Enea.

Benwold - A nation that shares a common descent from Djurian culture with Baegard and often allies with them.

Zakowa - A nation of Sumerland descent that often allies with Ha-Sypt.

North and South Vinaxi - Two nations of Sumerland descent that are in constant conflict with their sister nations.

Xen'tia - A powerful republic of Oessa, the continent to the west of Enea; sometimes participates in the wars between Baegard and Ha-Sypt.

Jin'to - A widespread empire of Oessa, the continent to the west of Enea; sometimes participates in the wars between Baegard and Ha-Sypt.

CITIES OF BAEGARD

Oakharrow - Formerly ruled by its jarl, Bor Kjellson.

Petyrsholm - Ruled by its jarl, Petyr Petyrson.

Ragnarsglade - Ruled by its jarl, Ragnar Torbenson.

Djurshand - Ruled by its jarl, Hother Alverson.

Greenwuud - Ruled by its jarl, Siward Jonson.

Skjold - Ruled by its jarl, Harald Sigurdson.

Aelford - Ruled by its jarl, Alrik Adilson.

OAKHARROW

The Squalls - The poorest district; primarily populated by Vurgs.

The Dusty Wares - The street-side markets along the main thoroughfare, the Iron Road.

Oakheart - The richest district; primarily populated by Thurdjurs and Balturg highborn.

Greenstead - The primary gathering place in the city for large-scale events.
Dawnshadow - The cliff that looms over Oakharrow.
Harrowhall - The former bastion of the last king of Baegard and the home to the present jarl; the center of Thurdjur power.
Vigil Keep - The citadel of the thane and center of Balturg power.
Honeybrook - The river that runs through the city.

EILDURSPRALL

Heim Numen - The compound of the gothi located within the Yewling town of Eildursprall. The center of the Inscribed religion in Baegard.
The Silvers - The three leaders of the gothi who rule from Heim Numen.
The Etching Wall - Every gothi contributes to carvings of the Inscribed.

CITIES OF HA-SYPT

Qal-Nu - The border city that was sacked by Baegardians just over twenty years before the start of the story.
Annax-Nu - The capital of Ha-Sypt, where the karah reigns.

CLANS

Thurdjurs - The ruling clan of Oakharrow; their clan color is aqua.
Balturgs - The secondary ruling clan of Oakharrow; their clan color is red.

Vurgs - The poorest and most oppressed clan of Oakharrow; their clan color is yellow.

TRIBES OF THE TEETH

Yewlings - The settled people of towns such as Jünsden and Eildursprall, who are on generally peaceful terms with Baegardians.

Skyardi - A nomadic tribe with a tenuous relationship with Baegardians.

Woldagi - A seasonally nomadic tribe with a hostile relationship with Baegardians.

Ovaldi - One of the tribes who has joined the Jotun's army.

Haddik - One of the tribes who has joined the Jotun's army.

Telduri - One of the tribes who has joined the Jotun's army.

Roks - One of the tribes who has joined the Jotun's army.

MAGIC

Volur - The Old Djurian word for one who can use magic.

Seidar / **The Sight** - Magic as Baegardians know it; involves the ritualized use of runestones. When employed, it is called "Seeing."

Khnuum - A mysterious substance contained within drascale ore that causes hallucinations in those susceptible to its influence, such as *Volur*.

The Hall of Doors - the place seers visit to access the power of runes; appears as a shadowy corridor lined with doors that are inscribed with runes. Open the doors and their powers are conferred. *Hael Ek'dyrr* is the Hall of Doors in Old Djurian.

BAEGARDIAN CULTURE

Jarl - The highest social position in present Baegard; the ruler of a jarlheim and leader of the ruling clan.

Thane - The second highest social position in present Baegard; the next-in-command of a jarlheim after the jarl and the jarl's heir, and the leader of their clan.

Lawspeaker - The primary judge and arbiter of justice in Oakharrow.

Warden of the Watch - The primary leader of the city watch.

City Sentinel - One of the captains of the watch, focused on the protection of the city.

War Drang - The leader of Oakharrow's patrols and, in times of war, its warriors.

Drang - A leader of a company of warriors.

Huskarl - A man-at-arms, such as a guardian of the Harrowhall, or a keeper of Vigil Keep.

Gothi - Once a group of people dedicated to keeping old Djurian traditions alive, they have become in the modern era a codified priesthood. They have a centralized compound located in Eildursprall, where the three Silvers oversee the religion.

Yeoman - A man who holds and manages a small estate of land.

Thrall - A slave, often of Sypten descent and captured in raids.

SYPTEN CULTURE

The Ascendant Empire - Syptens' name for their country. Also refer to it as "the Plentiful Land" and themselves as "the People of Dust."

The Holy Karah - The god-king of Ha-Sypt; often referred to as "Divine One."

Ohkweht - The sister to the karah; translates to "Royal Sister."

High chanter - The highest priest dedicated to a specific Sypten god; referred to with the honorific "nautjer."

Vizier - The foremost advisor to the karah.

Chief general - The head general of the Sypten armies; honorific for generals is "baka."

Paragon - A notable champion addressed as "lion."

Afterlife - Syptens believe they either descend to the Jackal's Blight or receive an everlasting life in the Jackal's Delight, both ruled over by the god Gazabe.

Apostates - Those who defy the will of the Divine, including the karah.

Duaat - A Sypten game modeled after the real-life game "Senet," in which the aim to move one's pieces across a long board and into the afterlife.

Nomes - Districts of Ha-Sypt, ruled over by governors called "nomarchs."

Khopesh - The preferred Sypten sword; is curved halfway up its length like a sickle and single-edged.

DJURIAN PANTHEON: THE INSCRIBED GODS

Djur - The Wild God, the Greatbear, the God of the Stars and Wrath; father to many of the pantheon.

Nuvvog - The Trickster, the Dragon God, the God of the Sun and Deceit; father to the other half of the pantheon.

Skirsala - Goddess of the Harvest; one of the three Wild Wives of Djur.

Yusala - Goddess of the Forest; one of the three Wild Wives of Djur.

Lerye - Goddess of the River; one of the three Wild Wives of Djur.

Ovvash - Goddess of the Underworld; the daughter of Nuvvog and the surtun Finyurrle.

Lavaethun - God of the Sea Moon; thought to take the shape of a giant sea serpent.

Skoll - God of the Blood Moon; thought to take the shape of a giant wolf.

Baltur - God of Poetry and Justice; the son of Djur and Skirsala.

Volkur - Goddess of War and Glory; the daughter of Djur and Lerye.

Mostur - God of Stone and the Forge; the son of Djur and Yusala.

The Spinners - Three immortal beings who are said to spin the thread of each person's life when they are born and determine the timing of their deaths.

SYPTEN PANTHEON: THE DIVINE

Pawura - The Dreaming Antelope; Goddess of Art and Love.

Yeshept - The Prowling Lioness; Goddess of the Hunt and Wealth.

Qa'a - The Wise Scarab; God of Justice and Foresight.

Bek - The Red Behemoth; Goddess of Might and War.

Aya - The White Cobra; God of Cunning and Deceit.

Gazabe - The Black Jackal; God of Death and Decay.

Hua - The Bright Maker; Father of the People of Dust; Mother of the mighty Huame; Creator of All. Also known as the sun and claimed to be the mother of the huame, the southern giants.

OTHER

Jotunar - Giants of Frost The mythic behemoths of the Witterland

Surtunar - Giants of Fire; the mythic behemoths of the Sumerland. Known as "huame" to Syptens, or "Children of the Sun."

Jotunmen - Barbars who have have been changed into bestial men that resemble the Jotun

Nuvvog's Rage - The mysterious inferno that appears to manifest from Chasm-dust

Woolith - A livestock animal that resembles a mixture between an aurochs and a wooly mammoth.

APPENDIX II
CHARACTERS

OAKHARROW

Thurdjurs

Aelthena Of'Bor - Daughter to the jarl of Oakharrow.

Bjorn Borson - Youngest son to the jarl of Oakharrow.

Bor Kjellson - Jarl of Oakharrow.

Bestla Of'Bor - Wife to the jarl of Oakharrow.

Annar Borson - Eldest son of the jarl of Oakharrow; the jarl's heir.

Yofam (Yof) Borson - Middle son of the jarl of Oakharrow; the war drang.

Frey Igorson - A guardian of the Harrowhall.

Yaethun Brashurson - The lawspeaker of Oakharrow; son of the deposed jarl.

Brashur Felson - Former jarl of Oakharrow; deposed and executed by Bor Kjellson.

Egil Yaethunson - Son of the lawspeaker; a sentry of the watch; a member of the Hunters in the White.

Vedgif Addarson - An elder of the Thurdjur clan; first drang to the Hunters in the White; known as "the Rook" for commanding role in the Sack of Qal-Nu.

Keld Erlendson - Youngest member of the Hunters in the White.

Morif Morifson - The warden of the watch.

Brant Elofson - An elder of the Thurdjur clan.

Fiske Yarison - An elder of the Thurdjur clan.

Raldof Koryson - Blademaster of the Harrowhall

Menif Laethson - A sentry of the watch.

Skarif Graynson - A guardian of the Harrowhall.

Menith Karlson, or "Pine" - A guardian of the Harrowhall.

Pestur Yroelson, or "Ratclaw" - A guardian of the Harrowhall.

Balturgs

Asborn Eirikson - Son of the thane of Oakharrow.

Kathsla Of Eirik - Wife to the thane of Oakharrow.

Eirik Havardson - Thane of Oakharrow; leader of the Balturg clan; known as "Bloodaxe" for his ferocity during the deposing of Brashur Felson and the Sack of Qal-Nu.

Loridi Kelnorson - The self-proclaimed "Lord Sword"; a jester of the Hunters in the White; Balturg.

Seskef Gulbrandson - Named "Skiff" by Loridi; companion to Loridi and member of the Hunters in the White; Balturg.

Tait Knudson - A young keeper whom Bjorn attacks and injures.

Snornir Baelson - A city sentinel of the watch

Hervor Halvorson - Known as "Silverfang" for his silver

false tooth; an elder of the Balturg clan; also a wealthy merchant and owner of drascale mines.

Vurgs

Skarl Thundson - Known as "the Savage" and "Dragon-skin"; leader of a rebellion.
Troel Magurson - A sentry of the watch.

Thralls

Uljana - The loyal servant to Lord Bor.

Other

Yonik Of' Skoll - A gothi (priest) of Oakharrow; famous for his greatbear cloak won from a hunt.
Ilva Of' Skirsala - The head gothi (priestess) of Oakharrow.
Bastor, or Alabastor Ragnarson - A rogue first encountered in the Wolf's Den, revealed to be the Heir of Ragnarsglade.

PETYRSHOLM

Ipu - A thrall young woman who works in the Elkhorn kitchens.
Pyhia - The thrall head cook of the Elkhorn kitchens.
Bennu - A young thrall girl.
Neith and Soben - Two young thrall boys.
Ragnar the Younger - Bastor's younger brother and the youngest son of Ragnar Torbenson, Jarl of Ragnarsglade.
Thorpe and Kustaa - Two guards of the Elkhorn.

Destin - A huskarl to the jarl Siward.
Helka - Lord Siward's eldest daughter.
Olle - Lord Siward's infant son.
Yerrik - A wall captain.
Endre Kettilson - A huskarl to Lord Ragnar.

EILDURSPRALL

Tyra - An acolyte at Heim Numen who works in the library.
Flint - The captain of Eildursprall's sentries.
Wuldof and Dagar - Two sentries of Eildursprall.
Embla - A priestess stationed at Heim Numen.
Torvald Geirson - The Last King of Baegard. Legends tell of him wandering into the Teeth and never returning.

The Silvers

Mother Sign - An enigmatic older woman skilled in the Sight.
Mother Iron - A bold older woman who positions herself as the de facto leader of the Silvers.
Father Temperance - A cautious older man who counsels a conservative approach.

JARLS OF BAEGARD

Bor Kjellson - Jarl of Oakharrow.
Ragnar Torbenson - Jarl of Ragnarsglade.
Petyr Petyrson - Jarl of Petyrsholm.
Alrik Adilson - Jarl of Aelford.
Harald Sigurdson - Jarl of Skjold.
Siward Jonson - Jarl of Greenwuud.

Hother Alverson - Jarl of Djurshand.

Wives of the Jarls

Sigrid Of'Harald - Wife to Lord Harald, the Jarl of Skjold.
Iona Of'Siward - Wife to Lord Siward, the Jarl of Greenwuud.
Olga Of'Petyr - Wife to Lord Petyr, the Jarl of Petyrsholm.
Inkeri Of'Hother - Wife to Lord Hother, the Jarl of Djurshand.
Nanna Of'Alrik - Wife to Lord Alrik, the Jarl of Aelford.

HA-SYPT

Sehdra - The "ohkweht," or "Royal Sister," of the karah, the ruler of Ha-Sypt.
Hephystus III, or Physt - The karah, or god-king, of Ha-Sypt.
Oyaoan - The leader of the huame, the southern giants.
The Ibis - The Suncoaster translator to Oyaoan.
Teti - A servant and friend to Sehdra.
Zosar - The vizier to the Karah.
Renab - The high chanter of Qa'a.
Nekau - The first chief general.
Amon - The second chief general.

ACKNOWLEDGMENTS

Dozens of folks have generously sacrificed their time, effort, and, if I did my job right, emotion into making this book all it can be. A huge round of thanks to:

Kaitlyn, my wife, first reader, and patient ear for all my harebrained ideas.

Shawn Sharrah, my keen-eyed proofreader.

René Aigner, my stunningly talented illustrator.

My parents, who long ago fostered a love of reading and creativity in me that they have unfailingly supported since.

My siblings, who take the time out of their busy lives to read and listen to their baby brother's stories — I'm sorry you'll never be able to catch up.

And lastly, to my advance reader team, *the Chapter*, whose reviews and encouragement ease the travails of book publishing. A special thanks to: Marc, Pamela Bickford, Emma, Jackie Tansky, Steve, Debbie, Dennis, Laura, Andrew, Angela, Deanna, Jen, Sandra, and last but certainly not least, Chris.

BOOKS BY J.D.L. ROSELL

Sign up for future releases at jdlrosell.com.

THE RUNEWAR SAGA

1. The Throne of Ice & Ash
2. The Crown of Fire & Fury
3. The Stone of Iron & Omen

LEGEND OF TAL

1. A King's Bargain
2. A Queen's Command
3. An Emperor's Gamble
4. A God's Plea

RANGER OF THE TITAN WILDS

1. Ranger's Rebellion

THE FAMINE CYCLE

1. Whispers of Ruin
2. Echoes of Chaos
3. Requiem of Silence

Secret Seller (*Prequel*)

The Phantom Heist (*Novella*)

GODSLAYER RISING

1. Catalyst

2. Champion

3. Heretic

ABOUT THE AUTHOR

J.D.L. Rosell is the author of the Legend of Tal series, The Runewar Saga, The Famine Cycle series, and the Godslayer Rising trilogy. He has earned an MA in creative writing and has previously written as a ghostwriter.

Always drawn to the outdoors, he ventures out into nature whenever he can to indulge in his hobbies of hiking and photography. Most of the time, he can be found curled up with a good book at home with his wife and two cats, Zelda and Abenthy.

Follow along with his occasional author updates and serializations at jdlrosell.com or contact him at authorjdlrosell@gmail.com.